Wynne's gun barked. The flash was right in front of my face. I flinched as the bullet went right past my ear.

I went for the pistol concealed at my side, but Wynne shifted the muzzle over a tiny bit and it was aimed at my nose.

"It's not time to kill you yet." The words came out of Wynne's mouth, but it sure didn't sound like him anymore.

Slowly, I moved my hand away from my gun. I risked looking behind and saw Albert sinking to the floor. There was a red hole in his shirt.

"You did exactly what I wanted you to do, daughter of Eve."

One thing I've learned in this business is that when someone starts addressing anyone as *daughter of Eve* or *son of Adam* they are evil with a capital E and there's usually all sorts of weird culty demonic crap behind it.

Albert was in big trouble. He needed help fast or he was going to die. I kept my voice calm. "What do you want?"

"You'll find out . . . Oh, you'll find out."

When I was really young, my dad had told me the way to know if someone is about to use the gun they're pointing at you is to look at their eyes. But he'd never told me what it meant when they started glowing . . .

MONSTER HUNTER
GUARDIAN

Larry Correia
Sarah A. Hoyt

Monster Hunter Guardian

This is a work of fiction. All the characters and events portrayed in this book are fictional, and any resemblance to real people or incidents is purely coincidental.

Copyright © 2019 by Larry Correia and Sarah A. Hoyt

A Baen Books Original

Baen Publishing Enterprises
P.O. Box 1403
Riverdale, NY 10471
www.baen.com

ISBN: 978-1-9821-2504-2

Cover art by Alan Pollack

First printing, August 2019
First mass market printing, December 2020

Distributed by Simon & Schuster
1230 Avenue of the Americas
New York, NY 10020

Library of Congress Control Number: 2019017278

Pages by Joy Freeman (www.pagesbyjoy.com)
Printed in the United States of America
10   9   8   7   6   5   4   3   2   1

To Uncle Timmy

Thanks to Kacey Ezell for helicopter advice. And thanks to Herb Nowell and Larry Bauer for their advice on submarines.

MONSTER HUNTER
GUARDIAN

CHAPTER 1

Take it from someone who grew up in this business. You should never, ever, ever hunt vampires in a dark basement as the sun is going down.

Crash.

Something broke in the dark basement where I was hunting vampires at sunset.

Yes, I know. My grandpa would have hit me upside the head for even considering this job, but I had my reasons. Sometimes a girl's got to do what she's got to do, and I had ignorant college kids to protect.

My fellow students lived in a kind of dream world, filled with comforting lies and pretty fairy tales. I'd grown up in the real world, where monsters exist and are out to destroy humanity. My youth was spent in shoot houses and eavesdropping on autopsies. My first monster kill was when I was ten, and I'd been a member of the family business ever since. My classmates, if they thought of monsters at all, thought of them as sexy, or tragic and misunderstood. Personally, I'd found there were few misunderstandings that couldn't be cured with a sufficient quantity of silver delivered at a high enough velocity. I'd been to way too many murder scenes to buy into any of that pro-monster propaganda nonsense. Monsters were evil, and evil needs killing.

Which was how I'd ended up alone in the creepy basement of the science building, armed to the teeth, and surrounded by vampires. The high narrow windows meant that there was still a little light getting in, but despite that, some of the vamps were already awake and moving. Retreat would've been the smart thing to do.

Only the infestation could not be allowed to go on, not even for one more night. No more innocents would die. Not on my watch.

Technically, it wasn't *my watch* anymore. This wasn't supposed to be my responsibility. Private monster hunting had been banned. Both tactically and legally speaking, being down here was stupid.

Only none of that matters when monster hunting is in your blood.

It's what I do.

It had started in the library where I was studying with my friend Cynthia Anne Aiken. Well, sort of my friend. She was younger than me, naïve, having trouble adapting to college, and she sort of clung to me like a bird with a broken wing. We sat at a table with a pile of art books between us. I was a grad student in anthropology, but I was picking up an art history degree while I was here too. When you've worked as hard a job as I'd had, going back to school was a piece of cake.

"No, I don't think vampires are romantic," I told her, as I had many times.

Cynthia Anne sighed. "You're no fun."

I shoved some books aside and looked at her. Really looked. She was just a baby. Granted, I was older than most other students in my classes—education gets delayed when you've already got a good paying job—but Cynthia Anne Aiken was just a round-faced little freshman with big blue eyes and wispy blonde hair. She wore a blue headband and little flower earrings, and had *He listened, like we dream of others listening* tattooed in fancy script around her wrist. She reminded me a bit of the youngest Hunters who'd ever shown up for our training classes, meaning those who'd had their first supernatural encounters when they were just kids but had to wait until they were adults to join. Only without their cynicism. Or guts. Or perspective. Or, you know, the scars of having survived an encounter with homicidal monsters.

I'd noticed she was reading Anne Rice's *Queen of the Damned* and had to comment. "Vampires aren't sexy, or cute, Cynthers. They want to eat you, and not in a good way."

She had stared at me, mouth open like a guppy. She hadn't said vampires don't exist. That should have been my first clue. Instead, she muttered something in a tumble about the tragedy of living forever and not having anyone to understand or love you because people would think you were a monster.

"That's because they *are* monsters, evil spirits animating the soulless undead husk of a human." I started to tell her the truth, but then her wide-open eyes told me I was out of step again, unable to communicate with people who hadn't grown up like I had, or seen the things I'd seen. Regular people can be so exasperating at times.

For a hundred years, my family's business had been eradicating the things most people didn't think existed. For generations, we had killed vampires, werewolves, and weirder. We'd kept people safe and collected the bounties—quite good bounties—until the government had decided to shut us down. Okay, the government had a reason, and I'd been there for that event, but I still didn't like to dwell on it.

After I'd been put out of work, I'd come to Auburn to study and to be *normal*. Not to think of the Christmas Party or dwell on my dead brother or insane father. I failed at that a lot. I constantly had to remind myself about that *being normal* thing. A normal person had no reason to blow up little Cynthers' illusions. The Monster Control Bureau was still keeping tabs on all of the former employees of MHI, and they'd love to throw the book at a Shackleford for violating the Unearthly Forces Secrecy Act. It was illegal for someone like me to speak frankly to someone like her. If she started blabbing about how crazy Julie Shackleford believed vampires were real, the MCB wouldn't hesitate to further ruin my life. They really weren't messing around right now, not after the Christmas Party. Nobody was getting let off with a warning nowadays. I'd be looking at prison time minimum, or more likely a bullet to the head and a fake suicide note.

Besides, if she wanted to dream of vampires as fairy princes, that was innocuous. After all, odds were most humans would never run into a vampire.

So I chickened out, shrugged and said, "Whatever" and "Aren't you going to study for the test?"

She shoved the novel aside with a sigh and allowed me to share my flash cards with her. We drilled each other on art history and the ability to recognize different styles from just a portion of the painting.

I left the library at five P.M. to go to another class. She stayed behind. It was the last time I saw Cynthia alive.

She didn't show up for the test the next morning.

I didn't think anything bad had happened to her either, really. I thought I'd just pushed her too hard studying and she'd finally lost it and driven back home to Mommy and Daddy. In fact, her little sporty red Mercedes, which she'd told me had been her eighteenth birthday gift, was gone from the parking in front of her dorm. Mom and Dad must be talking her out of the dismals right now.

Because that's the sort of conclusion a *normal* person would come to.

I didn't have to be normal. It's not like I didn't keep getting job offers to join teams operating in other countries. Despite my dad's screwups, I still had a good reputation. It's not like I couldn't have left the US and made a bit of money. But after losing so much, I'd just wanted to walk away. I'd lost my brother. I'd lost my best friends. Talking to the ones who were still alive just reminded me of the dead. So I'd cut myself off and moved on.

Even though I was actively trying my hardest not to think like a Hunter, I couldn't help but keep my ears open. Another girl had gone missing recently, but she was one of those types where disappearing for weeks to "find herself" wasn't odd. Then the day after Cynthia, another girl didn't show up to class, and the next day, another.

That was when people began to panic. Photos of the missing girls got plastered all around campus. There was no evidence of any wrongdoing, no witnesses, and no bodies had been found, but the police had started talking about a possible serial killer operating around the Auburn campus. Like a good normal, I told myself they were probably right and all the disappearances were because of a run-of-the-mill psycho killer and, trust me, by my jaded standards those were practically cuddly, they were so nonthreatening. They were also not my problem, so I could leave it to the police.

Still, I felt prickles of discomfort about Cynthers almost immediately, but I kept telling myself not to be paranoid. She was deluded about vampires, but that wasn't uncommon. Half the girls on campus were crazy for stupid, fake, sexy movie vampires.

But as the number of disappearances rose, it got harder and harder not to think like a Hunter.

Since I was the last person who'd seen Cynthia, I was interviewed by the local police. They weren't read in on the supernatural, so I couldn't even risk warning them what they might be up against. They'd just think I was crazy.

While the locals formed search parties to walk through the woods looking for dump sites, I was a good citizen and called the MCB to report my suspicions. That wasn't a number that was listed in the phone book, so they took all their tips seriously. However, after I gave them my last name, they said they'd look into it, and then promptly hung up on me.

A few days after Cynthia went missing, I stayed at the library late, studying for a linguistics test. Linguistics is kind of like math without any numbers, and you need to dislocate your mind to fit it. That's the best I can describe it, and back then I was still having some trouble with it. I loved it, but it just took some effort. Afterwards I ended up having to cross the whole campus after dark.

Maybe subconsciously I was looking for trouble, I don't know.

Auburn has all these tall brick buildings that look like they were built by homesick Englishmen. Between them, the lush vegetation of Alabama grows rampant. There was this trimmed area with topiaries, but it had to be trimmed constantly because one thing Alabama vegetation doesn't do is "restrained" or "civilized." The path home wound past the topiary garden and through an area with really thick trees.

With the serial killer scare, there weren't very many people out after dark, and those who were traveled in groups. That was smart. I was alone but wasn't worried about getting kidnapped. I'm not really the victim type. If we did have a serial killer, I'd just drop him and consider it a community service.

I confess I wasn't even thinking about that at the time. I was thinking of the set changes that had taken Middle English to modern English. I needed to translate "Our Father" from modern English into some defined century of the past. It's harder than it sounds, and because you were required to explain the transformations, just memorizing the thing wouldn't solve it. So I was doing it in my head, and had got to the fourteenth century with *Oure fadir that art in heuenes* when someone slid out of the trees onto the path in front of me and started in my direction.

It was Cynthia.

The light was bad here, but it was definitely her. A normal person would have reacted with joy, probably just thinking she was coming back with her tail between her legs, wanting to know if I'd help her sweet-talk the art history teacher into letting her take the test late. Like Professor Clark would listen to me any more than to her...but the Hunter part of me read things differently.

In that second, I noticed several things. Like, if she'd gone home, why was she still wearing the same yellow top and artistically torn jeans she'd worn last time I'd seen her at the university? I'm a good observer and those weren't just similar clothes—they were the same. Also, she was walking differently, like she had a lot more self-confidence all of a sudden. Maybe she'd found a boyfriend and had been shacked up with him for a few days. It has that effect on some women. Hell, maybe she was just on painkillers or something.

But since I've already said that the library was the last time I saw Cynthia Anne Aiken alive, you know how this is going to go.

I said, "Cynthers, you're back," friendly as could be, as I moved my hand to my gun.

Of course I was armed. I'd never understood why most universities banned concealed carry. I mean, if they wanted to provide targets for killers, couldn't they buy some clay pigeons? You can hide a Colt Officer's Model .45 inside a waistband holster beneath a baggy War Eagle sweatshirt really well.

She didn't say anything, just smiled, as she kept closing distance. I could feel something coming off her, as if she were trying to send thoughts my way, suggesting she was inoffensive. Vampires do that thing where they project right against your mind. I always hated that feeling.

Normal people would tell themselves that they were imagining things, that they were being fanciful. But it turns out I wasn't normal, no matter how much I'd tried to pretend I was.

Cynthers charged and I was sure. No human could move that fast.

I shot her in the face.

She jumped back, startled, blinking, as if she hadn't expected me to resist.

I'd been a little off. That's what I got for being out of practice. I lined up the night sights and immediately put my second bullet through her eye socket.

Sadly, guns aren't the best thing for killing vampires, which was pretty obvious since shooting her twice through the brain only made her stumble.

She might not have been alone. There could have been more vampires hiding in the bushes. I should have run away, but honestly that thought never even crossed my mind. Cynthia was hissing and squirting blood. When I saw her remaining eye glowing red and a sneer that revealed sharp fangs, I was committed. This monster was going down, no matter what.

The night had been still so the whole campus must have heard the noise. People or vampires were sure to come running, but I didn't think about that as I dumped the rest of my magazine into her.

My slide locked back as I fired my last round.

Cynthia had a bunch of new holes in her, but the instant the gunfire let up, she lurched in my direction.

I wished I had a flamethrower. And body armor. If you don't have something belt-fed or explosive, stakes and decapitation work best. I swung my book bag around, ripped open the side pocket, got ahold of my big knife, and yanked it from the sheath.

Milo Anderson had made this blade, hammering it from a truck's leaf spring over an open fire, just to teach himself how, and given it to me for Christmas. I intended to take her head off with it.

Cynthia was wounded and pissed. She also had super vampire strength, but like most new vampires, she was too stupid and clumsy to use it well. The bullet wounds had screwed her up, so I might have a chance.

She leapt at me.

In my head was the story of how the Maasai hunt lions with just a sharpened stick. They crouch when the lion jumps, then run out of the way when the lion falls, preferably on the stick. No-longer-Cynthers was the lion, and a Milo-forged blade was a whole lot better than any stick.

She tackled me. Cynthia wasn't very big and Milo's knife was huge. We landed hard, her on top of the knife, and I split her wide open. It was a mess. With my free hand I pushed against her face to keep her snapping fangs away from my neck. With my other, I just kept twisting and sawing, aiming for her heart. She shrieked and snapped, nothing but an undead animal. Thick black blood was gushing everywhere.

She smelled like road-kill death.

We rolled until I somehow wound up on top. I jerked the knife out of her torso and slashed it hard against her neck. Fluid sprayed out like a geyser. That took the fight out of her.

Vampires are incredibly tough, and if you give them any time at all, they'll heal. So I hacked her head off.

It wasn't pretty. Everything was slick, and I'd let myself get out of shape. My arms were on fire. It took me several tries to remove her head.

At the time I felt nothing. My friend was gone. This was just evil animated meat.

The overgrown area was quiet again. There was a bunch of noise and commotion around the rest of campus, but my gunshots had been so rapid that they must have been hard to pinpoint. The whole fight had taken like thirty seconds, but I was breathing hard, pulse pounding, sitting on top of a headless corpse whose flesh immediately started softening into black goo. I knew that pretty soon all that would be left were bones covered in ooze, but some idiot might stick the head back together with the body, and that would be bad. So I picked Cynthia's head up by the hair and carried it back to my book bag. I shoved her in on top of my expensive textbooks... Well, those were certainly ruined now.

No, you don't need to know how I disposed of it. Suffice it to say no one ever found her head.

I got out of there fast, before whatever vampire had turned Cynthia came to feed—or worse. I'd get caught by the cops covered in blood with a severed head in my bag. That would be tough to explain. I avoided the arriving police cars and hurried home off campus.

My place was the top floor of a Victorian. I'd bought the house with my savings left from the bounties I'd collected. The bottom floor was two apartments, which paid a good portion of my tuition. The top floor was all mine, with a secret addition where I stored a bunch of my old equipment. It was well hidden. I could even have friends over for parties—not that I ever had parties—and they'd never have guessed that room was there. The first thing I did was open up the safe room to pull out some real hardware in case I'd been followed.

Then I stripped off my blood-soaked clothing. While I showered was when the guilt really hit me. I could have saved Cynthers. I could have warned her, told her the whole truth...something. It was my duty to protect the lambs who couldn't recognize a wolf. Really, I had barely known her, but I cried more right then than I had when my brother Ray had died, because at least with Ray, I had tried to save him.

Grieving over my family and friends had made me selfish. Being normal was a foolish dream. It was too late for her, but not too late for the rest. The Feds be damned, it was time to go back to work.

Normally when a vampire moves into an area, it takes victims and then stashes them, bleeding them slow, feeding over a period of time. That kept the number of disappearances low enough to not attract the attention of Hunters. When their helpless blood bags eventually died, the vamp would usually rip their heads off to keep them from coming back; less mouths to feed that way. Only this one was actively creating new vampires. That kind of escalating behavior was extremely dangerous. They'd still need a place to sleep during the day. That's where I would find them and kill them.

Solo hunting is stupid. It's reserved for people with a death wish or nothing to lose. I didn't think about that. This was personal. Nothing makes you dumber than anger or guilt, and right then I was feeling plenty of both.

I spent the rest of the night preparing. I had a ton of guns, but with the MCB breathing down my neck,

I was actually trying to obey the law, so I didn't have any explosives. So I made up some Molotov cocktails in my kitchen. They would have to do. While I worked I kept asking myself where, on or near campus, was a place where vampires could hide from the sun without anyone seeing them?

I came up with a few ideas and made a list. I had lockpicks, bolt cutters, and a crowbar. The minute the sun came up I got busy breaking and entering.

I burned way too much daylight before I found my winner. The old science building was the fifth place I checked that day. It had a deep basement that had been closed off years ago. Theoretically, some people had keys for it, but nobody ever went down there, something about exposed asbestos. There had been articles in the student paper about all the stuff abandoned, including decaying books and science instruments long out of date. There were jokes about the philosopher's stone forgotten in some cardboard box down there.

I had put loose clothing on over my armor and stuck my equipment into a duffle bag, just enough of a disguise that someone seeing me on campus wouldn't wonder when Auburn had added a Commando 101 course. I expected someone to challenge my right to go into the science building basement, but no one did. Since it was closed, there wouldn't be any innocent people getting in my way.

As soon as I found a bunch of dried bloody handprints and scratches where they'd dragged some poor struggling victim down the stairs, I knew I'd found the right place.

❖   ❖   ❖

There were a lot more of them than I'd expected. This dirtbag had been building an army.

Young vampires are sluggish during the day, but they're not entirely helpless. So every time I found one, I'd slam a stake through their heart to paralyze them, then immediately go to work chopping their heads off. Surprise them one at a time like that and they're not too bad.

The hard part is they like to hide. Vampires can sleep in the weirdest cramped conditions. In those cases, I'd toss a rope over whatever was sticking out, then drag them into the open to stake them. It's time-consuming work.

These were all weak, barely more than incoherent ghouls. They might have survived if Cynthers hadn't gone off the reservation. A couple tried to fight me when I woke them up, but I'd shot those with a suppressed carbine until they were practically Swiss cheese. Then I dragged them out and finished the job. New vampires can hardly talk, but one tried to beg for mercy. I didn't have any to give her.

Vampires have a stink to them. Decay and blood. Their presence makes your skin crawl. They suck the warmth out of a room. They leave all that stuff out of the romance novels.

I killed vampires all afternoon. They'd been collecting here for a while. There had probably just been one to start. That was the one I was really worried about. The longer vampires live, the tougher and smarter they get until the old ones are practically a nightmare.

I never found him, but I found where he'd kept his captives: chained to a toilet in an old bathroom. He'd probably picked that room because it had a drain in the floor. But as the people he'd fed on died, he'd let them come back, and their numbers had grown. I really wanted to make him pay.

As the sun went down, I knew the rest would wake up and swarm me. There was no way I'd make it out alive. Then the surviving vamps would escape to inflict this same horror on some other unsuspecting place. I was angry, guilty, and really tired, but I'm not dumb.

So I lit my Molotov cocktails and burned that whole son of a bitch to the ground.

My name is Julie Shackleford. My family have been Monster Hunters for over a hundred years. My job is to keep the sweet little idiots who don't believe in monsters safe.

And I'm okay with that.

CHAPTER 2

There was fire and screaming. The smell of gasoline stung my nostrils. I stood outside the burning building, the university campus behind me as dark shadows—the distorted bodies of vampires—threw themselves at the windows of the science building. One of them broke through.

It was looking for me. Not to kill me, but worse. To steal my soul and make me like her.

And someone had taken my baby.

This made no sense, as my dream self didn't have a baby—college had been a long time ago—but nonetheless I knew someone had taken him, and I was desolate.

And then the shrieking started. Fire and vampires vanished.

I woke up in the dark, shivering, with my baby screaming nearby. He'd saved me from a bad dream, a twisted version of what had happened years ago in school. We were having one of those winter nights when the temperature dips into the thirties, which would make people in more northerly states laugh, but it shouldn't. It's one thing to be in the teens or negative temps when you are in an insulated house that's ready to take the cold, but in Alabama, no old house is really ready to take the cold.

I had spent half the night not fully asleep, but too sleepy to get another blanket, and now I stared stupidly at the red glow of my alarm clock: four A.M. This was a problem because everything ached, and I was more tired than I've ever been, including times when I'd been out on a contract for weeks on end. But the baby's screaming continued—loud, disconsolate, and demanding.

"All right, all right." I probably didn't sound maternal at all as I dragged my tired ass out of bed and put on a robe. The crib was in my bedroom, both because I was sleeping alone and because . . . well, given the things that had been known to happen to my family, I still wasn't too comfortable about letting my son too far out of my sight.

Raymond Auhangamea Pitt was a big baby. He was also adorable, responsive, and just now a handful. How someone could be a handful when the sum total of his accomplishments were rolling over, drooling, and smiling was somewhat of a puzzle, but my son managed it.

The minute he saw me appear over the edge of his crib, the crying stopped and a kind of amused gurgle came out as he waved his hands at me. Thing was, even this early in the morning I wasn't even mad. There was something about my son's laughter that melted my heart. It was a sort of chubby laugh, a rolling happy sound.

He had reason to wake me, which I realized when

I took a deep breath. He quit crying and gurgled and laughed through the changing, and then, when I sat on my bed holding him, he fell asleep, still smiling.

He'd been a big baby—a super baby, as my husband had predicted/hoped, ten pounds plus at birth, and 22 inches long—and three months ago, I'd started supplementing his feedings with solids and he'd sort of given up on breast feeding. He was so big and perpetually hungry that my body couldn't really keep up with him. The kid was probably ready for protein shakes. By six months he was done nursing but I still loved holding him and feeling him close to me, and the way his baby head was all heavy and warm in my arms.

Owen had never even seen his son yet. I hadn't signed up to be a single mom, and I told myself I wasn't. I couldn't be. But it was getting harder and harder to believe my husband was going to make it home and everything would be as it had been before.

A shiver ran up my spine. Four in the morning is a terrible time to start thinking about your missing husband. I'd last heard from Owen right before Ray was born. In an underground city belonging to an ancient chaos god, he'd crossed a portal to a nightmare world—quite literally a place made out of nightmares—on a rescue mission, and hadn't been heard from since.

Owen was, like me, a Monster Hunter. More than that, he was a protector, a man who would always instinctively try to help others. It was part of the reason I loved him. Hyperresponsible, competent, and a protector. How could anyone not love that?

But even the best of us lose sometimes, and he

might not be coming back. That was part of what we signed up for, right? Hunters often married Hunters. It's too much effort to stay married to someone who didn't understand the truth, too difficult to keep up a façade about your job. Some of us told our spouses all about what we did, and others lied because they didn't want to put their loved ones at risk. There's no way I could've done that. Owen and I understood each other. Still, when you marry a Monster Hunter, you know you could end up widowed early.

I looked at the ring on my finger and shook my head. No. Owen wouldn't let that happen. I wasn't going to be alone, and little Ray would know his father.

It wasn't just Owen either. I had a bunch of friends and family on that mission. I'd not heard from Owen for six months, but the rest—who were at least still in this dimension—checked in daily, or whenever the weather allowed at least. Yet whenever a day went by without a check-in, I had the forlorn thought that everyone on Severny Island had been killed, and that if only I'd been there, they'd be okay. I realized that was stupid. They weren't lost, and I wasn't some kind of superwarrior who could have made that much difference. Never mind that I had a duty, and that was to keep superbaby—or as Earl tried to call him, Little Bubba—safe and sound.

Still . . .

I must have dozed off, sitting up in bed holding my son, because I dreamed that Owen was right there with me saying, "Oh, man, he's so chubby!" And I woke up feeling like I was about to drop him and clutched Ray tighter. He woke up, too, and fussed at being held so tight. The evil-red alarm clock said it was after seven A.M. and I was going to have to go to work.

I showered in really hot water, but still felt cold. The nightmare about the science building basement had left something behind, some sense of foreboding. I should've been able to shrug it off and say *it was just a dream* but I couldn't.

Because I'd remembered the feeling that my baby was gone, I'd brought the little dude into the bathroom with me, sitting in his little car seat. He kicked his legs and chortled at himself, the way babies do, as if they knew some joke that they're just not willing to share. When I was done showering, I washed him, then put a fresh diaper on, and dressed him in his little onesie with the MHI logo on the chest, a green smiley face with horns. By the time I'd dressed, he'd started to fuss, so I went downstairs to prepare a bottle.

The big old house was quiet. It was a landmark, owned by the Heart of Dixie Historical Foundation— which was basically me but for tax purposes. The house was also currently a mess, with tape and tarps everywhere. I'd been renovating this old place for years. I don't really know why. Maybe because of all my family memories growing up here, and if I was the one doing the work, it meant I got to keep the best and get rid of the worst.

We'd been making real progress too. Owen was terrible at anything requiring a delicate touch, but he was great for manual labor. Because I'm not very good at staying with one task, various rooms were in different states of renovation at all times. And because varnish, paint, and particulates are almost as bad for pregnant women and babies as monster hunting, I hadn't been able to do much for over a year now.

And then of course, stupid Franks had shown up,

and he and Earl had trashed the place. I'd hired contractors to fix the worst of it so the house would at least be livable again. I could have kept them on until the whole house was done, but that didn't seem right. That was my job to finish.

I really wanted to get back to it too. And back to monster hunting. When you actually like what you do, maternity leave kind of sucks. Being a mother makes you feel both really powerful and really helpless at the same time, which was a mind twist I hadn't been looking for.

With Ray on a crossbody sling, holding his bottle and drinking with horrible grunting slurping noises, I went to check on the other resident of the house.

My grandfather is Raymond Shackleford the Third, grandson of the legendary Bubba Shackleford, who founded Monster Hunter International back in 1895. I didn't remember a time when I hadn't looked up to Grandpa. He was tough, competent, and what he said went. Everyone respected him. The scariest, toughest Hunters in the world were a little afraid of him. This was the man everyone called the Boss, with a capital B. With that scarred-up face, missing an eye, and a hook for a hand, he was intimidating to most, but I loved him.

It's kind of funny, but it says about lot about Monster Hunter families. I'd been pretty young when he'd lost the eye and got the hook, but I'd baked him a get-well cake with a pirate on it. He'd thought it was hilarious. He'd gotten disfiguring and crippling injuries, and he'd just had a laugh about them, then gone back to work as fast as he could.

You've got to understand. This man has always been

my rock. But now there was something wrong with Grandpa, beyond the scars and the old wounds. If I was to believe the doctors, he was dying of old age and...well...tiredness. His body had taken all the beating it could take and was just done. He hadn't been well for a long time, and though he'd tried his best to hide it from us, even before the others left for Severny Island it had gotten obvious.

I'd asked him to move in, ostensibly for me to have another adult to help with Ray, but really it was so I could keep an eye on him. Except he'd really started to deteriorate over the last few months, and there wasn't much I could do for him. When he'd gotten to where getting around was a challenge, I'd had to hire a very nice nurse who specialized in geriatric cases.

I'd put him up in one of the finished suites, a room that connected to another room next door by an inside door. It had either been a suite for a married couple or a nursery next to the parents' room. Now it did very well for a dying Hunter and his caretaker.

Her name was Amanda Fuesting. She'd once been a surgical nurse who had the misfortune to be helping with surgery on someone who'd been bitten by a zombie, and when the patient died on the table and came back chomping, she'd beaten his head to a pulp with the IV stand. She'd saved the life of the doctor and the other nurses, but when the Monster Control Bureau had needed a cover story and she'd refused to cooperate, they'd just said that she'd lost her mind and killed a patient. For some reason, this was the sort of thing that tended to blight one's official career.

MCB had gotten her labeled insane, but a kindly read-in judge made sure she was sent to Appleton

Asylum, where people who had monster encounters could find affirmation and healing. That place was run by my old friends, doctors Lucius and Joan Nelson. They'd helped her out, taught her how to not piss off the MCB, declared her rehabilitated, no longer a threat to society, and I'd been happy to give her a job.

As I approached the hallway, Ms. Fuesting came out of her room. I swear nurses are some form of supernatural creature, both because they hear everything and because they can move without making any sound, like some sort of haunt. She was short and petite, dark-haired and pretty and frankly looked like she was about fifteen years old, so every time I saw her, I wondered what she was doing here, looking after a cantankerous, dying Hunter. It was only when I saw her being stern but reasonable at Grandpa that I realized she was more than capable for the task.

"Morning, Julie. He's just waking up. He'll be happy to see you."

She spent much of her time encouraging everyone around to hang out with Grandpa while they could. It supposedly made things much easier for both parties, if you knew you'd spent as much time together as possible.

"Sure. I'm going into work in a bit, but I've got a while."

"Oh good. Talking with you is the highlight of his day."

Sadly, right now I was all the family the Boss had nearby. Everyone else was laying siege to the City of Monsters. I aimed my formless worry and guilt vaguely in the direction of someone up above and asked Him to keep my friends and family safe. I wasn't brought up particularly religious. It's just that no one can go toe to toe with evil so often without getting a very clear idea that there is something else up there, and that He has a soft spot for humans. Otherwise, we would've lost a long time ago.

"Is he doing okay?" I wasn't stupid. I knew he was dying. And yet a part of me, the part who'd been little and knew that the Boss could do anything and was immortal, still hoped for a miracle, for something extraordinary to happen to have him be fine and live a long time, and run the company and get to help me raise little Ray.

Ms. Fuesting shrugged. "Well. He's not doing too badly today. I've got him on something for the pain and shortness of breath, plus liquid Ativan for anxiety, and we have his cough under control with Duoneb nebulizer, cough drops, and Robitussin. He didn't want breakfast, but he had some water."

The no breakfast but some water made *me* anxious, but I wasn't about to ask. I didn't want to know if this meant he was near the end. I wanted that miracle. I wanted Grandpa to be there. If I'd lost everyone else, I'd still have him.

"Just go on in."

He was sitting up, but his eye was closed. His hand and his hook were resting atop the turned-back sheet. He looked so tired. It seemed unfair that someone could fight through so many battles and end up dying in bed. I always wanted Hunters to survive every fight, but it seemed like it was better to go in a big blaze of glory than to fade away. We lived hard, and it seemed like we should die loud, a shout of defiance against the dark forces in this world and the next.

As I walked up to the bed I could see that he was breathing, his chest rising and falling, but he was so still. I put my hand over his. It was cold. Not cold like he was dead, but cool, like his circulation was failing. When I leaned forward and kissed his cheek, he opened his eye and looked at me.

"Julie." His voice was low, as though dampened. The doctors had said something about his damaged lungs making it difficult for him to have enough breath to speak. "Any contact with the mission?"

I loved how he got right down to business. "Nothing in the last twenty-four hours, but don't worry. A really big snowstorm is covering the island so comms are probably just down. I'm sure they're fine."

He looked at Ray and smiled. "Hey, you brought Little Bubba."

"Now, Grandpa," I said with mock severity, sitting on the side of the bed. There had been a video call shortly after Ray's birth, to introduce him to the Hunters who were away, and Earl had insisted on referring to him as Little Bubba. I really didn't want that nickname to stick.

Grandpa laughed, a low chuckle that edged into cough. "Well. Dad—Earl says little Ray reminds him of Bubba Shackleford. He's got a very dignified bearing."

"Oh, that's just Earl being Earl."

"I don't think it is," he said slowly, as though he'd taken a long time considering it. "I think Earl really thinks that Little Bubba looks like Bubba. And it makes me feel good in a way, you know? If this little fella could remember me later, he'd just remember *old.*"

"Come on. You're going to get better and live ten years more, and get to teach Little Bub—now you've got me doing it—little Ray how to shoot and fight and all the same tricks you taught me."

He patted my hand. His skin was like paper and I could feel his finger bones beneath. "Honey, you know that ain't gonna happen. A body should know when he's dying. Lord knows I dodged it enough for a real long time. Little Bubba won't remember me at all. That's fine. I've lived a long, full life. I built something to be proud of. I can't ask for more. It's only decent to move off the stage." He had a faraway look and his jaw worked. "If only..."

"Earl was here?" I asked.

Grandpa laughed. It was a dry, raspy laugh, and he started coughing again. He took his hand away from mine and fumbled on the bedside table with a little package. I got hold of it. It was maple-flavored hard candy. The nurse had told me earlier that hard candy worked just as well as cough drops, and Grandpa liked the maple flavor. He sucked on it until the cough subsided, but there was still laughter on his face as he looked at me. "I wish he was here, but he'd probably hate it. His curse is its own punishment and its own reward."

"If you start telling me of the pain of outliving everyone else, like some teenage vampire groupie, I'm going to be very upset."

He smiled. "Oh, hell no. Besides, Earl don't sparkle. No, but there's something in it. I know my daddy loves me, as much as ever, but there is...ah. There's a distance between us, because this isn't supposed to happen. No father should have to see his son die. But no father really should have to see his son die of old age." He was silent a moment. "No father should see a son die," he repeated. "And I sit here, you know, and I can't sleep, or else I'm between sleep and waking much of the time, and I wish—how I wish—that I could go back in time just a few moments and tell my younger self to watch out for my boy, for your father. To watch out for him, and to keep Susan safe. But I can't now, and I couldn't then."

"It wasn't your fault, Grandpa." And it wasn't. My mom had been lost on a mission, and the grief had driven my dad to do some desperate and crazy things. Now he was dead and my mother was a powerful vampire whose goal in unlife was to turn the rest of her family so we could be together forever. The evil thing that had replaced my mother was a real piece of work, and as far as I knew she was out there somewhere, plotting.

"You did what you could. Dad made his own bad decisions."

Grandpa shook his head. "I know that. Don't make it any easier."

Little Ray had finished eating and was lying there in the sling, holding the empty bottle. His head was drooping sleepily. Grandpa ran a finger down the chubby cheek, producing no more than an eyelid flutter. Then he turned his gaze towards me, very serious. "It's being a parent, you see. I know my son made his own decisions. I know there was only so much I could do with him. He was what he was. We're not born blank slates; we're born with capacities, inclinations, ways of behaving. Ray was always insecure. Smart, mind you, honey, I'm not putting your daddy down. He was damned smart, and a good family man, and a good Hunter. He wasn't a coward, but he always needed an anchor, and that was Susan. When your mother was lost . . . Well, he made his own decisions, but being a parent makes you want to fix things for them forever." He looked at me and sighed. "You'll learn. Even when this little one is bigger and taller than you—probably by five or so the way he's growing—you'll still want to protect him from everything. And if something happens to him, you'll never forgive yourself, even if it's not your fault."

Grandpa was going to be stubborn to the end. That was just the Shackleford family way. He inclined his head a little, then sighed again. "At least I'm leaving MHI in good hands. Shackleford women have always been pretty as flowers, but made of steel and determination. You'll do fine."

"I don't want to do fine. I'd rather do just okay and keep you around longer to make sure I'm doing it right. It's all so new, this mom thing." The next thing I said was really dark, but we were a monster hunting family, so we didn't tend to dance around ugliness. "If the mission fails and no one comes back, the company's gutted. I'd have to rebuild from scratch. I can't do that."

He laughed again, then sucked hard on his candy. "No one is ever ready. I sure wasn't. There's tough times, lean times. But we survived those, and you're at least as tough as I was. Maybe more, and certainly better trained. You'll do fine." He lifted his hand again. My son was now fully asleep and didn't stir as Grandpa smoothed the fine, silky hair on his head. "And Little Bubba will be fine. We're Shacklefords—even if his name is Pitt, still counts—and we do what we have to do."

That made my lip quiver, but I wasn't about to let Grandpa see me being sad.

"You take care of Little Bubba. Not too much care. You don't want to protect him too much, makes 'em soft. Someday, many years from now, he'll be ready to take over MHI. And then . . ." Grandpa's voice seemed to fade. "His kids, and his kids after him. It's what we are. It's what we do. We live, we die, but the hunt goes on."

He didn't so much fall silent, as his voice faded out completely as he nodded off. His chest rose and fell slowly. And I realized that my cheeks were moist. I didn't remember crying. I wiped my face impatiently with the back of my hand. I'd make him proud, no matter what the world threw at me.

Supporting little Ray's sling, I stood up and stooped to kiss grandpa. When I did, his lips moved, but I couldn't tell what he was saying, if anything.

I got out of the room and found Ms. Fuesting hovering. Nurses do that. "I'm afraid I tired him out a bit."

She shook her head. "No such thing. It's good for him, and good for you too. The more time together you have, the more you talk. It eases the transition."

"Yeah," I said, because I didn't know what else to say. When she used words like *transition,* it made it sound like he was just going on a trip. And maybe in a way it was just that, as Grandpa said, this was the way things were supposed to happen.

The problem was that for the Shacklefords nothing ever happened like it was supposed to. Great-granddad was a werewolf. My parents had turned into vampires. And I—I lifted my hand and touched the dark mark on my neck—well, I wasn't sure what was happening to me.

I'd been terrified the mark of the Guardian would

taint little Ray, like I might pass that curse onto him. It didn't seem to have. He seemed about as normal and happy a baby as you could get.

Thing was, in this family, you never knew.

Grandpa was slowly dying, but that was lucky. He was the only normal one among all of us. What was it they said about those who fight monsters having to be careful lest they become one? Well, we'd been careful, but it hadn't mattered. Some of us fell by the wayside, and some of us became something else.

I couldn't protect little Ray from things like that forever either. One day I would have to let him face monsters on his own. But not yet. No. Not for a long time yet. My cheeks were unaccountably wet again. I wiped my eyes, got my car keys, strapped little Ray into his car seat, and went to work.

CHAPTER 3

MHI company headquarters was usually described as a *compound*, which was fine by us, because images of crazy militia rednecks out in the Alabama woods kept the riffraff out.

The whole place was fenced in. There was one main building, which was sprawling since bits got added to it when needed, without any regard for how it looked. It was built of heavy brick and steel. Though it was technically an office building, it had served as a fort, and we'd successfully defended it from attacks before. Most workplaces don't have a portcullis.

The parking lot was nearly empty. The compound was usually a busy place, but most of our regular people were on the mission, and we were between Newbie classes. It kind of had an empty vibe that made me feel a little lonely.

I went straight into the office with little Ray in his sling. The first thing I checked was to see if there had been any contact with the mission, but still nothing since they'd been hit by the latest storm. There wasn't cause to worry yet. They were on a crappy island north of the Arctic Circle in winter. We lost contact every time the weather turned bad. These sorts of things happened. They were probably fine. *Probably.*

So rather than fret uselessly, I got to work. I've always been the person who did general planning and contracts for MHI, because most Hunters have all the business acumen of a baby opossum. No, seriously. You get all these tough guys and gals who risk their lives in really scary ways, but not too many of them could make a budget, and paperwork confused and frightened them.

I think when my husband took over as MHI's finance guy most of our team leads were handing in their receipts in a shoebox: weapons, ammunition, Big Macs, clothes to replace the ones shredded by a monster, parking fees, oil changes, and that one time they took their team out for ice cream—just in case, throw it all in the box. Then they'd dump these on Earl's desk, which he'd ignore until they'd reached a height of three-to-five feet, then sweep them into a file cabinet where he'd continue to ignore them.

Luckily that hadn't been my problem. During those years, I'd stayed busy trying to book our gigs, negotiate our contracts, and generally keeping us in business. The tax side of it . . . well, I did the best I could, but there's not much you can do with stacks of shoeboxes of unorganized receipts compiled by angry gorillas.

Okay, I could have made a wonderful bonfire.

But the IRS wasn't likely to believe I'd *accidentally* burned all our records, just like the ATF tended not to believe us each time we told them we'd lost a machinegun in a tragic boating accident. But even the idea of a bonfire had often warmed my heart in those days before Owen.

Then my husband had come along and set everything right just by the force of his personality. He was just tenacious like that. It was the same spirit he used to drag himself through death and back—sometimes literally—to win the day for the good guys.

Damn it, I loved that man. When they'd made him, they'd broken the mold, and there was no way, no way at all that I would resign myself to him being lost in some chaos dimension. If he didn't come back, I'd go find Owen and drag him back myself. I'd just have to get little Ray to the point I could entrust him to someone to finish raising him.

Maybe Owen's mom? She'd come to visit after Ray was born, but she'd still been grieving her husband and had been kind of an emotional wreck. Her offer to help however she could had been appreciated, but after staying with us a week she'd gone back to Europe to visit her sisters, to "get her head straight." I knew she'd rush back if I asked, that's just how she was, but I wanted to give her time to heal.

Headquarters was too quiet nowadays. With most of us off on the siege, the big place felt empty. I'd moved my office into one of the larger rooms because there needed to be accommodation for little Ray.

How much accommodation does a six-month-old infant need?

Ah. It wasn't so much accommodation that he needed as it was entertainment, so that he wasn't crying, complaining, and trying to get me to play with him every minute.

Luckily, his entertainment was orcs.

MHI's orc tribe lived nearby, in their own little village, but in a heavily forested area where the chances of anyone stumbling across them were virtually nil. They'd moved in with us after Earl had rescued Skippy's tribe in central Asia, and they'd been crazy loyal ever since. The orcs considered MHI their adopted tribe, and there was nothing they wouldn't do for their tribe.

Thing is . . . Baby Ray was very special to them, and not just because he'd been delivered by an orc healer. Why would I go to a hospital when I had perfectly good orcs? It wasn't even that he was the nephew of Mosh Pitt, whom they called "Great War Chief," because orcs loved heavy metal music more than anything else in the world. No, they treated him as if he were special, really special, in his own self. Which, of course, he was to me, but I hadn't been able to figure out why he would be to them. I mean, sure, he was a pretty wonderful baby, and really, despite a tendency to wake screaming at four A.M., I couldn't think how he could be better.

But why did the orcs hang around every chance they got, adults and children both coming over to spend time with him all through my workday? Was it some instinct he'd someday be the boss? Orcs were big on the whole bloodline thing. Or was it just the way they treated all babies? Probably not that, because they had a ton of their own. Heck, I think Skippy by himself had like a dozen kids.

Anyways, one side effect of few humans around meant the orcs were more comfortable visiting. My new and improved office, about twice the size of the old one, had filled up with orcs before I'd even finished checking my emails.

It was always the same. Somehow they'd get word Ray was here, they'd run over from their village, I'd get a knock on the door, and there would be some squat little children in ski masks and heavy metal T-shirts asking, "Baby?" and "Play now?" Orc kids have gravelly voices like their parents—and they'd always be followed by a couple of patient, burkha-wearing mothers.

It used to be that the only orcs who ever came around the compound were Skippy, Ed, and Gretchen, that was only ever for work, and they were always shy while they were here. Ray's arrival had changed that big time. Now I couldn't get rid of them. Normally all the orcs hid their faces around humans, not wanting to cause any freak-outs because of their pointy ears and tusks, but once they were in my office they were in friendly territory and they'd ditch the masks and sunglasses.

Ray started chortling the minute he saw them.

I had a hanging swing chair, a playpen, and a high chair for him. But it didn't really matter which one I stuck him in. He wouldn't be in any of those for very long. A minute later they'd be dancing around with him, or lying on the floor making fight noises while they wiggled Ray's arms and legs like he was punching and kicking their enemies. I've learned quite a bit of their language over the years, so apparently my son had a warrior spirit "pleasing to Gnrlwz," the orc god of war. Which was good, because I think Gnrlwz had officiated at my wedding.

My workday went something like this:

I sat down and started filling PUFF paperwork, looking up around my third form to say, "Stop bouncing him around like that, he's going to urk up his break—and there it goes. Thank you for cleaning that up, guys. Play more gently, okay?" By the fourth form, I'd hear "I warg!" shouted by one of the juveniles, getting down on all fours, while another one held little Ray on the back of the pretend giant wolf. And then they'd ride around slaying imaginary monsters. I'm pretty sure once Ray was older he'd end up riding a real warg like the orc kids did, but right now, he was just too small for it, and I'd already put my foot down: no way in hell were they putting my baby on the back of a giant killer wolf no matter how much they promised to *hold him tight good*.

I went back to my forms and actually managed to concentrate for a few hours, despite the fact that the orcs were singing horribly distorted versions of metal songs the whole time. They were surprisingly gentle with Ray, and he absolutely loved them.

"Julie! Damn it, girl, how many times do I need to call you before you hear me?"

I looked up past the pile of orc kids, to the door of the office, where a forbidding figure stood: Dorcas.

Okay, not really a forbidding figure to anyone who didn't know her. Some people who weren't very good at reading people might mistake her for a sweet Southern grandma. But in this office, we both knew her cantankerous, take-no-prisoners persona too well. She could be a mean old lady, but she was utterly devoted to MHI and loved us like her own kids. Unless, of course, one of us had been stupid enough to eat one of her pudding cups she kept stashed in the break room fridge, because she'd straight-up kill you for that.

The reason someone might unwittingly mistake Dorcas for a kindly grandmother was that she was kind of plump and cheerful looking—when she wasn't yelling at anyone—and her white hair was neat and obviously carefully combed. But she always had a slightly manic gleam in her eye and a big revolver in a shoulder holster under her purple knit sweater. Dorcas had been a Hunter until she lost a leg in a fight with a werewolf, and then she'd been our "receptionist" ever since. Mostly that meant she herded us into shape and looked after us in her own demented way.

Right then she was glaring at me as she maneuvered around the orcs. "What's so fascinating about Fed forms that you'd ignore me?"

I was her boss but there was no point in debating it with her. She'd known me since I was a baby, and I think in her mind I was still a lot like Ray: a little kid making other people's lives difficult. So I just said, "What can I help you with, Dorcas?" And then because my heart picked up all of a sudden and I thought maybe, just maybe she'd gotten word. "Is it—did you hear anything from the siege?"

Dorcas went from cheerfully annoyed to sad in a second. "Sadly, no. Hunters on the mainland checked in, but the island's still getting hammered by that blizzard. We just got a tip there was a monster attack down in Philpot."

"Alabama?" That was only an hour's drive away. "What kind?"

"Swamp lurker."

I pushed the forms aside—damn it, why did the federal government still insist these be on paper—and went back to my computer, already running through my mind who might be available to deal with an incident. Not a lot of people, that's for sure. We weren't only a skeleton crew, but the skeleton was picked clean. With over half our employees off on the other side of the world, we were down to some very overworked pros, Newbies, and the people who normally wouldn't be sent on missions at all, covering the whole country. "I don't know who we can send—"

"Whoa, slow down. This went down a couple days ago. It's contained."

I took a deep breath. *Okay. That was good.* I was dying to get back to hunting, but it's hard to charge off to kill monsters when you need to find a sitter first. "We're just now hearing about it? That's practically next door. What're we bribing all these public officials for anyway?"

Dorcas shrugged. "It got stopped so fast nobody got hurt. Some local had a bunch of guns in the back of his truck and took care of business. Those things are freaky as all get out, but he kept his cool and got shit done. By the time the cops were notified, it was all green guts as far as the eye could see."

"Hmm. That's good work. Those are tough."

"Yep. That's showing some initiative." The way she said that meant Dorcas had obviously been thinking the same thing I'd been thinking. MHI recruited almost exclusively from the survivors of monster attacks. Come to think of it, that's how I'd first met my husband. With all the government-mandated secrecy, it wasn't like we could post help wanted ads.

"You got a name for this local hero?"

"And an address. Philpot isn't far. I think somebody needs to go interview this guy and see if he's proper Newbie material."

"Right." I looked over at where my son had fallen

asleep and was being tucked into his little crib by one of the orc women. Checking out potential recruits was a delicate job, usually reserved for team leads. You've got to get a good feel for the individual before you start telling them too much, especially about the money, and you had to make sure they had the flexible mind necessary for this job. I sure as hell couldn't send Dorcas. She'd pop off her fake leg to explain about what killing werewolves was like and scare him off. "I don't know who I could send to talk to him just now..."

"Hell," Dorcas said. "You should go yourself. It's a nice drive. You're obviously bored out of your mind. This paperwork can wait."

"I'm not sure—"

"Well, I am. You're looking like one of them caged lions. When I was little, the zoo had this lion, and in those days they didn't know any better, so they put the creature in a cage barely bigger than she was. My mom and dad took us kids to see the lion, and she'd just pace around and look sad."

"I don't know what the heck you're talking about."

"Because you didn't let me finish. That lion was so bored she eventually died. You've had that same look in your eyes as that lion. And you've looked that way for months."

"I'm not caged. I'm only—"

"Beating yourself up you couldn't go and fight in the biggest mission ever, while everyone else you know has."

"Someone was going to have to stay and run the day-to-day operations no matter what. The pregnant lady was kind of the obvious choice."

"I'm too old and crippled and I'm pissed off I couldn't go either. You're doing what you've got to do. When you choose to become a mother, you're putting yourself in a cage of sorts—leastways if you give a damn about your kids, because from the moment you have a kid, the kid comes first. You know what I say?"

I waited with bated breath for her to tell me what she said. Dorcas was a great source of off-color aphorisms, but it was hard to think of anything she'd ever said in particular on the subject of the costs of motherhood.

"I say that it's time you get back to work."

"I'm at work, Dorcas." I gestured at my cluttered desk.

"I mean *real* work. This is the crap that happens after real work gets done. When's the last time you practiced with a gun?"

I scowled. She had a fair point. In the field, I was usually the one on precision rifle. Honestly, I was really good. Or had been... It wasn't like I could haul Ray out to the range with me. Babies don't like to wear earplugs.

"Too long and you know it. Okay, I'll admit I'm bored. I'm sleep-deprived to the point of brain damage, and I'm either on mommy duty for Ray or mommy duty for this company. I'd love to do *anything* different. But what am I supposed to do? Put Ray in the car seat and drag him around to interview a prospective recruit?"

"That would make us look like serious professionals." Dorcas snorted. "All them mothers in other jobs, they go back to work when the baby's done nursing, and stick 'em in day care, and go about like they don't have a care in the world."

"I'm not going to put Ray in day care." For one, it

wasn't even a sane alternative. Given the things that tried to get at Hunters through their children—I'd had to fight off an incubus at my junior prom—the last thing I was going to do was drop him off somewhere I couldn't keep an eye on him. Second, most kids in day care didn't have a vampire grandmother with deranged ideas about reuniting her whole family as happy bloodsuckers. "And you know he wouldn't be safe."

"Look at him. He has the best day care in the world right here, with all the wards and protections of the compound. They'll watch him while you go and talk to this prospect."

"The orcs? Who's going to watch them watch Ray?" Still, it was sorely tempting to get *out*. "I don't know. What if we have a call for help? Or what if our people call?"

"I might be old, but I'm still competent enough to patch through a call from your husband if he happens to show up. So, you go talk to this prospect. You can be there and back by closing time. I'll man the phones and the orcs would love to mind the baby."

"But if I run late—"

"I'll take Ray back to your house and meet you there. I'm a good babysitter"—she patted the Ruger Redhawk in her shoulder holster—"and a better bodyguard. Come on, kid. You need to get out. You look like crap."

I tried to fight the temptation. The day had warmed up somewhat, and it was nice without being hot. Outside, the sun shone and the day was bright. And I was probably the worst mother in the world, because after months of being tethered to Ray night and day,

I just wanted to go somewhere by myself and do my own thing. Even if it was just talking to some random stranger who'd shot up some swamp lurkers. But I had all those forms to file and I really shouldn't leave my son alone. He was my primary responsibility.

An orc was singing a lullaby that sounded suspiciously like Black Sabbath, and Ray was passed out on his back, his cheeks rosy, and a little smile on his lips.

"You know if you don't go now, the MCB will get to him first, and either intimidate the hell out of him, or outright send him to a mental hospital, pump him full of drugs, and convince him he dreamed the whole thing."

"Well, that's true," I admitted.

"Of course it's true or I wouldn't have said it. Take Albert with you," Dorcas suggested. "I don't think he's left the library in months. That boy's been working himself to death researching everything the mission's come across. He's been drinking more caffeine than Melvin. I think he's the only other person who got left behind who took it even harder than you. He needs some fresh air now and then before he turns into a mushroom."

I didn't demur that time. She had a point. "Okay. You win. I'll go."

Dorcas grinned. "Girl, I always win."

"Get back to work before I fire you."

I got on the phone and dialed the extension for the archive room in the basement, and when Albert Lee answered, I knew he too sounded exactly like that lion Dorcas had described. It wasn't being physically confined, but stuck—either by motherhood or a physical disability—while all your friends were off doing something dangerous and important. It was the sort of thing that brought up the toddler complaint *but it isn't fair*. Only we weren't toddlers, so we just tried to do the best we could while dying a little inside. It had made me grumpy, but it had left Albert downright antisocial.

So I told Albert what we were doing. And since I was his boss, I didn't really give him a choice. Like me, he was driven by a sense of duty, but even then, the best he could manage was "Gee, I don't know" in the way of objecting.

"Come on, what are you doing that's so important right now?"

"Cross-referencing the latest monster sightings on Severny Island with historical accounts of arcane energies cutting off radio communications, seeing if there's any commonality."

"Fascinating," I lied. It sounded like he was stuck and bored until the teams checked in, so he was passing his time looking for haystack needles. "Would a few hours make that big a difference to your research? Come on. Road trip. And I'll buy you lunch at Big Cove Barbecue!"

I could hear him waver. For a man of Asian extraction, Albert Lee has a wicked fixation on Southern barbecue.

"Oh, all right," he said at last. "But I'm going to call Melvin and get everything on this survivor dude so we can read up on him on the trip."

I had no argument with that. "That's what I pay him for."

"I don't think he actually gets paid..."

"Whatever. Dress business casual."

"I'll even comb my hair." Albert hung up.

While he was getting ready I wrote down a list of everything that needed to be done with Ray for Dorcas. I knew everyone knew this stuff by now, from where I kept his formula (in the drinks fridge in the office) and his clean bottles (on the top cabinet across from my desk) and the fixings for the cereal he liked (on the bottom cabinet) and that he was on no account to be given raw egg or honey because his immune system couldn't handle that yet, even though I often suspected that the orcs were feeding him lizards or snails or whatever leaves looked appetizing. My theory was based on the smells I encountered while changing his diapers. Mind you, just like with Gretchen's disgusting potions, they didn't seem to do him any harm; on the contrary, he was a shockingly hardy baby.

So I knew my instructions would probably be ignored, but I had to leave the note to make myself feel like I wasn't a horrible mother for skipping out on my infant.

I drove while Albert read the files Melvin kept emailing him. After a while I got tired of the silence and said, "It's good to be out, isn't it?"

"Sure." Albert didn't sound sure. He sounded like he wanted to be sullenly hiding in his library, trying to feel useful.

"Come on. It's a nice day. Though . . . I do feel a little guilty."

He looked up from his phone long enough to give me a sickly smile. "Because the women, children, old folks, and cripples who got left behind haven't heard anything from our friends who are busy risking their lives?"

"Don't remind me, but I was actually talking about Ray. This is the longest I've ditched him since he's been born."

"Oh." Albert looked a little sheepish at that. He'd volunteered to go on the siege and was assigned to Cody's big brain squad, but Earl had changed his mind and shot him down at the last minute. It had been gentle by Earl's standards, with him saying that Albert and his skills would be more valuable here, while his messed-up leg would be a liability on Severny Island. So not particularly gentle, but this was Earl we were talking about. "Sorry. I didn't mean it like that."

Maybe it was just a Hunter thing. Even though there had originally been over a thousand men on that mission, each of us was big-headed enough to think that we alone could have made all the difference by being there. Albert Lee had to wear a brace and walk with a cane, and he'd still fought for a spot. To be fair, he probably would have been way more effective than a really pregnant sniper.

"It's cool, Albert. I'm with you. You can vent."

"Okay. This friggin' sucks. I could've spent the last six months manning a gun turret on that boat or on one of the supply convoys just as well as anybody. But no, I'm sitting at a desk all day waiting for a call, just in case they need help figuring something out. How dorky is that?"

"Not dorky at all, considering how many times something you looked up saved someone's ass in the field."

"I'm going to remind you that you said that when it comes time for annual bonuses."

"You do that." But considering that I knew he'd moved back into the company barracks like a Newbie, just so he could be close to the archives 24/7 in case someone on Severny Island had a question, Albert was getting a good bonus this year. "In the meantime, I feel like a teenager sneaking out of school."

He grinned at me. "I guess it does. I did need to get out of that basement. I've been down there so long that Melvin is starting to make sense."

"That can't be good for your mental health."

"Probably not. And just so you know, I'm still looking into that other thing for you, but I've got nothing."

I nodded. He meant the Guardian curse. What the marks meant, and what they'd eventually do to me were still a mystery. I'd put out feelers to all our scholarly types and asked Ben Rigby to have his people check with Oxford. Yet, even with centuries of collected monster hunting wisdom, it was like nobody knew a damned thing about the Guardians.

"It's all good, Albert. I wasn't getting my hopes up."

It was a nice day for a drive. Philpot wasn't quite as hidden in the middle of nowhere as Cazador was, but I remembered how to get there. They were Cazador's Pee-Wee Football's rivals. Both my brothers had played.

I changed the subject. "Anything of use on our potential recruit yet?" I asked. "Anything that I should know, at least?"

"Melvin's last email was titled *I bored* and had this guy's tax records attached. It's like central casting called for a small-town white guy from Alabama."

"Hey, you just described most of my relatives."

"Except for the werewolf..." Albert muttered as he scrolled through. "High school quarterback, married his high school sweetheart who was a cheerleader. Worked as a mechanic. Took over his dad's auto shop and been there ever since. Never been arrested, never even had a speeding ticket. The most interesting thing about him is that he shoots guns on a friend's farm after work, and Melvin only knew about that because they posted pictures on Facebook."

"He seems pretty normal."

Albert looked up from his phone and scowled. "Julie, serious question: how many monster-encounter survivors have you interviewed would you describe as *normal?*"

"It's about half and half. For every guy from a stereotypical overachieving Asian immigrant home whose uptight parents expected him to be an engineer, but who rebelled and joined the Marine Corps instead..."

"I like this guy. He sounds like a badass."

"Let me finish. Who then got a job as a librarian, until he nuked the county library because of a giant spider infestation, and got interviewed by me right after the MCB was threatening him into silence with felony arson and bomb-making charges...for every one of those interesting types, I interview a Johnny Football Hero who took over his daddy's auto body shop."

"Brakes and mufflers mostly it looks like from their webpage," Albert corrected me. "But fair enough. I don't usually do interviews. I just figured most of us would be weirder."

"Oh, they're weird too. They just hide it better."

CHAPTER 4

Philpot, Alabama, is not a one-horse town, mostly because no one rode horses anymore. Once we got off the highway it was all winding country roads. Here and there was a house, a good bit back from the road, half hidden by trees covered in kudzu. Once, a pickup truck passed us, the echoes of the music it was playing wafting behind like a ghostly presence.

"Wow, there really is nothing much out here, is there?" Albert stifled a yawn.

"I grew up in Cazador. This seems completely normal to me."

Moments later, on the route to the main street, we passed a—well, for lack of a better word—a "convenience" store. It looked beaten and grey, like no one had bothered to paint the white façade in a long time. There were no gas pumps. There was, however, a sign in the window advertising boiled peanuts. Tempting as that was, we kept going.

The town was really just one main street, but it seemed to have everything you'd need: grocery store, gas station, barber, and doughnut shop. There was even a little Italian restaurant tucked in at the other end.

We followed the GPS past the end of the strip, and after a couple of miles turned off. At the end of that road was a building that might have started life as a barn. Parked around it were a bunch of cars waiting to be worked on or ready for pickup. They certainly weren't hurting for business.

As I parked, Albert noted, "This is isolated enough for a swamp lurker attack, but normally they like a swampier climate. That's kind of in their name. He's in for a good PUFF though."

"Yeah, about that. We'll hook him up with whatever bounty he's owed no matter what, but let me get a feel for whether I want to make him a job offer before you mention how much money he could make. Too many Newbies who show up with dollar signs in their eyes wash out during training." Money is a fantastic motivator, and this career usually paid really well, but a good Hunter needed other qualities too.

"You're the boss."

Albert meant that in the nicest possible way, but it just made me think of Grandpa. He was still *the* Boss. That was and always would be his title as far as I was concerned. When I opened the car door, I could hear country music coming from inside the shop. Not really loud, just perfectly audible in the surrounding silence.

The barn doors were open. I noted that the inside of the mechanic's shop was more modern than expected. There was a lift—with a car up on it—and there was computer equipment on a roller cart. The whole place smelled strongly of cleaners and disinfectants. Swamp lurkers stunk, and he'd probably been scrubbing up their oozy, sticky blood for hours.

The guy was standing by the computer doing something. At least I presumed he was our guy because there was no one else around, and he looked a lot like the driver's license photo Albert had shown me.

He must have heard our car or our footsteps because he yelled toward us without looking. "I'll be right with you."

This guy was . . . standard issue. Blond, looking like he'd once been very athletic and now gone a bit to seed. Not fat, as such, but no longer looking like he played sports anymore. He was handsome, too, the sort of generic handsome that a small town guy might be without pretensions. Square chin, but his most striking feature was nice eyes, so green they were almost emerald. The name tag on his coveralls read CJ. When he finally looked up from whatever he was doing, he immediately realized we were strangers, then gave us a polite smile and said, "What do you need?"

"Mr. Colin Wynne?"

"That's me." The smile remained polite, kind of noncommittal, but I could tell he was nervous. He'd just dealt with some really weird shit but wasn't curled up in the fetal position sucking his thumb, so that was a good sign. I also didn't know if, or how much, the MCB had yelled at him yet about not talking about his supernatural encounter. "Who are you?"

"I'm Julie Shackleford." I still used my maiden name for MHI business. I'd built up enough of a professional reputation that switching now would cost us money. My husband was too much of an accountant to be offended. "From up the road in Cazador." I added that last part, so at least he'd know I wasn't another carpetbagging MCB goon. "This is my associate, Albert Lee."

I went to shake his hand, but he made a big show of cleaning his hands on a rag, so that he couldn't. "Okay."

"We wanted to talk to you about what happened here."

Wynne muttered something under his breath as his expression shifted to annoyance. "Who are you?" He looked at me first, then over at Albert. I was wearing slacks and a blouse, and Albert had on a nice button shirt. "Newspaper reporters? I've got no comment. Are you going to slander me? Because if you are, I'll sue. I grew up here. Everyone knows me. I've never done drugs, never even smoked pot, but now some government types are saying I got high and hallucinated. And them saying it was the result of prescription meds doesn't cut it. I don't take any prescriptions, either. Do I look like I need prescriptions?"

That meant he'd gotten a call from the MCB already. "We're not newspaper reporters. Besides, prescription drug abuse wouldn't explain the slime left from the swamp lurkers."

His eyes narrowed. "What are you? Someone from that New Age place over near the doughnut shop? No, ma'am. It was probably just a deformed giant crab. My grandpappy disposed of some weird stuff back there a long time ago, you know, all the refrigerants and stuff. The old barrels must have leaked, made it look like that, like a mutant or something."

"That's some potent chemicals if it's making their blood turn green," Albert said as he walked to the side and poked his cane at a wet spot on the floor. It had obviously been sprayed off, but there was still some splatter that needed to be scrubbed.

Wynne pushed a button on his computer and the music cut out. "Look, lady, my day was weird enough. I don't need to be on the front page of some UFO

magazine any more than I need rumors of my doing
drugs going around town, hurting my business. I'm just
a mechanic. I do good business. I don't need rumors of
anything weird around here. People could start driving
to the next town over for service."

My grandpa always liked to say that the single most
important thing for a Monster Hunter to possess was
a *flexible mind*. From the way he seemed to be trying
really hard to convince himself that nothing too odd
had happened here, he might not be a good fit. Oh
well. Not every prospect was right for MHI.

"We're with a company that deals with these sorts
of events. From what we've gathered, you handled
yourself well. I wanted to talk to you about a job."

"Fixing cars?"

"No." Though come to think of it, even if he wasn't
mentally suited to making the jump to full-fledged
Hunter, it might be handy to have someone else in the
region we could bring in to service the fleet vehicles.
When your office has got pictures all over the walls
of supernatural things that are actually illegal to even
talk about with regular people, it makes little things
like hiring a plumber really hard.

I handed him a business card, the one with the green
smiley face with horns, and a number that would go to
Dorcas' reception desk. "What we're about to say may
sound a little weird, but after your recent experience,
you of all people will understand we're not crazy. Albert
and I represent a company called Monster Hunter
International. We handle monster-related problems."

He looked down at the card in his hand as he ran
one callused hand through his hair. "So, you deal with
things like . . . those things?"

"Yes, we do." This part was delicate because even though the MCB knew damned good and well we cherry-picked survivors, if they didn't join up and they later talked about stuff that I'd told them, it could complicate both our lives. Plus, I didn't want to scare the hell out of the poor guy and start talking about elder things. "And many more."

"What kind of *more*?"

"Vampires, werewolves, zombies," Albert supplied. "You know, the usual stuff."

Wynne gave a little laugh, like he thought that was a joke; then his eyes got really big when he saw that Albert was totally serious. "Naw. No way, man. You're crazy."

Albert could have been a little more diplomatic on the reveal, but my gut was telling me we hadn't struck pay dirt here. A good potential Newbie, there was always that little spark of curiosity. I'd done so many of these interviews that my instincts were seldom wrong.

"Look, Mr. Wynne. I don't want to waste your time. I'm betting that you were contacted by some government agents already."

"Maybe." The way he said that meant that he had been, but that they'd made it real clear that talking about them was a bad idea.

"They'll probably follow up with you again soon. What they probably didn't tell you is that there's a bounty system to deal with creatures like the one you killed."

"What do you mean 'bounty?'" He sounded even more suspicious about the money than he did the existence of monsters.

"Killing a swamp lurker is worth a significant amount of money to the federal government." I looked to Albert. I hadn't checked the latest PUFF table before we'd left.

"About twenty-five grand for a little one," he said. "I've got some paperwork in the car you can fill out, and when those federal agents call you back to make sure you're being good, tell them you want your bounty payment. They'll act dumb, but if you give them the forms, they're legally obligated to process them. Then you'll get a reward check."

"Really? That's a lot of money."

"You earned it." Even if this wasn't going to work out for MHI, the guy had done a good deed and deserved to get paid. In some cases we'd just go ahead and file all the paperwork for them, like we did for Owen. But then again, he'd killed a werewolf with his bare hands and we'd gotten to watch the whole thing on video. That's the stuff of legend. My future husband had been more like a first-round draft pick, so of course we'd put in the extra effort. "Albert, would you grab those PUFF forms?"

"No problem." He began limping back toward the car.

Wynne obviously liked the part about reward money but was also really suspicious. I know I'm charming enough to get Eskimos to buy snow, but some folks are just a hard sell. I'd let him percolate on it.

"Well...thanks, Ms. Shackleford."

"If you have any questions about that paperwork, you've got our number. When you get paid, you can see that this isn't some sort of scam. If you're interested after that, give us a call. We're always hiring. It was nice to meet you."

"Nice to meet you too."

I turned on my heel to leave. That's when things got weird.

First there was a sound from the car lift. It jerked

up and down several inches, two or three times. There was a loud beeping from the computer. The lights flickered on and off. The beeping and hydraulic humming all stopped at the same time. And suddenly the garage was cold as hell.

It hadn't been very warm to begin with. The temperature outside was in the fifties or so, and he had the bay doors open. But suddenly it was so cold that I turned toward Albert and could see his breath puffing out of his mouth in a cloud.

Shit.

Don't even ask me why, but when there's something powerfully supernatural going on, the temperature often heads down to freezing depths. I'd guess it is the magic, or whatever, sucking all the energy available in the surrounding air. Maybe that's why it seems to get so quiet too.

You know all those little sounds you don't even think about in the South—often the sounds of insects? Or the sound of the computer fan running? Or birds? Maybe a dog barking in the distance? It had all gone suddenly and deathly silent.

I turned back toward Colin Wynne. He looked the same except...except his features had gone rigid is the only way I can describe it. And he was aiming a big stainless steel revolver at me.

"Whoa, easy there."

The gun barked. The flash was right in front of my face. I flinched as the bullet went right past my ear.

I went for the pistol concealed at my side, but Wynne shifted the muzzle over a tiny bit and it was aimed at my nose. His finger was on the trigger. He had me dead to rights.

"It's not time to kill you yet." The words came out of Wynne's mouth, but it sure didn't sound like him anymore.

Slowly, I moved my hand away from my gun. Over the ringing in my ears I could hear the rasp as Albert's back slid down the wall. I risked looking in his direction. My friend was sinking to the floor. His teeth were clenched, trying not to cry out. There was a red hole in his shirt.

"You did exactly what I wanted you to do, daughter of Eve," Wynne said, except it didn't sound at all like the man we'd just been talking to. This voice had... a buzzing undertone is the best way I can describe it, as though each word was being conducted through a cloud of bees.

One thing I've learned in this business is that when someone starts addressing anyone as *daughter of Eve* or *son of Adam* they are evil with a capital E and there's usually all sorts of weird culty demonic crap behind it.

The revolver was trained on me, but it would only take the smallest movement to put it back on Albert. Neither one of us could risk making a move. My friend had pressed his hands to the hole, but from the way there was a streak of blood on the wall behind him, there was an exit wound. The bullet had passed completely through his upper torso. Albert was in big trouble. He needed help fast or he was going to die.

I kept my voice calm. "What do you want?"

"You'll find out... Oh, you'll find out."

I was almost certain that Wynne was, in fact, a regular human being. I'd just been having a conversation with a normal person. His skepticism hadn't been faked. This wasn't a psychotic break. With the lights and the cold and the voice change, this was a straight-up possession. Wynne might still be in there, but he wasn't in charge anymore.

I stared at that gun. We were close enough that tiny black flecks of unburned gunpowder stuck to my glasses. I could see the hollow points in the cylinder. When I was really young, my dad had told me the way to know if someone is about to use the gun they're pointing at you is to look at their eyes. But he'd never told me what it meant when they started glowing.

"What are you?"

The thing inhabiting Wynne's body laughed. It wasn't a horror movie laugh, but just a laugh. This new voice was a few octaves deeper and somehow Wynne had picked up an accent that made him sound like he was from Africa. "My identity is not important. What I can do for you is. I know you're the Guardian. In your possession is an item of great value, an artifact known as the Kumaresh Yar."

"What?" My mind froze for just a moment. I hadn't told anyone I had stashed that thing. Even my husband didn't know I had it. For good reason too. Last time he'd used it he'd turned back time and nearly blown up the world. That thing was stupidly dangerous. And power-mad idiots kept trying to use it for things like bringing back the dead or opening portals to other dimensions. "Go to hell."

The now obviously glowing eyes were looking right through me. "I suspected that would be your answer."

I laughed. I wasn't aware of laughing, exactly, and I certainly wasn't amused. Albert was still burbling and gasping for air. The instant Wynne looked away

I'd go for my gun and hope that the Guardian's curse would save me if I got shot in the brain.

"I expected defiance like that from the Guardian. You would not have been chosen if you did not possess the courage of a lioness."

"I don't have it. The last time I saw that thing was when Lucinda Hood and my mother were fighting over it. You should take it up with them."

Wynne smiled, but the expression didn't fit right on his contorted face. "Guardians do not break. Torture, physical suffering would make no difference. But what would you give in exchange for the life of your child?"

"What?" The word came out of my mouth before I could even fully process the threat.

"I have your baby."

That didn't make any sense. How could it threaten Ray's life? Ray was at the compound, surrounded by orcs who would die to defend him. "You're lying."

The thing laughed again, and the already freezing air seemed to get colder. Supernatural creatures lied all the time. Did it actually have my child? But it had possessed Wynne. Could it possess other people? Dorcas?

"If you've done anything to my son, you son of a bitch, I'll eradicate you."

The shots came out of nowhere. I'd been staring at the creature's evil green eyes and that unnatural rictus grin in its face, trying to decide if it was telling the truth or not, when the pair of bullets struck him in the center of the chest. Wynne tumbled backwards.

As soon as he was sure the monster wasn't watching him, Albert had pulled his pistol and put a controlled pair center of mass.

I drew my gun as I moved over. Wynne was on the floor, gasping for breath. I stepped on his fingers, pinning the .357 Magnum to the floor.

"Tell me what you meant! What've you done with my son?"

His teeth were bloodstained and little bubbles of blood formed on the edge of his lips. "You'll find out soon," said the creature. "We'll be in touch."

In that instant, the sounds of the outside world seemed to come rushing back. I'd not realized that the lights had turned dim and weak, but the garage brightened as they returned to normal. The temperature jumped.

And then it was the real Colin Wynne who was staring up at me. The glow was gone, and these were just normal eyes, blue and frightened. His expression was one of total confusion, as if he couldn't remember what had happened or how he'd wound up on the floor or why I was standing over him or why everything hurt, but then he was dead.

I rushed over to Albert. "Damn it, damn it, damn it."

He was pale and shaking, his whole face contorted in pain. I holstered my gun, grabbed a big rag that was hanging from a hook, and pushed it hard against the wound. There was blood everywhere. While I kept pressure against the wound, I got out my phone and dialed 911.

"Get out of the office," Albert wheezed. "It'll be fun, you said."

"You're going to be fine," I lied.

The last thing Albert said before passing out from blood loss was, "I didn't even get barbecue."

CHAPTER 5

As I ran back into the garage carrying the big med kit from the car, a cell phone began to ring. It was sitting on top of the diagnostics computer.

I grabbed for it before I could think. If I'd thought, I'd have realized that the call would probably be for the dead guy. But as I picked up the phone, I saw that the screen read *Guardian*.

"Son of a bitch." I couldn't believe they had the audacity to be calling me right now. I wasn't in the mood to talk, what with my friend bleeding to death. So I shoved the still-ringing phone in my pocket and went back to Albert. I got compression bandages on the entry and exit wound. He'd gotten hit up high on the chest, and my biggest worry was that the bullet had nicked the superior vena cava.

He was losing too much blood and I couldn't stop it. We were in a rural area. There was no way that an ambulance would get here in time. "Come on, Al." I wrapped my arms around him, hoisted him up, and pulled him towards the car, feet dragging. Luckily Albert wasn't a big dude. I was actually an inch or two taller than he was and running on desperation strength.

I got him into the passenger seat, slammed the door, ran around to the driver's side, got in, started the engine, and shot out of there so fast that the tires sprayed gravel everywhere.

"Hang on, man. I owe you that lunch."

We'd passed the closest hospital on the way in. At regular speeds it had been twenty minutes from the garage. I floored it. I was going to try and get there in ten.

The phone I'd taken had started ringing again.

I pulled it out, put it on speaker, and dropped it on the dash so I could keep both hands on the wheel. That's kind of necessary when you're doing over a hundred on a twisting country road. I didn't say anything. Apparently I didn't need to. The African-accented voice that I'd last heard from Wynne's mouth came on the line. *"Listen carefully, Guardian."*

I was dealing with a monster that was capable of possession and projection. Usually that meant something incorporeal, and those were rather weak, but this thing didn't strike me as weak.

"You will give me the artifact—or your child will suffer." It went silent, and in that silence I heard a scream.

Look, there are so many things weird about being a mother that if every woman didn't have the capacity to become one, motherhood might be considered a supernatural condition. One of those things is the ability to know our kids from a glimpse or a sound. Objectively, all babies look a lot alike, even if mine was supersized. But mothers can always tell when it's their baby crying.

And coming through that phone was my son's cry.

I couldn't talk. My heart clutched. My mouth went dry.

"Now you understand that I'm telling you the truth. If you give me the Kumaresh Yar, I will return him to you unharmed. If not . . . I have interesting plans for your child."

The call ended. I screamed—a prolonged primal scream.

A firefly glowed in front of my windshield briefly, then exploded on impact with green goo. I hit the windshield wipers and washer fluid. Damn things were out earlier every year. We didn't used to get them till May.

"Julie, go back to the compound," Albert rasped. He'd come to and had heard that phone call. "I'll be fine. You need to save—"

"Did I ask you to talk?" I said, taking my impotent fury out on my wounded friend. "Hospital first. If you die, Albert Lee, I'll never forgive you. I'll go back to the other side and kill you again."

"Okay."

I couldn't even risk looking at him, but he really didn't sound good. Instead, I took out my phone. "Call Dorcas." It rang several times and then went through to her voice mail. "Damn it." My eyes were burning. A pickup pulled out in front of us. I had to lay on the horn and drive through the grass to keep from T-boning him. That would have extra-sucked considering I hadn't taken the time to buckle Albert in.

"Call headquarters." That number was for the front desk. Again, no answer. Normally that wouldn't be too surprising. There was no Newbie class going on and most of the Hunters who normally worked at the compound were off on the siege. If any team leads needed anything important they'd call me directly. But right now, the lack of answers was terrifying.

Inside me, something was ticking like a frantic clock. You know that biological clock people talk about? It's nothing to the mom clock that tracks every second her baby might be in danger. I was going to kill the assholes who'd taken him. I didn't even care if this possessor was incorporeal. I'd make it a body just for the purpose of taking it apart molecule by molecule.

I was just glad no dogs or kids got in my way because I wasn't stopping for anyone.

The next call warned the hospital we were on the way—Asian male, thirties, gunshot wound to the chest—and that they'd better be ready.

"Blood type B positive," Albert added through clenched teeth. "Heh... Be positive. Good advice."

I told that to the hospital, hung up, then went back to trying everyone else. No one answered. Not even my home number. Neither Amanda Fuesting nor Grandpa answered the phone. Instead I got my own, annoying voice, saying, *"This is the Heart of the Dixie Historical..."*

I looked down at my hands, clenched and smearing blood all over the steering wheel. Right. Of course no one was there. Because when I got there, if I found anyone in the compound alive and well and my son gone, I was going to personally injure them.

I took a deep breath and remembered that Skippy's tribe had a couple cell phones. We'd even put them on the company plan, but the orcs didn't particularly care for the things and only used them grudgingly.

"Call village."

It rang only twice before a voice answered, *"Eh?"*

This was going to be tough. Our most conversational orcs had all gone on the mission.

"This is Julie. No one is answering the phone at the compound. Is my son okay?"

There was a silence, then the orc said. *"Hello, Jool-eee. I Shelly."*

I hadn't even realized I was talking to a girl, but I knew Shelly. She was one of the younger orc females, and I could always pick her out even in disguise because she was the one with a lazy eye. She'd been learning English and was probably better with it than my mediocre Orcish. "Is Baby Ray okay?"

There was another voice talking rapidly behind her in their rumbling language. *"Uh . . . Dorcas take baby. Great Chief call her . . . The Boss sick, Dorcas say. She go your house. Baby Ray go your house."*

"Okay, listen carefully, Shelly. Baby Ray is in danger. How many warriors do you have?"

"Urk great warriors! All!"

That was pride talking, not reality. Most of their experienced warriors had gone with Ed to the island. They'd only left enough to guard their village. "Yeah, okay. I need you to gather all your warriors and go to my house. Protect the baby. I'll meet you there."

The hospital was visible in the distance. I'd made it in eight minutes. Good thing MHI didn't skimp on our company fleet cars. I was so desperate I thought about calling the cops—our local sheriff was read in on the supernatural; you kind of had to be when you were in charge of the county MHI had been head-quartered in for the last century—but I was dealing with a monster that was organized, had a plan, and was capable of possessing people. This was way over their heads, *and* that thing might have my kid as a hostage.

Not to mention once the authorities got to Wynne's garage, I'd probably be a murder suspect. I hadn't thought of that.

I jammed on the brakes right in front of the emergency room doors. There were already doctors and nurses waiting outside. This was a quiet part of the country. They didn't get a lot of emergency calls about incoming gunshot wounds.

Luckily there weren't any cops here. Yet. But I wasn't going to stick around.

"You're going to be okay, Albert."

"Get your kid," he mumbled as they pulled him out of the car.

Someone was coming around to my side. Their lips were moving. Asking something about me being hurt. Why would they think that? And then I realized I was covered in Al's blood. But it didn't matter, because the second my friend was out of the vehicle, I was driving again. A nurse had to jump out of the way to keep from going over my hood. The passenger side door only got closed by the air flow.

And that is the last I remember of that drive. I drove as fast as I could, breaking every speed limit, and I might very well have evaded pursuit too. Nothing registered, nothing made any impression on me beyond the memory of my son crying through the phone.

I hadn't thought about what I was going to do yet. My son was my son, but surrendering the Kumaresh Yar to an evil force meant the entire world, including my son, would be in danger. In the wrong hands, that thing was crazy dangerous. It was a time-traveling weapon of mass destruction.

No. It was a false choice, I thought as I started down the gravel road toward my house. It was a wrong choice. A stupid choice. I wasn't going to choose. I was going to get my son back, not give them anything, and the evil assholes were going to regret the day they'd messed with my family. There's only one thing that we Shacklefords take more seriously than killing monsters, and that's defending our families. This was both.

This creature was going to find out he'd picked on the wrong mother.

There were orcs—a whole bunch of them—in the back of a pickup truck in front of my house, and more of them milling around on my front porch. They weren't masked, and they'd rolled up so fast that they'd not even bothered with their war paint. I could tell from their dejected expressions that it hadn't gone well.

How bad was it?

I got my answer as I ran inside. There was blood splattered across my living room. Dorcas was lying on the carpet with two orc healers kneeling over her.

"Is she—?"

"Lives," said one of the orc ladies quickly. "But much hurt."

Then I realized that Dorcas was missing her artificial leg. It had been yanked off and was lying in the hall. From the look of it, she'd been beaten with her own leg.

I ran towards the stairs following a trail of blood droplets and stopped, aghast.

Lying there was my grandpa, in his pajamas and socks, holding an old 1911 in his one hand, the slide locked back empty, surrounded in spent brass.

"No, no, no."

Orcs moved out of the way so I could reach him. Grandpa was dead. The Boss, Ray Shackleford the Third, was dead.

I registered several things at once. He'd been stabbed multiple times in the chest. I didn't know with what, but there was a lot of blood. I looked around, but there weren't any bullet holes in the walls, which meant Grandpa had hit whatever he was aiming at.

He'd been in hospice care, practically at death's door, but when he'd heard the commotion, he'd cowboyed up one last time and gone out fighting.

Oh, Grandpa.

There wasn't even time for my heart to break. I ran past his body and into my room. The crib was empty. I went from room to room shouting Ray's name. There was no sign of my baby. I half expected to see Amanda, the nurse, dead somewhere too, but she wasn't.

The orcs were looking at me, confused and sad. They tried talking to me, but I was having a hard time understanding anything. I'm a professional. I've been through some terrible things. I don't panic. But this time, I was on the verge.

I couldn't think about Ray being in danger. I had to focus on piecing together what happened so I could find him. My house had a security system. The doors were always locked. Hit a button, the armored shutters would drop, and this place was practically a vault. Only Dorcas had a key and knew the codes.

She'd taken Ray from the compound and then gotten jumped by something on the way in here. Grandpa had heard and tried to help, and it had gotten him killed. Whatever had done that had then left with my baby...

Shelly had said that Dorcas had gotten a call, something about Grandpa. They'd been friends for forty years; if she thought Grandpa was about to pass on, of course she'd come. And since Ray was her responsibility, obviously Dorcas would take Ray with her.

Damn, this thing had been organized.

That also meant there was only one possibility who could have convinced Dorcas she needed to come here.

The nurse's room was empty too. Her things were all there. Nothing looked like it had been packed, but there was also no sign of a struggle. Had Amanda been willingly complicit...or possessed like Wynne?

I rushed back downstairs to where the orc ladies were still tending to Dorcas. With her face all bruised and bloody, she looked really messed up.

"Got hit with own foot," explained one of the healers.

"Can she talk?"

As I knelt next to her, I saw that Dorcas' eyes were open and for a moment had the horrible fear that she was going to be dead, but then she blinked at me, coughed—I noted that the orc had just given her something from a cup. There was a strong stink of burnt leaves coming from the tea. Dorcas gasped and said, "Goddammit, son of a bitch, no-good motherfuckers."

When that lady got spun up, she could cuss for five minutes straight without repeating herself, so I hurried and cut her off. "Dorcas, listen to me. I need to know what happened."

"I'm sorry, girl, I'm so sorry." She must have been concussed, but whatever potion the orcs had given her was keeping her focused. "The nurse called, said the Boss was on his way out, asking to see his great-grandson one last time. I had to. I didn't think—"

"I know. It's okay. Where's my son?"

There was a panicked look. "I don't know."

I shook my head, realizing that, of course, she must have been knocked out when it had left. "Ray's been taken. Grandpa's been killed."

"Son of a bitch!" Dorcas started coughing and the orc gave her something else to drink, and then started smearing something all over her head. There was so much blood from Dorcas' scalp that it was making a real mess on my carpet. "I parked out front, everything looked fine. I unlocked the door. It must've come out of nowhere and clocked me."

"Tell me what happened," I said. "Everything you remember."

"I had Bubba in my arms, so I remember turning to protect him from the fall. I didn't even have a chance to draw my gun. I'm slower than I used to be, but not that slow. Whatever it was, it's fast... Did that bitch nurse set us up?"

"Maybe." That hurt. I was furious. We'd sort of become friends while she was looking after Grandpa.

"Hang on." Dorcas winced and closed her eyes. "Room's spinning again."

For you and me both.

I dealt with a lot of crises. I knew freaking out was useless, but right then I couldn't help it. I was on the ragged edge. My kid was gone. My grandpa had been murdered. My friend had been shot. I wanted to scream at Dorcas for failing to protect my baby, but that was just stupid anger talking. Whatever this monster was, it was clever, and it must have been planning this for a long time. Wynne's monster encounter had been a setup. The distance, the setting, it was all a perfect lure. If I hadn't taken that bait, it would have been something else. It had watched and waited, exploiting our weaknesses. It was smart, murderous, and had my baby.

I'd lost a lot of people. I knew the grief about Grandpa would hit later. As long as I had business to focus on, I'd be fine. If I started thinking about my baby, though, I'd crack. I had to keep moving.

I went back outside. Amanda's car was gone. Of course it was. That bitch had stolen my kid, and she had at least a forty-minute head start.

Several orc warriors were there armed with a motley assortment of guns—mostly hunting rifles and shotguns decorated with feathers and small animal bones—and contact weapons—axes, swords, and a baseball bat with nails in it.

Shelly was short, squat, and ugly, even by orc standards, so I recognized her immediately as she waddled up. She was wearing a serape and carrying a pair of six-shooters like something from a Clint Eastwood movie.

"No baby find. Who we go kill?" Shelly demanded.

"I don't know yet." All orcs had a gift, something that they were truly world-class amazing at. Skippy could make a helicopter do things that were supposedly impossible. In close combat, Ed was like a walking blender. "Are any of you a tracker? I think Ray was taken away in the nurse's car. Can any of you follow Ray's trail?"

"Shelly, shoot good," she said apologetically. Then she

turned and started shouting in Orcish. I understood about three quarters of what she said as she repeated my questions, but apparently none of them had that talent. One snapped something back. I understood the part about *wargs*.

"Maybe wargs track? Good nose warg."

They were giant wolves after all. It was worth a shot. "Can you go get some?"

Shelly nodded vigorously and then took off running.

That was everything I could think of to do right then. This was a kidnapping. I had something he wanted. He'd call with instructions. I went back inside and stood there, seething and useless, still covered in my friend's drying blood. I went into the bathroom and washed my hands. My clothes were still blood-soaked, but they could wait.

I went back upstairs to say goodbye to Grandpa. Thing was, he didn't look upset. He even had a contented look on his torn-up face, like he'd died doing what he loved. Or maybe I was just imagining it. Going out fighting was the Shackleford way. Even though he was in pajamas and socks, he had, in fact, in every other way but the literal, died with his boots on.

Then I noticed something. While he'd been lying here, he'd scratched something into the wood with his hook. It wasn't very clear. He'd been running out of time and blood pressure, and hadn't been big on penmanship to begin with, but it looked like he'd tried to write A-L-U and the beginning of another letter.

Grandad must have held on, staying alive so he could leave me this message, and bled out before he was done. And I had no idea what it meant. His message was unfinished. It was a dead end.

Just then the phone I'd taken from the garage rang. I pulled it out of my pocket. Through the bloody smears on its screen I could barely read *Guardian*.

I answered with "You son of a bitch—"

"No time for pleasantries, Guardian. Do you hear that?"

He must have held the phone close to my child so I could hear his cries crystal clear. I cringed. It was his "I'm scared" scream, not just his "I'm hungry" or "I'm dirty" scream.

"You know what's at stake. Do as I say or else."

"Or what? My baby dies?"

The guy—well, whatever he was he sounded like a guy—on the other side, laughed as if I'd said something funny. *"Is death truly the worst thing you can think of? We both know there are worse things than death. Far worse. Use your imagination."*

There was a short silence during which I did my absolute best *not* to use my imagination. Instead I said, "I'm listening."

"Very well. I want you to go to your kitchen. I left something for you there."

I went downstairs. There were bloody footprints on my otherwise clean kitchen floor. The prints were from small shoes, and the blood was from Grandpa and Dorcas. Hopefully just them, and none of it was Ray's. Just that thought made me sick.

"I'm in the kitchen."

"Open the first cabinet on the right."

I did. There, atop my familiar plates was a small length of unfamiliar rope. It had that kind of *fizz* feeling I get from something magic. It took me only a second to figure out what it probably was. It had to be one of those transportation spells used by the Condition cultists. In fact, this entire operation was smelling more and more like the work of the Sanctified Church of the Temporary Mortal Condition, founded by the necromancer Martin Hood, and now run by his batshit-crazy daughter, Lucinda.

"I assume you know how to use the portal rope. When you place it down, it will be too small for a person to come through, but the artifact will fit."

I was thinking frantically. Working alongside Franks, Milo had come up with a way to use the Condition's teleportation magic against them. By using their existing, preprogrammed length of rope, he'd spliced a bunch more on, and then opened a path big enough for us to fly a helicopter through. But that had taken lots of time, and I didn't have lots of time.

"How do I know you'll give me my baby back when I've given you the artifact?"

There was hesitation. I could sense I'd taken it by surprise. It's not that evil is stupid exactly, but every evil thing I've ever dealt with tends to have this unique inability to think outside its own very narrow parameters. This particular evil was used to being obeyed.

"You have no choice."

"How do I even know he's still alive, and you haven't just recorded his cry?"

"You do not. Once you send the artifact through, I will pass your baby back."

I was the company negotiator for a reason. "No. You're not putting my kid through some evil portal. I need proof he's alive. I need to see him in person. Then we hand off."

"The artifact must be delivered through the portal. That is the only acceptable outcome."

"Fine. Then agree to meet me somewhere I can see my kid in person, I'll drop the rope and put the artifact through it, then I walk away with my kid. If I can't see him alive and in person, then you get nothing."

The thing was quiet for a long time as it thought over my counteroffer. *"I will call in thirty minutes with a location."*

"Wait." If I could get more time I might be able to splice the rope thing and go through with a rescue party full of orcs and guns blazing. "I need more time to retrieve it."

"Do not lie to me. I have no idea how you managed to hide it from everyone, but I do know that the Guardian would be compelled to keep it nearby."

Damn it. I hated when evil things were thinkers. "It's under a magical lock. It takes time to open. I need more time."

"You have thirty minutes." The call ended.

I stood in my kitchen, trying to think. I was shaking so hard, I could hear my teeth chatter. It wasn't fear, it was absolute, blinding anger that I had nowhere to put. If I could, right then, shoot all the evil bastards, my hand would be as steady as ever. But that's not what I had to do. I had to think. There was no way I could hand the artifact over to His Evilness.

In the wrong hands, the Kumaresh Yar could literally destroy time. I knew this because my husband was one of those wrong hands, and using it once, he had erased several minutes from existence for everyone in the whole world. Not to mention that had also woken up an ancient chaos god. It was the kind of thing that powerhouses like Lord Machado, Martin Hood or, yes, even my mother, could use to accomplish all sorts of evil.

After the Arbmunep incident, everyone else had thought the Kumaresh Yar was missing. My taking it and hiding it away had seemed like the logical choice at the time. MHI didn't need to know about it because eventually there would be a big enough threat that someone with good intentions—like Owen—would be tempted to try and use it. And I definitely didn't want the MCB to get it, which had turned out to be a good decision considering what a power-mad asshole Stricken had turned out to be.

So I'd stashed it and not told anyone, the whole time telling myself that it was my choice, and not that I'd been somehow compelled to protect that thing because of the Guardian's curse. I didn't think that the marks were messing with my mind, but magic could be weird and subtle.

Cursed obligations aside, there was no way the kidnapper would turn over my baby without at least seeing the artifact first, and bringing it out of hiding at all risked losing it. However . . . if I did have to turn it over, they might not be able to use it. From what I understood, it was always useful for dark magic, but it took someone special like Owen to unlock its full potential, and from everything we'd learned, someone like him—or Lord Machado—only came around once every five hundred years. Luckily, the only man in the world right now who could use the Kumaresh Yar's full power to tear holes in space and time was a good man who wouldn't touch it with a ten-foot pole. So I'd have to trust that this murdering, baby-kidnapping asshole would at least need a little time to figure out how to use it at all, and five centuries before they could find another special person to end the world with it.

It probably wasn't a good idea to pull out the potential world ender, but I needed my baby back and I was on the clock. I grabbed the length of rope, shoved it in my pocket, and ran for the back door. I stopped by the tool shed to get a sledgehammer and a crowbar.

The evil dude had guessed right. I did keep the artifact nearby. In fact, it would probably have driven him insane if he'd realized how close he'd been, also how unguarded it was. Most of its protection was in misdirection and secrecy.

There is a building on the grounds of the old plantation that had been slave quarters. When I was little I'd set fire to it, but there were parts that didn't burn. Back then I'd been teaching myself how to make homemade explosives. In fact, it had been that same melted packing peanuts in gasoline mixture I'd later used in college on those vampires. Owen says that it's a common mark of a future Hunter to have caused unimaginable destruction with improvised explosives while they were young and didn't know any better.

The slave quarters didn't have anything to do with my family. Bubba Shackleford had bought this property a long time after the Civil War. His branch of the family had always been dirt-poor farmers, treated like trash. Once monster hunting had made him wealthy, he'd returned and bought the biggest, nicest, most historically significant plantation house in his home county. According to family tradition, Bubba didn't even like fancy things, other than guns obviously, but like a lot of men who'd grown up with nothing, spiting those who'd once looked down at him was a hell of a good motivator.

But the slave quarters had been part of the history of this place, and even the ugly parts of history shouldn't be forgotten. All the people who wanted every reference to the bad things we'd done in the past removed were fools. They were just trying to signal that they were better than their ancestors, but in fact, we're no different. We've just got hindsight and their mistakes to learn from. If we forget the atrocities of the past, we'll repeat them in the future, just with prettier names and new justifications.

Which is why as an adult, I felt bad for burning down a historical landmark. As a kid I'd thought it was kind of awesome how the melted burning Styrofoam had stuck to everything.

There were a few things that hadn't burned, like the really solid prison room that had served as Earl's full-moon retreat for decades, but most of the slave quarters had been totally destroyed. Except years later, my brother Ray and I had found something while poking around in the ruins.

I had no idea what the secret chamber past the trapdoor had been used for or who had built it. The locking mechanism was intricate and well hidden. You had to push on different stones in order, like a spy movie. I'd once tried to sound Grandpa out about the secret room, without giving too much away, but he'd shown no sign that he'd known what I was talking about.

Since it was newer than the building which had burned down on top of it, it had probably been Bubba Shackleford himself who'd designed it to hide something important. Ray and I had figured with Bubba it had probably been buried treasure. Literally. But whatever had been in there was long gone by the time his great-great-grandkids broke in. When I'd checked Bubba's writings in the archives, there was no mention of this room. And apparently Bubba had never told his son, because Earl hadn't known about it either.

As kids, having a secret clubhouse like that is kind of amazing. Ray had thought it was dorky, and he'd thought he was too mature to crawl around narrow muddy tunnels, but he'd sworn to never tell anybody what we'd found. I'd stashed my diary in there, because that's the kind of thing teenage girls do. Except now that Ray was long dead and I'd found something far more important to hide, I'd put that secret chamber to better use.

Beneath the trapdoor was a narrow hole, like an old well, stone-lined, with iron rivets stuck into the stones which could be used to climb down. At the bottom was a tunnel which had been a lot easier to navigate when I was a kid. Now, it took getting on all fours, and then squeezing past a half-moon opening on the wall. I crawled along with my flashlight in one hand. It looked so rough and small that I suspected anyone who got this far would think it was just an opening to an old cistern or well, and would turn back. The whole place smelled musty. The air was humid. It felt like if you kept going you were going to get stuck, and die trapped down here.

But that was just to set the ambiance. Once you squeezed past the half-moon opening, there was an actual stairwell. Each step was of a different height, as if the people who'd built it had either not cared the least bit how it looked or had used the materials at hand without any thought. My flashlight illuminated the signs I'd posted all over the walls, signs that read KEEP OUT and TURN BACK and skulls and crossbones and DANGER HIGH EXPLOSIVES, that sort of thing.

Not that I'd normally warn people they were about to step on a land mine, but I was afraid that Owen or someone else—Owen had a talent for finding things no one wanted found or blundering into places no one wanted him to go—would come in here without the slightest notion of what it was. So I'd taken precautions.

I now disarmed the precautions as I went, avoiding the spring-loaded spikes and being careful not to pull the trip wires that would set off the silver-loaded claymore mines. I wasn't joking when I said I really did not want this thing to fall into hostile hands.

Then it occurred to me that I might be putting it directly into hostile hands, and I shuddered. Hopefully not, but if I did, only for a very short time. *A very short time.* Certainly too short for them to get up to anything interesting with it.

After getting past the booby traps, I unlocked the heavy wooden door at the bottom of the stairs. The door looked positively medieval. I'd replaced the Bubba Shackleford-era locks with some new ones, mechanical and electronic. Then I had to disarm the second layer of booby traps. No, you don't need to know what they are because I might need to use them again. It took me a little while and quite a bit of concentration. If I'd forgotten any of them, I'd get killed, and then Ray would be on his own.

The room was relatively small, probably only large enough for Bubba's treasure chests or whatever it was he'd hidden down here. The walls and floor were made of big stones mortared together. I had a few things left out in the open, and I'd made sure some of them were valuable enough that if someone did manage to get in, they'd think that was what all the booby traps were trying to protect. But the real prize was under the floor.

I'd tried to destroy this damned thing. A bullet had chipped it once a long time ago, but it must have *wanted* that little piece to break off to go and cause mischief, because bullets sure hadn't worked when I'd tried again, including some *really* big ones. I'd tried melting it, crushing it in a hydraulic press, acid, and a plasma torch. I'd even thought about going old-school and throwing it in an active volcano, but then it would probably send out a signal and some kind of fire demon would find it.

Evil has a way of attracting evil, which was why I'd put the artifact in a lead cube with an outer one of cold iron. I figured that would stop it from sending out any negative waves. Then I'd buried that, mixed up a few buckets of cement, and put that on top so that even if someone did find this place, they might not know they were walking on top of it. I had done what I had to do to keep psychos like the Condition or my evil vampire mom from sniffing it out. Now I had to get it out before my baby ran out of time.

I set down my flashlight, pried up one of the floor stones with the crowbar, and then went to work with the sledgehammer. I took out my anger and frustration on the cement. Pretty soon sweat was running down my face and dripping inside my glasses. The labor made my muscles ache. I'd been on soft mommy duty for too long, so blisters formed on my hands.

Once the concrete was smashed, I hooked the iron box with the crowbar and dragged it out. It weighed a ton. I thought I was going to pop a blood vessel, but you know there is some truth in those old wives' tales about desperate moms being strong enough to lift a car off their baby. I started smashing open the nested boxes.

When they were finally opened, the thing inside—the thing I'd taken such trouble to protect—was just sitting there, looking innocent. It really didn't seem like much, just a hunk of stone, old and dusty, about the size of a deck of cards with slightly ragged edges.

It was so much more than that. It was a weapon created by beings beyond our understanding, from another dimension or before time or who the hell knows, and left here to really mess us up.

The power of this thing had also given me back my life... I realized that I'd unconsciously moved one hand to the black marks on my neck, and then I quickly snatched my hand away. It had changed me in ways that I couldn't even begin to understand, except that those changes had saved my life from mortal wounds a couple of times now. But I wasn't about to thank it. Everything supernatural came with a price. I was sure it would make me pay with interest.

During my pregnancy, we'd been deathly afraid that the artifact would change little Ray, make him into something not human. That hadn't happened but—but now it might cost me little Ray himself.

With shaking hands, I got the artifact out. It felt

like a boring old chunk of stone. As usual, nothing weird happened when I touched it. I wasn't one of those special people who could use it to blow up the world. I was just the poor sap who'd been drafted to keep it from falling into the wrong hands. I checked the time. He would be calling me back soon.

Now that it was physically in my possession, my mind recoiled even harder at the idea of giving it away. I wondered how much of that feeling was me, and how much of it was the curse that had made me responsible for it. I took a deep, shaky breath. Spell or no spell, first I'd take care of my family. After that... I'd do what I could to keep the artifact safe.

As I turned to leave, my flashlight beam fell on something I'd almost forgotten. In a corner of the room there was a big stainless steel container which glimmered under the light. It had been a right pain to get that container down here just because of the size. It had warning stickers on it, but unlike my booby trap signs, these were from the factory: DANGER, MEDICAL WASTE, and DANGER, LIQUID NITROGEN.

I'd written a letter explaining everything to Owen or Earl, or whoever survived me and eventually found this place, because if they opened the container and saw what was inside they would be really confused. The Kumaresh Yar wasn't the only thing I'd smuggled back from New Zealand. The envelope containing that letter was in front of the container and labeled READ THIS.

It gave me an idea. I was probably going to have to drop the artifact through the portal rope to who knows where before I could get my baby. The kidnapper was sure to be jamming things like tracking devices, so I could be sending the thing off to Antarctica for all I knew. Once it went through that rope I'd never find it . . . but the thing in the container on the other hand . . . The kidnapper would be on the lookout for electronic tracking devices, not biological ones.

It was an idea so crazy it might just work. Or it might turn out horribly. But I was desperate and running out of time. So I unscrewed the cap. Normally you had to top this stuff off every so often, but I'd paid a whole lot of money to an elf to stick a rune on the lid to ensure endless cold. There was a hiss and a bunch of white vapor as the freezing liquid nitrogen hit the atmosphere. Then I dumped the contents on the floor.

It was a frozen black blob, only about the size of a hamster. Almost immediately, I started having doubts about the wisdom of this.

As the nitrogen evaporated in tendrils around the blob, all I could think was that he was dead or, if not dead, completely ineffective. He'd still been alive when I'd frozen him. Or at least, the tiny, partially-burned-to-ash piece of him I'd found stuck in my body armor had been alive. I think it had even tried to communicate . . . right before I'd dunked him in liquid nitrogen. Where was the—limited—intelligence of an amorphic creature housed? And if it was a matter of mass, would this little lump be literally brainless?

The blob didn't move for a minute, and I didn't have minutes to spare. Okay, so that plan was a dud. I needed to get outside because I doubted I would get a cell phone signal down here. The fact that tears were stinging in my eyes was just a sign of how many shocks I'd withstood recently. I was certainly not crying for a servant of the Old Ones, even one who'd been a childhood friend.

I was just about to turn away when the blob wiggled a bit. From the little black lump a tendril extruded, a baby-blue eyeball appeared on the end of it, and the blob asked me a question with a tiny little squeak of a voice.

"Cuddle Bunny?"

CHAPTER 6

One of the things I really hate about intelligent monsters and the kinds of bad guys who work for them is that they're creepy all the time. They never give it a rest. You know, they can't arrange a meeting at Sunny Street or Happy Fields. No, anything to do with them will be in Mount Gloomy or Darkness Alley.

Even so, I groaned under my breath as I entered the address into my GPS: Crybaby Bridge. I knew the place. MHI had caught a bubak at that site.

What is a bubak? Ah . . .

People joke that every small town in the US has a legend about a crybaby bridge. There's always some story to go with it too, a dark tale of infidelity and illegitimacy, and of a baby who was born only to be killed by its mother or father, or some stranger who'd absconded with it because of its origins. The standard legend was that on certain nights, but particularly when the moon was full, you could still hear the ghost of the baby crying under the bridge.

Like most such legends, it wasn't exactly wrong. What often happened, in fact, was a bubak, a kind of Czech boogeyman, had set up shop there. They loved to make a noise imitating a helpless infant, to lure would-be rescuers to the dark place under the bridge, where the bubak could then eat them.

While a bubak was dangerous and ugly as sin, looking like a ghoulish, green version of a scarecrow, they really weren't that dangerous comparatively. But, yep, that was exactly where the creature who'd taken my baby wanted me to meet him.

"That bastard," I muttered under my breath.

Two eyes on tentacles pushed out of the bag where I'd stowed Mr. Trash Bags. "Cuddle Bunny mad?"

I looked down at the tiny shoggoth, and he looked back at me with an adoring expression. I turned my eyes back on the road. "Yes. Very mad."

I'm not going to complain about my childhood. I'm a Shackleford and there were more important things for my family than making sure a little girl has play friends. I was older than my brothers, and there had been no other kids around. Back then we didn't even have the orc village. I remembered endless days of playing in the woods near the house, making up stories and entertaining myself, while my parents were busy with much more important business.

Again, not complaining. I'd been very able to keep myself amused. And when I was four I could read and then make up stories off the stories I read. Most of the time when I was playing alone in those woods, I'd been conquering fantasy kingdoms, exploring the wilder parts of Earth, and taking spaceships to unknown planets.

But every kid needs friends, and for the longest time when I was little, I'd thought I'd had a play friend named Mr. Trash Bags. Granted, most children's imaginary friends didn't look like a pile of black trash bags with lots of eyes, but I'd been a weird kid. I remembered Mr. Trash Bags very clearly, how sweet and friendly he'd been, and how he'd played all the parts I assigned him in my play scripts. He would play monster or friendly rescuer, and he'd even play stuffed animal. And it always ended in hugs.

Then one day he had just disappeared.

It wasn't until a few years ago that I had found out Mr. Trash Bags was neither imaginary nor...well, nor something you'd want around your kids.

You see, Mr. Trash Bags was a shoggoth, the manual-labor and odd-job slaves of the Old Ones. They run errands, eat people, dig tunnels, and so on. Some guy who went by the charming name of the Mad Arab said that "To look upon their hideous thousand eyes is to invite horror and the suffering of infinite madness, within tombs of blackness where the innocent are devoured for eternity." So on and so forth.

Shoggoths are amorphous. They change shape, but they're normally about fifteen feet across and weigh around two tons. They talk, after a fashion, but they're never going to win any prizes for eloquence. And they eat *everything*.

Except Mr. Trash Bags hadn't eaten me. For whatever reason he'd taken a liking to four-year-old Julie Shackleford. And when we'd met again, a few years ago, in a showdown between me and the death cult who commanded him, he had chosen to side with me. In payback for his treachery, Mr. Trash Bags had been burned to ash.

Well, except for this damaged little chunk that I'd found afterward, seemingly still alive.

I could have finished the job. He was a shoggoth after all. Any of my teammates would have. But Shacklefords pay their debts and don't desert allies. However, I couldn't just leave him free to roam. Nobody knows much about shoggoth physiology. I didn't know if he would grow back to giant size, and if he did . . . Well, Mr. Trash Bags loved me personally, but he was still a shoggoth. Which meant he would go back to running errands for the Old Ones, digging tunnels, and most of all eating everything, including people. Which I couldn't allow him to do.

So I'd frozen him.

But with all my friends gone, and me alone and facing a threat to my baby, I could use something that could run errands for me and, well . . . eat whoever I told him to eat. It was probably the desperation talking, but having a friendly shoggoth sounded like a great idea at the time.

As I drove toward the meet, I tried to fill in my new, tiny ally. "Cuddle Bunny is angry at people who took away my bab—her cuddle bunny."

The two little blue eyes on tentacles crossed. "Cuddle Bunny has cuddle bunny?"

It was weird. The last time we'd spoken Mr. Trash Bags' voice had been extremely, violently loud. Now he sounded like a cartoon character, but to be fair, Martin Hood had burned a few thousand pounds off him.

"Yes. I have a little cuddle bunny. He's very small and helpless, and bad men took him away." I left aside the complexities that these probably weren't exactly men, and there was no way the guy I'd been talking to on the phone was human. But the thing was that Mr. Trash Bags had never exactly been a genius, and being frozen for years couldn't have improved his mental performance.

I have no illusions. Shoggoths are still bad guys, the enforcers for the Old Ones, but Mr. Trash Bags loved me, and could be an enforcer for *me*. At least potentially. Hopefully. I was heading into a meeting with really bad guys, guys who probably wouldn't hesitate to pull a double cross. My only ace in the hole was a hamster-sized, recently unfrozen Mr. Trash Bags. And I planned to use him.

I reached over and grabbed Mr. Trash Bags—a warm pulsating blob in my hand—and yes, he did say "whee" as I grabbed him and shoved him into the pouch which held the artifact. The blue eyes looked up at me, confused, and a tentacle reached out to pat my hand.

I looked at the GPS and left the highway at the required exit. I was driving fast and it was still going to be tight. I hated this. The kidnapper's deadlines were keeping me reacting instead of acting. If he kept me moving, it minimized my chances of getting help, or having time to prepare, or getting anyone to the meet early. He'd given me the expected instructions: come alone, come unarmed, or else. I hate smart monsters.

"The bad men want me to give them the artifact in there. So they can give me my baby."

"Cuddle Bunny Cuddle Bunny!" the little shoggoth squeaked.

"Right. And I'm afraid they'll take it but not give me the baby. Or they'll use the artifact to hurt me."

The eyes looked slitty. "No hurt Cuddle Bunny! Or Cuddle Bunny Cuddle Bunny."

Really, for Mr. Trash Bags this was genius. We were firmly in the realm of nuclear physics as far as Mr. Trash Bags was concerned. "We have to protect my Cuddle Bunny at all costs, or I can't love Mr. Trash Bags anymore."

Another eye joined the other two, and the tentacle wrapped around my wrist. "Cuddle Bunny love Mr. Trash Bags?"

"I sure do. But it is very important to me that you protect my Cuddle Bunny." The little eyes looked so sad; I felt awful using emotional blackmail on the little eldritch abomination.

"Number 786 of Horde became exile. After failure to consume target mammals exile became *Mr. Trash Bags.*"

"Okay, then."

"Protect Cuddle Bunny!" A fourth eye joined the others and they all blinked at me, which was very distracting as I drove a winding country road. "How?"

"That pouch you're in? The bad guys will take it. You've got to flatten yourself so they don't find you. When you get to the other side, if my baby is there, you protect my baby. Eat the bad guy."

"Consume!" Then Mr. Trash Bags' now five eyes looked confused. "Mammals too big?"

Right. He was a fraction of the mighty shoggoth he once was. "Well, you can eat their nose or something. Whatever it takes to distract them and keep my Cuddle Bunny safe."

"Keep safe Cuddle Bunny."

"Right. When baby is safe, you can do whatever bad stuff you want to the bad guys. As small as you are right now, ears, eyes, toes, fingers, those are all good targets."

"Do bad stuff to bad guys."

I kept repeating my instructions, making sure he understood that the primary mission was protecting Ray and the secondary was getting the artifact back. By the time we rounded Dead Man's Turn—aptly named, there were lots of accidents there—leading up to the bridge, I was teaching Mr. Trash Bags my phone number and he was chanting it back to me enthusiastically.

I had no idea where they'd take my baby. In the past, the teleportation spells of the type used by the Condition had led to places around our world. Wherever the artifact wound up, I wanted him to be able to call me and tell me where to go. Once he'd memorized the phone number, he asked me what a phone was, then I had to explain that too. And how to use one.

"On box with numbers summon Cuddle Bunny. Purge. Destroy. Consume!"

"And?"

Mr. Trash Bags had to think hard. "Protect?"

"Good."

I was so screwed.

I finally got to Crybaby Bridge. It seemed like it had taken forever, but my watch said I still had a few minutes.

The bridge was a fairly normal metal, arched one, the sort you find down a lot of country roads in Alabama. This one was pretty big, and I presumed at some point it had led from somewhere important to somewhere else important. Right now, there was an old abandoned house behind me, a straggle of farms on the other side, and trees everywhere.

Across the bridge was a woman, holding a baby in a blue blanket. I recognized Amanda Fuesting, *that child-stealing bitch.* The blue blanket had been made by Holly during her downtime on the siege. Since quilting wasn't in the main body of Holly's skills, it was pretty special to her, and seeing it there just made me even angrier.

Had Amanda been a traitor all along?

At this point I didn't trust anybody except for myself and the truckload of orcs who'd been following me, who would now be hiding out of sight. Well, I had to trust Mr. Trash Bags . . . kind of.

The kidnappers knew I was a shooter, so Amanda was standing on the edge of the bridge. A head shot would flip her off switch, but then she'd take my baby over the side with her. We were maybe twenty feet over the river; a drop was more than sufficient to kill poor little Ray.

I shut off the car and waited a second. Amanda didn't move. There were good hiding spots all along the river. I could be walking into an ambush. Maybe the second they saw I had what they wanted, it would be my switch that got flipped.

Mr. Trash Bags was in the pouch with the artifact, so I stuck my hand in to check and found that he'd become as thin as the lining. He was warm, and I felt a bizarre tickle on my fingers, like he was licking them or something. When it came to shoggoths, it was better not to think too clearly about what they might be doing. I wiped what was probably spit on my pants, then got out of the car.

I started walking toward them, slowly lifting my hands, one empty, and from the other dangled the bag. My stomach hurt from the tension. "I've got what you want."

Amanda stood very still, and the baby lump in the blanket didn't move either.

"Amanda," I said, in case she was another victim, and not a traitor. "I'm glad you're alive."

There was no hesitation in the response, as the thing in Amanda's body laughed, the full, rich sound of a much larger person. "She's only alive in the basest sense, Guardian. The process of taking over a human mind is a rather violent one. I'm afraid once I release my puppets, there's usually not much left of their mind. This body is merely a convenient vehicle. You have no friend here, merely a negotiating partner. Now, that's close enough."

We were fifty feet apart.

"Did you bring the payment for your baby?"

"Hang on. I need to—"

"Too late," the thing in Amanda's body said. It moved fast, grabbing the baby by the ankle, and suspending him over the side of the bridge.

"No!"

It was Ray. No doubt about it. He looked unharmed and very surprised, and as the little quilted blanket Holly had made fell into the river below, Ray gave vent to a scream of outrage and fear, his little lungs laboring overtime to let me know all was not right.

"Not a step closer, Guardian. You see he is alive. Don't make me change that. Payment. Now."

"Stop, stop. I've got it." I opened the pouch and let him see the evil thing.

"Excellent." Ray went on crying, pumping his little arms and legs with a wail, and the thing that spoke through Amanda's body raised his voice to be heard over the wail. "Now put the rope down. When the portal forms, place the artifact inside. I must warn you—those waiting to receive it will recognize a fake."

I threw the rope on the bridge. When it hit the metal, it began to wiggle like it had a life of its own, gradually arranging itself into a circle. When the two ends met, there was a hiss of sparks, and the part of the bridge inside the loop disappeared. It was like a window had formed. The other side was too dark to tell where it went.

I'd seen these before, even gone through them. This one was only as big around as a basketball. It made me wish I had a hand grenade to toss through to whatever greedy bastards were waiting on the other side. But it was give up the artifact or Ray, which was no choice at all. I went to drop the pouch, but then my hand wouldn't let go.

It was as though the curse that bound me to the thing was stronger than even love for my baby. Amanda's face contorted in a horrible, unnatural grin as I struggled to let go.

"It's difficult being chosen. What is stronger, I wonder? A desperate mother's love or a Guardian's curse? Hurry. This arm grows weary."

Ray was screaming, upside down, all the blood rushing to his head. I needed to hold him and comfort him and stop his fear. My fingers were clenched so tight that my hand was shaking. I tried to tell myself it couldn't be used to destroy the world for another five hundred years at least . . . Talk about kicking the can down the road.

I'll get this back. I promise. Right now I have to save my child.

It took all my willpower to force my fingers to open and drop the artifact into the portal.

As it vanished I realized I could breathe again.

"It's done! Give me my baby!"

"Not until I receive confirmation they have received the real thing."

"At least turn him upright. You're hurting him! Please. I'm begging you."

But the thing wasn't paying attention to me; it was like he was listening to someone else. Could this thing inhabit more than one body at a time? "Delivery confirmed... It was a pleasure doing business with you, Julie Shackleford."

And then Amanda stepped over the edge.

Hands outstretched, I began running toward them, but horrified, I watched Ray fall, screaming, from sight.

I reacted without thought, flinging myself over the side after them.

The water wasn't very deep right here. There was barely enough to break my fall, but then my body hit the rocks below. I came up, thrashing and spitting, searching desperately.

I'd lost my glasses on impact, but I spotted the blue blanket floating away. Then I saw Amanda, face-down... and then *Ray!*

He was beneath the water, unmoving, being swept along by the current.

I beat all speed records wading after him. When I grabbed hold, I lifted him out of the water, and started back toward the bank.

Thankfully he began to cry.

Stumbling, I climbed to where it was only ankle-deep, standing on slick rocks. "It's okay! Hush, dear, hush.

Ahhhh!" My leg nearly buckled when I put weight on it. I'd hit it hard on impact and not even felt it at the time. It didn't matter. I didn't care what I had to give up, the world included, to hold him in my arms again.

"Mommy's here," I tried to turn him over to examine him for injury, but he felt oddly lumpy. He was wearing the little outfit with the elephants that I'd put on him this morning, but suddenly it was like all his bones and joints were in the wrong place.

I got him turned over and found that all similarity to my son had vanished. The thing I was holding was like a hideous, hairless monkey. Its filthy claws raked down my face as its baby screams turning into something like hysterical laugher. I tried to drop it, but it clung to me and went after me, claws scratching my face, going for my eyes. I lost my footing and fell. It immediately started snapping at my face and trying to drown me. I got hold of one of its arms, now wiry strong, and tried to force it away, but it grabbed my ear with its other hand and tried to twist it off. I bit its arm. It tasted terrible, but I kept biting until it let go. I threw it away as hard as I could.

It hit with a splash, but popped right back up and loped toward me.

Even blurry, I recognized what it was now, a tokoloshe, an African water spirit, known for luring women and children to a watery death through its power of illusion. They could look and sound just like a baby, helpless and trapped, and then it would murder whoever tried to help it.

I'd been conned. Furious, I picked up a big rock out of the water, lifted it overhead, and smashed the evil little imp flat. I lifted the rock in both hands and started smashing it down, over and over. It was said a tokoloshe could curse you, an ill wish they called it. I wasn't going to give it the chance. "Ill wish this, bastard!" Its skull splintered and cracked, gushing purple ooze.

By the time the orcs reached me, I was stomping what remained of the thing flat with my shoe. The water churned with mud and purple slime.

Shelly slid down the steep embankment and nearly fell in the mud. "No baby?"

I shook my head. "No." My face and every bit of my exposed skin were all scratched to hell. I'd gone from terrified, to relieved, to furious, to disappointed in the span of a minute. This was exhausting. I just wanted to sit down and cry, but I wasn't about to do that. Hell, no, I wasn't about to do that.

He'd used a decoy. That meant Ray was still out there, and now the rat bastard had the artifact too. I didn't know what I could do.

Neither did the orcs. Most were standing there, confused, but a couple of them had jumped off the bridge into the river—each landing far more gracefully than I had—and they'd swum after Amanda, who'd been floating off downriver.

"We follow," Shelly said apologetically as she helped me out of the water. "We too late."

"No. The baby was never here. I got duped." Which just shows you that motherhood does things to people's heads. How long had I been dealing with evil things? I should have known better.

Shelly picked my glasses out of the river and helpfully handed them over. "What do now?"

"I don't know..." I just stood there angry, freaked out, soaked, and in pain. "I need a minute to think."

I looked toward Amanda. A young male orc was pulling her body onto the mud. I limped over to her. I was going to have one hell of a bruise on my leg, but I'd worry about that later. I'd thought maybe I'd be able to question her, but she was obviously dead, eyes empty and staring at the sun.

Shit. I'd liked her. She'd been kind to Grandpa. But thinking of him just made me suddenly feel a lot more lost and alone.

The young orc had a short sword at his waist. I didn't know if his life gift lay in combative arts or he was trying to emulate the infamous Edward, but he seemed pretty comfortable with the blade. And as much as I'd liked Amanda before she'd turned out to be a mind-controlled kidnapper, my number one suspect right now was the Condition, and their people often came back from the dead, and they did so quickly.

"Cut her head off." The male looked at me funny, but I don't think he spoke English. So I stuck my hand out toward Shelly and said, "Can I borrow a gun?"

Shelly obediently handed me a single-action Army reproduction. She was like an orcish Annie Oakley. I was almost never unarmed, but I'd followed the kidnapper's instructions because I'd not wanted to give him an excuse to bail or hurt my son. I cocked the hammer, aimed, and shot Amanda right between the eyes.

The young male orc jumped back and gave me an angry glare, like *warn me next time so I can plug my ears.*

"Sorry," I said to him as I handed Shelly back her gun. My ears were ringing too. In my defense, I had a lot of stuff on my mind.

What was I going to do now? The kidnapper still had Ray. Ray was still valuable. The kidnapper's phone was still in my car. Maybe I could call him and offer something else. The problem there was assuming the kidnapper had sane and rational motivations, and what else could he want? I'd just stupidly given him a magical super weapon....along with Mr. Trash Bags, who might still come through and call me...

It's pretty sad when your best hope is a shoggoth. Then I began to panic as I realized Mr. Trash Bags had memorized my phone number, but I'd just jumped in a river. It was with great relief when I fished it out of my pocket and found it was still working. That had been close. I couldn't imagine him calling Information.

"Flortz," said the male orc. He was pointing at the messy bullet hole in Amanda's forehead.

"Glowy bug," Shelly translated helpfully.

A *firefly* had crawled out of the wound.

"What the hell?"

It was unusually large, shook itself in a tiny shower of blood, and then promptly flew away. The yellow light was visible until it disappeared into the trees.

Then I gasped as I remembered the other glowing firefly that had hit my windshield as we'd left Colin Wynne's place. March is too early for fireflies, and they don't normally glow during the day. Not in any way you can notice.

"I know what kidnapped Ray," I said as I began climbing up the bank.

"What bad thing is?" Shelly demanded.

"An *Adze*." The orcs shared a confused glance. Shelly's googly eye turned back to me as she shrugged. They'd never heard of that. "Never mind. Take her body back to the compound, and I'm going to need what's left of that magic rope."

From the mists of my memory, I'd dredged up the probable creature I was dealing with. The *Adze* was a vampiric monster, rarely seen at all and almost never outside of Africa. The presence of fireflies and the possession fit. From what little I knew about these things, they were really bad news. An *Adze* was always described as powerful, cunning, and greedy.

By the time I got back on the bridge, I could hear a phone ringing. I ran over to my car and retrieved the phone the kidnapper had left me. The screen read *Guardian*. This asshole had never even mastered the fact that the call should say from whom it was, not whom he was calling. And yet he was smart enough to fool me. I hated my brain just then.

A booming laugh came from the phone as soon as I answered. "Did you think I ever meant to let you have your son?"

I spoke, though my lips felt like stiff cork, and my voice came out hoarse, as if I'd been running for miles and miles without a drink of water. "Is he alive?"

"Oh, yes, your spawn is alive. He is far too valuable to kill. I intend to sell him. Those who hired me didn't care what happens to the baby. Think of it—the child of the Guardian and a Chosen? Such a thing has never happened before as far as I know. Such blood will fetch a high price at auction." He sounded insanely pleased with his own cleverness.

My stomach lurched. I felt cold, very cold. I'd never been so cold in my entire life. My voice must have sounded just as cold, just as impersonal, as I said, "I'll pay whatever price you want."

"Ah, I'm afraid you can't. You don't deal in the currency I trade in. But someone else will. They will pay very much indeed."

I snapped. It felt like a physical snap, like something within me had cut loose, like an overstretched cable that held me to sanity and humanity had let go. It's not right to say I was furious. I'd left fury way behind. This was to fury as a nuclear explosion was to a slap. This was fury's older brother, the one who looked all calm but could beat fury five ways from Monday.

And even I was surprised at how cold and composed the words came out, "Listen carefully. You think you know me, but you don't. You don't know what you're messing with. I will hunt you down. I won't just kill you. I'll obliterate you. I'll make you wish you'd never existed."

I expected a snappy comeback, or that taunting laugh, but there was no sound from the phone. I finished through gritted teeth, "Enjoy what passes for life while you can, because you'll be dead soon. I'm coming for my son."

The line went dead.

CHAPTER 7

I stood at the edge of the bridge shaking. I wanted to kill things. I wanted to wreck worlds. But I had to think. I didn't know where my son's kidnapper was. I had almost nothing to go on. I was still covered in my friend's blood, I had traded away a doomsday artifact for nothing, and my baby was in the clutches of someone who intended to trade him to something probably even worse.

I took a deep breath, then another. I was simultaneously angry and terrified, but then I focused on my training and experience. I had a job to do. Normally I was the Hunter who comforted the victim's family. In this case I was both. I knew all the assurances and platitudes by heart, and I also knew the odds of recovering a victim. That didn't change the Hunter's job one bit.

So I shoved the emotions aside and got down to business.

"Okay, noble orcs. We're going to get Baby Ray back. But first, do any of you know how this works?" I held up one end of the now scorched and useless rope.

All the assembled orcs shook their heads in the

negative. I'd been hoping that one of them might. It might not lead to where Ray was, but it would at least get me to whoever had received the artifact. Milo had reactivated a used one of these before, but that had been with Frank's help—and that freak of nature knew a lot more about magic than he liked to let on. And they'd powered it with the ward stone—which we didn't have anymore.

"Maybe shaman?" Shelly suggested. "Two at village. Much wisdoms."

"Call them. It can't hurt to try."

Milo knew how, only everybody on the siege was unreachable. But he'd documented the process and put it in the archives . . . except I'd need to look it up myself because Albert was in the hospital—I didn't even know if he was still alive—and Dorcas probably wasn't in any shape to do it either.

"Okay, everybody, back to the compound."

One of the orcs handed me the little blue blanket.

I'd broken so many speed limits today that it was a miracle I hadn't been pulled over yet. Which was good, since I was still blood-stained, both red and purple, drenched in river water, there were scratches all over my face, I was probably a murder suspect by now and, oh yeah, there was a dead nurse in my trunk, so I'd have a hell of a time talking my way out of a ticket.

I called Melvin. Normally that shifty troll would let everything go to voicemail, only answering texts or emails, but by now he must have known we were in the middle of a crisis, so he actually answered.

"Why interrupt Melvin's—"

"Shut up and listen, troll." Normally when dealing with him, I remained polite but firm, but not today. "I don't have time for your usual bullshit."

My tone must have conveyed how grave the situation was because shockingly enough he only said, "How may Melvin help Julie?"

I quickly told him about the portal rope. "Find Milo's notes and figure out how to power this up again."

"Seen Milo scribbles. Melvin will have to search troll net for empower spells. Good thing you pay for fast connection. But wait . . . you would put your body through *portal* . . . created by *Melvin*?"

Yesterday I wouldn't have trusted him to mow my lawn, but right now I was desperate enough to let him play with the fabric of space-time. "Yes." And saying that really must have accentuated how serious this was. "I'll be there in fifteen minutes."

The next call was to one of MHI's lawyers. This time I did get voicemail, which was good, because I left a breathless forty-second recap, accentuating how if Albert Lee lived through surgery, he was going to be arrested for gunning down a local businessman, so get on that.

From what I'd read about the *Adze*—keeping in mind they're so rare a lot of our info was based on folklore and guesswork—it took them a little while to work their way inside someone's head. They were sneaky and nefarious about it, and the details about their methods were fuzzy, but working through dreams and telepathic pressure, they could subtly begin to guide a person's thoughts and behavior. After the *Adze* was fully established, they could then take their victim over completely, basically using them like a puppet.

As far as MHI knew, they could only get their psychic hooks into a few people at a time, and only fully possess one. Or at least that was our best guess based on their prior behavior, but that was based on the handful of cases where we'd encountered one of these things. I had no idea how much any good specimen could vary in that ability.

One thing we did know for sure, once they fully possessed someone, if they ever let go, the host's brain was done, fried, dead or going to the cast-off wing at Appleton. The guy in the garage had been as good as dead before Albert had shot him. I felt fractionally better that at least we weren't responsible for killing some little boy's daddy unnecessarily.

Of course, the question remained how long it had been working on Amanda without any of us noticing that she was being taken over by a monster. That was another thing for me to feel guilty about later.

I hesitated before making the next call, even though it was the logical thing to do. The presence of the rope suggested that the Condition was involved. It was one of their signature abilities. Lucinda Hood had lost her hand over the artifact, so it was looking likely that she was the one who'd hired the *Adze* to get it back. Because Lucinda had been involved up to her eyeballs in the events at Copper Lake, she was on the Monster Control Bureau's hit list. They had far greater resources than we did, so if anyone had an idea of where Lucinda Hood was, it would be the MCB.

The problem was, if I involved the MCB, I was done. They barely tolerated MHI's existence on our best day. There was no way they were going to allow the mother of the kidnap victim anywhere near that case. They'd take over, and worse: Their primary mission was keeping monsters secret; rescuing hostages was way down their list of priorities.

However, there was one MCB agent I could reach out to, who might know something that could help, and keep this on the down low, at least for a little while. It was odd, but putting my body through a portal to who knows where created by an insane troll was easier than calling my ex.

I sighed and swallowed my pride. "Call Grant Jefferson."

Grant had once been one of us, a respected employee of MHI, with a prestige posting on Earl Harbinger's personal team. Plus, well . . . we'd sort of been engaged, too. Okay, just dating, but we'd talked about marriage; only then I'd met Owen.

Grant had a lot going for him back then. Smart, handsome—I'm talking *really* good-looking—suave, cultured, went to the best schools, been all over the world, and had lots and lots of impressive accomplishments; but after I'd gotten to know Owen, nothing Grant was, nothing Grant did mattered.

In a way, we'd treated him shabbily—I still feel bad about how we'd broken up—but to be fair, he'd been kind of an asshole to my future husband. But it wasn't until my crazy vampire mother had kidnapped him and a supernatural warlord had almost sacrificed him to dark gods that Grant had given up on MHI.

He had decided that monster hunting really was too dangerous for private organizations and belonged only in the hands of the government. As repugnant and idiotic as that idea was, I thought that at his heart Grant was still a nice guy. I'd known him well, and understood that he was an idealistic guy, even if he'd grown up in a pretty shitty environment, with a rich, self-centered father and a never-ending rotation of trophy stepmothers. He still wanted to kill monsters and keep people safe, and if he couldn't do it with MHI, then what other choice did he have? I hated the intimidating witnesses and destroying their lives part of the MCB's job, and for the good of his soul, I sincerely hoped that Grant did too.

It rang three times, and then I heard Grant's voice. "Julie?" So he still had my number programmed in. I was going to try not to read too much into that.

"Grant, I need your help."

"What?" He sounded out of breath, as if he had been running. Of course I caught him exercising; he ran marathons for fun. "Look, if this is business you need to call the director's office or the hotline. I've got no—"

I didn't have time for him to go all official on me. "My baby's been stolen by an *Adze*. I need your help. Is this line secure?"

"Whoa . . . okay." There was a moment of silence, then he said, "Hold on." After a while he came back on-line, sounding more composed. It also sounded like he was someplace small and bare, because I could hear a weird echo. "Now it is. What's happening?"

"This is off the record, just between me and you. I need your word."

There was a lumbering old farm tractor ahead of me, taking up way too much road on the way into Cazador, so I laid on the horn, slowed down to eighty, and passed him on the shoulder.

"Are you driving?"

Like a maniac. "Yes. Promise me, Grant! They've got my kid."

"Okay, okay. I promise."

He might be lying and would call his bosses the second I hung up, but I was committed now. I told him, as rapidly and succinctly as I could, everything that had happened. Only I left out the incriminating part about me keeping an illegal magical superartifact in my possession. Also Mr. Trash Bags. I can't even imagine how badly the MCB would freak out about keeping a shoggoth popsicle in the fridge.

"I know I'm a complete idiot. I shouldn't have given them the . . . the price without them giving me my baby back."

"No." I could feel him holding back from asking me what the ransom was, something for which I was eternally grateful because Grant wasn't stupid. "I completely understand doing whatever's necessary to rescue someone you love. I'd do the same for—for someone I love."

I really didn't have time for awkwardness right then. If he started talking about his feelings, I was going to wreck the damned car. "Great. I need to know where Lucinda Hood is."

"You and every supernatural law enforcement agency in the world."

"I'm on the clock, Grant!"

Thankfully he didn't ask me what I was in a rush for. Black magic portals were probably super illegal too. "Lucinda was last seen in Europe."

"Where in Europe?"

"All over. London, Paris, and Lisbon mostly."

"That's helpful," I said sarcastically.

"Look, I know it's not, but it's all I have. We've got

reports that she and her loonies are rebuilding there. They're setting up cells in every major city. The Condition is rejuvenated since Lucinda found them a new god, and their recruiting is way up. Every so often she'll dump a truckload of zombies somewhere, just to be a bitch. Our equivalent agencies in Europe have had the hardest time hiding the evidence of her activities."

"Any idea where someone would hold an auction of a potentially magical baby to evil cultists and monsters?"

"Shit, that's terrible. I've got no idea. I've never even heard of anything like that. If a bunch of supernatural entities are going to congregate somewhere, we usually hear something, but there hasn't been anything on the radar. Let me call my friends in intel—"

"You promised. I'm not getting shut out of this. He's my son!"

"Calm down, Julie. I'm a federal agent. If I find out an *Adze* is stealing children and killing people on US soil, I can't just—"

"I'm going after him. Don't try to stop me." I was getting close to the compound when I got another call. It was Melvin. "Hang on, Grant. I've got to take this."

"Julie, wait. Don't put me on h—"

I flipped to the troll. "Go."

"Nice orc ladies came over to help Melvin. Red beard's handwriting sucks and is lame, but you bring rope, we get you *close* to last place it used."

"Define close."

"Walking distance . . . hmmm . . . Melvin hopes they weren't on boat. Heh-heh-heh . . . You drowning is funny. Anyways, Harbinger has old treasures in basement with magic inside. You mind if Melvin breaks them to power the—"

"Go for it. How big will the portal be?"

"For such little magic? Only one go. And tight fit for you. Having babies makes humans fat."

I swear if I didn't need him, I'd have shot him just on principle. "Get ready. I'm almost there." Then I switched back to Grant.

"Julie?"

"I'm back."

"Okay, we're not the bad guys here. My people are good at what we do. You don't need to keep us out of the loop."

If the portal rope actually worked, even if the MCB tried to stop me, there was no way they could get here in time. I'd be off to who knew where, beating the *Adze*'s location out of whoever had hired him to steal the artifact. "I don't care. Talk to your agent friends. Tell your boss. The only thing that matters to me is that Ray comes home safe."

Putting him on hold must have given him time to think. He actually sounded a little contrite. "I'm sorry about your grandfather. I always respected him, even if he didn't like me. I can't understand what you're going through right now, but rest assured I'll keep looking for where an auction could take place, okay? In the meantime, don't do anything stupid."

"Ha!"

I put my finger on the button to hang up when Grant yelled, "Julie, please be careful. Be safe."

Fat chance of that. I hung up.

The "nice orc ladies" turned out to be two of Gretchen's sister-wives, who'd been called by Shelly. For whatever reason, magic comes far easier to species like orcs, elves, trolls, and gnomes than it does for humans. Between them, Melvin Google searching troll magic, Milo's notes, the frayed rope from the bridge, and the magic *sucked* out of some miscellaneous knickknacks we'd stored in the archives, they were fairly certain this would work.

They were using the middle of the cafeteria. The tables had been shoved off to the side to make room. It was rare to see him outside of the basement, but Melvin was sitting on the floor, huge, green, and hideous, drawing troll runes on the floor with a Sharpie.

They needed a few minutes to stitch more rope onto the old one to make it big enough for me to fit through. Melvin's cracks about my mom bod aside, the problem wasn't one of dimensions, but of available power. Apparently none of the trinkets they'd used up could hold a candle to our old ward stone. It had been the magical equivalent to a nuclear power plant; this was more of a double-A battery. The more mass that moved through, the faster the energy was drained. When that power was used up, the portal would instantly snap closed like a quantum guillotine.

"How instant?" I'd asked. Melvin had suggested that just in case of technical difficulty I go head first, rather than feet first. Because feet first, I might get decapitated, but head first, at worst, I'd only leave my feet in Alabama . . . but probably not, though it would be close. Troll shrug. Since trolls can regenerate lost limbs, they're pretty flippant about amputation and don't understand why humans get so upset about it.

Fantastic. I hadn't even said a word to that revelation. Since it was going to take them a little time to get ready, I decided to take a shower and get into some dry clothes. Since the lunch I'd promised Albert had never happened and it had been a stressful few hours, I was starving, but I was scared to eat because those extra ounces might cost me my feet.

In the shower, I watched the blood run pink down the drain. That little monkey monster had scratched the hell out of me. There was a huge, purple, spreading bruise on my leg. It felt good to be clean, but unfortunately not being in motion gave me too much time to think of all the horrible things that could be happening to my kid. I had to keep moving.

As I dried off I went over equipment. The problem with portals is they could lead anywhere. Dress light and I'd probably land in a blizzard. I thought about armor, but armor was heavy, and heavy meant it was going to use up magical energy. So I went with cargo pants and a black Under Armor shirt. I'd risk frostbite in hopes of getting a gun through instead. Then I'd have the rest of my gear staged and they could toss it through after me until the portal closed. Maybe I'd get lucky.

While the orc shamans sewed on enough rope for me to fit through, I set up my kit. They could send me, then my pistol, and then—fingers crossed—a rifle, then my armor and equipment. But getting all that would be like winning the lottery. Hopefully, the portal wouldn't land me directly in front of the bad guys, but that was a risk I was willing to take. I kept my phone on me because I was still hoping Mr. Trash Bags would call, but he hadn't yet, so that wasn't looking likely. Whoever had received the artifact had probably just squished him and finished what Hood started.

That thought made me cringe. Mr. Trash Bags was a monster, but he was also my childhood friend. I'd kept him frozen because I hadn't known what else to do with him. I really hoped I hadn't condemned the poor little guy.

I left the kidnapper's phone with Melvin in the hopes that once he had the chance he could maybe glean some useful information from it, but that was a long shot.

By the time I was ready, Skippy's wives were still working. More orcs had arrived, except for the members of the tribe who were taking Amanda out of my trunk to give her a *Hunter's funeral*—as in decapitation and cremation. It's safer that way. They'd already done the same for Grandpa.

The wait was killing me. I checked my watch and discovered that only a few hours had passed since Ray had been taken. Then I thought better of it, pulled my watch off, and tossed it on the floor. I'd rather have that weight in bullets.

Then one of the orcs gave me a nod. It was time. "Will this work?"

She spread her hands apologetically, as if to say *maybe?*

Melvin placed down the rope. Unlike the Condition one, it didn't have the cool snake-wiggle effect, so he had to arrange it into a circle himself. But then he cackled with glee as it ignited and some of the cafeteria floor disappeared. "It work! Melvin brilliant!"

Just in case, I went head first.

CHAPTER 8

I dropped from a hole in the sky onto a ratty lawn. My impact woke up some sleeping geese who waddled away protesting.

It was nighttime but there were plenty of street-lights. Nearby, staring at me, was a guy in virulent yellow tights and the sort of tabard that medieval people used to wear, also in violent yellow with blue polka dots. He wore a crown with antennae and—I hoped—a false nose about the size of an eggplant and the same color. And he was looking at *me* like *I'd* lost my mind.

The woman with him, wearing a sort of ballet outfit in the same colors, striped tights in black and white, fake plastic glasses, and a headband with eyes attached to it, glared at me and grabbed his arm. It probably looked like I'd just appeared out of nowhere.

They said something in fast German. Where the hell was I? And why were they dressed like crazy people? I spun around, saw a cathedral dominating the sky, and immediately realized where I was. *Köln*. Cologne, the eponymous city of eau de cologne.

I'd kind of been expecting to land in the middle of nowhere, not a crowded city. Then I had to turn back to catch my pistol as one of the orcs tossed it through. I quickly shoved the compact .45 into my waistband and covered it with my shirt before the locals noticed.

I'd been through this area before, but just briefly as a tourist. The view was dominated by the largest cathedral in Germany, visible from everywhere in Old Town. I'd landed on the grassy verge near the river walk. Down from me, the bridge was brightly illuminated. The river walk was full of outlandishly dressed people. I could hear drunken singing nearby. I swear the entire city smelled of beer. And the little bit of road I could see from where I was looked like it was chockablock with . . . floats.

Fasching. This was Köln's answer to Carnival and started sometime in November and lasted all the way to Ash Wednesday, achieving its most frenzied celebration just before then. I wasn't Catholic, which meant I had no idea when Ash Wednesday was, but from the look of things right now, it must be just around the corner.

Then Melvin screwed up the order and sent through the gear bag with my armor, which I caught with a grunt. And before I could drop my kit on the grass, my rifle fell through, but only half of it, because that's when the portal gave up the ghost. There was a flash of sparks as my custom M-14 was instantly sheared in two. The front half hit the grass with a thud. The magazine had been sliced through so the spring shot out, spilling .308 rounds everywhere. The receiver was glowing like it had been hit with a cutting torch and the plastic stock was smoldering.

I turned. Eggplant nose and his googly-eyed girl-friend were still standing there, so I resurrected my very rusty German to say, "Magic show! I'm an assault commando. Good costume, hey?"

It shouldn't have worked. It wouldn't have worked if Fasching didn't amount to the world's largest beerfest, and if everyone involved hadn't by now, for sure, drank enough to believe just about anything. By the magic power of beer, both of the witnesses to my arrival smiled wide and started clapping.

That was one problem solved, but it left me with others, such as how to find a cult of weirdos in a city that was going to be overflowing with people dressed like weirdos. Worse, while I wasn't very conversant with magic, I knew that events like this, tied to a religious festival and probably having roots in pagan festivals long ago, were the kinds of things that cultists loved to infiltrate. So of course it made sense that this was where they'd sent the artifact.

I looked around. The road near the river walk was filled with floats built on flatbed trucks. I had a vague memory that at some time or other in the last few years there had been floats depicting American politicians, which had upset a bunch of people. Upset me too, truth be told. If anyone was going to mock our robbers and con artists, it should be us, and besides, from across the ocean, they didn't know what the hell they were talking about anyway.

But the floats I could see didn't have anything to do with politics, and it was late enough the parade was over. It was party time now. There was a float parked nearby that seemed to be an autonomous beer garden, complete with maidens in dirndls and men in lederhosen dancing around what had to be the world's largest beer stein. The float behind that one had a huge dragon which looked like it was made from some sort of plastic; only three guys were on top of it, drinking beer. And behind that was a truck carrying a big Cthulhu, or at least what they imagined Cthulhu looked like, because this one was kind of cute. Guys and girls who looked much the worse for wear were sitting on some hydraulic-powered tentacles which bobbed up and down, and from where I stood, I swear they were singing, "Ph'nglui mglw'nafh Cthulhu R'lyeh wgah'nagl fhtagn."

I shuddered a little because, unlike these idiots, I knew what the Old Ones were really like.

But none of this brought me close to saving Ray. It simply wasn't possible that the artifact had been sent into the middle of this madhouse. Melvin had said he could get me *close* to where it had been delivered. They would have wanted a secure place, one they could guard.

Where around here was a place like that?

There were businesses, apartments, and hotels all around. It had been years since I'd been in Cologne and I'd just been a tourist passing through. I had no idea where criminals or weird cults gathered around here, or where a group of people who relied on the supernatural and stitched together automatons out of dead creatures would find a safe hideout.

With nothing to go off of but instinct, I put my bag over my shoulder and just started walking. There was one obvious landmark. I looked again at the cathedral, remembering how much evil likes places of power, but then again some types of undead couldn't go near a consecrated place, and the Condition—assuming that's what I was chasing—loved making undead servants. So I went in the opposite direction, toward where the floats were parked.

The sidewalks were packed with bodies, most of them in colorful costumes. The buildings through here were all four or more stories tall, so I thought about trying to get up high for a better look. Every available balcony already had people on it so I wouldn't stand out, but then I dismissed that idea. The cultists were probably hunkered down inside somewhere, and if they weren't, it would take a miracle to pick them out of this mob. Assuming they'd not already left the area entirely.

I was dying inside. I might have already lost the artifact and, with it, my only leverage to get Ray back.

Okay, think. I'd been drafted to be the Guardian. I didn't know what the hell that title actually entailed, but I was connected to this stupid artifact. Maybe it would show me the way.

So I stopped right there, closed my eyes, and concentrated...

...and a minute later gave up because absolutely nothing happened, and I felt stupid. I don't know how my husband put up with that mystical psychic nonsense.

I checked my phone. Because I traveled so much—or at least I had before the baby—I had an international plan, but there were no new messages. I started thinking that Mr. Trash Bags had let me down after all—and feeling guilty as hell because, for all I knew, the little deranged shoggoth was dead because of me—when I saw a car driving erratically.

It had lurched out of an alley by a hotel, forcing

crowds of drunken spectators to get out of the way, and generally acting like the driver was drunk off his ass, which probably wasn't unusual during Fasching. It could only fit between the floats because it was one of those dumpy, tiny little things...a Smart Car they called it, which meant it had been named on Opposite Day.

But as the car got closer, through the open window I could hear the men inside, and their panicked screaming about *"Finger"* and *"Beissen."* As bad as my German is, it's remarkably easy to understand when somebody is freaking out about something biting his fingers.

Oh no. I pushed my way through the crowd until I found a gap, then sprinted toward the car. Then there was a high-pitched battle cry that sounded like you'd imagine a hamster would sound if it could talk.

"Cuddle Bunny made of stars!"

The passenger was thrashing around and wrestling with something in his lap. The driver looked over at me, and I caught sight of an adolescent face with an uncertain growth of beard. I almost pulled my gun to shoot him, but I needed them alive to question. Plus...it was Mr. Trash Bags. Considering he might not be super reliable at target identification, this could just be some poor kid who'd picked up the discarded bag. But his eyes grew very wide as I grabbed hold of the door handle. He stomped on the gas and drove right across the crowded sidewalk.

The car didn't have much in the way of guts or acceleration, but the people got out of the way. Mostly. One woman in a bright green costume went over the hood and landed in the street. The door was locked, and I had to let go before I got dragged.

But one thing was crystal clear in my mind before

I let go: there had been a squid necklace—the symbol
of the Condition—dangling under his vapid face.

For one brief instant, I had the shot, and I could
have plugged the driver through the back of the head,
but then they were crashing haphazardly through
the crowd. The car didn't seem to be hitting anyone
because people were jumping out of the way and there
were shouts of drunken offense, but no screams of
pain and no thumps. Then they hit a clear patch of
road and started making distance.

They were getting away from me.

The nearest float was the Cthulhu one. It wasn't
nearly as fancy as some of the others here, mostly being
a giant papier-mâché monster on the bed of a Mercedes
truck. I ran over and opened the door; the chime told
me the keys were in it. The burly blond behind the
wheel barely had time to open his mouth before I
pulled him off the seat and shoved him into the road.
It wasn't as hard as it sounds because he seemed really
drunk, which was good, as he was a lot bigger than I
was, and I didn't have time to fight random Germans.
I tossed my gear bag on the passenger seat, got behind
the wheel, slammed the door, started the engine, ground
the gears, and then laid on the horn and the gas. The
driver was sitting in the gutter, staring at me as I
drove away, seemingly baffled by this turn of events.

The float gradually built up speed. The already angry
crowd didn't like getting out of the way again, but they'd
already been bested by a Smart Car. They weren't going
to stand up to a truck, even a stupid-looking one with a
cartoon Old One dangling over the roof. They got out
of the way, though a few chucked their beer bottles at
the cab.

"Move, assholes!" Normally monster hunting was all about protecting the innocents, but right then I truly would have run them down. Luckily, I didn't have to.

I got it up to a whopping twenty miles an hour by the time the Smart Car made a right at the end of the street. I made that turn in a vehicle so top heavy that I thought for sure it was going to tip over. Then I realized that I still had people riding on the back, now clinging to Cthulhu in terror.

Most embarrassing car chase ever.

I made that corner, and then the next one too, though that one was only on two wheels. It's not a drive I'd care to make again. It had been easier to drive a van across Alabama with giant, animated gargoyles on my tail.

We were moving away from the main party streets, but it was still crowded with pedestrians. The car sped along erratically, forcing people to jump out of the way. And then, just as they started to gather up behind the Smart Car to talk about how weird that was, I charged in, honking, driving a truck loaded with Cthulhu and frightened drunks. The crowd screamed, the Germans on the tentacles screamed, and I probably got called a lot of names.

The Smart Car sped ahead, around a set of sidewalk tables. Fortunately, that warned the occupants of the tables enough that they were out of the way by the time I crashed through them. And there was no way, no way at all, in the world, that I could squeeze this thing into the space the Smart Car had. Nor did I intend to. Instead, I plowed into the tables—crunch, crunch, crunch—making the good people of Köln run—scream, scream, incoherent insult—while the tentacles of Cthulhu waved madly in my rearview mirror and men in lederhosen jumped off, and I tried very hard not to kill anyone.

At the end of the sidewalk, the car darted onto a climbing side street, and I plunged after them. Now that we'd left the main parade area behind, this road was a lot more open, so I floored it. I just had to be careful not to run over the Smart Car and kill all the disgusting cultists before I could ask them where the hell they'd taken my baby. Seriously, I remember my brothers playing with Matchbox cars bigger than that thing.

I bumped it once or twice, trying to make them spin out, and each time I smacked into it with controlled force, through the open window I could hear their panicked shouts and the little hamster voice screaming, "Consume!"

With me on their tail and Mr. Trash Bags in their laps, the cultists tried something desperate. Ahead was the entrance to a parking garage. There was no way I could fit. The Smart Car didn't even slow down as it crashed into the plastic arm blocking the entrance.

I had no time to check my progress, nor would I. Yeah, yeah, the garage top said something about nothing over three meters, and I was damn sure my vehicle was taller, but I didn't care. I crashed into the garage with an awful ripping sound. Cthulhu pretty much exploded. Hopefully all the passengers had jumped off before that.

Only when I looked in my rearview mirror, I realized a sedan was tearing into the garage after me. There was no siren, so it probably wasn't cops. But I'd worry about my pursuers after I cornered my target. All of a sudden my side mirror shattered as they started shooting at me. Probably not the *Polizei* then.

Even freed of my float, the truck was less maneuverable than the Smart Car in this confined space. The garage was packed with parked cars and the turns were tight. The cultists went down a floor on a sharply curving ramp. My truck hit the side and I left a shower of metal sparks and tearing concrete. They were going to shake me in here.

But then Mr. Trash Bags must have turned his attention to the driver because suddenly they turned hard to the side and smashed directly into a big concrete pillar. I don't think those little cars had a lot of crash protection because the cultists flopped out of it like the contents of a smashed egg. I needed one of them alive to interrogate, to tell me where my baby was.

I slammed on the brakes. The chase car was trapped on the ramp behind me. *Screw those guys.* I put it in reverse, stomped on it, and smashed the rear of the flatbed into their hood.

Like Earl always said, "When in doubt, be aggressive." Bailing out, I pulled my .45 and ran back up the ramp to the Smart Car, using the side of the truck as cover.

They were rattled, but trying to get out of the wrecked car. One, two, three, four, five, six...what the hell had this been, a clown car? They all had that pale, fanatical, scraggly look the Condition loved, only this time with a skinny-pants Euro-trash vibe. My aim point was just below that squid necklace. The first one out of the back seat went down with two holes in his chest.

This next part is going to sound callous, but it was

like shooting fish in a barrel. I've got a reputation as one of MHI's most precise shooters and it isn't because I'm that talented, it's because I'm efficient.

My next target was passenger side, and he got priority because he was behind cover and lifting what appeared to be a sawed-off shotgun. I leaned around the rear of the truck, aimed at his face, and fired. I don't know if I got him, but he dropped behind the car.

The driver hung a pistol out the window and started cranking off wild shots in my direction. I shifted back a bit and put a pair of bullet holes through the glass right over him. His pistol clattered to the concrete. Movement to the left, but that one was running up the ramp, trying to get away. Movement to the right, and another one fell out of the back seat. *Gun!* So while she was on her hands and knees, I shot her in the side, and then when she rolled over, chest.

My slide was locked back empty and I still had threats. My hand instantly went to my side for a spare magazine that wasn't there. *Shit.* So I calmly went back to the cab of the truck, grabbed my gear bag, dragged it over, got a spare mag out, and reloaded.

Before I could go back to finish the job, I heard sirens.

I was in the country illegally, didn't even have my passport, and had just shot a bunch of people after stealing a truck and driving it through a crowd of pedestrians. And I still needed to take a hostage, so it was time to go.

The two from the Smart Car were messed up, but still moving. There were more cultists on the ramp, and I didn't know how many were dead, wounded and still dangerous, or perfectly healthy and ready to shoot me. They'd be coming after me, but there was also an incendiary grenade in my bag and a giant flaming truck was one hell of a barricade. So I fished in the bag for the grenade, threw the bag over my shoulder, pulled the pin, dropped the grenade onto the floorboards, and trotted away.

The grenade went off with a *foom,* and the truck cab was instantly engulfed in flames. It turns out all the leftover Cthulhu bits were exceedingly flammable, too, because within seconds the entire ramp was a giant fireball.

Gun up, I stalked towards the wrecked Smart Car. One blood-spattered cultist was lying on the concrete floor and didn't look like he was up to answering any questions. The driver's airbag had deployed, and that one was groaning.

"Cuddle Bunny?" a voice called from inside the car, followed by a human scream as the driver came to and realized he still had a shoggoth on him. He struggled to open his door while a little creature who looked like a very small blob made of oil, eyeballs, and teeth crawled around his head and greeted me through the window with, "Cuddle Bunny!"

The bad guy got the door open and fell out, screaming and swatting at Mr. Trash Bags. It was doubtful they'd ever had Ray—there was no sign a baby had ever been there, and not enough space to hide one—but lying there on the seat of the stupid Smart Car was one of the most powerful magical artifacts in the world.

"Amateur hour," I snapped as I reached in, grabbed the Kumaresh Yar, and stuck it in my pocket. I stood over the driver and aimed my gun at his face. The cultist stared at me, eyes wide in horror. He was very young, for sure not even twenty, and ran true to type for Condition recruits. He was skinny, had mouse-colored hair all shaved down one side of his head and long on the other, and so many face piercings that it looked like he'd run face-first into a conveyor belt full of metal castings. He wore tightly fitted leather pants and a shirt, which in a healthier human would showcase muscles, but in him just showcased the places where he hoped wishfully that muscles would materialize.

He started to cry and plead for mercy.

He also had a shoggoth on his head, pulling at his hair with the style and élan of a cowboy busting broncos, and there was a chunk missing from his ear, which probably meant Mr. Trash Bags might have got carried away.

"Good job, Mr. Trash Bags. No more biting for now."

I pulled out my knife. The cultist screamed and raised his hands, and mumbled stuff in German, then yelled, "It wasn't my fault!" in English, then shrieked as though I'd cut him as my knife flashed towards his throat.

Of course, what I'd actually cut was his squid necklace.

We'd run into these before. They were the Condition's way of making sure their members didn't talk. When they did, the necklace would come to life and strangle them. I was going to nip that in the bud.

The cord actually gushed some weird black liquid as I cut it and must have tried to come to life, because it sort of writhed, then tried to grasp my hand as I flung it aside. It landed, slithered a bit like one of their portal ropes before burning up with a green fire, and ended up looking like a line of melted tar.

The garage was filling with smoke. I couldn't hear the sirens anymore over the crackle of flames, but this place was going to be swarming with cops soon. "If you try anything, I'll shoot you in the dick." I assumed he would understand that well enough.

Like most Germans, he spoke decent English. "It wasn't me," he said, staring at the necklace in a sort of fascinated wonder. "I was just joining the club because it was college and they said they had much beer and I could live forever. And they made real magic, which was being cool."

I ignored his babble and patted him down quickly. All he had was a knife which, to be honest, was one of those pseudo-cabalistic pieces of junk you can get at every New Age store, and which would probably break to pieces if he tried to stab anyone with it.

Then I noted that the passenger had dropped his cell phone. So I went over and picked it up, which was when he started to rise, scattering safety glass. Since he made a very zombielike groan suggesting that he'd expired and his magic necklace had brought him back to unlife, I promptly shot him in the head.

The living cultist shrieked. Seeing how casually I'd blown his friend's brains out must have driven home the point that I meant business.

The iPhone was locked, so I stuck the dead guy's thumb on the button. *Bingo.*

"Get up." He did. I nodded toward the AUSFAHRT sign over the stairs and shoved him. "Move."

CHAPTER 9

I walked my captive, Mr. Trash Bags in one coat pocket, away from the garage, seeing police cars and fire trucks converging on the scene the whole time. Because of the nearby super party, there was a massive crowd of curious witnesses gathering to see what was on fire.

This was a blessing in disguise because it enabled me and my looking-worse-for-wear prisoner to make it through without being noticed by the authorities. I stayed a step behind the cultist the whole way and made sure that he knew if he tried anything I'd kill him. He must have been tempted to run a few times, but he was too chicken. I didn't even need to have my gun out because of Mr. Trash Bags, so the cultist kept walking obediently. While we moved, I went into the settings on the dead guy's phone so it wouldn't lock again. There could be something useful there.

A really drunk man, who I think was supposed to be dressed as a vampire, had taken off his red velvet cape and hung it on a fence while he watched the fire trucks. I grabbed the cape as I walked by, threw it on, and put the hood up. I probably looked like a militant Little Red Riding Hood, but it hid my face from street cameras, and the gear bag, too.

We headed away from the party zone. Once there was nobody around, I told him to turn down a dark alley behind a closed-down restaurant. It was much like any witness-free alley in America, just cleaner. I made him take a seat behind some little wheeled dumpsters and started asking questions.

"Where's my son?"

My captive blinked at me stupidly, so Mr. Trash Bags said, "Wheee" and bit his nose.

The cultist flapped his hands and smacked at his own face, missing the shoggoth who climbed on top of his head, pulling his hair like reins. I really should get Mr. Trash Bags a little cowboy hat.

"Eat noses, eat toes, eat ears!" Mr. Trash Bags declared, while the cultist gave up a babble of German and English from which was most audible: "It wasn't my fault."

I was getting a headache. And even though I didn't care if Mr. Trash Bags terrorized this scum, I needed to know what was going on, and I wasn't going to get anything useful out of him if my shoggoth was making him crazier.

"Mr. Trash Bags, please, stop for now. Only bite if he doesn't answer questions."

"Mr. Trash Bags no eat noses?"

"Not yet," I said to him. Then to the cultist, who was stupid enough to try to crawl away with Mr. Trash Bags still on his head like a stylish and very strange hat, "I asked you a question. Where is my son?"

The cultist just shook his head.

"Eat toes!" Mr. Trash Bags said dancing down his head and shoulder headed for the top of his cheap fantasy high boots.

"No. Not yet. Wait."

Mr. Trash Bags stopped, poised where he was, tentacles extended to the top of the boot, little eyes on stalks turned to me hopefully.

It was time to try good cop/bad cop. Even in the mood I was in, I could still play good cop. We Southern women are good at being cordial even when we hate someone. "If I were you, I'd talk. He *really* wants to eat your toes. He's been frozen for a while, and I guess that builds up an appetite."

The cultist's eyes filled with tears. Blood was dripping from where a dime-sized piece of flesh had been bitten off his nose. His lips trembled. "I'll talk." His voice was all watery and childish. "But I don't know anything."

"Let's start with your name."

"Benno Jurgen."

"Right, okay, Beano—"

"Benno!"

"Sorry. I know this is really traumatic, but I need to know what you have done with the baby your guys stole."

The tears multiplied. "We never got a baby. We just wanted the artifact."

"Fine, okay." It was neither fine nor okay. I'd recovered it, but what I really wanted was my son. "So you wanted the artifact, and what did you do?"

"We should never have done it!"

"Undoubtedly." I couldn't roll my eyes any further without risking their falling out. "I mean, yeah, mistakes were made, you should never have done it, but what did you *do?*"

"The high priestess, Lucinda, she told us if we had it, we could cast a spell that would mean none of us would ever die, and also make everyone our servants and us kings of the world."

"Of course she did." Every religion in the world warns that evil is corrupting, evil is seductive, evil is all sorts of bad things, but they never tell you that evil is *boring*. Still, the evil ones always all want the same thing: control. They're predictable. They prey on naïve losers like this. Benno looked very young and that was playing havoc with me. I wanted to wipe his face and tell him to sin no more, but he'd messed with my family, so I was fresh out of pity. "Then what?"

He snuffled, wiped his nose—blood and snot—on his sleeve and said, "I can't tell you."

"He's going to eat your toes."

"No, be listening to me. I can't tell you or they'll kill me. They said if we left for any reason, they'd kill us. I liked it when it was just cool parties and drinking, but I didn't like to do things to people, and all the dead robots. All the robots made from parts of dead people and things." He shivered. "But they said they'd kill me. They'll use my flesh to make more automatons."

"Well, bless your heart," which was Alabama woman for *wow, you're an idiot*. "That's one of the risks you take when you join a death cult."

"Toes?" Mr. Trash Bags yelled, and he began slithering inside the boots.

Benno shouted. "I'll talk, I'll talk! We hired Brother Death."

That was a new one on me. "Keep your voice down. If you attract attention, Mr. Trash Bags might eat your tongue. Nod if you understand... Good. Tell me about this *Brother Death*."

"We hired him to retrieve the artifact. So we could give it to high priestess Lucinda. Our leader wanted to impress her. He messaged her as soon as it arrived, very proud. She's coming to Köln tomorrow to get it."

Since the artifact was in my pocket, Lucinda was going to be pissed. "Where's your leader now?"

"You just shot him in head! I was only his driver."

"In that clown car?"

"Wilhelm said it's easy to park and good for the environment."

I resisted the sudden urge to shoot him in the face.

"The high priestess didn't know about our plan. It was to surprise her so our church could gain favor. We are a new chapter, but we would be first among the Condition, and blessed with power and riches. Wilhelm just told her so she can come and get it."

"You guys are ambitious. Who is Brother Death?"

He hesitated too long. Mr. Trash Bags now had more than a few tentacles down Benno's boots and was looking at me, bouncing gently, like a dog waiting for the order to eat the treat on his nose; like a toddler with his hand in the cookie jar, waiting for the go-ahead. "Okay, but just his pinky toe."

"No! No one knows much about him, even in our circles. He's an entity, from Africa originally, but he'll work anywhere for a price. He's very old, older than humanity. Dirty jobs you want done, you summon him, make a deal, and he does them. He can sneak in places and take over minds. To kill things or take things, he is the best. Very dangerous, very smart. So we made a contract and signed it in blood."

As Benno said that, a chill ran down my spine. I remembered the voice on the phone saying I couldn't pay the price he charged. "How did you pay him?"

"Souls, human sacrifice, magic, pain, whatever."

It sounded like they'd hired a top-tier supernatural hitman. It was obvious that this was a new and fairly inept branch of the Condition, but they'd made a deal with something truly dangerous. "Why did you think of hiring something like him?"

"I don't know. Lucinda taught Wilhelm how to summon him. Other groups of the church have hired him before, so we thought—"

"You'd promise my son in payment?" My voice must have had some kind of edge because Benno blanched and Mr. Trash Bags said "Toes?" hopefully.

"No, no, nonono! We didn't know he was going to get your son, I swear!"

I was sure he wasn't the mastermind of this plan, and he certainly wasn't even one of the big wheels in the small group he belonged to. Hell, it was quite possible that he had been desperate to quit the Condition ever since he'd realized they were more than a drinking club, but that didn't mean I didn't want to gut-shoot and leave him to bleed out in agony. Because of their stupid idea, their impulse no more serious than giving an apple to a teacher, my grandfather had lost his life and my baby was missing.

I noticed the night had grown uncomfortably cold.

"How do you contact Brother Death? Where can I find him?"

"That was Wilhelm's job! I don't know. I only met him once when we signed the contract."

"You signed the contract too? What did it say?"

"It was . . . I don't know . . . hard to read. The language was weird. It was written on a piece of skin. I was scared but Wilhelm told us we all had to sign or else!"

I realized that fog was gathering in the alley.

"Oh shit." I could no longer hear the noise of the party. Something weird was going on. "You never sign a contract with monsters!"

"Danger, Cuddle Bunny," Mr. Trash Bags warned as he crawled off of Benno and toward me. "Collection imminent."

Benno was still lying on the ground. The fog collecting around him had begun to glow red, and it was as if the light was coming from *beneath* him.

"What?" he shrieked. "What's happening?"

What was happening was that their magical contract with Brother Death had probably had a nondisclosure clause, which Benno had just violated the hell out of, and now hell was going to violate *him*.

The streetlights dimmed to nothing. Now the only thing illuminating the darkness was that eerie red fog. All my instincts told me to run, but I stayed. The ground around him seemed to fade away. From beneath, rusty chains appeared, acting with a mind of their own, curling around Benno's body and pinning his arms to his side. They'd come literally out of nowhere. It happened so fast all I could do was leap back.

"Help! Help me!" Benno screamed as the chains tightened.

What came from below to collect him was lumbering, simultaneously slimy and furry, a mix of discordant parts which I had too much sanity to identify. To collect him to *where*, I had no idea. That had probably been specified in all that supernatural legalese these cultists hadn't bothered to explain to Benno.

The dim light spared me a good view of the creature. All I got was hints, and that was enough to make me nauseous. Benno started screaming, but a black hand with six fingers clamped his mouth shut. It had several heads. One of them—the closest approximate description would be *boarlike*—turned toward me.

This does not concern you, Hunter.

The way that terrible swarm of wasps of a voice assaulted my brain, I knew that this wasn't the thing I'd been talking to on the phone. This was sick and wrong. Its presence on Earth was trespassing. Standing in front of that terrible, otherworldly horror, I should have been frightened, but I was a mother on a mission.

"I think it does concern me."

The trade was made. It traded itself to the Adze. *The* Adze *traded it to us. We will claim what is ours now.*

That was the kind of terrifying shit right there that nobody was going to put on a parade float.

"The *Adze* called Brother Death. He's stolen something of mine. I need to find him."

While Benno kicked and thrashed and tried to get away, the demon thought it over.

We could trade for this information. Only that which we collect, you cannot give. The Guardians already claim you.

This thing was about to swallow Benno's soul and could probably flay me alive with a thought, but I was angry and desperate. I didn't know what being a Guardian entailed, but all these cosmic horrors seemed to. "Tell me how to find him or I will hurt you."

You would not even know how.

"I might not now, but if I can't get my kid back then I'll make it my mission in life to find a way."

A snake head slithered over and whispered something in the boar's ear. The sound could best be described as gibbering madness. Just hearing a little bit of it made my nose bleed.

Brother Death is a valued seller . . . However, strife in the mortal realm amuses us. And we owe you. You have done us a favor.

There was no way I'd ever do a favor for something like this. Just the idea made my skin want to crawl off.

By recently killing a few of those who signed the contract, we did not have to wait for them to age and die before collection. By making this one violate the terms, we may rightfully claim both spirit and body. They are more useful to us when they still have flesh.

Useful for what, I didn't want to know. "Then tell me how to find Brother Death."

In the place of power you'll find him, where evil dwells beneath. In the country of the sea.

I almost thanked it, but something warned me that would be a mistake and I started walking away instead. "Come on, Mr. Trash Bags." Country of the sea. So probably not Germany. I mean, it had shores, but no one ever called it a seafaring country primarily.

Farewell, Guardian.

The poor, stupid, condemned cultist pleaded for help with his wide, tear-filled eyes. "Sorry. You're on your own, Benno."

It felt good to be back under the electric lights. By the time I'd reached the street, the fog had dissipated. I turned back to look, and the alley was empty.

Where Benno had been, there was just a damp spot on the pavement.

That's what you get for not reading the fine print.

It's always been my experience that if you walk along looking like you know what you're doing and are precisely where you're supposed to be, few people will call you on it. But the area was crawling with cops and there had to be eyewitness descriptions of me circulating—5'11" Caucasian female, dark hair, glasses, athletic build—but luckily that description wasn't that unusual here. I had no idea if I'd been caught on Europe's ubiquitous cameras, and then I started worrying about anything I might have left fingerprints on. I tried to remember how I'd touched the Smart Car, and then I really started hoping that the fire had spread to destroy the evidence.

I wasn't in the country legally. Germany was super strict about monster hunting, and I didn't have a license for the gun I had tucked beneath my shirt. I'd just committed at least a couple murders, a bunch of attempted murders, arson, and grand theft float. In the US it was legal to kill anybody who qualified as a necromancer, but even then, local law enforcement was going to assume you were a psycho and roll you up until the MCB arrived to sort it out. I wasn't sure if it worked the same way in this country, or if they even had a necromancer exception at all. If they caught me, I could be looking at prison.

The problem was that for every minute I spent answering police questions and waiting for rescue, it was that much longer Ray would be in the power of a supernatural assassin, and that I could not abide.

So I kept walking and tried not to get noticed, which was easy amid the crazy costumes. I moved in behind a group costumed as zombies and shambled along with them.

"Dead are not real dead. Confused." Then Mr. Trash Bags climbed up on my shoulder for a better view, and he must have enjoyed the wind on his half-dozen eyeballs. "Whee."

That was just too unnerving. Whatever survival instincts Mr. Trash Bags had when he'd been huge and fearsome must have gotten burned away with his bulk. Monsters were usually smart enough to hide. "You can't let anyone see you, for both our safety. Don't make a sound, and hide in my gear bag until I tell you otherwise." Somehow the little blob managed to look disappointed, so I told him, "And good job back there. You did great. Thank you. Because of you we're one step closer to rescuing Cuddle Bunny's Cuddle Bunny." That seemed to make him happy, and Mr. Trash Bags oozed down my shoulder to drop into the bag.

I was exhausted, hungry, needed to get off the streets before I got arrested, and had to plan my next move. Benno had said Lucinda was on the way to Cologne to get the artifact. She was the one who'd taught their leader, Wilhelm, how to summon Brother Death. I got out the phone I'd stolen and read through his texts while I walked. My German was rudimentary so I couldn't understand most of them, but Lucinda was British, and sure enough there was a text—no names—in English, a few minutes after I'd sent the artifact through the rope that said *I have found something very special for you. I hope you will be pleased.*

And then the response. *Don't waste my time.*

Then poor stupid Wilhelm tried again. *It was your father's most precious thing. I have it in my hands. Dawn. Meet at the river.*

That was infuriatingly vague. Cologne was a big city on both sides of the Rhine. So all I had to do was figure out how to find the cagey leader of a death cult who was really good at not being found, in an unfamiliar foreign city.

I needed help.

MHI took the occasional job in Europe, but for the most part, hunting here was dominated by governments and a handful of private companies. The biggest and most successful of those was Grimm Berlin. They virtually owned private monster hunting in Germany and were our biggest single competitor when it came time to compete for foreign contracts in countries that didn't have their own monster hunting companies. We'd teamed up a few times now and had a pretty good working relationship, but that was mostly with their leader, Klaus Lindemann.

Only Klaus and most of his top-tier personnel were at Severny Island with my husband and friends. But monster hunting never slept, so to speak, not even when most of us were off saving the world. They surely would have left behind enough staff to look after things while they were gone. Like MHI, it would probably be the young, the old, the half-trained, the nearly retired, and all those they could spare from the really dangerous and important business going on up north.

Even if they were the B team, they would still have access to resources I didn't. This was their home turf. If Lucinda was coming here, Grimm Berlin was really my only hope of finding her, and she was my only hope of finding Brother Death.

There was a little outdoor café where a bunch of hipster types were hanging around smoking, drinking, and talking. So I stopped there, waiting at the edge of the tables but not sitting down, got out my phone, and called Grimm Berlin's main line. I keep all the different company contacts ready in case of emergency. The phone rang so long that I was revising my opinion of whether they had left anyone behind. Then an irritated voice answered, *"Yah, yah, Grimm Berlin, was ist los?"*

It seemed like a less-than-professional way to start the conversation, but who was I to judge. We had Dorcas. Her greeting was dependent upon her temper, her pudding coefficient, and whether they'd interrupted her all-important game of solitaire. Plus, even though I was still on Alabama time, it was getting late here.

I hoped this lady spoke English, though not doing so was actually surprisingly rare in this country. "This is Julie Shackleford from Monster Hunter International."

That sure got her attention because she started shouting into the phone. "You've heard then? From Severny Island?"

Of course that's what she thought. Why else would MHI be calling? Their people were just as much in danger as mine. I knew how she felt, having spent all these months waiting anxiously for every check-in, and being worried that I was about to be given news of my husband's death, like this, with no preamble, over the phone.

"I'm sorry. I haven't heard anything. That's not why I called."

"Oh." She sounded disappointed. "I hoped you had news of Klaus and the others."

"Me too. I'm afraid I've not heard anything since that blizzard started. I'm in Cologne pursuing something, and I could use your assistance."

There was a long pause. "Our teaming agreement with MHI states that you must inform us when taking a contract in our territory. Not to mention foreign Hunters must register with the government twenty-four hours before entering the country, and we've received no notification of—"

They sure loved having their papers in order. "Listen. I don't mean to be rude, but an hour ago I was in Alabama. I fell through a portal to get here, and at the time I didn't even know where *here* was. A few minutes later I walked right into an active cell of Condition cultists and shot them with a gun I'm probably not supposed to have, and now I need to know if you're going to help a sister out or turn me over to the police."

"Why—"

"Because I just found out that Lucinda Hood is on her way to Cologne right now." That caused an audible gasp and then a really long pause. Long enough for one of the local studly-looking young guys to wander over to try and flirt with me. Flattering as that was, I moved the phone away from my mouth and said, "Buzz off."

As the dejected hipster wandered away, the lady from Grimm Berlin said, "Excuse me?"

"I wasn't talking to you. But from your shocked silence I'm betting your government's got as big a bounty on Lucinda's head as mine does. I'll tell you what I know to help you catch her, and MHI doesn't expect a single Euro of the reward money."

"What do you want in return?"

"A chance to question Lucinda. And no police, no SJK." That was their equivalent to the MCB. "I don't have time for them. Hunters only."

"We have a man in Cologne right now."

"Only one?"

"Like you, we are a little short-handed right now. All of our teams are currently occupied. We have one man there in an advisory capacity. There were some reports of unusual activity there tonight."

"Oh, it was definitely unusual. Could I have his phone number?"

"Just a moment please."

And then there was a long silence, the kind of dead silence you get when you've been muted. I knew exactly what the person on the other side was doing. In our career, there are things we have to worry about that no other field of endeavor would even think of. When you meet an old friend, especially in an odd situation like this, you want to make sure they are who they say they are. There are things like doppelgangers. I had some experience being fooled by one, and I knew Grimm Berlin did too.

I figured calls were being made, at least to the MHI office, to make sure I wasn't at home. I hoped there was someone on the other side to answer. How was Dorcas? Had Lee made it? *Crap . . . I really needed to check my messages.*

A few minutes later the voice came back. I must have checked out. "Where in Cologne are you?"

"By the riverside. Near . . ." I had to lean over and read the names off the nearest street signs.

"Ah . . . by the disturbance. Our man is at a parking garage—"

"Yeah . . . I was just there."

"I presume you don't wish to meet him there?"

"Good guess. Have him meet me in front of . . . Hang on . . ." I found the name of a bar a ways down on the other side of the street that I still had a good view of. That way if they ratted me out and a bunch of cops rolled up, it would be the wrong place.

While I waited, I checked my texts and voicemails. Dorcas was awake, in pain, and really cranky, but holding down the fort. A Hunter from our Atlanta team was on the way to help her out. Albert was out of surgery, wasn't awake yet, but stable. *Thank God.* There were a bunch more messages I didn't have time to go through from Grant, Melvin, and other stateside Hunters who'd just heard something had gone down who were ready to kick ass and take names. Too bad they were on the other side of the world. By the time they got here, it would probably be too late.

I sent Dorcas a message telling her where I was, and she'd pass that on. Then I decided to power it off. If the police did identify me somehow, they'd be able to track my phone. But before I did, I realized I was staring at the background photo because it was a picture of my little guy. "Oh, Ray." I wanted to hear his fat, rolling, satisfied giggle. And I needed—with a near physical craving—to know he was safe and well, and that he would grow up safe and well, my son, Owen's son, a happy young Monster Hunter who'd inherit the company, just the way Grandpa would have wanted it.

I needed kin and comfort. Neither was available. What I got instead was a black Audi with tinted windows pulling up in front of the bar down the street.

Shutting my phone down, I looked around. No sign of uniforms and nobody I could pick out as a plain-clothes cop or SJK agent trying to blend in, waiting to pounce. But then again, I was a Monster Hunter, not a professional criminal. What did I know?

Since there wasn't an open parking spot, the Audi was blocking traffic. Other cars were backing up behind it, but the Audi didn't move. People got impatient and started to honk, but the driver didn't give a shit... That was a very Hunter-like attitude.

I ran over to the passenger side door. He must have seen me coming because the window rolled down.

The driver was a young man with longish hair. "Julie?"

"Yeah,"

"I'm Fabian. Get in."

And we were moving before I even got the door closed.

Surprisingly, he didn't immediately start to grill me with questions. Instead we drove in silence.

"Where are we going?"

"A safe house."

The idea of being able to stop running for just a moment, to be able to eat something, to stop and think sounded wonderful. But then I was hit with this frantic sense of guilt. Yes, I was still worried about my son and, no, I couldn't waste time on my way to finding him. I was tired and vaguely dizzy, yet the thought that I probably would have to take a break, maybe even sleep before I found him was strange and revolting. You have to be a mother to fully understand why. It seemed selfish that my body would even have necessities while Ray was missing. The minute he'd vanished, as far as my back brain, my mommy brain, was concerned, I should have become a perfect titanium automaton, needing no food, no sleep, no rest, no slowing down until I found him.

In a way I wished it were really like that. It would make life much easier.

But here, in the slightly cold spring night of Cologne, listening to the mournful metallic clangs from the motion of some sailboats anchored nearby on the darkened Rhine, smelling the beer and the fresh pretzels, I felt as though my arms and legs were made of lead, my stomach an empty hollow composed of hunger and fear, and my mind a muddle from lack of sleep. I rolled up the window so I could tune out those distractions.

"A safe house, huh? And not the local SJK office?"

"Sonderjagkommandos? I was told you requested no government interference."

They wouldn't care about Ray nearly as much as they'd care about killing the threats to their national security. "My son...my *infant* son has been kidnapped by an *Adze* that calls himself Brother Death."

"I'm terribly sorry to hear that." He was slim, and as young as Benno and the cultists. I could tell his hair had been cut to frame his face in a way that women would think "so romantic." He wore tight black pants and the sort of loose white shirt that belongs on the cover of a romance novel. But his eyes were sharp, and the look he gave me then was one of respect. He knew I was dangerous and desperate. For whatever reason, that little bit of recognition meant a lot.

As if to prove he had no ill intentions, Fabian started talking. "My office called your office. The woman there told us of your predicament. Anything I can do to see your baby returned to you, I will do. Grimm Berlin is dedicated to protecting the innocent from monsters, and there's no one more innocent than an infant."

"Your kindness is much appreciated, but I can't go to a safe house. I need to keep moving."

"To where?"

I didn't have an answer for that.

He was an unknown, and I didn't have the inclination to get betrayed, arrested, or otherwise screwed with. I kind of wished that international Monster Hunters, who had to face diabolical deceptions in the course of our everyday business, could've worked out some system of sign and countersign, or secret rings or something so we were sure we were speaking to the right people. But that was just the tired talking because it wasn't like the smart monsters, or the mind-reading ones, or the ancient chaos gods wouldn't just learn all that stuff in short order to screw with us anyway.

So I'd just have to trust my gut.

"Mrs. Shackleford, if I may. Germany is a much smaller country than the United States. Not just in size, but in how far apart things are. I have experienced the American way of monster hunting, having fights in public or on the Autobahn. It can't be that way here. Anything publicly experienced will get around fast because everyone has an aunt in the next city over, and the next city over is less than an hour away. Our SJK makes your MCB look gentle as a lamb. Unlike back home, you can't just go off half-cocked."

"You're pretty good with your American euphemisms."

He shrugged. "I did my post-grad at MIT. Grimm

Berlin avoids using public accommodation unless it's strictly necessary; instead, we have safe houses or chapter houses, perhaps you'd call them, where we can stay when a disturbance occurs in the area. In major cities like this we always have one or two, with disguised entrances and exits, or neighbors who aren't particularly observant...and, of course, some additional protections against the supernatural. I was going to drive to the nearest one, so that we could have a meal and discuss our strategy."

"*Our* strategy?"

"Yes. You've only been here a couple of hours and already burned a parking garage at a major cultural festival with thousands of potential witnesses. I am in no way exaggerating the merciless nature of the SJK. They are efficient. They will surely find you, and then they will put you into a very dark hole for a very long time."

Good thing I hadn't told him about the collector from another dimension showing up.

"So, if you do not wish for me to take you to the safe house, where would you like to go?"

The mystery meeting with Lucinda wasn't for several hours, so I didn't actually know, and that was killing me. I just shook my tired head.

"Safe house it is then."

CHAPTER 10

The place Fabian took me was on the outskirts of Cologne. It looked much like a warehouse district anywhere else would, except that the big, bulky buildings were older and made of stone, interspaced with the occasional younger looking prefabs with metal roofs.

The road was potholed and bumpy, and the old warehouses had faded painted signs that said things like BEST WINES and METAL AND HARDWARE. The lights shining at the street corners seemed yellowish and dim. Except for some trucks and panel vans parked in front of some of the warehouses, there was no sign of life or modernity. There was a fog coming in, rising from the ground up, the tendrils reaching upward and around the car, like living things. I was kind of waiting for that fog to turn red. Thankfully it didn't.

Fabian touched a button clipped to the visor, and iron gates I hadn't noticed before opened. He drove the car down what looked like a narrow alley, but I suppose was really a long and winding driveway hemmed in by trees on either side.

As we drove through the iron gates, I felt something

that wasn't quite a jolt in my neck, right along the Guardian's mark, as though a very slight electrical field had been broached.

"This place is warded."

Fabian seemed surprised I could tell. "Nothing nearly as potent as a ward stone, simply some spells drawn by an elf we contracted with. It merely warns us if anything otherworldly breaches the perimeter, but it does not give us any details."

I'd heard European elves were different from ours, but that would have to wait for another day. "Well, I'll tell you now, it's going to warn you that something just did." If I'd felt it in the marks, I probably qualified. Not to mention Mr. Trash Bags—and I wasn't going to say a word about him. Bringing a shoggoth into somebody's house wasn't exactly polite. "It's just me."

"Oh really?"

I'd been thinking paranoid thoughts about things like doppelgangers, and I'd never stopped to think he was probably thinking the same thing. So I pulled back my hair so he could see the black mark on my neck. "I got cursed. It's a long story. Don't believe me, you can let me out here and I'll walk to a hotel."

Fabian sighed. "Very well."

There was another old warehouse at the end of the lane. Fabian touched a different button and a corrugated metal garage door rolled up in front of us. It moved far more quietly than expected, probably so no one would hear late night comings and goings.

We pulled in and the door shut behind. I realized I had, once more, put my hand under my shirt to rest on my .45.

"I suppose paranoia is a perfectly normal reaction

to what you've been through," Fabian said pointedly. "But now you're just being rude."

"Yeah... Sorry. It's been a long day."

The interior of the warehouse looked almost mundane. There were an assortment of cars, a panel van, and shelves with the sorts of things you expect in a garage: oil and stuff for automotive maintenance.

There was a door in the back. Fabian went over and held it open for me. I entered and found what looked and smelled like a suburban home.

We'd come into what appeared to be a mudroom, with a row of shoes on mats. A big shaggy dog came running in and jumped on Fabian. "Down, Prinz, down!" Fabian said, but in the sort of tone a person uses to a very spoiled animal that they know won't get down. He patted the great, untidy head for a moment, then said, "Now, where are your manners? Say hello to the lady."

The dog plopped down and lifted a paw in such a polite and intelligent manner as to make me wonder if it was something supernatural. I shook his paw, then looked up at Fabian, who must have read my thoughts, because he smiled. "No, no, he's just a dog."

He led me and the dog—whose wagging tail was a weapon of mass injury—out of the mudroom and into such a brightly lit room that it took a moment for my eyes to adjust. It was a large, well-appointed kitchen, and the source of the smell that permeated the place: soup and bread.

"I left my dinner simmering on the stove when I heard about the fire. A well-informed detective saw the squid necklaces and called me for a consult. You should eat."

"I'm fine," I muttered. Now that I had a chance to slow down, I felt nauseous.

"You don't know if your child is eating, so you think why should you get to? Don't be irrational. Here." Fabian got out a bowl and began ladling soup into it. The way he held everything struck me as odd, and that's when my tired brain finally realized that he had an artificial hand. In my defense, it was so lifelike it was hard to notice.

He saw me looking. "Ah, this . . . It is why I'm here and not on the siege with my colleagues. Notice, this is a big place. Normally there would be five of us here. But with the siege, we only have a few full teams traveling constantly, and a single coordinator, such as myself, everywhere else. So they left the one-handed man home."

"I was having this same exact conversation with a friend before my day went sideways." Seeing that fake hand reminded me of Grandpa, and that thought just made me sad. "How'd it happen?"

"I've not had it for long. Do you remember when your government offered that obscene bounty on Special Agent Franks of the MCB?"

"How could I forget? Two hundred and fifty million dollars, biggest PUFF bounty in history."

"I was one of the fools who tried to collect."

"Oh . . ." I'd heard that had gone really badly for Grimm Berlin. "Sorry."

"Franks easily picked us off one by one. It could have been worse. He spared our lives, but not all our limbs." Fabian handed the bowl to me. "Sit. Eat."

It did smell good and I needed the calories so I could keep going. I pulled up at a spot at the kitchen table and started eating. I didn't know how good of a

Hunter he was, but Fabian was a great cook. While I shoveled food in my face, he got a text. Fabian read his phone, then scowled.

"It's my grandmother's recipe. Good, no?" He sat down across from me.

"Excellent," I mumbled with my mouth full.

"So now for the bad news. SJK just sent out a wanted notice with your name and a street camera photo of you and a cultist."

"That's fast."

"I told you they're efficient. Facial recognition software is truly a marvel."

Dead Condition and shell casings from American-manufactured silver bullets at the scene had probably drastically narrowed the SJK's search parameters too. "Now what?"

"They take great personal offense to foreign companies working here without approval. If you attempt to make contact with any of us, you are to be detained for questioning." He began texting back, typing with one finger.

"What're you doing?"

"Telling my superiors that you never arrived at our meet. You must have gotten spooked and run off." He even held up the phone so I could see the words. Then he hit send.

"Why would you do that?"

"The SJK can pound sand. They're efficient at everything except for action. If they detain you for questioning, your baby will be ready for kindergarten by the time they let you out. And what my employer doesn't know can't hurt them. I'm on my own. It's just me and the dog."

"So you're helping me because you're lonely."

"And bored. Now let's talk about how to get your baby back."

Long before the sun came up, I was lying on my belly behind a rifle, in a little stand of trees overlooking the Rhine.

Fabian was twenty yards away, dressed in a stolen uniform that I think was their equivalent to the park police, and he'd brought in two other men—not Hunters—but I think they were some sort of city workers who owed him a favor. Either that or he'd bribed them well. My command of the language wasn't good enough to keep up with his side of the phone conversation. They'd set up cones and barriers to keep people away, with warning signs about air and soil collection taking place in the area.

"We'll tell people it's to evaluate anthropogenic global warming," Fabian had said with a smile. "People always fall for that one, at least in Europe." It's funny, all the different tricks Hunters come up with to take care of our business without freaking out the locals.

It was a really quiet morning. The day after the Fasching parade I expected it should be almost deserted, with everyone sleeping off their hangovers...but did Germans even get hangovers? As much as this country drank, it was like they had a genetic gift for metabolizing alcohol. Not me. I'm a lightweight—a glass of wine and I'm ready for a nap.

It was shaping up to be a cold day. Good. That would also cut down on the number of innocent bystanders who might get in my way. The only people I'd seen out and about so far were a few hard-core runners. And seeing them just reminded me how I'd *not* been doing that for a long time. Normally I took a great deal of pride in how physically fit I was, but motherhood had screwed that up too.

It had also severely cut into my training time. I was rusty. But if Lucinda went where we expected her to go, then she'd only be six hundred and fifty yards away. If the wind was mild, I could make that shot in my sleep, even with an unfamiliar rifle.

Fabian had hooked me up with an old Steyr SSG with a Schmidt and Bender scope on it. It wasn't the most advanced rig he'd had in the safe, but it had a suppressor, which should keep the noise to a minimum. And more importantly for him, they'd found it on a job a long time ago, so there was no paper trail leading back to Grimm Berlin. I loved how even the most law-abiding of Hunters, in a country that loved it some gun control, still managed to have a throwaway sniper rifle on hand.

Lucinda had said to meet her at the spot by the river. Since our German counterparts also paid a lot of bribes to various people and things to keep tabs on monster activity, they'd found out where Wilhelm had met her last time. In this case, they were paying off brownies. Those annoying little shits were totally PUFF-eligible, but it sounded like Grimm Berlin had a relationship with them like we did with our orcs. By the time they'd been told though, Lucinda had been long gone.

I could only hope from her vague message that she was consistent.

If she showed up, I was going to threaten her into giving up Brother Death; then I was going to shoot her in the head.

I always felt a little sorry for Lucinda. Not enough, mind you, that I wouldn't drop the bitch—particularly if she were standing between me and my baby—but still, she hadn't chosen to whom to be born, she hadn't had any kind of normal or sane influence in her life, and she hadn't ever had a chance to develop a moral system that wasn't messed up. That said, she'd been offered the chance to turn back from her path any number of times, including by us after we'd defeated her father. She'd chosen to be the demented queen of a bunch of cultists and dead things instead. Her involvement in the massacre at Copper Lake had sealed the deal.

It was perfectly possible to be sad for the person that Lucinda Hood might have been, while still thinking the horrible person she actually was needed to get put down like a rabid dog.

But not until after she told me how to get my kid.

The sun was coming up behind and to the right. It was one reason why I'd picked this spot on the map during planning. Glare on your scope can mess you up. There were buildings around where I could've gotten an elevated position, but that would have required breaking and entering, or Fabian tricking somebody into letting us in, but that meant more potential witnesses which made it more likely I'd get picked up by SJK. Vacant properties are great for shooting from, and if I'd had more time, we could've gone through property listings and done some scouting, but we'd only had a few hours, and I'd managed to sleep for a couple of them.

It had been a fitful, nightmare-plagued sleep. Thinking about Ray made me fret, so instead I concentrated on the technical parts.

I think the reasons I'm MHI's best contract negotiator are the same reasons that I'm one of our best precision marksmen. They're both about knowing the details in advance. I'm meticulous. It's the little things that make you miss, or screw you up and cost your company a whole lot of money. It isn't about emotion. It's about repeatable precision and knowing your job in and out.

Since Melvin had screwed up and sent my gear bag first, I'd at least gotten some useful equipment. Particularly my laser rangefinder, and my Kestrel. The rangefinder told me that I was 447 yards from the opposite bank, but since the little sitting area we expected Lucinda to use was downriver a bit, she would be anywhere from 620 to 650, depending on which bench she went for.

The Kestrel is like a miniature weather station, and it told me the barometric pressure, the humidity, and that the wind was moving at a leisurely three-to-five miles an hour. Of course, that could only measure the wind at my position. Looking across the waves of the Rhine told me that it was pretty calm all the way across. The two pieces of yellow surveyor's tape I'd tied to the fence on the other side told me that the wind was about the same—speed and direction—over there.

Before leaving this morning I'd shot a few rounds across Fabian's chronograph to get the velocity, and a five-shot group on paper to check the zero. The SSG had put them all in under an inch, so it would do. It was a good thing that their warehouse was long enough. My high-tech backstop had been a few cardboard boxes full of printer paper.

Then I'd measured the scope offset to the bore

and looked online for the ballistic coefficient of the bullets Fabian had provided. Once I'd had all that information, I'd plugged it into my ballistic calculator to tell me how many clicks of adjustment I'd need to hit my target, first try. One shot, one kill. Precision, long-range shooting is basically weaponized math.

Milo had told me he was trying to coach my husband on all this wonderful stuff while they were up in Alaska, but knowing Owen, I doubted it would stick. Good as he was at math, when push comes to shove, that man always goes for volume over precision. I suppose that's why we make such a good team.

Lastly, I'd written my data card on a little piece of paper, did a poor man's home laminate job on it—as in sticky tape on both sides—poked a hole and zip-tied it to the side of the scope so I could read the numbers without having to move my head off the stock while I was prone.

Now I was in position, hidden beneath a tarp in the miniature construction zone that Fabian's buddies had set up to combat global warming or whatever. Watching. Waiting. Ready. The only thing moving over there were some pigeons.

As the scene got brighter, I got more nervous.

What if we'd come to the wrong place? What if Lucinda had figured out it was a trap? Was I just wasting my time?

What if Ray is already dead?

Shut up, shut up, shut up.

But after ten minutes of second-guessing myself, Lucinda appeared in my scope. She was late because she'd stopped for coffee and a pastry. The leader of the Sanctified Church of the Temporary Mortal Condition took her sweet time walking into the little park. She was just strolling along, looking like a young woman out for a nice walk. Lucinda was rather pretty, in a blonde, waifish sort of way, and today she was wearing a long coat and sunglasses. Her long hair was free, which was good, because that was one last indicator of wind direction and speed.

She looked around for a minute. It was hard to accurately read facial expressions at over six hundred yards on only 14 power magnification, but she seemed annoyed that Wilhelm wasn't already there. For a second I was worried she'd just keep on walking, but she took a seat on the first bench and nibbled at her breakfast.

Six hundred twenty yards then. I adjusted the focus a bit, checked parallax, and watched as pigeons immediately began to cluster around her, hoping that she'd share some of her food.

Fabian had supplied me with some cheap cell phones. I had one in front of me and I'd left one beneath each bench.

I dialed the first preprogrammed number then went back to my scope. I had a Bluetooth earpiece in.

Lucinda seemed startled. She looked around, like maybe she was just going to bolt. I really hoped she didn't because I needed her to talk *before* I shot her. But her curiosity must have gotten the better of her, because she reached beneath and found where I'd taped the phone.

"Who's this?"

"Hey, Lucinda. This is Julie Shackleford. We need to talk."

"I don't think so."

The line went dead.

She started to stand up, but I'd been prepared to send a message.

One of the pigeons near Lucinda's feet exploded in a cloud of feathers.

A .308 round does a real number on a little bird. I couldn't see from here, but I was betting she'd gotten peppered with pigeon bits. She'd spilled her coffee, and the rest of the pigeons began fighting for her discarded pastry. The flying rats didn't even have a moment of silence for their fallen comrade. Lucinda calmly raised her hands to the surrender position and stood still. The sun gleamed off her metal hand... What was it with me and people with one hand lately?

The suppressor had taken care of most of the noise. There was still the sound the supersonic bullet made flying over the top of the river, but just the one by itself, most people weren't going to hear that and think gunfire.

I worked the bolt to chamber another round, then hit redial.

Through the scope, I watched her sullenly move the phone back to her ear. "You made your point."

"Then sit your bony ass down."

She did. "What do you want? I don't have anything to say to you."

"Oh, I believe you do. A member of my family has gone missing, and I want him back."

Her eyes swept the bank of the river. "Where are you?"

"Where I can see you... and kill you if needed."

"Very well." I had to hand it to her. She'd matured over the last few years and had really perfected that whole British stiff-upper-lip attitude. She was as cool under pressure as her father had been. "If you wanted to shoot me, you already would have, so I'll humor you. What do you want?"

"I want my son back."

"I wasn't aware you'd misplaced him."

"Don't play coy. Your loony cultists, Wilhelm and friends, hired an entity called Brother Death to kidnap my son, so I would exchange him for something you want very much."

"Ah. I had a hunch you were the one who had the Kumaresh Yar. And did you make that exchange?"

"Briefly. But I wasn't given my son, so I took it back."

"Did you now? That's fascinating. And what happened to my friends during all this?"

"Dead or picked up by the SJK, except for one poor bastard named Benno who got his soul collected by a creepy . . . something . . . hell if I know what it was."

Lucinda took a deep breath. "Benno was a numpty, though unfortunate about Wilhelm—he had real potential. Bloody unfortunate turn of events all around, but I don't see what it has to do with me."

I was dialed in. The whole time we were having this conversation, I had the crosshairs sitting on the top of her chest. They barely quivered as I spoke.

"This was started by your people. I hold you responsible."

Lucinda laughed. "That takes some gall. I hold your people responsible for killing my father, but you don't see me being a bitch about it. Go home, Julie. Make other sons. Count your blessings that you haven't also lost your god, or a part of your body."

"Your father was a lunatic necromancer, his god

tried to take over the Earth, and your hand got ripped off by a vampire who I wouldn't trust further than I could throw a stake. I'm trying to be diplomatic here, Lucinda, but either you talk or I shoot you. Tell me about Brother Death."

She thought about it for a moment. So long in fact that I'd moved my finger back inside the trigger guard.

"Brother Death is from Ghana originally. He's hundreds, if not thousands, of years old. Various tribes worshiped him as a god or feared him as a demon. Either way, they made sacrifices to him... virgins, children, that sort of thing. He sometimes chose to live among them, appearing as a human, carrying out tasks in return for blood sacrifices or other items of magical value. During the colonial era, he discovered that Europeans were exceedingly eager to pay for services such as his. He has been a mercenary ever since."

"He's an *Adze*, isn't he?"

"A near meaningless term from folklore, trying to identify and quantify a creature beyond mortal understanding, but fine, that'll work. He works primarily in Europe now, but will take contracts anywhere and is very good at what he does. Back in the day, King Leopold hired him to do things to people in the Congo the likes of which sound heinous even to me. My father used his services on occasion, as have I. But not this time. This whole thing was as much a surprise to me as it was to you. I neither told him to take your child, nor do I know where he is now."

"Then I have absolutely no reason to let you live." I let that obvious threat hang there.

"You Americans are so trigger-happy. Calm down. I didn't say I don't know how to contact him. Though extremely powerful and deadly beyond your imagination, Brother Death's defining characteristic is greed. At his basest level, he's a simple creature. It isn't about spending his wealth, it's about accumulating it. As long as your child can be sold to someone, then Brother Death won't harm him. And the brat of Julie Shackleford and Owen Zastava Pitt? I can guarantee something out there will pay dearly for blood like that."

The sad part was that as she said that, I knew she was telling the truth. My family had made a lot of enemies. There would be no shortage of evil things who'd love to hurt us . . . or worse . . . What if my mother found out?

"That makes me want to shoot you more, not less," I snarled.

"It boggles my mind that there is so much about the real world you Hunters still don't know. There's a whole underground economy. Brother Death will surely auction off your child. He's done it before when he's come across something of great value to people like me. Once he gets set up, he'll send out invitations to a very select clientele. He might already have; I've not checked my email yet today. There's no way you can get an invite to that table—you've got to be able to pay in suffering or necromantic power—but I can. In the dark market, I've got an excellent credit rating. So be a dear, put the gun down, and I'll buy your child back for you."

"Uh-huh . . . That sounded like a reasonable offer from a totally trustworthy source." I was tempted to wipe the smug off of her face with a bullet.

"You didn't let me finish. I wouldn't do that out of the goodness of my heart. Frankly, the idea of some horrible being from the nether realms buying your child because Earl Harbinger wronged it generations ago is pretty damned funny. The things I associate with can hold a grudge like you wouldn't believe. But poor beautiful Wilhelm was right about one thing: I want the Kumaresh Yar more than anything else in this world. I'll buy your child back, and then we can exchange him for the artifact."

I'd already made that deal once, with the devil I didn't know. The devil I knew was already aware that I'd made that trade before, so I'd probably do it again.

"It's not like any of the other bidders would be willing to work something out with a goody two-shoes like you. Come on, Julie. This is a win-win situation. We both get what's rightfully ours."

"Until you use the artifact to blow up time or whatever half-baked insanity you've got going on this time."

"Don't worry, love. The Kumaresh Yar's not that easy to use unless you're one of the rare mortals it was meant for. It takes a considerable amount of time and effort for the rest of us to harness even a small bit of its power."

"You killed a *town*, Lucinda."

"That was just an experiment. My new boss is busy now because your friends are mucking about in his business. You've already seen, he's taking his time. I'm sure you'll have plenty of opportunities to stop him, but only one chance to get back your boy. Or tell it to yourself however you have to so you can justify it enough to sleep at night, but I'm your best chance."

"Tell me how to reach him myself."

"As a display of my good will, fine. Brother Death always works through an intermediary called *Le Marchand*. He manages the affairs of several powerful beings in Europe. When one of us wants to hire Brother Death, we send a message to Marchand, he passes it on, and if his client thinks the offer is sufficient, he'll take the job. But Marchand won't respond to someone on the side of the angels. Contact him and see what happens. Mark my words, the sale will be announced soon and the fact is I'm the only bidder you could possibly make a deal with...though come to think of it, I bet your dear old mum shows up."

The thing that had been my mother was a nefarious, well-connected, extremely powerful vampire now. She'd offered to turn all her loved ones into vampires so we could live together forever, and when I'd turned her down, she'd tried to do it by force. She'd surely want the same messed-up fate for Ray. And in Lucinda's terms, my mother probably had one hell of a credit rating.

"I know what you're thinking, Julie, but Susan Shackleford is a solo act. I inherited my father's estate. I can outbid her."

"How could I possibly trust the likes of you?"

"You can't, really." Despite the prospect of getting sniped, Lucinda seemed annoyingly confident. "The only thing you can be certain of is I don't give a damn about some stupid baby, but I'll pay anything to have the artifact. I'm leaving now, Julie. You can either shoot me in the back, or let me go buy your son."

Lucinda threw the phone into the river. Then she started walking away.

The crosshair rested right between her shoulder blades. My improvised wind flags were hardly moving. I put my finger on the trigger and slowly exhaled.

Lucinda was a monster. She'd hurt hundreds of innocent people. I had the shot.

I didn't take it.

"Shit!" I took my finger out of the trigger guard and put the safety on. "Shit! Shit!" I got up, wrapped the rifle in the tarp I'd been hiding under, and started back toward Fabian.

"What are you doing? Take the shot, Julie!"

I turned back. In the distance, Lucinda was already gone. She'd probably had a magic rope on her just in case. The crazy, cult-leading murderess was once again in the wind.

Fabian looked at me with disbelief and disgust. "You were supposed to kill her!"

"I couldn't." The next part made me sick to say aloud. "I need her alive."

CHAPTER 11

Fabian was sullenly silent toward me for most of the drive back to the safe house. We'd had a deal, and I'd explained my reasoning, but Grimm Berlin was out a giant bounty and a magical lunatic was still at large. I bet Fabian felt like he'd gone against both the SJK and his employer for nothing.

He was still pissed at me when we parked inside the garage. I finally broke the awkward silence.

"Look, I had to make a call. Was it the wrong call? Maybe."

"She could have made up the whole thing," he snapped.

"Like I said . . . maybe. I'll find out. She either lied and I screwed up and all the future horrors she causes are on my head, or she wants the artifact bad enough to keep her word."

"And all the future horrors she inflicts are still on your head."

Ouch. But it only hurt because he was right. "You got any kids, Fabian?"

"No."

"Then maybe one day you'll understand. Until then, judge away. I've got work to do."

Fabian was ticked, but he wasn't a bad dude. The concern was obvious. "What do you intend to do next?"

As mad as he was, I didn't think he was going to betray me to the SJK. Plus, really, there was no way he could do that without incriminating himself in the process. "I'm going to find this Marchand and make him tell me where Brother Death is."

"With what resources?" Fabian was still dressed as a police officer because Hunters always knew how to get by in their area of operations. Unlike him, I had no clue how to blend in here. "The minute you use your credit card or turn your phone back on, the government will be on you. You can't use your ID. You've got no passport. You can't go to your embassy because they'll just hold you for the MCB."

"I'll figure it out."

Inside the mudroom, I noticed the dog bowl had a new owner. Mr. Trash Bags must have gotten hungry because he'd crawled out of my bag and was eating Prinz's food. The bowl was nearly empty, and the shoggoth had grown from hamster- to puppy-sized. Poor Prinz was standing a few feet away, growling at the thing that was absorbing his breakfast.

"Cuddle Bunny return." His voice was getting less high-pitched the bigger he got.

"*Scheisse!*" When Fabian saw Mr. Trash Bags, he went for the pistol in the cop holster at his hip.

"Stop! The blob's with me."

"What the hell is that?" When Prinz saw how upset his owner was, he took that as a good indicator it was okay to start barking wildly.

"That's Mr. Trash Bags." I didn't want to say he was a shoggoth because that sounded really evil. Besides, when Hunters thought of shoggoths, we thought of two-ton wrecking balls of Old One-powered destruction, not things that could fit in a soup can. "He's a friend and the only reason I found the Condition."

"Whatever it is, it's menacing my dog."

I was just glad he'd not eaten the dog. "Let me grab my stuff and I'll get out of here."

"Ah"—Fabian waved his artificial hand at me—"I've seen weirder. I'll still help you. I don't like being screwed out of a bounty, but that doesn't mean I want your baby to get hurt. Come on."

The map we'd used to plan the Lucinda meet was still on the table. Fabian went to a bookshelf and got out a heavy binder. He dropped it on the map. "I've heard of Marchand. It just means dealer in French."

"Local?" I asked hopefully.

"Sadly no. France. And I think I know how to find him. Lucinda Hood is a lying psychopath, but what she said about an auction does sound plausible. What do you know of the Affair of the Poisons?" Fabian asked as he got a beer out of the fridge. "Want one?"

"It's seven in the morning."

"Eh, it's a German thing."

"More like an alcoholic thing. But I've heard of the Affair of the Poisons." You can't get an art history degree without picking up a lot of trivia about European royalty. "It was something about people making poisons and selling them to noblemen to kill each other."

"It was in the reign of Louis XIV. It was believed that Athenais de Montespan, Louis' mistress, was part of the ring, but he stepped in and it was never really investigated. Or at least that was the public version of events."

I felt that weird hollow feeling in my stomach again. This is how stories among Monster Hunters start. It's always, *Yes, that's what the public was told, but*— which wouldn't be nearly so disturbing if this didn't involve my child, and if my recollection was correct the Affair of the Poisons had involved a whole lot of sacrificed babies. Like babies burned and reduced to powder to make potions and mind-control substances, behaviors that made absolutely no sense in a normal world where monsters didn't exist and magic was make-believe, but knowing how things really worked, I felt the hair stand up on the back of my neck.

"What's the real story?"

"Unpleasant," Fabian said. "Necromantic rituals and pacts with otherworldly forces in exchange for power. The affair was simply the temporary surfacing of something that has been going on in Europe for a very long time, and which continues in secret to this day. You know how in the mundane world there is human trafficking for immoral purposes?"

"Of course."

"The supernatural world is far worse. It's a scourge on this continent. I imagine there is some in America, too, but you're a young country, with new traditions, and these things are old. You have some bad actors, and bad actors often use children for sacrifice or worse. But you don't have the history we do. I speak of organizations, cultures, and practices going back to the Neolithic."

I must have given him an incredulous look.

"No. Really. It's like the saying goes, Europeans forget how big America is, but Americans forget how old Europe is. The ring revealed during the Affair was ancient. We don't know how ancient for sure, because Hunters of the time didn't keep precise records, they just speared monsters and burned them at the stake. However, many of the participants escaped and there are still established networks that traffic in innocents for necromantic purposes, especially infants or pregnant women."

"That's disgusting."

"Which is why Grimm Berlin fights them. Klaus has a special hatred for such creatures, and we disrupt them at every opportunity." He shoved the binder toward me. "Take this. It's everything we know about these groups."

I flipped through. It had names—both human and other—locations, dates, and the descriptions of their crimes... I quickly closed the binder.

"What does the Affair of the Poisons have to do with Marchand?"

"He participated in it." Then his phone rang. "It's my superior. I've got to take this." He answered, and the lady on the other end started yelling at him so loudly and angrily that I could hear most of it.

Fabian responded defensively. My German wasn't good enough to get all of the rapid-fire conversation, but I got enough of it to know that something bad was happening. Fabian began protesting that he hadn't seen me, but then he shut up when the lady said something about his car on video.

Then he hung up on his superior. "Bad news..."

"I gathered that."

"SJK found a security camera that recorded you getting into my car. They just called my employers and demanded to know the addresses of all our safe houses in Cologne."

"Your bosses just gave you up?"

"Of course they did. Klaus is the only one of them with the spine to spite authority, and he's not here. I'm lucky they called to warn me that SJK is on the way at all. They're rather cross about one of their employees harboring someone wanted for murder."

"They were death cultists!"

"Germany is not so loose on the subject as your country. You must go now. The best I can do is get you a private flight to the Ile Sainte-Marguerite, where you can talk to Vincente Ducharm."

Something about the name tickled my memory and there was some kind of unpleasant association, but I wasn't sure what. "Who?"

"The government calls him a consultant. I consider him a snitch. There is a dossier on him in the binder. It'll explain. Take the Volkswagen in the garage. It's my teammate's personal vehicle. She's about your size and keeps a suitcase in the trunk with clothing and some Euros. She's at Severny Island so won't miss it until she gets back." Fabian took a Sharpie out of his pocket and scribbled an address on the binder. "Go to this airport, ask for Max. He's got a small plane, is discreet, and owes me a favor. You can't fly into Sainte-Marguerite as there's nowhere to land, but you can go to Cannes and then hire someone to take you across on a motorboat. You must keep a low profile in France, too, though because all the government monster control agencies in the EU cooperate."

I didn't know much about the SJK, but by rep they were similar to the MCB and, if an American Hunter had crossed the MCB like this, they'd be in deep shit. "What are you going to do?"

"If the rabbit runs, the wolf chases. I'll stay here, lie for you, and stall them."

I grabbed my gear bag and saw Mr. Trash Bags was already hanging onto one of the straps. "If Grimm Berlin fires you over this, MHI is always hiring."

"Wonderful. I shall look you up after I get out of prison."

I really hoped that didn't happen. "You went out of your way to help me and I won't forget it. Thank you."

As my hand landed on the door knob, Fabian said, "Julie." I turned back to find him looking solemn. "Good luck with your son."

CHAPTER 12

The Ile Sainte-Marguerite is just off the coast of Cannes. I'd never visited, but I'd read about it. It was one of those tiny places that packs a ton of history.

It was little more than a square mile total, but it had been held by Romans and Moors, still had the remnants of German gun emplacements from World War II, and had been the place where the Man in the Iron Mask was held.

Now that was one of those legends that always made me wonder exactly what had really been going on, and what kind of monster needed an iron mask. It would certainly subdue—and torture—certain kinds of fey, that was for sure. Hunters found partial truths showing up in fiction all the time. I was half convinced that Dumas had just run into some old-timey Hunters telling stories in a bar. One rumor was it had been some kind of doppelganger who had tried wearing the likeness of a king, but the details were long since lost.

During my long flight in a tiny, slow plane, I read through the entire binder. It turned out that Klaus Lindemann and Pierre Darne had been working together to really put a hurt on human trafficking cults in Western Europe. A bunch of the monsters had big red Xs through their page.

Vincente Ducharm, however, was off-limits.

He wasn't a monster, cultist, or a trafficker. He was human, but he was a *monster rights advocate* which, trust me, is way more annoying. They were the useful idiots who lobbied for equal rights for monsters, which was fine, if you were talking about things that were happy to leave people alone—like Sasquatch or orcs—but those assholes inevitably wound up pushing for leniency against unrelentingly evil things like vampires. Oh, they don't mean to be blood-sucking monsters, look how charming they are! Can't we all just get along?

Darne and Lindemann both believed that Ducharm was in contact with Marchand. I could believe that. It was common for gullible, monster-rights types to secretly rub shoulders with the horrible things they defended. However, because Ducharm was super rich, politically connected, and occasionally fed the government some monster intel, the EU agencies had declared that Hunters weren't allowed to bother him. The last who'd tried had gotten busted for harassment. They'd been warned that they'd get the book thrown at them just for making contact with the man.

I was already wanted for murder, so there wasn't really a significant downside for me.

Now Marchand, on the other hand, was a beast, not human. It had been involved in a bunch of killings and disturbances over the years, but had been off the grid for the last few. The government didn't even know what it was, just that it was a shadowy broker of secrets and dark magic, and that it had been around for a very long time, as in centuries. It served as the go-between for evil people who wanted terrible deeds done, and the worst kind of supernatural predators, in exchange for a cut. Only a very select group knew how to contact the dealer.

It took a special kind of asshole to get one of Marchand's business cards, but the European Hunters figured that Ducharm was just that kind of asshole.

We landed in Cannes or, rather, in a private airport at the edge of it. My French is better than my German and for a few euros I got a ride to the sea, where for a few more euros, a cheerful young man with a broad smile said he'd take me across in his boat.

We motored across the maybe half mile separating the mainland from the island. I didn't need to encourage him to go fast. My driver was already in a hurry because storm clouds were coming in, and he warned me that I was probably going to be stuck there for the night. It was early in the afternoon, and I'd be damned if I got stuck here that long, not with my baby out there. I'd question Ducharm, then swim back if I had to.

I'd ditched my gear bag at the airfield in Germany and traded it for the far-less-militant-looking backpack Fabian's coworker had left in her car. It turned out whoever she was had a fashion sense that tended toward the whimsical, because I'd wound up wearing a hoodie that said *"Das einzige gute Monster ist ein totes Monster"* or "the only good monster is a dead monster" and had a cartoon vampire with a stake through the heart on it.

My armor, I'd left behind. It was heavy and basically

impossible to use without sticking out like a sore thumb. Same with all the mags of silver .308—I had nothing to shoot it out of. But I'd kept all the equipment that had been stored *on* my armor and stuffed that into the backpack just in case. Along with Mr. Trash Bags, of course.

Fabian's friend had also left a Walther PPQ and some spare mags in the center console, so I'd borrowed that too. I didn't have a holster for my 1911, but the PPQ had been in a Kydex appendix rig, so that way I could hide a gun on me and not walk around like an idiot with my pistol sliding around loose in my waistband. My 1911 went in the bag. It saddened me to ditch the sniper rifle, but it's hard for a tourist to walk around France with one of those unnoticed.

The boat kid knew who Ducharm was. Apparently all the locals knew him. Nobody knew what he did— just vague ideas about being some kind of consultant for the government—but he was really rich, though humble about it, and mostly kept to himself.

As we motored across the water, the island grew nearer, and it seemed to have a split personality disorder. Nearby, nearer the water, it looked like a standard Mediterranean holiday village, with tiny colorful houses, moored boats, and festive flags and signs. But farther up, forest loomed, with squarish cement protrusions that I assumed were the remains of the Nazi gun emplacements. And at the top, there was the medieval fortress where the Man in the Iron Mask—whatever he really was—had been imprisoned until death.

Under the roiling dark cloud, it all looked dark and ominous. "There's going to be a massive storm," the kid said, his words sounding odd, buffeted by the wind. "By the time we get there, I'm going to have trouble seeing to come back."

Once we docked, he pointed me at a path and said, "Take that to the right, then up the first flight of stairs you come to. You can't miss them. At the top, it'll be the first house on the right."

Of course I missed the stairs. In my defense, it had started to pour, and the place wasn't particularly well illuminated. The path was along what remained of the beach. I say what remained because it looked like it had been eroding and, in an effort to stop it, someone had dumped a bunch of trash on it. I wasn't even sure what the trash was, but it looked and felt like shredded Styrofoam that had gone grey with age and contact with seawater. It *gave* unpleasantly underfoot, but also bounced back in a way that wasn't normal for plant matter, let alone for rocks or sand.

I scrambled along it for a good while, until I came upon what seemed to be a little street front of small houses. Only from the look of them they were actually touristy shops and were closed. The realization that if the stairs were past these, these would likely have been mentioned, hit me. I backtracked my way along the unpleasantly bouncy, weirdly crunchy, very much unstable path until I found the stairs.

They were wooden, sounded rickety underfoot and were dark as pitch. At one point the railing went away, and I couldn't tell if there wasn't a railing there on purpose, or if it was broken. I only knew I'd arrived at the top because the feel underfoot changed, and running my foot one way and another, I determined I was on a dirt path. The first house to the right had lights glimmering faintly through curtained windows. I headed that way slowly because the path was unexpectedly narrow, and there was a deep drop-off on one side.

It seemed to me that if this Ducharm wanted Hunters to leave him alone, he shouldn't live someplace so scenic and easy to visit.

The house appeared to be one of those low-slung Mediterranean cottages, with two or three windows and a narrow wooden door fronting right onto the street. It might have been built any time from a hundred years ago on back. From the boat man's description, it wasn't at all what I'd expected. I'd been picturing a mansion with a perimeter fence and armed guards with Dobermans.

The knocker on the door was a Fatima hand. I pounded it and was in the midst of raising it to pound again when the door opened, pulling the knocker from my grasp. To be fair, I might have pounded a little energetically.

The man who opened the door was shorter than I, with dark hair, a receding hairline and an aquiline nose on either side of which shone very bright hazel eyes. He was wearing a brocade robe and grinned at me, displaying an overbite, and rather large, very white teeth. "Ah, Mrs. Shackleford. I've been waiting for you. Please, get in out of the rain."

Also not what I expected. And here I was thinking I might have to kneecap him and then beat him until he talked. "Ducharm?"

"Indeed. Come in, come in."

The room behind him was suited for a home-and-garden magazine. It was one of those great room arrangements, very large, with a peaked ceiling. There were railings indicating a stairway going down, which meant the house was built into the mountainside. I could see a kitchen with an eat-at counter all gleaming granite and warm polished wood at one end. The floor was also pale and clean. It looked like original pine, but someone had done a wonderful job on it, kind of like what I was trying to do in my home: refinish the floor so it looked good, but also so that it had the modern finishes, which would allow children to play on it without hurting it.

Children...

Back to work. "How did you know I was coming?"

"I did not for certain, but I am a well-informed man. When I heard about your situation, I thought a visit might be possible. I'm a noted expert, and you are in need of expertise. Please, come inside and make yourself comfortable," he insisted. "I am happy to assist you."

As I crossed the threshold, for just a moment there was a feeling like there had been when I had gotten close to the Grimm Berlin safe house. This one was more heat than electrical shock, and for a sharp, short moment, all the marks imposed on me by the Guardian's curse burned. It was overwhelming but thankfully brief, and then gone. I showed no more outward indication than taking a deep breath, which could either be justified by admiration at the décor, or the feeling that I had been in the cold then had come into the warmth, and the contrast had caused me to draw in air.

Ducharm's eyes were on me, attentive, a little worried, but he smiled again. "You've come a long way.

May I offer you refreshment?"

"No, thank you. I just want to talk."

"Of course." The smile flashed again and, inexplicably, I saw him as a very large rodent with greedy eyes, though he tried to make himself look sober and severe. "There are rumors flying about your predicament, and that a creature took your infant son."

"Was it the creature in question who told you that?"

"No, of course not." He gave an offended sniff. "I may believe in the equal treatment of supernatural citizens, but I do not associate with such violence."

One reason I wound up as the company's negotiator was that I could tailor my behavior to deal with different kinds of people, regardless of how I actually felt about them. Sometimes I played the sweetheart, sometimes the hard case, but since Ducharm was a monster rights activist, he was probably a smug and egotistical asshole who liked to feel important, so I'd give him the *opportunity* to help me. I didn't trust Ducharm in the slightest, but if there was a chance he could point me in the right direction, I'd take it. Or at least that was my opening strategy.

"Of course. Forgive my tone, I'm really tired."

"No need to apologize. On the contrary, as the leading expert on supernatural societies, I've developed a close working relationship with various government figures. The authorities are very worried about you."

"They're worried about me causing trouble, but I'm more concerned with the welfare of my son. I need your help to find him."

"Do you know what this creature is planning to do exactly?" He guided me toward one of the overstuffed leather sofas, and I sat down.

"He said something about selling him for a price I couldn't pay."

Those hazel eyes looked speculatively at me. "I see. It is very bad," he said this in the way certain European language speakers have of saying that sort of thing, implying it is a terrible event, but not one they can plausibly do anything about. He sat heavily on the armchair facing my sofa. It seemed to me that as he sat down the chair creaked and groaned as though he were much heavier than he looked which, I thought, just went to tell you exactly how flimsy this antique furniture was. My admittedly rather large husband had complained during his visits to Europe that the entire place was filled with dollhouse furniture which would break if he so much as looked at it.

"I don't suppose that I could convince you to give up the search and leave this to the professionals."

"I am a professional."

"Not on this continent you're not. We have specific ways of doing things here. You see, the network you're dealing with— I suppose you've learned something of it?"

"I don't really care how powerful or nasty they are. This is my son. I'll do whatever it takes."

He opened his mouth, closed it. His smile flashed again, now with overtones of disdain or perhaps dismay, as though I'd picked my nose at him. "Ah, yes, the famous American can-do. But you see, you are a very young country, a very young—if you pardon me the term—race. You haven't learned yet that sometimes there are things you can't do, things that all your bluster, all your guns, all your . . . attitude can't manage. There are things beyond your power."

"Are you telling me to turn back and forget Ray?" I heard a faint threatening edge to my voice. That was a good indicator of how weary and stressed I was. I'm usually better at keeping a smile on my face as morons lectured me.

"Yes, that is what I was telling you, but I see it is useless, is it not?" There was a crack of thunder outside. The heavy rain made a distinctive sound as it banged on the roof. "Very well. How can I help you?"

"What do you know about Brother Death? Where can I find him? And where would he auction off a baby to a bunch of evil magical creatures?"

Ducharm waved his hand dismissively. "Oh, the answers are straightforward. Almost nothing, I don't know, and I don't know. Now, will you listen to me?"

"Not yet." Appealing to his sense of importance wasn't working. Maybe it was time to get a bit more direct. "Tell me about Marchand then. Or are you going to pretend you don't know anything about him either?"

"Not at all. Due to my work I have had some contact with Marchand." He got up, walked to the corner, and opened what looked like a standing globe, revealing a set of glasses and row upon row of cut glass decanters. He picked up one filled with a ruby liquid and poured some into a tiny glass, sniffed it with obvious satisfaction, and said, "Are you sure there is nothing I can offer you? Some brandy? Madeira? Sirop de cassis?"

"No, thank you." I had never acquired a taste for wine, though I would drink it at a party or if somebody was giving a toast. But even if I'd been desperate for a drink, I wasn't about to take one from this guy, who more and more had started to impress me as a smooth and smug prick.

"Your loss. It is excellent."

"Monsieur Ducharm, tell me what you know about Marchand." I didn't add *or I'm going to switch gears and waterboard you with your fancy wine collection* but I suppose my tone implied it.

He brought his drink back to his chair and sat down, again causing a bunch of groans and creaks from the furniture. "Where to begin . . . You see, Europe is very old."

"So I've been told."

"You've been told because it's sometimes not readily apparent to you people. You come over and see the old buildings and the ruins, and you go how romantic, *très chic, très* . . . how you say, sophisticated. And you go back and talk to all your friends about the European palazzos and cathedrals, and you sigh over them, but you don't see the other things that go with living in a place that has been thickly settled ever since there have been humans. You don't see it because most of it isn't visible. It is said our monsters are more complicated than in America. Sure, sure, you get monsters from all over, but the monsters you get there, like the humans you get there, have to an extent fled their roots and left their origins behind. They have gone to America to be something else, something different."

"Something amazing."

His lips twisted in what was either amusement or disgust. "We know what happens to gnomes and elves in America: they adopt new identities. That doesn't happen here. As the humans who stay behind are still bound by their history, so are our supernatural citizens. They are held within the bounds of their culture which limits the amount of harm they actually do. Because we have dealt with fey, demons, ghosts, and much weirder things from the time the first men climbed out of their caves. They will never change. So, we live with them. We coexist."

My lip was curling upward. There was nothing I could do about it. In America we also have monsters we coexist with. Like, say, Earl or the orcs or even— shudder—trailer park elves. We don't even set out to eradicate every gnome, even though, honestly, some urban neighborhoods would be a lot safer without them. In the backpack resting under my arm, I could feel the lump of Mr. Trash Bags through the fabric. But I'm no hypocrite. The issue was that *monster* is a really broad category.

We can give a pass to monsters who agree to be good. That's the whole concept of PUFF exemptions: behave and you're fine, step out of line and we shoot you full of holes. Though I suppose Monsieur Ducharm, who advocated a friendly detente with monsters, would be overjoyed that I carried a miniature shoggoth around. I didn't test that theory, although the temptation was huge to dump him on the floor and yell *eat toes*.

I got what Ducharm was saying, loud and clear. In Europe the governments put up with even harmful monsters, as long as they kept within certain bounds. But all the same, I wasn't from around these parts, and I didn't have to tolerate anything.

"So you're telling me," I said, my voice very frosty, "that you'll tolerate traffic in babies as long as it keeps the peace?"

He gave me what could only be called a Gallic shrug, all exaggerated shoulder motion and politeness. "Tolerate? Not precisely. But we've come to accept there are certain things we can do nothing about."

"You mean people like you say there's nothing you can do. I bet if the EU let people like Lindemann or Darne do their jobs, they'd take care of the problems real quick."

"Doubtful." He opened his arms, as though to signify impotence. "Look at me. For three decades I have sought peaceful resolutions between the mortal and the supernatural worlds . . . and that I have achieved. There are now fewer than five children stolen for human sacrifices a year." He puffed out his chest. "Yes, I see you look surprised, but yes, it is true. Only five in all of Europe. It is a great improvement from the hundreds that used to go missing just half a century ago, never to be found again."

I didn't say anything. Five was better than five hundred, but that didn't make it *acceptable*.

"The thing you must understand, Mrs. Shackleford, is this: you talk about it as if this cannot be tolerated at all, but remember, many of the beings who have been doing this have been around for a long time . . . hundreds, sometimes thousands of years. It is impossible for us mere humans to know how many of them there are, much less to find them all. Once a child disappears into that network, it is more or less impossible to find even a trace of them. You have unusual abilities, but have you found a single trace of your son yet?"

Monster rights advocates were always the same. They were quitters and appeasers who hid their cowardice under a cloak of smug. I'd tried to be reasonable, but negotiations required time, and that was the one thing I didn't have to spare. Getting really tired of his games, I stood up. The rain was coming down hard enough that the neighbors probably wouldn't hear him screaming.

"Tell me about Marchand or I'm going to lose my temper."

"You know, it's very fine to say you want to find your son and bring him home, but the chances of that are very small, as are the chances of your doing anything but dying in the process. Think about it. It used to be, in the old days, before giving birth was made safer, that often the doctors had to give people a choice between the mother and the baby because only one can live. This is what I'm doing to you now. Yourself—or the baby? Who do you think your husband would most willingly sacrifice?"

"Neither, you son of a bitch," which was, of course, the only answer.

Ducharm frowned. "Marchand is a procurer, a dealer, a businessman. He would never be so rude. You should leave now. Return to your home."

"And get on with my life? Have other children? Yeah, I've heard that. Your opinion has been noted." I lifted my novelty shirt and put my hand on the stolen Walther. "Marchand. Now."

"I am an important man with important friends. You cannot come into my house and threaten me."

I pulled the gun out and let it dangle at my side. "Wanna bet?"

He rose. There was an effect of shaking himself and straightening his clothes, though he didn't do more than a vague dusting at his pants, as though his liquor might have dropped crumbs. "If you can't be persuaded to see sense, so be it."

"Mr. Trash Bags. Eat his toes."

There was no response from the backpack, which was surprising, because he seemed to really like tormenting people's appendages.

He noted my surprise. "Your little companion is temporarily stunned. There are spells upon this dwelling beyond your comprehension. Surely you felt them when you entered? You are, after all, the Guardian."

There was a tingling in my neck. It felt like my vision was closing in on me. The edges of the room were getting dark. The lights flickered, and it wasn't because of the storm.

Damn it.

I'd been given bad intel. Grimm Berlin had thought Ducharm was just another misguided human being, but he was obviously something else.

"So what are you really? Wizard or monster?"

"I prefer supernatural citizen."

I raised the gun. "Just tell me what I want to know and I won't have to shoot you."

"You come into my home and threaten me? You're a barbarian, Mrs. Shackleford. It's throwbacks like you that keep us from coexisting peacefully."

"To hell with your peace. I just want my boy." Whatever Ducharm was, I still needed him alive. So I aimed at his foot and pulled the trigger.

But he was no longer there.

The 9mm round put a hole in the nice hardwood floor. I backed up, scanning all around me for threats. Ducharm was nowhere to be seen. It wasn't that he'd moved that fast, it was more like he'd simply vanished.

The house creaked. Someone was moving down the stairs.

Gun raised, I swept in that direction. "Come out, Ducharm. Or should I call you Marchand?"

I heard his obnoxious laugh somewhere below me.

It was dark down there. And he wanted me to chase him. *Screw that.* "How do you play it?" I shouted as I reholstered the 9mm, and went back to my backpack and took my .45 out, because I had a flashlight clipped to its frame rail. *Much better.* "By day you lobby for your kind, and at night you hook up contract killers with cultists to steal babies?"

"I'm merely a facilitator," he shouted back. "But more importantly, I am an organizer. I unite buyer with seller. There is no haphazard killing. I manage the herd, so only the minimum lives necessary are taken. After six hundred years I've gotten it down to a science. You should be thanking me."

"You're an asshole, but give me Brother Death and I'll let you live."

"He is a valued client. How dare you assume I could be intimidated into breaking such a trust?"

All the power in the house went off. The timing was too convenient for it to have been the storm. More likely the breaker box was in the basement and Ducharm had just flipped the switch. I started down anyway.

I turned my SureFire flashlight on. A thousand lumens is crazy super bright. *Suck it, forces of evil.*

Gun up, I made my way down. I'd partly been expecting some sort of wet, stone, torture dungeon, but the next floor was finished as nicely as the first. There was a lounge with big couches, shelves stuffed with books, and a truly gigantic fireplace.

"Come out," I ordered, but Ducharm was hiding now.

Past the lounge was a hall with several doors. I went to the first door. Inside was a princess room. No, I mean a *princess room*, with frills and a canopied bed and all. It was perfect, provided the princess was about six and obsessed with lace and pink which, frankly, I'd never been, even at six.

The room was small and smelled like someone had crushed candy all over it. My light illuminated a pile of mismatched dolls. The door locked from the hallway side.

You can't call it a guest room if it was intended for prisoners.

As Ducharm, he was paid money for his services. Is this how the monsters paid Marchand? What kind of creepy shit was he into?

The problem with searching a darkened house is that there are a lot of places something can hide. Lurking behind furniture, around a corner, in the closet, under the bed...and for all I knew, Marchand might be some kind of shapeshifter. He might *be* the bed.

"Cuddle Bunny?" The tentative little voice came out of my backpack. The spell that had frozen him must have been wearing off. "Bad place. Bad. Bad thing. Bad."

My hair tried to stand up at the back of my neck. What did it take to make a shoggoth think of something as *bad*?

I flung open the closet. *Clear.* There was little girls' clothing hanging, but I realized that the styles were wildly different. There were modern-looking clothes in front, but the outfits aged as they went, with styles that were obviously from the eighties, seventies, sixties, and even older behind those.

There were bloodstains on many of them.

Furious, I stepped away from the closet. I was going to question this thing, and then *he was gonna die.*

Suddenly, the door to the girls' room slammed shut.

I spun around, ready to shoot, but there was nothing there. The door had been opened inward and nothing had touched it. Magic shit like that just pissed me off.

If he thought he was going to lock me in like his other helpless victims, I wasn't some unarmed kid. One of us here was the Hunter, and it certainly wasn't Ducharm.

Then I heard the sound. It was like something snuffling along the hallway. Not a human, or even a dog, but like I'd imagine a dinosaur snuffling if there were dinosaurs. Again, the Guardian's marks on my body got warm. My neck and the three claw lines down my abdomen began to burn.

Mr. Trash Bags was wide awake now, as he fearfully warned, "Bad thing. Bad thing come consume Cuddle Bunny."

The handle turned... very slowly. Something pushed against the door.

I fired two fast rounds through the wood, chest-high.

The door stopped moving, but I didn't hear a body fall. Instead, I heard him out there, breathing, wet and heavy. The silver bullets had hit him, but all they'd made him do was hesitate.

"What are you, Ducharm?"

There was a strange sniggering laugh, like he had air leaks in his vocal apparatus or something, but the smug and pleased with himself still came through loud and clear. "For one, not Ducharm. That fool has been dead for years. He thought he could *reach out* to me, to *negotiate,* as if I was some lesser being. However, he had influence and contacts, so I absorbed his mind, ate his bones, and still wear his skin. Ironically, he became a far more effective lobbyist that way."

As he'd been talking, I'd been tracking his voice, and when I was pretty sure I knew where his mouth was, I fired a round through the wall.

"Ouch. Such rudeness. Please, Mrs. Shackleford. I'm much harder to kill than that. Now come out here, and we'll discuss terms. I'm not an unreasonable beast, and I can even negotiate to let you have a chance at your son. In return, you leave me alone and don't tell anyone what and where I am."

Sure . . . "While you continue eating five children a year."

"Five. Ah. Forgive me for that. At the time I was still trying to make nice. Those are only the ones that are tracked. And I make sure that no more are tracked. But they are all bad children. It is my duty and my obligation to eat bad children. That's why I was created, I think, almost as soon as humans appeared."

He might actually be telling the truth. Every culture talked about monsters born or summoned by fears of its children. Thankfully, those types of creature are rare because they are usually hard to put down. This was no longer about questioning him, it was about survival.

I knelt down behind the princess bed and shrugged out of my backpack. There had been two grenade pouches on my armor. I'd already used the incendiary, but I still had the frag. Mr. Trash Bags was there when I unzipped it, watching me with several eyeballs.

"Flee, Cuddle Bunny. On your pathetic leg limbs, flee."

I smooshed him out of the way and retrieved the grenade.

"My offer was time-sensitive, Mrs. Shackleford. I'm afraid my children are awake and wish to play. It's too late for you now."

There was another noise from the hall, like the skidding of dog claws across the hardwood. The door exploded open. I swung my gun over the top of the bed, and the light hit what looked like a hallway full of fat boxer puppies, but only if boxer puppies were three feet tall, with no fur, and human faces with big pointy teeth poking out of their open, loose, droopy mouths.

The light seemed to temporarily disorient them. I started shooting. Blue guts and blood splattered on the pink wallpaper. The first one let out a half-human, half-canine *yelp*. But there were so many of them, and they came flooding into the room, trying to surround me.

The instant my sights landed on a dog thing, I blasted it, and then switched to the next. Only they weren't just coming in from the ground level, they were clinging to the walls and climbing across the ceiling.

A silver hollowpoint splashed blue brains across the chandelier. The monster fell and smacked against the floor. My slide locked back. The spare .45 mags were in the bag so I dropped my gun on the bed and went for the Walther on my belt. The flashlight beam bounced wildly across the bed as I backed toward the corner, shooting again.

One of them had crawled under the bed. I felt a pain across my ankle as it clawed me. I stomped the too-human fingers, but in that moment of distraction, one of the ones on the wall launched itself. They weren't very big, maybe fifty pounds, but getting hit in the chest with fifty pounds of furious, biting, clawing dog-child will still knock you back.

I crashed against the dresser, scattering porcelain ballerinas and antique music boxes, but I didn't go down. Instead I held the monster back by a handful of neck fat, while I jammed the Walther into its ribs and fired. Blue blood splattered my glasses.

The one that had clawed me was scrambling out from beneath the sheets. It was about to reach me, but then a tiny black blob leapt from my backpack onto its head. "Consume!"

The creature began to roll around, screaming and clawing at its face, before it tried to get away, running for the hall. I went back to shooting the others, so I only caught what happened out of the corner of my eye. I know what I saw but to this day I don't believe it: Mr. Trash Bags ate the thing. I don't even understand how because he was a fraction of the size of the evil hellhound, but he crunched right through its skull.

And as fast as it started, Marchand's children were lying dead or twitching in blue puddles. Somehow I'd dropped nearly a dozen of them. I was breathing hard and had lost track of how many rounds I'd fired.

Then a vast shape materialized directly behind me. "Disappointing."

I tried to turn, but Marchand shoved me hard. And when I say *hard*, I mean I left the ground, crossed the room, and bounced off the wall. My back shattered a mirror. I think I might have broken a rib.

Dazed, I lay in a pile of broken glass as the world

spun. Something gigantic lumbered in front of the flashlight beam. It was as big as a gorilla and sort of the same shape as the "pups" but it was walking on two legs, and its face was, horribly, that of Vincente Ducharm. He'd shed the robe, revealing a body made out of pustules and fat rolls, and was walking toward me, on feet that looked like giant pink hands.

I didn't think I'd lost consciousness—not even for a brief moment—but Mr. Trash Bags had climbed onto my chest, several eyes telescoping near mine, several mouths open and screaming "Doom. Run. Doom." He made himself thin and long, and wrapped himself around my arm, like a very stylish avant-garde bracelet. "Flee. Flee now!"

I'd lost hold of the Walther, but it had landed only a foot away in a puddle of blue. I rolled through the glass, cutting myself in the process, scooped it up, and started shooting. I'd emptied most of the mag already, but there were still a few rounds left. I hit Marchand right in the temple, but it was like hitting putty. While his children had exploded all over the place, this one just showed a blue hole for a moment, then the hole re-formed, he shook his head, and it was perfect again. He laughed. God, I hated that laugh.

"You should try to run," he said greedily. "It's more fun when they try to run."

Everyone runs away and lives to fight another day, but Hunters don't like running from monsters. We run at them.

I let out some sort of incoherent battle cry as I got up and launched myself at him.

Marchand had to be over triple my weight. My actions seemed to amuse him greatly, until the big shard of glass I'd picked up got rammed into his pendulous belly. I'd cut the shit out of my left hand, but it was worth it to see the look on his face. He'd felt that.

But then he grabbed me by the neck, lifted me off my feet, and tossed me again. Luckily the bed broke my fall. I bounced off the mattress hard enough to break the frame, but at least I was still in one piece. Impacting the floor still knocked the hell out of me. I wound up on my hands and knees next to the backpack where I'd started. Everything was blurry, but it was from getting my glasses knocked off, not repeatedly banging my head on the wall.

"You killed my whole litter, but you will find I am far more difficult to harm." There was a sucking noise as he pulled the chunk of glass out of his fat. It broke into smaller pieces when he dropped it on the floor. "They were just juveniles, young and innocent."

Yeah, no, I'd seen those teeth. And his children? I shuddered to think of that thing reproducing. "Little bastards deserved it," I croaked.

"I could say the same thing about the missing baby who brought you here." His voice was back to sounding like human Ducharm: educated, pleasant, slightly accented, a man of the world complaining of a slight problem in social relations. "You wouldn't take any of my nice drinks, which could have put an end to this impasse with no unpleasantness."

The monster lifted the bed and flipped it out of the way. As I struggled to my feet, he stomped over to finish me off.

"This will be such a pleasure." And even though that was spoken in the Ducharm voice, he wasn't inviting me to tea. He reached for me, but I dodged to the side and launched a snap kick at what would be a vital spot in a male human. I didn't expect the same result, which was good, because I didn't get it. Instead, I got an *oof* as though I'd kicked its breathing apparatus.

I was so angry I went after the son of a bitch with my bare hands.

My husband is a slab of a man whose preferred form of cardio is eroding knuckle holes through leather punching bags. He might have had a chance here. I'm fairly tough, but the laws of physics didn't give a shit about my feelings.

I punched Marchand over and over in the eye, but my fist just bounced off his rubbery flesh. Ponderously, he swung at me, but I ducked under that and kneed him in his gut. Blue juices squirted out the glass hole, but I might as well have been kneeing a tractor tire, he was so solid. Then he connected, and it knocked the air right out of me. I hit the ground, flat on my back, gasping.

My bounce across the bed had landed my .45 on the ground, pointing back toward me. It was blinding, being in that beam, but there was one oblong black shadow between me and the light, shaped just like a hand grenade. I reached out and snagged it.

Marchand lifted one foot-hand to stomp my guts out. I yanked the pin. At least I'd take him with me. Except that was when Mr. Trash Bags started attacking the side of his head. Imagine crazy miniature shoggoth tentacles, beating like whips. I'd not even realized he'd jumped off my arm.

I think it was surprise that did it, but Marchand

reared back, batting at his head, and I saw my chance. I kicked with everything I had for his one planted knee. Marchand bellowed and fell forward. I rolled like a lumberjack trying to dodge a tree.

He belly flopped on the grenade.

If I suddenly ran for cover, he might realize what was happening and do another vanishing act. I couldn't give him a chance to get away, so I jumped onto his back and clung to those greasy fat rolls for dear life, gritting my teeth and hoping that his huge bulk would be sufficient to save me from the blast.

The grenade went off.

Pinned beneath over four hundred pounds of rubbery, supernatural blubber, the grenade made a terrible world-consuming *whump*. The blast lifted him straight off the ground. I wound up a few feet away, ears ringing.

And then it started raining. Squishy, fleshy blue bits dropped from the ceiling. A hand grenade produces a ton of smoke in a confined space and I began to cough. I started checking myself. By a miracle I hadn't blown off any of my limbs—but then a terrible pain snuck through my shock. Marchand's body hadn't stopped all the shrapnel. The blood that was coming through the side of my sweater wasn't blue. It was red. I pressed my hand to the wound. Then I realized there was another gaping hole in my thigh.

When it stopped raining monster goo, I tried to take stock of the situation. My flashlight was still working. I picked up my empty gun and shined it at where Marchand had been. There was a star-shaped explosion pattern that had torn the shit out of the nice hardwood. As for my host, he was in pieces.

The biggest one was the back half of his torso which, apparently, I'd ridden across the room like a rodeo bull. His ribs had gotten launched so hard that some of them were embedded in the wall. There was so much blue that it looked like someone had run the Smurf village through a wood chipper.

It wouldn't be the first time a monster had reassembled itself from near-molecular pieces, but the shreds of this one seemed to be just that—shreds.

Then one of the blue flesh chunks moved. I glared at it, trying to figure out how I was possibly going to be able to fight anymore, when an eyestalk lifted and Mr. Trash Bags declared, "Bad thing all gone."

Master of understatement, that Mr. Trash Bags. Then the blob oozed over to me, helpfully dragging my glasses. A little tentacle hoisted them up so I could reach them. "Cuddle Bunny hurt?"

"I blew myself up."

"Mammal blood should stay on inside," he told me helpfully.

CHAPTER 13

There was a ton of blood coming from my leg wound. That probably meant that my femoral artery had been hit and, if so, I'd be dead in minutes. My head was swimming. I wanted to throw up. I was afraid, but not for me. I was scared for Ray because he was counting on his mom.

Focus, Julie. I swear I heard that in Grandpa's voice.

I crawled through the blue remains of Marchand and his brood, got the backpack, found the med kit inside and got out the SOF-T tourniquet. I popped off the rubber bands, got the loop over my foot, and pulled it up my leg. I can't even explain how much moving it hurt. When the loop was past the wound, I started cranking the handle. If it hurt before, this was a whole new level of pain.

Once I got it cranked as tight as I could, I locked the handle in place with the triangle... Yeah, these things are awesome. People who think they'll be able to improvise a tourniquet out of household items on the fly are really lucky they don't have to actually test their bullshit shoelace method.

Okay. That was one problem temporarily handled, but I was still screwed up, in so much pain I could barely think, and bleeding from a hole in my side. The neighbors might have heard the gunfire or the explosions, but it was raining hard, and I had a feeling this basement had been soundproofed so the neighbors wouldn't hear children getting eaten.

I could call for an ambulance, but then the cops would just arrest me in the hospital, and by the time this got worked out, Ray would be lost forever. No. I had to handle this on my own.

Lights and a sink would be a huge help. So I pulled myself up the wall and screamed when I put weight on my leg. That caused Mr. Trash Bags to start fretting, but I could barely hear him over the buzzing in my ears.

I limped down the hall, found the breaker box, turned the lights back on, and then found the bathroom. It was as nicely done as the rest of this place. Ducharm's tile guy did excellent work. It's weird what goes through your mind at a time like this. All I needed to do now was stop the bleeding from multiple shrapnel wounds before I lost too much blood pressure and passed out. I turned the sink on and took a deep breath.

"Mr. Trash Bags, would you guard the door in case there's any more of them, please?"

I gritted my teeth and peeled my shirt off, examined the abdominal wound in the mirror, and realized I was totally screwed. It wasn't a laceration. It was a puncture wound and the chunk of shrapnel was still inside me, which raised the question: what had it hit? It was far enough to the side that it could have hit a kidney. If that was the case, I wouldn't be able to stop internal bleeding. Was I better off trying to get it out or leave it in?

I needed to decide fast because I wasn't going to be awake for much longer.

But my decision was made for me when that jagged chunk of metal *fell* out and hit the porcelain sink with a clatter.

Then the wound was simply gone. The flesh was sealed. I rubbed my hands across my skin, smearing the blood. Sure enough, there was a black circle, big around as a quarter, dark as night, where the hole had been.

"Well... Huh."

It was another Guardian's mark. I turned so that my front was facing the mirror. I could see the three long, black vertical lines running down my belly. I'd had those for a while now, since they'd replaced the claw marks the last time the Guardian's power had saved my life. They seemed a bit bigger. Then I lifted my hair and checked my neck where the original mark was.

It was obviously growing. I watched as the mark went from a line to forming several new edges, like the crest of a wave or the edge of a serrated knife, and then it stopped.

I pulled my hand away in fear. Then I remembered my leg, and the throbbing awful pain above it because I'd cut off all my circulation. I undid the tourniquet handle and slowly relaxed it. Electricity shot through my leg as blood began to flow again. No blood came spurting out though, so I undid my belt and dropped my pants.

Sure enough, there was another black line across my thigh.

I checked the palm of my hand, where I'd cut it with the glass. It looked like a perfectly normal injury, no magical black lines. The other cuts, bruises, and scrapes on my body hadn't changed either. I guess the Guardian's magic only activated for potentially fatal injuries.

It had saved my life again. But each time, there was a little less of me. I was a little less human, and a little more something else. I didn't know what it meant, or where it would lead, but probably every cosmic power that knew about this thing kept calling it a curse for a reason.

The other two times it had saved my life, I'd cried afterward, wondering about the mysterious cost I'd have to pay... But not today. Today I had to save my baby.

I put my fingers against the now longer, angrier-looking mark on my neck. It was still hot to the touch. "Let's do this."

After I showered off the blood and blue slime, I changed into the last of my stolen clothing. I kept the artifact close at hand the whole time. Mr. Trash Bags hadn't seen any more monsters, and the cops hadn't kicked down the door—the neighbors must have not heard the explosion—so I had time to search the place and plan my next move.

Inside the downstairs fireplace, I found ash and bones. Little bones. I wasn't going to look any closer and see if some of those rounded rocks were baby skulls. There are things you can know but don't need to see, because if you see it, it will never, ever, ever leave you alone.

In my circuit of the house, I discovered the master bedroom wasn't arranged for humans and looked like a cross between a kennel and an animal's den at the zoo. In addition to the pink room, there was another decorated in blue and outfitted with a large TV and game system. There were discarded toys and clothing from several decades in the closet...and fingernail scratches on the inner door. I had no doubt these rooms had housed many victims who'd never left this house alive. Perhaps the rooms were the equivalent to those aquariums in seafood restaurants, where lobsters are kept in a semblance of their native environment until they can be eaten at their freshest.

The Guardian's mark had stopped the life-threatening wounds, but from the nausea and dizziness, it didn't do much for blood loss. Mr. Trash Bags, now the size of a toy poodle, came along by my side, dragging himself along on pseudopods. He didn't shout any warnings, and his eyes were interested but not pleading as they had been.

"Cuddle Bunny sad."

"No kidding." I was terrified for Ray, scared of what the curse was doing to me, overwhelmed, and exhausted. I wanted to scream and break things, but that was no excuse to snap at my clueless but loyal childhood friend who'd gone above and beyond to help me. "You saved my life, Mr. Trash Bags. Thank you. You're the best."

He seemed positively gleeful at that. "Mr. Trash Bags is best."

When we found the kitchen, I told him, "Don't eat anything. Might be poison."

Or human, but if I told him that, he might fail to see the problem.

I won't tell you what I found in the fridge, but suffice it to say that I'll have it in my nightmares to the day I die. One thing, though, none of them was Ray. I had to make sure, even though it broke my heart to look.

After I was done vomiting in the kitchen sink, I went back to searching. Ducharm seemed to be an organized beast, so there had to be some clues to his business dealings around here somewhere. I smelled the bottles in the living room. I had no idea what they actually contained, but it's safe to say it wasn't Madeira, or brandy, or sirop de cassis.

Upstairs had an office and a computer. It was on, but password protected.

I'm not a computer genius. Actually other than shooting, I don't really have any special talents. I'm a relatively smart, relatively competent human being, but I knew absolutely nothing about breaking into a computer. That's what Melvin was for.

I couldn't risk turning on my phone, because then the government monster hunting agencies would be all over me. However, Ducharm had a landline, and since he was a consultant, him placing a call to an American hunting company wouldn't be seen as suspicious.

Dorcas picked up on the first ring, which was saying something since it was like five in the morning there. "This is MHI." Of course, companies that operate under legally mandated secrecy can't just say "Monster Hunter International" to any random caller from an unidentified number.

"How's the head?"

"Julie! I'm down to seeing double, which is nicer than triple was. Are you okay?"

Fifteen minutes ago I'd been bleeding out, but instead I said, "I'm fine."

"Where the hell are you?"

"France."

"France! Did you find Ray?"

"Working on it."

"Listen, you don't sound fine. Be careful. Use your brain. You won't do Ray any good if you get yourself killed doing something stupid. I rounded up who I could to back you up. The B team we've got covering New York was the fastest I could get someone to help you. They'll be landing soon, but in the wrong country. They're heading to where you were in Cologne."

"They're probably going to get detained as soon as they land by the SJK. It's a long story. Can you reroute them?"

"Only if they hijack the plane. They're on commercial, not private. It was the quickest thing they could find at the time." I should have figured that. We could've chartered a trans-Atlantic private flight, but that had been really short notice to hope somebody was available. "Did you find Ray?"

"Not yet. Grab Melvin. I need his technical expertise."

Dorcas began shouting, and from her tone I didn't expect the troll to give her any of his usual sass. While she waited for him, I gave her a quick update.

"MCB has been calling to scream at me. Sounds like you've caused an international incident. There's still no word from the Hunters at the siege. The blizzard is over, but comms are still out. It's like the Russians are jamming the whole area."

"That can't be good." While Dorcas kept talking, I

began rifling through Ducharm's big desk. Most Hunters were even lesser computer geniuses than I was, and the number of times I had to guess someone's password didn't bear thinking about. It was particularly heartbreaking when one of us died, and I had to try and guess their password to get into their files . . . but if that process had taught me anything, it was that people liked to write down their passwords.

I started going through drawers. It was all very normal stuff, office supplies, lots of papers in hanging file folders, but there was an oddball scrap of paper squished to the side of the bottom drawer. It had a single word on it: Athenais08.

It was hard to type with my left hand wrapped in a bandage, but the computer accepted that password. *Jackpot.*

It was entirely possible that the monster I'd just killed had actually been Athenais de Montespan in an earlier incarnation, or perhaps he'd been one of the lowlifes who'd killed babies to supply her with her potions. Or at least, he had killed the originals and taken over playing their roles, like he'd done with Ducharm. Grimm Berlin had thought Marchand had been around at least that long.

"Dorcas, listen. Tell Melvin never mind. I need to go. I'll be in touch as I can."

"You'd better. I'm depopulating the entire Eastern seaboard of Hunters to try and get you some backup. In the meantime, want me to call the French Hunters?"

"Not yet." They'd either turn me in or end up in the same boat as Fabian. "By the way, call the lawyer and tell him I'm wanted for some murders."

"Oh, honey, you're on a roll, ain't you?"

The first thing I clicked on was Ducharm's email. The child-eating shapeshifter still used Yahoo. The last email he'd sent had gone out last night. I could read French well enough to tell it was announcing the upcoming auction of a very special . . . *piece of livestock?* I gritted my teeth so hard I nearly cracked them. If I could kill him over again right then, I would've. It said this particular animal was of two unique and portentous bloodlines. Only the teaser was in French. The rest of the message, probably including the time and location, appeared to be in some manner of alphanumeric code.

"Julie, are you still there?"

I checked who the email had been sent to. They all looked like random, anonymous addresses . . . but there had to be at least fifty of them.

"On second thought—have Melvin call me at this number. I'm going to give him remote access to all the files of a really bad dude to pick through."

"Bring Ray and you both home safe, girl."

I ransacked Ducharm's office. Amid his papers I found a tattered old children's book from Portugal. It was curiously out of place, but as I flipped through, I realized it told me what manner of creature I'd just killed. The book was about a *bicho-papão*, aka an "eating beast" in Portuguese. It was one of those moral, scolding books about how this shape-changing monster would devour recalcitrant children, like those who refused to do their homework, say their prayers, or take their naps.

I'd heard about such creatures through other Hunters. They existed around Mediterranean countries and had been terrorizing people since Roman times. They were mostly solitary creatures, and though they spawned litters every century, the cubs would fight and eat each other until only one remained. Then when that one was an adult, it would find its own territory to torment.

Albert would love to add this book to the library... assuming he was alive. I'd been so preoccupied I'd not even remembered to ask Dorcas how he was doing. I was a terrible friend, but I had a lot on my mind.

This whole place was probably a treasure trove of monster information. It wasn't very often we found something this old, knowledgeable, and organized. As much as I wanted to set fire to the house because it was so unclean, that would be a waste of valuable intel. After I was long gone, I'd tip off the French Hunters so they could loot the place, and maybe even collect whatever the equivalent to PUFF was here.

Melvin had impatiently walked me through a few websites that had let me grant him remote access to the computer. While I broke open drawers and went through the papers, the computer screen kept changing as Melvin stole everything. Marchand had lists of emails and phone numbers attached to codes that had to represent names. He saw customers. I saw potential targets. One of these was Brother Death.

I found that the repulsive monster had kept a handwritten diary. I didn't read it all. Evil, besides being unimaginative, is long-winded. It whines or brags at length for page after page that no sane person would want to read. I'd heard that serial killers often had pages and pages and pages of confessions and admonitions and explanations that no one ever bothered to read, not because they were horrible—though they often were—but because they were amazingly predictable and boring. This was like that. I skipped to the end and skimmed enough to see my son wasn't mentioned. He was very proud, however, of his new thirteen-meter yacht and the dock he'd had built for it. So at least now I knew how I was getting off this rock.

The desk phone rang again. Hopefully Melvin had found something. But just in case it was one of Ducharm's friends or customers, I didn't say anything when I picked up.

"Hello. I am looking for Julie Shackleford-Pitt of Monster Hunter International." The caller had a very polished, educated, resonant voice.

I thought about just hanging up and making a run for the dock, but something told me to hold on. "Speaking."

"Ah, what an incredible pleasure. I've made your husband's acquaintance and provided a great deal of funding to your company's current operation, but the two of us have never been formally introduced. I am Management."

Holy shit. I was talking to an actual dragon.

Owen had met Management in his secret cave beneath Las Vegas. The mysterious billionaire was something of a collector, more like a hoarder. But Owen liked him, he'd helped us against the Nacht-mar, and he'd bankrolled the siege against the City of Monsters. But I was still bewildered how he'd found me here, and for just a moment I thought that he might somehow be involved with Ray's kidnapping. But that made no sense.

"Why?"

"If you will recall my reputation, I pay a great deal of attention to current events. In particular, it behooves me to keep track of my investments."

"I'm an investment?"

"In that I believe Monster Hunter International is the single best hope of keeping Asag from destroying the world, yes. And with the death of your grandfather—my utmost and sincere condolences by the way—you will be named the CEO."

With everything else on my mind, I hadn't even really had time to dwell on that new weight on my shoulders. I was still suspicious. "How'd you find me here? Did you know Ducharm?"

"I knew of him, as I know of many things, though I did not know what he truly was. As for how I found you, I've been keeping my eye on MHI."

"You've tapped our phones?"

"You don't have to *tap* them if you own enough stock in various telecommunications companies. I've been investing since you humans invented the concept of capitalism. I still have shares from the Dutch East India Company around here somewhere. I'm seeing these files before your troll does. I will admit Ducharm's records make for fascinating reading. I've gone through fifteen of them while we've been having this pleasant conversation."

Owen had said that the dragon liked to watch all the news channels simultaneously. It wasn't a surprise he was a speed reader too.

I was still suspicious though. "And it wasn't because you just got an email from Marchand about an auction?"

"Well . . ."

"I knew it!"

"Just a moment now. As you humans say, hold onto your horses. I am on many mailing lists, but because I am a collector of things, not people. All sentient life should be respected. Well, except for gnomes. To hell with gnomes... But I have a love of antiquities and items of power. The sources of such treasures are often the most unsavory sorts."

My husband had said that his cave had been packed with a Smithsonian's worth of stuff. It wasn't like you could just buy moon rocks on eBay, so he was probably telling the truth. "If you knew these monsters were trading in humans, why didn't you rat them out?"

"To whom? The MCB, who would destroy me and confiscate my treasures? You forget, Mrs. Shackleford-Pitt, that though I have a great deal of fondness for humanity's artistic achievements, I hold no loyalty to your species beyond our mutually beneficial business arrangement. You are not the only intelligent life upon this world. To speak to human authorities about the dark markets would mean forever being excluded from them. I am the last of my kind. I've survived because I have resources, but mostly because I pay attention. If I am caught helping you, then I will be cut off from that source of information forever."

"I get that, but please, I'm begging you. You've lived thousands of years. My baby hasn't even had one. I need him back."

"Please, do not cry."

"I wasn't."

"Apologies, it is difficult to tell with humans. You all sound very squeaky to me. You want him back. I do not disagree. I engage in many activities your species considers immoral, such as stealing information or eating large numbers of gnomes, yet I have no love for fiends who would steal eggs or babies. I will help you. As a former client, I am privy to the cipher to Marchand's code. I know where the auction will take place."

My mouth went dry. I didn't even want to allow myself to hope. Instead, I held my breath.

"It says the auction will be in Lisbon. Marchand arranged it on behalf of an entity called Brother Death. The asset in question is a human male, aged six months, the offspring of the Guardian and a Chosen, both from a long line of Hunters. If it makes you feel any better, he is being advertised as in excellent health and temperament."

I was speechless for so long that Management asked, "Are you there?"

"Yes," I answered, and then, "The auction is going on now?"

"It begins at midnight. One must be present to bid. I suspect it will gather representatives of many of the power players in the supernatural world capable of trading in the currency this creature seeks."

No wonder they needed so much secrecy. If Hunters, government or private, got wind of a meeting like that, they'd hit that place hard. Depending on who or what was in attendance, the bounties could be astronomical. Only Hunters tended to go in guns blazing. They'd be interested in surviving first, killing monsters second, and hostage rescue a distant third. It was rare to get back someone who'd been taken by supernatural creatures. That was just the nature of the things we dealt with and something we had to accept.

Screw that.

"Tonight. Lisbon. Portugal. I don't know how, but I'll get there."

"First, permit me to offer you the use of a private jet. I have access to one which is currently in Cannes. Second, I will send one of my employees to the meeting as my proxy. I will instruct him to bid for your child to try to win the auction."

Lucinda had made the same offer, only she was in it for the artifact. "Why—why would you do that for me?"

Management chuckled. Over the millennia of doing business with humans, he had, doubtless, perfected the art of reading us. "Fear not. I do this because your child is the scion of a legacy. Those of us who have practiced high finance for thousands of years are aware that it is not merely business transactions which move fortunes, but what is owed and what can't be paid. Favors, madam. Obligations. Debts of powerful beings to powerful beings. I plan on living a very long time. Someday, perhaps one of your descendants will return this kindness to a poor old dragon."

"Thank you."

"Do not thank me yet. The type of assets Brother Death most desires, I do not keep. I am far from the wealthiest participant when it comes to the currency of the dark market. I will offer up treasures that I believe may interest him and hope for the best."

"And if your guy doesn't win?"

"If a price cannot be agreed upon, you'll simply have to rely upon your fertile imagination and capacity for mayhem."

With Mr. Trash Bags bouncing along around my feet like an enthusiastic puppy, I went to investigate the arrangement for Ducharm's boat. I'd stolen the keys and a few thousand euros I'd found lying around.

Turned out the mechanism for lowering and getting the boat down the ramp was push-button, which figured, since evil was stupid and lazy. I didn't know much about yachts, but the controls seemed incredibly simple. There was gas in the tank. I was good to go.

I set course for Cannes, which was a fancy way of saying that I drove in the general direction of Europe. The rain had let up a bit, and the waves weren't too rough. I was in bad shape. Everything hurt. The Guardian's marks had stopped the life-threatening wounds, but didn't do anything for the dozen or so smaller ones. The cut on my hand was the worst, and it was bleeding through the bandage.

While I was piloting the boat by guesses, Mr. Trash Bags had climbed on my head and made himself thin, so that I was in fact wearing a Mr. Trash Bags hat. The shape he had assumed was somewhat reminiscent of a Napoleonic hat, albeit a Napoleonic hat with a lot of crazy little eyes and mouths.

He was just being protective. I suppose I was getting used to the little guy again. He'd saved me from getting my guts stomped out by Ducharm, and he only seemed to leave drool or slime when he wanted to. Most of the time he had the consistency of silly putty and the loyalty of a really good dog. More people should get miniature shoggoths. It turns out they make great pets. At least mine did.

Management had given me some landmarks to look for and said he'd provide a driver to get me to the airport. There were binoculars on the boat, and I was able to pick out a restaurant that had a dock in front of it. Management's description had been pretty good, especially when you considered that he'd never actually seen the place with his own eyes and was going off of photos on the internet.

Not knowing what I was doing, I made a mess of docking, bumping and scraping the expensive boat against the wood until I got it close enough I could jump across.

Nobody was eating at the outside tables because of the weather, so I'd not drawn too much attention, but I told my shoggoth companion to take cover anyway. Mr. Trash Bags wrapped himself around my neck like a stole while I trudged up the stairs. A waiter came running out waving his hands at me while shouting something about how I couldn't park there.

I tried to ignore him and keep going, but as he drew close to us, Mr. Trash Bags extruded several eyes and opened several little mouths to scream, "Eat noses, eat toes, eat EYES!"

The poor kid ran for his life.

After years of having humans break out the torches and pitchforks whenever they saw him, Mr. Trash Bags should know better about attracting attention, but he cared about me so much he was willing to risk exposure when he thought I was in danger . . . either that or freezing him had given him brain damage.

"Please, don't do that. You've got to stay hidden until I tell you."

I staggered out to the road in front of the restaurant just as a limousine rolled to a stop and a uniformed driver stepped out. Since I was the only person walking in the rain, he asked, "Julie Shackleford-Pitt?"

Since Management was the only person I knew

who insisted on the hyphenated last name, I knew this wasn't a trap. *"Oui."*

He opened the door for me. *"Je suis ton chauffeur."*

"Fantastic."

In the back seat there were packages of snacks, and I was dying, but before I could open one, a phone began to ring. A cell phone had been left on the seat across from me. Of course, the display read *Management.*

"I hope this method of transportation will suffice."

"Oh yeah. It's super low key. Did you miss the part where I'm wanted for a bunch of murders?"

"I did not. Did you know that the man you kidnapped is the son of a member of the German parliament? What happened to young Benno anyway?"

"Eaten by cosmic horrors." That would also explain why the SJK and, by extension, all the EU monster agencies really had it in for me.

"The plane is being prepared now. These hirelings have no knowledge of your business, but they will do anything I ask. Do you have any requests?"

"Guns. Lots of guns. Ammo, preferably silver. Explosives. Night vision. Body armor. I can give you a detailed equipment list, but I'm not choosy."

"Ah . . . these humans are my employees, but I'm afraid they are from legitimate businesses. They only know Management as the mysterious majority shareholder of their various companies, not as the fearsome dragon I truly am. However, the man who will represent me at the auction is a capable sort. He will meet you in Portugal. I will instruct him to see what he can do. You will attend as his plus one. I have ordered suitable attire for you."

"Suitable attire?" What did you wear to a monster gathering? A flying purple people eater costume?

"These events are formal occasions, almost festive."

"I can't imagine what kind of horrible assholes would have fun at an event selling babies."

"The most horrible you can imagine, but they will abide by certain covenants during the event. There is often a great deal of animosity between the various attendees, but Brother Death's security team keeps the peace. This one will be taking place in the Convent of Our Lady of Mount Carmel, which he has rented for the night."

"A convent? Am I supposed to dress up as a nun or something?"

When a dragon clicks its tongue, it's a really loud click, even when you're just getting it over the phone. "No. It is no longer a consecrated building. It was abandoned after the 1755 Lisbon earthquake. The convent building itself has been renovated and used for various purposes over the years, but the church has never been recovered and is left in ruins. All the stone parts are extant, but it has no roof, and everything that was wood has been burned. For a while in the 1970s it was boarded up, and some tourists who broke in were eaten by rats."

"Not rats," I said, speaking from my internal certainty of how these things worked and the stories that were made up to cover up monster outbreaks.

"An excellent guess. Only a fool believes the news. In actuality, there is a lair of lamias beneath the abandoned church."

Lamias are sort of like the Romans' idea of vampires, only—well, I know this is going to sound weird considering that my mother is a Master vampire whom I loathe, and that my family has fought countless different kinds of vampires and has yet to find one that isn't a horror—lamias are nastier than vampires.

To begin with, they're not fully in human form. They're all female, but from the waist down, they have the body of snakes. Kind of like a more repulsive form of mermaids though, frankly, mermaids are also nothing to be friendly with or to have Disney movies about. The best that can be said about mermaids is that some of them are just not evil enough to earn a PUFF exemption if they work really hard at it. Lamias—no. Like other forms of supernatural monsters that are completely unredeemable, lamias have no human qualities. They're the embodiment of cruelty and blood lust.

"I trust that nest has been cleaned out." I couldn't imagine whoever owned the place was renting it out if people were likely to get eaten.

"Not precisely. I believe they've been given other outlets, and they are spared as long as they stay out of the nice part humans still use, and they only prey on undesirables."

"Fantastic. If those scrubs aren't going to be near the party, why share the trivia?"

"Because, if you do have to make a hasty escape with your purloined baby, Brother Death's security would not expect you to exit through a lamia den."

"Good point. Any chance you've got a map of the building I could study, or some interior shots you could send me?"

"It will be arranged. Anything else?"

I realized that we were going really fast. The

chauffeur wasn't messing around. And then I realized I was getting blood all over the nice interior. "Okay, I do have a request. Can you get me a doctor, nurse, or somebody who can do good stitches? I've got a couple of cuts that I can't get a good angle on or I'd do them myself."

"My dear, I already have a seamstress, makeup artist, and hairdresser waiting to help you in Lisbon. You should have led with needing a doctor. I shall summon one immediately to the plane. Oh, and please keep this phone. It is untraceable. We shall speak again soon."

If I ever had a chance of being someone's kept woman, I'd want to be Management's kept woman. Never mind that he's a dragon and doesn't, so far as I can tell, even understand sexual attraction behavior in humans. But if Management kept a kept woman, he'd do it right.

The limousine had a minibar, from which I got three water bottles, because I hadn't been able to drink anything since I'd arrived at Ducharm's place. I didn't even trust his tap water that much. The limo also had little cheese crackers, which right at that moment felt like the finest ambrosia. I leaned back into the comfortable seat and watched the narrow streets and stone walls of Southern France pass by, while Mr. Trash Bags absorbed a container of cookies, plastic wrapper and all.

Our destination was a private airfield. Before we got to the plane, I warned Mr. Trash Bags, "You need to play it cool."

"What is cool?"

"Don't let people see you. You need to try and stay hidden. Quit freaking out."

"What is freak out?"

"Just hide in the bag until I tell you otherwise, please."

Though Management had said jet, I'd assumed it would still be a small plane, like the one that had gotten me to Cannes, but with better engines. But this was a *jet*, as in the nicest thing money could buy. I didn't know enough about airplanes to guess the make or model but it was way bigger than anything MHI had ever chartered.

There was a stewardess who greeted me at the bottom of the stairs. She'd probably been told to expect some super important business executive, not a scratched-up lady bleeding all over her German novelty sweater.

As I went up the stairs I found that the cabin was basically a living room. The interior was like how I imagined Air Force One looking, but this was a little more upscale. Even on hunting money, it had never occurred to me that we could buy this sort of flying palace to whisk us swiftly around the world. MHI's cargo plane had been bought used from the Post Office.

Honestly, though, I had no desire left to travel. I just wanted to go home. Perhaps years from now, when the kids were grown, Owen and I could take a tour of Europe, hitting up all the museums. He'd be horribly bored but would get over it. And for just a moment there was a very clear picture of "the kids" in my head: four of them, two boys and two girls, with Ray the oldest, getting ready to step in to command Monster Hunter International when I retired.

Then my heart clutched at the thought that it was all a dream, all uncertain, that my husband might already be lost, and I'd have to fight for every bit that was left.

I took a seat on one of the sofas, and a young man in a black tie bowed to me and asked if there was something he could do to make me comfortable. I ordered a sweet tea, mostly to have something to hold in my hand, and he gave it to me seconds later, the frosty glass sweating, the tea perfect.

The doctor arrived right after I did. I don't know which of Management's companies he worked for, if any, but he didn't even bother to ask me any questions. Hell, I didn't even know if he spoke English. He just unfolded his kit and started gesturing impatiently at the red stained bandage on my hand.

The doctor frowned when he saw how deep the cut was. He'd probably been expecting this to be easy. He gestured at the waiter who stood by—I wondered if he had a place to strap in—and held up two fingers. A moment later he was brought a short, heavy-bottomed glass with amber liquid at the bottom and he took a sip. I didn't think it was iced tea. Behind me, I could hear the sound of the door closing, and then the plane started moving. I noted that the waiter remained standing and didn't so much as sway.

The waiter brought me another sweet tea—I'd not realized I'd already chugged the first—asked if I wished to watch a movie or if I required anything else, and I shook my head no. I was too keyed up and nervous to concentrate on a movie.

"How long is the flight?"

"Just over two hours, madam."

"Awesome." I winced as I undid the bandage. "Hey, Doc, stitch fast so I can take a nap."

CHAPTER 14

I woke up, looked out the window, and realized we were landing in Lisbon.

It was sunset. The first thing to meet my eyes was unexpected: a giant statue of Christ, arms wide open, as if for an embrace.

"I thought that Christ statue was in Rio de Janeiro."

The doctor was sitting across the aisle, and it turned out he did speak good English. "The statue of Christ the King. No, there is one on either side of the Atlantic posed so that if they could be brought together they would embrace."

"Why?"

He shrugged. "I don't know. They were built to commemorate some kind of agreement between the Portuguese government and the church after the civil war. There are two, but Rio is more photogenic than Lisbon for the movies."

He was right, I think. After all, in Rio, the cameras could pan bridges and tropical greenery. As we turned in a wide circle, I did glimpse beaches, though they seemed deserted at this time of year, and there were briefly seen palm trees lining the city's avenues. There were a bunch of tall buildings, like the skyline of any modern city, glinting in the sun.

Respectable. But not nearly as photogenic as Rio.

I flexed my bandaged hand. "Thanks for the help."

"I was paid to aid you and not ask questions."

"Good. You don't want to know."

In a few more minutes we touched down. The kid in the tie tried to help me off, but I shooed him away. I had the impression that Management's regular guests were way more demanding than I was being. I didn't care. This wasn't a pleasure trip.

Turns out the other half really live differently. I'd been through the usual mess that is entry into an EU country. None of them except maybe Germany seem to have any idea of organization in order to go through customs and passport control. Instead, they dump everyone arriving from overseas into large rooms, willy nilly in no particular order, and then leave tourists, businessmen, families and presumably everyone else to elbow their way into one of the three or four lines moving at glacial speed.

There was none of that in this case.

As our door opened, Management's waiter got out ahead of me, which seemed out of character with his, up till then, very courtly manner. As we descended the stairs to the tarmac, we found a man waiting for us. He was small, slim, Mediterranean and he wore some kind of uniform. I didn't know if it was a security official uniform, or merely the uniform of the airport or some airline. All I know is he received us with a smile, the steward shook hands with him, and looked over passports that were handed him.

I didn't know what the passports were, or what the names on them were. My own passport was in Alabama. My only other ID was in the bag which now held the artifact, somewhere in the depths of Mr. Trash Bags'...depths.

Stamp, stamp went the man. Smile, smile, and gestured us toward a small building.

There was another man waiting there for me. He was wearing a business suit and had a briefcase in one hand. I knew right away that he wasn't just another servant. He was middle-aged, looked like an undefinable mix of European and Asian, with receding black hair and dark grey eyes. He exuded that air of assurance one expected from an executive.

"Mrs. Pitt?" He extended a hand to me. His handshake was firm, and mine was just as firm in return. I remembered my dad teaching me to shake hands in business occasions, when I was eight or so, and telling me that a firm handshake inspired confidence. It totally works. Daddies have more influence over their children than they'll ever know.

"I'm Gerard Hansel. Management sent me." He put his hand sort of around me, not really touching me, but guiding me, and at the same time conveying that I was under his protection. It was a gesture as old as time and accepted by most people instinctively. The building we entered was grey, utilitarian from the floor to the walls. There were broad doors leading to the outside.

We entered one, crossed the expanse of maybe two hundred feet, and exited through the other doors into a balmy evening with just a hint of a chill wind. I smelled a big city: fumes, the inevitable odors of human occupation, perfume and trash, cleaners and dirt, all together. Where we'd emerged, a long way from the main entrance to the airport, there was a stained, cracked sidewalk. Waiting there was a gleaming black stretch limo. The driver was holding the back door open for us.

As Hansel followed me in, I noted the interior was similar to the limo in Cannes. We sat back, leaning into the upholstered seats; the door was closed and we were off, down an avenue, into a tunnel, and out the other side as the lights of the city were starting to gleam against the fading light of the sun.

Now that we were somewhere we couldn't be overheard by normal people, he opened his briefcase and took out a sheaf of papers. I couldn't place his faint accent. "I have been deputized to bid on your son for you."

"So you're informed about what's going on?"

"I am an attorney who specializes in a very select clientele. I am very familiar with the supernatural world. Or as you Americans like to say, I am *read in*. Management has retained my services before."

"Good. And you know if you don't win the auction . . ."

"You will likely take more direct measures? Yes." He handed me the papers. "This is the contract for my services. Please look that over."

A quick glance told me that Hansel's standard agreement had clauses for things about how his clients weren't supposed to swallow his soul . . . select clientele my ass. He was a lawyer for monsters.

"I'm not signing anything. You work for Management, not for me."

"True. However, since I have been asked to serve your needs, this is to protect myself from liability should you take any actions which . . . let's just say, cause distress in certain communities."

The car started moving.

"Where are we going?"

"One of Management's properties. We have a few hours to prepare before the event begins. I have an RSVP for myself and one guest."

"They're going to recognize me."

"Perhaps not." He reached in his briefcase and brought out what looked like one of those carnival masks from Venice and passed it over to me. It would cover the entire top half of my face including the nose, leaving only eyes, mouth and chin free. "You will wear this."

It was a delicate concoction, a piece of jewelry clearly wrought by master craftsmen: the base was gold, but there was an ornamentation of silver filigree emphasizing the cheeks, a delicate inlay of reddish gold running a tracery-like brocade over all of it. The eyes were outlined in what I was fairly sure were real diamonds, and whose glitter would make it harder to see the eyes clearly. The whole was attached to a sort of veil, or cowl, of gold fabric, with tiny butterflies of ruby and diamond attached all over. It was a beautiful piece, it was embedded with magic, and it would be noticed.

"My employer said you are to have this. It has certain minor enchantments which will help conceal your nature."

"Won't people think—"

"That a disguise is strange? The other bidders? Or

Brother Death and his servants who will be managing the auction?" An ironic smile twisted his lips, lifting them up more on one side than the other. "You come from a more innocent world."

"Management told you what I do for a living, right?"

"Yes, you've witnessed monsters and mayhem your whole life, but even a vampire pit is cleaner than what you are about to see. Most of the mortal beings there will be hiding their faces. You must understand that these people have no honor, and that some of them are very prominent in the human world. Some of them have reputations as philanthropists."

"And what about your honor, Mr. Hansel?"

"I merely do what my clients ask me to do. This child? It is not the sort of thing my employer would normally bid on—"

"*He.*" My correction was sharp. This might just be a business transaction for him, but I wasn't going to let him dehumanize my son. "His name is Ray."

"Pardon. He is not the type of thing Management collects, and the dark magic human sacrifice enables is not something he partakes in. They will think, however, that he's obliging someone who is prominent in the human world who doesn't want to be known, who is paying him in currency he will accept. I started that rumor myself. You will play that part. I let slip that you are a rich and famous woman who can't afford a hint of scandal, but who wishes for a piece of this action."

"They'll buy that?"

"Yes. I am allowed to bring a guest; in this case, the famous woman who has struck a deal with my employer. It will be assumed you insisted on being present to keep an eye on me—there is, after all, no honor among evildoers—or, since you are a newcomer, you wish to witness the spectacle for yourself and to have the chance to rub shoulders with the supernatural set. I'm afraid you don't realize how *common* this sort of thing is."

"It sounds like you've worked with some real assholes." I'd noticed there was even a clause in his contract about how his clients weren't allowed to lay their eggs in him.

"Indeed, Mrs. Pitt, but I do not judge. More than likely some of my former, inhuman clients may be there tonight."

"If Management can send a proxy bidder, why don't all the supernatural players? Why risk the exposure?"

"Some would not trust a servant to retrieve something so valuable. Others? Pride. Hubris. I believe many of them enjoy the spectacle, displaying their riches and having their peers and rivals marvel at them. They really aren't so different from humanity in that respect. Now, our drive will take a bit, so we should discuss strategy. Our problem is that Management cannot field that many assets ideal for this type of transaction. Rich and powerful as he is, he is still shaken by the recent disturbance and his power is not what it once was."

"Beg your pardon?"

"Well, let's say that the assets we will be bidding with are not precisely . . . money."

"I got that part."

"Anything can be traded for money, even in the underworld, but the bids presented tonight will be in the form of things the bidders believe will be most pleasing to Brother Death, who is a notorious connoisseur of all things malicious. Management is many things, but he does not rejoice in evil or suffering, and much of his collection was destroyed in Las Vegas, so his offerings may be insufficient. Once the bidding is over, my work is done. If you take action outside the rules of the auction, you are on your own. I cannot be seen as aiding you. If your identity is revealed, I will deny that I knew who you really were and say that I was manipulated."

I was tired and emotional. I wanted to call him a coward... But no. That wouldn't work. "I understand. Your livelihood is at stake."

"Not my livelihood, my life. A secret society does not have many rules, but bringing a Hunter to a gathering like this is certainly among them. What their rules lack in number, they more than make up for with the quality of punishments. The only other help I can give you will be behind the scenes. If someone else wins, and you wish to trace the buyer and recover your child, I can perhaps do some research and arrange meetings."

I couldn't let that happen. This needed to end tonight. If someone else won this auction, it wasn't a job for lawyers or venture capital dragons. I'd have to make sure the winning creature didn't leave the place alive so I could go home with my son... though I didn't know how I was going to do that yet. Hansel wasn't kidding about being on my own. If we lost the bidding, it would be me versus a party full of monsters and cultists.

"I need to come up with a strategy. I don't suppose that you'd be willing to tell me more about what currency these supernatural underworld lords deal in?"

He frowned. "I don't see any reason to do so."

"Maybe I can bring some? Perhaps it could make the difference?"

Hansel shook his head. "It would not. In this, Management is moderately wealthy and you're a pauper."

"It's like this though. We Shacklefords pay our way and carry our weight. If Management is willing to exchange something very valuable for my son's freedom, I should know so I can repay him. This transaction is on my behalf. If the transaction's that dirty, I need to know."

"If you are certain, it's one of those things that once learned can't be unlearned. It's a world you Hunters know nothing of. Something that maybe even your government knows nothing of."

"Tell me," I said and was surprised at how firm my voice was.

"Very well." He touched the tips of his fingers together as he held his hands above the briefcase. "Here it is. What these creatures deal in is power and . . . well, humans."

"You mean like slavery?"

He sighed. "There is some of that, though perhaps not in the sense you mean. Not so much owning humans' bodies. That comes along with what they really own, which is their freedom and autonomy, their minds and, though the word is inadequate, souls." He continued, unaware—probably unaware—of the chill running up my spine. "But those aren't as valuable as you would think. After all, anyone likely to trade away his soul was probably already going to lose it anyway."

I thought about poor dumb Benno getting dragged off to whatever weird realm that had been. Then I looked down at the lawyer's contract in my hand and shuddered.

"There are other goods that can be sold in bulk. You get—how do I put this?—power from corrupting the minds of children. Say a being convinces millions of innocents that one of the cardinal sins is a virtue. That gives them power, and that influence can be traded. But there is more direct currency than that. Certain beings achieve mind dominion and control over multitudes, by magic or by illicit drugs or many other ways. Items of magical power, curses, books of spells, weapons of mass destruction, entire criminal enterprises—human trafficking and drug supply chains mostly—basically anything that supernatural creatures can control will be offered. Do you understand now?"

"Kind of." My voice failed. I understood enough to know it was probably immoral to be getting my son back at this kind of expense. I wasn't sure how this worked exactly, but whatever Management was going to give to Brother Death on my behalf was dangerous and immoral, and it would stain my soul.

I weighed it all, wishing I could be so fine, so noble, as to say, "No, no, I don't want to benefit from that." But I couldn't. My son was my family and mine to guard. I knew that my title of Guardian referred only to the artifact at my side . . . which was fine. But it didn't matter. I'd accept the stain on my soul, the feeling of becoming a little more of a monster myself, as long as it got my son back, costs be damned. I can say I was fine with dying or worse as long as innocent Ray was okay. At least one of us would escape this.

"Knowing Management owns some of those *assets* makes me like him a lot less."

Hansel pursed his lips. "Yes and no. Management has a diversified portfolio. Surely you understand, he couldn't have run casinos in Las Vegas without having his talons in various criminal pies. For the most part, he is one of my more virtuous clients. However, what he's actually bringing to the table are several potions, magically charged, some of which contain very dark magic, including several vials from one of the principals in the Affair of the Poisons. There are poisons there that will kill people in horrible ways, potions that will make people lose all free will and transfer all their financial assets to less than trustworthy kin, or to make them fall in love with the person who feeds them this. I am not sure you get all the implications or even—"

"I'm not stupid. I get it. If we bid them and we win the bidding, we'll be giving Brother Death—an extremely evil son of a bitch—a lot of power over innocents."

His eyes were very intent on mine, not letting me look away. "Yes, and I want to emphasize that with all that, winning the auction is still your best option. If you do not sign my contract, you'll be forced to go in, guns blazing, to a gathering of very high level power players, all of whom will have human security or some manner of supernatural protection. There is no assurance that you will get your baby out alive, and you will most surely die in the process."

Even with a full team a rescue would be dicey. To even be feasible it would have to be a team of our best, experienced Hunters. I didn't have that. The best Hunters in the world were—heaven willing still alive—on Severny Island, incommunicado, cut off from the world. The team Dorcas had scrambled to help me was probably being detained in Germany, and I couldn't risk contacting any of the EU-based hunting companies because that might end up with a bunch of government agents arresting me. I suppose I could have called on Grant again, but he was on the other side of the world, and *if* he helped, it would just jeopardize his position with the MCB.

"Fine. Winning the bid is plan A. It isn't like Brother Death doesn't already have mind control powers anyway. Once I get Ray back safe, then I can focus on hunting Brother Death down and returning Management's property."

"That isn't necessary—"

"Oh, it very much is."

Though Hansel was a lawyer rather than a cosmic horror, poor Benno was still a good reminder of what happened when you entered into binding agreements carelessly. So I read through the rest of the contract carefully. Hansel held out a gold pen.

"Okay. You try to win Ray. We'll pay whatever you can bring to bear, no matter how nasty it is. In the near future, we'll kill Brother Death and get it back before he can cause too much harm with it." That made me think about the artifact at my side and a very uncomfortable possible plan B.

He didn't say anything. I could tell from the way he looked at me that he thought it was futile and probably stupid of me to think I could simply kill all my problems away but, you know what, it had worked for us for many a year. If he thought it was a job too big for just me or even for all of MHI, he didn't know us very well at all. Once Ray was home safe and once our people were back from Severny—our people would be back!—I would make sure that everyone involved in this wretched auction scene died. That's what my family did. We killed monsters so normal people could sleep safe at home. I'd do it again, and if I failed to kill them all, then someday Ray would do it, or his sons, or their sons and daughters. Until every last monster was eradicated once and for all.

Because that's what Hunters do.

I took Hansel's pen and signed the contract.

CHAPTER 15

Our destination was a large home in a nice part of the city. It was three stories tall with a flat roof. The plaza grounds were made of that inlaid black and white stone you see on some older sidewalks in Europe; it was extensively landscaped, and palm trees swaying gently in the breeze.

Hansel escorted me inside, into a sort of atrium. From there, a hallway led to a staircase, big, marble and winding. It was truly a beautiful home, only from the lack of personalization or mess, it felt like no one actually lived there.

"This is one of Management's many investment properties," Hansel explained. "Though he can never visit any of his holdings, he enjoys collecting real estate."

It had a kitchen you could have fit an entire floor of my house into, and please keep in mind I lived in an antebellum mansion. "It must suck to be him."

"I will stay here and prepare while you get cleaned up and dressed."

"Speaking of preparations?"

"Ah yes, I was informed of your shopping requests.

I'm afraid I'm a lawyer, not a gun runner. I do not care for the things. So I could not get you a suit of armor and a bazooka, or whatever it was you wanted."

I was down to a few rounds of .45 for my gun, and a partially expended mag for the stolen Walther. "If we lose this auction, what am I supposed to use— harsh language?"

"Considering that some of the guests will possess claws, fangs, or magical powers, Brother Death's security won't look too askance at a human possessing a discreet handgun politely concealed. Anything more than that they would frown upon. I don't know much about such things, but I asked a favor of one of my other clients and he loaned me something that he described as rather *classy*."

I sighed. Since it was one of his asshole clients, that meant it was probably from a snooty billionaire's collection, so it would be covered in gold and ivory and, considering their goofy European gun laws, probably carry five rounds and be chambered in something odd and anemic like a .32 Pillow Fighter. Worst-case scenario I could put it in a sock and beat them with it.

"I'll take what I can get."

"I'll retrieve it while you are getting cleaned up." He sniffed disapprovingly at my blood-stained novelty sweater.

The staff was quiet, efficient, and perfectly trained. When they asked if I had any requests, I surprised them with an odd one. I showed the butler the artifact. Despite being super-ancient evil and capable of all sorts of craziness, it really didn't look like much in the hand. I might be able to use that to my advantage. "I need you to find me a rock or a piece of stone that looks close to this. It doesn't need to be perfect, just good enough that a quick glance could mistake the two. And I need it for tonight."

"I will see what I can do, madam."

A woman led me to a guest room. They'd even gotten towels warmed for me while I took a shower. Remarkably, in the time it took the limo to pick me up in Cannes, they'd picked out and bought a black cocktail dress for me, laid it out with the appropriate undergarments and a set of jewelry which was way more expensive than anything I'd ever seen outside of TV.

Examining myself in the mirror after the shower, I confirmed that the Guardian's marks on my abdomen and neck had grown a bit. The skin atop the new shrapnel wounds was perfectly smooth, but black as ebony. Other than that, I was covered in scratches, scrapes, and a whole bunch of bruises. I looked like crap.

Back in the guest room, I looked at the dress, thinking it was really pretty, and definitely not what I'd choose to go into battle in, but Management had tried to warn me about the dress code. I hated going into the fight of my life without so much as a bulletproof vest. The dress fit perfectly and really accentuated my figure, which made me wonder just how well Management kept tabs on us that he knew my measurements.

"May I help Madame with her hair and makeup now?" a young woman in a white smock asked, appearing—of course—at just the perfect time.

I nodded and sat down in front of the vanity while she piled my hair on top of my head, making it look way sexier than anything I ever managed to do on my own. It was obvious she was a top-flight professional, something that became even more obvious when she moved on to my makeup.

"That won't be necessary. I'll be wearing a mask."

"My employer's message was very specific that I must do my best."

I might as well make the dragon happy. "Can you hide these scratches?" I gestured toward where the Tokoloshe had tried to claw my eyes out.

"Easily." And she went to work.

I know that my husband thinks I'm so beautiful and amazing. Frankly, I've always thought I have an average face, but nothing to write home about. However, the way the makeup specialist outlined my eyes, and applied just a touch of color to my cheeks and the space between eye and eyebrow, everything just came to life. What I mean is, when you first saw me, I didn't even look made up. Just five years younger and a million times prettier than the real me.

While I was staring at the mirror, I felt her fingers on my neck, and turned, saying "Hey!" before I realized she was carefully applying some kind of concealer to the Guardian marks.

Her fingers stopped. Her eyes met my gaze in the mirror. "I was told Madame would be incognita... not under her own name or her own appearance. These tattoos are very distinctive, and I was told they must be hidden."

She was right. "Carry on." And she did. By the time she was done, the exposed skin on my neck looked smooth and exactly the same color as the rest of my body. I could still feel the marks there, warm and tingly, like a living thing. But no one would be able to see them.

As the hair and makeup virtuoso helped me put on my—or at least my borrowed—jewelry, it occurred to me it was like I was getting ready for the prom of the damned.

I wasn't wrong.

After refusing the several pairs of high heels that were offered to me—if I had to run for my life it would not be in stupid horror movie heels—I finally consented to a pair of easy slip-on flats. I'm nearly six feet tall. I can get by without heels.

There was a fur stole for me to use. It was shiny, sleek and silvery, and I'd bet real money it was made from the skins of baby seals who had been slowly clubbed to death. Slowly, to make the suffering last. When the makeup girl left, I told Mr. Trash Bags to make himself at home as a liner to the fur stole. If he complained, it was the sort of under-the-breath muttering where I couldn't even understand the words.

Management emailed me a map of the convent and some photos of the interior. He'd marked the route to the lamia den. Unfortunately, there were no maps of the underground passages, so if Ray and I had to go that way, we'd have to wing it.

This place had such a nice variety of rocks around it, the butler didn't take very long to find me one that was a close approximation to the Kumaresh Yar. It wouldn't pass even the most cursory close inspection by anybody who knew anything about black magic, but I figured it wouldn't hurt to have something I could flash to pull a fast bait and switch.

The real artifact went to Mr. Trash Bags with orders to defend it as well as he could. It probably made a slight bulge underneath the fur, but honestly, the fur was so thick that you'd have to look really close to notice it. Those clubbed baby seals have extra thick fur, possibly in a vain attempt to keep themselves from the clubbing.

"No matter what happens, you keep hold of this. Hide it. Don't let the bad guys see it. Okay?"

"Okay."

"Good boy."

"Mr. Trash Bags. GOOD BOY."

The lawyer had left a small metal gun box on the table downstairs. Expecting ostentatious junk, I opened it, looked it over—a pistol, a bunch of extra mags already loaded, so brand-new it still even had the invoice—then gave an appreciative whistle.

Hansel came in, now dressed in an immaculate tuxedo. "Is this to your liking?"

"Yeah." I pulled the pistol out and worked the slide to make sure the chamber was empty. I usually built my own guns—I'm a 1911 girl—but this was good.

"I was told this was a suitable weapon."

"No kidding. It's a Grayguns Compact custom P320 with a reflex sight."

"I'm afraid I do not know what any of those words mean."

"It means it's pretty damned solid and been worked over by someone who knows what they're doing." I didn't normally run a micro red-dot sight on my handguns, but I'd practiced with them enough to get over the learning curve. I checked the chamber again out of habit, picked a target—that potted plant would do—and dry-fired. *Click.* Flat trigger, good geometry, very nice.

"I assumed all your clients were assholes, but at least one of them has excellent taste in working guns."

"He has several of these. Like you, he is a professional, but in a very different and unrelated field."

"Come on, Hansel, you can admit you know John Wick."

"Who?"

"The guy, they killed his dog..."

"That sounds terrible."

"Never mind." There were ten magazines already loaded with 115 grain Federal hollowpoints. Great for humans, and I just had to hope there weren't any werewolves invited to the party. I took some mags out and started sticking them into Hansel's jacket pocket.

"What do you think you are doing?"

"Look at this dress. Where exactly do you think I'm going to hide all this stuff?"

"These are besom pockets. You'll ruin the lines! I am your bidder, not your Sherpa."

He was going to be my hostage if he didn't shut up, but the scowl I gave him must have convinced him that I meant business.

On the limo ride to the convent, I walked Hansel through plans B and C, then I used the untraceable phone to call back to base. It was late here, so it would be afternoon in Alabama...I think. I'd been in too many time zones in the last twenty-four hours to keep up. It was to tell them what I was about to do, but I was hoping for good news. I'd be ecstatic if somehow Owen had come back. As much as I hated to drop this in his lap, I would be so grateful to have him here.

But when I called, I got the young orc, Shelly. "MHI busy please hold for person talk."

If Dorcas had an orc manning the phones, things were tight. "Shelly, it's me, Julie. I'm still trying to get Ray back."

She seemed overjoyed to hear from me, distraught at my not having yet recovered my son, and told me, "Is much important get back great hero baby!"

I didn't know if she thought Ray was the hero, or that meant me, or Owen, or what. When I asked about Dorcas, Shelly immediately dropped the phone and went to get her. I gave her the quick version. Dorcas, too, was disappointed that I didn't have little Ray with me, and by disappointed you should read mad as fire and swearing up a blue streak.

"Goddamn no good monster motherfuckers." And that's even angrier in Southern-grandma voice. "What would a bunch of greasy assholes want with our baby?"

That was a rhetorical question. She'd seen some horrible things in her time. "I'm going to try and win him back, but I'm willing to bet my mother will have a representative there. She might even be there herself."

"That bitch is not your mother. Your mother was one of the most wonderful women who ever walked the Earth. That's a demon in your mother's body."

"I know," I said patiently. "But it thinks she's my mother and is trying to be a great mother, just like the real one was, which means she wants little Ray to bring up her way and not mine." I waited till the cursing stopped, and then I asked, "How's your head?"

There was a cackle. "I'm fine, girl. It takes more than a concussion to sideline me."

I could tell she wasn't telling me the truth. "Dorcas..."

"Okay, he hit me hard enough I've gone blind in one eye, but, don't worry, one of the orcs said my vision will probably return, and it ain't even my shooting eye. By the time you bring Ray home, I'll be back to normal. And you'd better be back here with that little boy, you hear me?"

"Yes, ma'am." From how jittery she sounded I suspected she was running entirely on coffee and energy drinks. "How's Albert?"

"You want to speak to him? The egghead is back in his library, ready to help."

I thought I must have misheard. "He got shot in the *chest*. Like yesterday! He can't possibly be back at work."

"Well, he wouldn't be if the MCB hadn't stepped in and told the cops to make the whole thing go away. Next thing I know he stumbles in here, pale as a ghost, still wearing a gown, bleeding through his bandages, carrying his own IV, and that tough little bastard declared, 'somebody get me an orc healer, 'cause Julie needs my help.'"

"Wow."

Hansel was sitting across from me. He recognized my shocked expression. "What is wrong?"

"My coworkers are incredibly badass," I told him.

"One of Gretchen's sisters mixed up some evil-smelling potion to slather him in, complaining about how useless human doctors were the whole time. He looks like shit, can't hardly move, but says he's ready to go."

"I'd love to talk to Albert, thank you. And you take care of yourself, you hear?"

Moments later Albert picked up.

"What the hell is wrong with you?" I demanded. "Why aren't you in the hospital?"

"I could lay in a bed there useless, or I could be here ready to help. I'm hopped up on orc potions, I've got a chair with wheels, and a troll for an assistant... I'm ready to rock."

He didn't sound good. He sounded like death warmed over. He sounded like he was trying to talk without moving too fast.

"You lost a lot of blood."

"And they put more in. Now you want to talk about business or our feelings?"

"You're brave when you're on painkillers."

"I'm flying high, boss. I got your last report. The thing you blew up in France is a *bicho-papão*. It's a category of fey who get called upon to correct egregious crimes. Stuff I found was that he punishes children who refuse to take naps. Our ancestors must have been crazy. What are you going after now?"

I gave him the quick recap.

He was quiet a long time. "I don't want to rain on your parade, Julie, but while Management isn't one of the bad guys, that doesn't necessarily make him one of the good guys either. He's helping fund the attack on Asag, but he's still a dragon. How many stories do you know from history where the dragon was the good guy?"

I looked over at Hansel who was politely staring at the window. "I think he's okay. Speaking of..."

"Nada on Severny. The way it's locked up, either the Russians are jamming it or there's a supernatural communications lock."

"Or our people are dead."

"If they were dead, there wouldn't be anything to block. When have you heard of a bad guy not gloating?"

"Oh. True." That gave me hope for the first time in a long time. "Is the New York team still stuck in Germany?"

"SJK arrested them. They can hold them for another twenty-four hours without charges, and if you're not caught by then, they'll probably just make some charges up. The French government is pissed off too. You blew up their favorite informant."

"He deserved it."

"Sounds like fun."

"You know very well I'm not having any fun. Did you get briefed on my main target?"

"Brother Death. From the mind control and the fireflies, he's probably an *Adze*. Problem is, they're super rare and almost unheard of operating outside of Africa. There wasn't a whole lot about them in the archives."

I knew how Al worked. He did this weird, hyperfocus thing, where he'd study something around the clock, chasing down threads. It shouldn't have surprised me that he wouldn't let a little thing like a sucking chest wound get in the way. "What've you got so far?"

"Sunlight doesn't harm them. The tribes who got tormented by these things didn't have a good way to stop them. Supposedly if you learned their real name, if you said it, it would stun them for a minute so you could get away. It was supposed to freeze them and stop them from using any of their powers, but not for long."

"Which is why this particular asshole uses a nom de plume."

"They're always described as petty, spiteful things. They would possess people and then use them to cause all sorts of trouble, then dump the bodies when they got bored. The sign that an *Adze* is getting to somebody is that their eyes turn a weird green."

I remembered that Wynne had oddly bright green eyes when we'd first met, and though I'd not caught it at the time, they'd been a normal blue as he'd died. "Did Amanda have in colored contacts?"

"Good guess. The orcs found them before they burned her, which means our bad guy is smart enough to use modern methods to compensate. That's just for the living though. Supposedly they can take over a corpse with impunity, so watch out for zombie meat puppets too. It's unclear how many living people an *Adze* can influence at once, but all the legends make it sound like the lazier and stupider you are, the easier you are to grab, while those with good character take a lot more time and effort to wear down. Of course, that might just be moralizing creeping into the old stories; you know how that goes."

"Amanda was solid, so assume he was right under our noses for a while."

"All accounts agree they can use black magic, so watch out for that. Some of the legends say they can summon ghosts if they're in a place with enough latent magical energy. They're supposed to be great at hiding, but at night the *Adze* would come out in their true form to sneak into the villages to drink blood and spread disease. Anthropologists thought that they were just stories to explain away malaria and bad luck, but I've got a partial handwritten report here that your grandpa fought one in the Congo back in the sixties."

For the briefest instant, I thought to myself, *Good, I'll just ask him about it,* but then I remembered he was dead. It was a sudden gut punch. "All I need to know is, is he killable and how?"

"I don't know. The Boss said they shot it with a ton of silver, but it turned into a cloud of fireflies and got away. It'll re-form if even one of them escapes. He thought maybe if it was stunned with its name first, it wouldn't be able to escape but he never got to test the theory. The contract got pulled and they had to flee the country. Political stuff. Very *Dogs of War.*"

"Look, Al, this might not go well for me. If I don't make it, we need to put somebody else on the trail. The only thing that matters is getting Ray back."

"Dorcas is piecing together another team from all over and will be flying them to Lisbon, and this time it's off the books. Screw the officials. They're just tourists. They'll find weapons when they get there. We've also got calls on the down low to European Hunters we trust to get there. You'll have help by tomorrow, but for tonight's party you are shit out of luck."

"It sucks being on your own," I muttered, then I looked over at the lawyer. "No offense."

"None taken," Hansel said. "I am content not to count in that particular equation."

"There is one weird possibility for help though. That douchebag Grant left for Europe after he got the charges against me dropped. I trust him less than the dragon, but he's already there, probably with the idea of helping you. Word is he went off on his own, without MCB approval."

That was kind of surprising. "He's probably going to get eaten by Franks when he comes back."

"He might have ended up with an official excuse though. Something is going on in Portugal. The area of Porto has had several supernatural incidents in the last few hours and it's now moving south."

"That's probably related to Brother Death's invitation."

"Regardless, they're having problems. Word is that ASS is asking for assistance."

Okay, now I knew I had misheard. "Ass?" I asked hesitantly.

"Oh, yeah, the Portuguese counterpart of MCB."

"But ASS?"

"Well, it doesn't mean that in Portuguese. It's the Agencia de Segurança Sobrenatural. Of course, the MCB call it PASS, i.e. Portuguese ASS, but Earl says that's nonsense and calls it Portass."

"Earl would." Horrible phrases were coming through my mind. *We pulled the information out of ASS.* If the MCB got a message saying *ASS got pounded this weekend,* would the sender be bragging or explaining why MCB should not count on backup?

"The important thing is that ASS called for advisory assistance, and an MCB agent happened to already be in the area, so Grant got seconded to them. From what I've heard he'd just barely gotten off the plane when the MCB director ordered Grant to help a private company there called Dark Fate on some containment."

In hunting circles, other companies were, as Earl said, either "assholes" or "all right." I didn't know where that company fit. "Dark Fate? That's a stupid name. I've never heard of them."

"I haven't either, but that should give Grant some official clout with the local officials. He might even be able to get the EU agencies off your back."

This would be a lot easier if I wasn't worried about getting arrested. "Maybe I should call him."

"Or he might just rat you out the second you talk to him, to curry favor with his bosses. Your call."

The auction would be held at the stroke of midnight. I couldn't let the government interrupt that and endanger Ray, but afterwards . . . I hated changing plans on the fly, but time was short and options few. "This is what you're going to do. At exactly ten minutes after midnight my time, I want you to call Grant, give him an anonymous tip, tell him where I'm at, and that the place will be swimming in monsters."

"Can do. He'll send in the cavalry."

And I'd either already be on my way to the airport with Ray in my arms, or I'd be dead and Grant could zip my corpse into a rubber bag.

"We are almost at our destination," Hansel warned me.

"Okay. Al, I've got to go. Don't work too hard."

"Don't worry. If I work too hard right now, I just pass out, so it's self-correcting."

"I'll remember this at bonus time."

"You'd better." Albert turned solemn. "Be careful, Julie."

CHAPTER 16

The houses started looking older as we got closer to the convent. Not old old, in the sense of dilapidated, just old in the sense that most of them had been built before the twentieth century and probably before the nineteenth. Knowing vaguely about Portuguese history, I thought that they'd probably been built in the eighteenth century, at the height of Portuguese wealth, when gold from the colonies was falling like a torrential rain upon the continent. These were the types of buildings that American tourists saw, and which greatly impressed them with the wealth of socialist systems, never mind that pretty much all of them had been built before Marxism was a glimmer in Karl's eye.

"This place we are going was partially destroyed in the great earthquake of 1755. The city lost a few hundred feet to the sea. There were stories of submerged churches, the bells ringing with the movement of the waves," Hansel told me.

So perhaps the buildings around us, four or five stories tall and made of pale golden stone were part of the reconstruction after the quake. They were clearly built to last, foursquare and solid, looking like they'd weather the centuries without a change. Around them, though, was superimposed the pattern of a modern European city: multilane streets clogged with tiny cars, tying themselves in knots around multilane, incomprehensible roundabouts. Despite the rock-steady driving of our chauffeur, the Portuguese had perhaps half the restraint and respect for human life of Italian drivers.

My mind wandered. There wasn't a car seat in the limo... Ray should ride in a car seat—I should have thought of that—but if there had been an empty one there, it would've just taunted me. And that was assuming that I'd get him back at all... My nerves were shot. At least talking to my people had kept me focused.

I put the decorative mask on and tied the silken cord tight. Sadly, that meant my glasses had to go into the purse next to the Grayguns Sig. Purse carry is stupid, give me a real holster anytime, but in a dress like this it was my only option. Without my glasses things were going to be a little blurry for a while. Looking up, I met Hansel's worried smile.

"Ready?" he asked.

"As ready as I'm going to be." I wouldn't admit my heart was speeding up in my chest, my hands were sweaty, and I just wanted my baby back.

I'd faced armies of monsters with less trepidation. I'd been fighting them since I was a kid. But this, this was more important than all those battles, all those dangers. This one was for my son. For my family. I felt Mr. Trash Bags tremble against me under the fur stole, and I wondered if he was going to give vent to his desire to eat noses and toes. But something—perhaps my tensing up—must have warned him and he stayed quiet.

The limo stopped. The chauffeur opened my door and handed me out.

We stood in a street with older houses, though some of them were not the towering golden buildings, but humbler ones whitewashed with tile roofs.

It was dark and a cool wind had picked up. I turned to look at the ruins of the ancient church.

That first glimpse was hard to describe. The earthquake, or a minor one later on, had stripped the church of all extraneous material, leaving only the bones of the building as it were: soaring arches rising to the sky, as though they were intended as a monument to despair, to portray all those who had asked for help from God and been denied. It was beautiful and cold and stark, with something faintly wrong about it, something that promoted thoughts of loss. I shivered.

Hansel adjusted my stole, as though he were a servant or one of those people hired to do hair and makeup. "Just be calm."

"I am calm."

"Your body language says you are ready for a fight."

"I'm calm when I fight."

"Please, just let me do the talking."

Other limos were stopping in front of the building. A crowd was forming. Sure enough, most of them were wearing decorative masks. We joined the line coming in behind a tall, squarish man who was speaking in rapid-fire Russian to another taller, squarer man. One of them said something that sounded like an insult, then spit on the sidewalk.

I wondered if these were human players, perhaps members of the Russian mafia—did the Russian mafia play in the supernatural? I'd have to ask Krasnov—or if these were supernatural beings wearing human disguise. Many creatures without a shred of humanity in them will wear the mask of humanity to do what they want to undetected. They got good at it because they had to. Anyone meeting the Queen of the Enchanted Forest would take her for a trailer park inhabitant, with all the usual vices. The fact that she was a four-hundred-year-old elf with actual working magic wasn't obvious. I remembered how many times I'd been reluctant to go to the trailer park, knowing I'd pay respects in the form of cigarettes and booze, and have to put up with the queen's incontinent dogs. In retrospect, the Enchanted Forest seemed downright homey compared to this.

The people, or whatever they were ahead of me, were all very well dressed, glittering like the cream of society, the apex of human life, when many of them probably weren't human at all. As we got further away from potential witnesses, the attendees got weirder. Ahead of the Russian speakers was a man who was a dead ringer for a Hollywood actor. His name escaped me because, frankly, I just don't watch that many movies. Owen does, and I sit with him because I enjoy his company. On the actor's—or disturbingly close look-alike's—arm was something so tall and thin that I knew she couldn't be human. Yeah, I know we all make jokes about how thin models are and how fragile they look, but trust me, in this case it really was impossible. If she was a human, she would have to carry her internal organs in a backpack or something. Her waist must have had a circumference of ten inches. She had wings coming off her shoulders, veined with red but otherwise looking much like fly wings. Without my glasses it was hard to tell, but I'm pretty sure those weren't decorative.

When they got to the head of the line, the two very large men who were checking the guest list motioned the star through but put a hand on the chest of his companion, pushing her back.

The actor turned around, putting his arm around her. "You shall not divide us."

The guard bent slightly and spoke to him in a quiet voice. The actor looked anguished. "But she must come with me. She's here to ensure I am safe."

The guard said something else, and the creature with the wings gave what sounded like a loud whistle, and then split apart. I don't know how else to describe it. One moment she was there, tall, blonde, and slender as supermodels dream of being, tottering on impossibly high heels and acting like she owned the Earth, with her creepy wings flapping in the cold wind, and the next moment she dissolved into countless pieces, each of the pieces an angry, buzzing fly. The flies held the shape of her body for a few moments, then spread all over, like black contrails over the crowd and towards the sky.

As the final flies zoomed away, the actor stared, dejected, like someone had broken his little red wagon.

We were close enough now I could hear the doorman. He spoke in English with an accent I couldn't place. "Brother Death stated that none of his kin are welcome. This auction must be carried out in the most aboveboard way possible."

There were whispers and talk up and down the line, and under the cover of the chatter, Hansel leaned close and said, "A goddess of the Salt River. Chinese. Very ancient. Older than mankind."

"Lovely," I said. If that was considered *kin*, that just meant that I knew even less about my target than I thought I did.

One of the Russians looked over his shoulder to check me out. He even elbowed his companion to take a look. To be fair, I really was rocking this dress.

As we got nearer, I hoped Management's mask would be enough to stop whatever magical scrutiny we were being subjected to. Not that I was an ancient salt goddess of the rivers or whatever, but I was probably something much worse as far as they were concerned: the true "owner" of the goods about to be put on auction.

The actor went through, his shoulders slumped, and the Russian speakers gave their names. I was now close enough to see that the door guards were, in fact, not human at all. I really missed my glasses. Instead of flesh, Brother Death's security seemed to be made out of a light tan clay. Golems? But they weren't clumsy like a golem. They were wearing black suits, and they were intelligent enough to communicate politely and read invitations.

My mind started flipping through all my monster lore. Lots of cultures had stories about animated creatures, though I didn't know of any from Africa. Not that they needed to be from Brother Death's original area of operations, of course. A monster could learn and obviously some traded with each other. If there was a good idea, they'd steal it. Anything that helped them survive or become more powerful would be adopted. A long-lived monster was usually big on multiculturalism.

More people had come up behind us, all black ties, beautiful dresses, and ornate masks. I wished I could tell who they were.

"What's wrong, Julie?" Hansel asked.

"I'm worried I'm going to bump into my mother." I wondered if she would recognize me. Sure, I was wearing a disguise, but what mother wouldn't know her own daughter?

"Do not fear. This is the *mundane* entrance. For guests of her stature, there is a special entrance."

"Stature, huh?"

"Yes. I'm afraid she's become something of a celebrity in this particular subculture."

Figures. As a human, Mom had always been an overachiever. Why would Vampire Mom be any different?

The golem—or whatever it was—took a gilt-edged card from Hansel's hand, then it looked at both of us. Despite it being dark out, they were wearing sunglasses. If it wasn't for their skin they would appear to be ordinary-looking men, shaved heads, bland features—in fact, they could be twins—but this close I could tell their flesh had the texture of a fired clay pot. Gargoyles were made of stone but had molten joints. I couldn't tell how these bent, but from the way they moved their fingers and elbows, and tilted their heads to read, they were flexible, though they looked dry and hard.

I had to resist the urge to reach out and poke one.

It was hard to tell with the shades, but it was clear that it was looking me up and down, then giving the same treatment to Hansel. He didn't check my purse for a gun, and he didn't pat down my stole to check for a shoggoth and a doomsday artifact. These things were less invasive than the TSA. At long last, it passed the invitation card to his counterpart across the doorway and said, in the tone of someone who had reached a conclusion, "An assistant of Management, and Management's guest."

The other one rumbled, a low, in-the-throat noise that sounded like the beginning notes of a song, and then they both stepped aside. Hansel and I entered.

We were walking on smooth, evenly cropped green grass, so smooth and evenly cropped it was obvious someone must cut it regularly and also seed it and look after it. The effect, given the attire of the people and creatures around was that of a high-class building with green carpet.

First I'll have to explain the setup of the ruined church. It had the traditional gothic layout, with two side naves and a central one. The naves were separated from the center part by columns which also rose up to support the multiple peaks onto which there had once been a roof. And both side naves were divided into multiple bays.

I supposed, when it had been in use, all of the main body of the building would have been filled with pews. Now there were none. There wasn't even an altar, though in front of where the two secondary altars would have been, there were interruptions in the turf that looked suspiciously like tombstones. Nothing strange there, of course, as ancient churches often had tombs in them, but for some reason it made a shiver chase up and down my spine.

There was no altar, but someone had put up what looked like a Lucite table. Behind that, there was a deep red curtain. I looked frantically around for Ray, but I couldn't see him. I couldn't hear him either. I realized my ears had been perked up for any sound of him since I'd entered the place. But of course he wouldn't be here, would he? I mean, there being no honor among monsters, the seller—Brother Death, I presumed—wouldn't bring him in until the auction was about to start. After all, what if some of the bidders had come prepared to take him by force?

Like I would if Hansel couldn't win this damned thing.

We were met by a little man as impeccably dressed as Management's servants and—from his body language— as well-mannered and devoted to service too. Except when I say *little man*, I mean little. He looked vaguely gnomelike, was maybe two feet and a half tall, but no beard or hat, was green, and had pointy ears. The ears were hairy. They flicked up and down as he bowed to us.

"Monsieur, madame," he said in unaccented French and then gestured for us to follow.

As we walked across the grass, I became aware of a strange phenomenon. There were portions of the side naves which were simply not visible. They weren't covered; there wasn't any kind of curtain obscuring them. There was just this sense that when you looked at them there was nothing there. By which I don't mean it looked as if the church ruins were empty, but more like they too were not there. Like there was nothing there. No stone, no grass, really noth-ing...just an empty space, devoid of matter. It was an interesting effect, and I was sure it was some kind of magic which would keep the auction participants from seeing each other.

Our guide asked Hansel if he cared to socialize with the other guests, or if he'd like to be shown to his seats. Thankfully the lawyer wasn't much for socializing.

There were more of the clay men inside, all of them dressed in identical black suits, looking so similar that I suspected they were created by pouring something into a mold. There was one of them stationed near each nave.

I tried not to get caught looking, but that wasn't hard, since a few of the other guests were openly gawking at the creatures. Those guests must have been new to this kind of thing. They were rich assholes wanting to play in a dangerous and mysterious world... If I did need to go to my gun, I wasn't going to worry in the least about collateral damage. I just followed the little man to a nave where there was a delicate golden table, small and high like you'd find in high-class cafes. Next to it were two chairs of the same design. The table had a tray set on it with what would be, in any other party of this kind—not the prom of the damned but just a black-tie party—appetizers. The triangles looked like some kind of chip covered in artistic bits of sauce of various colors and olives.

It was probably just regular food, but you know what? I had seen the contents of the *bicho-papão*'s refrigerator, and I had absolutely zero intention of partaking of anything in this place. Besides, my stomach was churning.

Either Hansel was too nervous to eat or he also didn't trust the food because he made an exclamation of disgust and thrust the tray aside before sitting down. Mr. Trash Bags probably would have eaten them, but he was being a good little shoggoth and staying hidden in the furs.

When I looked straight up, the starry sky was visible through the arches of the ruins.

While we waited, I tried to count potential threats. It was difficult because the same sort of thing that protected the other bidders from view also blocked our view in every direction save one: we could see clearly to the center back of the church, where the altar would normally be and where the strange table was now placed.

We could hear the other guests, but the sounds seemed unnaturally muted, like everyone was whispering. They'd probably done that for our privacy. The attorney was really good at keeping his expression neutral, but I noticed sweat droplets forming on his brow above the mask.

"How are you doing, Mr. Hansel?"

"I am merely thinking through the repercussions if this does not go as I hope. And you?"

"The same." Though I was sure we were coming to vastly different conclusions.

At one point, a tentacle, presumably from the nave next to us, came squelching and questing along the ground towards the base of our table. It looked like a normal octopus tentacle, only enormous, easily as big around as my arm, and it was dripping wet, leaving a puddle of salt water behind. It started towards my foot, and Hansel moved like lightning. He grabbed the appetizer tray and bought it down edge first onto the tentacle, in the process upending all the appetizers onto the grass.

The tentacle immediately curled into an offended shape and then retreated back to the other side.

"Sorry." Hansel told me as if he'd broken etiquette. "Such things make me very uncomfortable."

There was no complaint from the next partition, just a sort of wet snuffling.

Silence reigned for a long time.

A bell rang at midnight.

Then the curtain behind the table opened with a flourish and out stepped the tallest, darkest man I'd ever seen. He was shirtless, and every visible portion of his skin had been oiled so that he seemed to shine with a light of his own. He was physical perfection, too perfect to be human. And that was confirmed when he turned so I could see his eyes, too large and blood-red, and when he smiled, it revealed long narrow teeth that gave him the look of having a mouth full of needles.

It was Brother Death.

He was holding my baby.

CHAPTER 17

"Ladies and gentlemen, beings from other realms, Hell spawn, fey, and everything in between..." It was undeniably the same voice I'd heard on the phone. I couldn't figure out how he spoke so clearly with a mouth full of needles. "I am Brother Death. Welcome."

I took in every detail of my son's appearance. The weird thing is that he seemed so normal. You know, exactly like he looked at home. He was wearing a disposable diaper, a little blue T-shirt, and he looked chubby and contented, if a little sleepy. I wondered if it was a simulacrum, like how he'd deceived me earlier, but surely Brother Death wouldn't dare do that to this level of evil players, right? Surely he wouldn't. This really had to be Ray.

It took everything I had not to walk out of the nave shooting. I must have tensed up because Hansel reached over and put one firm hand on my arm. He shook his head. "Give me a chance. Please."

"I am pleased so many illustrious guests were able to join us tonight, as well as some newcomers. Others were unable to come themselves but have sent representatives in their stead. We have a few newcomers who simply wish to observe the festivities. All are welcome here in the spirit of peace and cooperation. I thank you for temporarily putting aside your differences. Let there be no conflict between us tonight."

Brother Death set Ray down, facing us, on the table, then took a package of raisins from his pants pocket and shook a few out in front of Ray. When he saw the raisins, Ray's eyes lit up and he started taking one at a time and putting them in his mouth, munching contentedly. Ray was acting like he couldn't see the rest of us—I'm sure he would have looked at what must be a really strange assemblage of people and things—but instead, he acted like he was alone in the church.

"I offer for auction a healthy baby male, six months old. This is the offspring of two faction champions. This is the son of a Guardian and a Chosen, blessed of mankind, descended from a long line of Hunters, imbued with all the magic you would expect from such a momentous bloodline. As you can see, he is in perfect condition."

He'd better be.

There was a question from one of the secret nave bays. It was a strange voice, high and balloon juicy with what seemed like an undertone of snickering. "How do we know he's the genuine article and undefiled? If he's been touched by magic, other than that of his breeding, his value is markedly lower."

Brother Death smiled and I wished he hadn't. "A good question, fine sir, a very good question. We assure you there is no trickery here. Since I would not ask such extraordinary confidence in my word alone—" The syringe came out so fast it was like a magic trick. One moment Brother Death was gesturing, the next he had jabbed a needle into Ray's leg. My son wailed.

You could see that for whatever reason he couldn't see Brother Death, wasn't aware of him or his movements. Then, out of nowhere, there was this lancing pain in his thigh. As the syringe filled with blood, Ray's face crumpled in a mix of outrage and shock. He opened his mouth to wail and raisins dribbled out.

It was the most woebegone countenance in the whole world, and I wanted to hold him so badly my arms ached. It took all my self-control to not leap up and run to him.

Brother Death handed the syringe to one of the little green men who scurried away. Moments later, a different one—I could tell because it was the same one who'd escorted us to the table because his tie was slightly askew—carried a tiny glass with some blood on the bottom into our nave. He set it on the table for our inspection.

I didn't know what we were supposed to do with it: sniff it, taste it, or merely test it for magic? As horrible and cruel as it was, the logical part of me appreciated the assurance that Ray hadn't been interfered with, but the rest of me still balled my fists into concentrated points of rage.

Ray was now snuffling gently, in that kind of offended way he had. He'd done that when I woke him up too early or when he didn't get something he wanted, even if the thing he wanted happened to be a train he saw passing by. His eyes shone with tears; there were tears down his face and I wanted to kiss those away so badly. He looked down, saw the raisins on the table, and picked another one up and shoved in his mouth, gumming it to death happily.

Brother Death waited a while before crossing his

arms across his muscled chest, looking smug. "I assume everyone is satisfied."

"Very much so," someone with a French accent declared. "A prime vintage."

"Only the best for you, my friends." Brother Death chuckled. "Now let the bidding commence."

What followed was a deranged—and magic-powered—version of *The Price is Right*. The curtains behind the podium closed. A shimmering partition, as of water running, came down in front of them.

One of the other bays lit up. The magical barrier that prevented us from seeing what was on the other side got a neon glow around the edges.

Across the shimmering curtain, two young women in shackles materialized, both pulling at their bonds, attempting to escape. They were probably around eighteen, though they might have been underage, and identical twins.

A gravelly voice grumbled something in a language I didn't recognize, explaining their offer. Brother Death scowled at the image for a long time before he said, "Very well."

The second partition lit up. I didn't understand this offer, which seemed to be a step pyramid of some sort, which looked ancient and gave off a sickly green glow. It was the sort of glow that made me think *Kill it with fire*. But from various tables around us, a mumble and a sigh arose. Apparently that was something impressive.

It was then that I realized I wasn't going to understand a damn thing about this auction. I'd thought it was going to be all numbers. "A million souls." "Two million souls" "Three million souls and a vanilla cookie." But apparently it was nothing like that.

As other booths lit up, other images joined those first two on the board: more images of people; one image of a grave with a fine mist over it that probably had something to do with ghosts; various artifacts, particularly swords and knives; one building; a—was that Elvis flipping pancakes? That was another one that got oohs and ahs and I had no idea what it was all about. And then it was the high-pitched thing's turn, and the picture that appeared was of what looked like an entire hospital ward of newborns. Yes, whatever that thing was, it was going to die too. I didn't know how or when but I was going to make it my life mission to rid the Earth all these monsters.

More people appeared on the board, some shackled, some with vacant eyes. This whole thing was sickening and depressing. A woman with a British accent started describing her offering, and I realized it was Lucinda Hood.

Giving her a chance to win Ray was the only reason I'd not shot her. She'd kept her word. Better her to win than any of these monsters, but she was a distant second choice to Management.

Her presence did complicate matters, because if we lost and I tried to grab Ray, Lucinda would certainly try to kill me. She had some powerful magic, and I'd be stunned if she was here on her own.

Brother Death seemed pleased at the Condition's offer, and the bidding continued.

Then I heard a familiar voice. I'd recognize it anywhere because she used to tell me bedtime stories with it. I've been told she sounds a lot like me.

"Is that...?" Hansel looked nervously toward the nave at the far end of the church.

"Susan Shackleford, Master vampire, and all around bitch."

She hadn't sent a rep. She'd come here in person. Of course! This was her grandson we were talking about. Mom was all about *family*. I'd been afraid she'd drop whatever she was doing to be here for this. The creature wearing the body of my mother offered up several slave pits and five young vampire slaves. I noted that Brother Death lingered on her offer for a long time.

My stomach was clenched. I was terrified. If Susan won, I'd never get Ray back. Worse, she was incredibly dangerous. Even though she was relatively young by vampire standards, she was more powerful than other vampires ten times her age. My best guess was that it was because she'd used her Hunter knowledge to track down, feed upon, and suck the potent life out of various mystical creatures.

Despite being a vampire, her personality was still basically Susan Shackleford. Even if it was a twisted, evil version, I knew exactly what she would do. Like me, there was no way Susan would accept losing this particular auction. If someone else won, Susan would strike. Brother Death's comments about temporary peace aside, she'd kill whoever won and just take Ray.

So would I. Only I wasn't a bulletproof superhuman killing machine.

I found that I'd subconsciously reached up and touched the mark on my neck. I hurried and snatched my hand away before I could disturb the makeup concealing it.

The tentacled monster next to us offered up . . . something. I couldn't tell what it was, but it looked like a box covered in lichen, only when the image was put on the board, the lid opened a bit, and a terrified, very large eye looked out.

Our turn came, and Hansel announced, "The missing box of vials from the Affair of the Poisons."

There was some muttering from the audience. This was the spiritual descendant of that event, and they'd probably thought it had been lost forever. Brother Death nodded, but he didn't say anything else.

I whispered to Hansel, "I thought you said we had more stuff to offer?"

He shook his head and mouthed back at me: "Save it for the next round."

I hadn't realized there were going to be *rounds* of bidding. This was horrible already.

The two booths after us offered, and neither of them elicited much response from our host.

And then Brother Death went from game show host to a bridezilla surveying her gifts. He turned toward one image, put his hands on his hips, and said, "You insult me." He started making a swiping gesture with his finger, and images vanished. Swipe, the girls were gone. "And what is this trash I could buy at a thrift store?" Swipe, goodbye to various pieces of arcane jewelry. "What do you expect me to do with souls already this broken by torment?"

Swipe, and the grave with the mist over it vanished.

The tentacle monster was off the board. So, too, was the first offering with the bound-up identical twins, and the one that I guessed was from the actor—an image of a dozen or so women with vacant eyes—and the high-pitched thing's offer of something that looked very much like the contents of Marchand's refrigerator, only much older and, oh yeah, somehow still alive despite being in pieces.

Left on the board were the bids from Mother Dearest, Lucinda and the Church of the Temporary Mortal Condition, and Management.

"Now for those remaining," he said, grinning at the audience while my son blissfully ate raisins on what might very well end up being a sacrificial altar. Just like a Pitt, eating in the face of doom. "How do you wish to sweeten the pot?"

Round two, the remaining naves lighted up.

"Excellent," Brother Death crowed. "Hold nothing back, my friends, for this is your final chance to sway me."

We offered a gently smoking bottle filled with a red liquid. "Circe's potion," Hansel said. It looked exactly like the kind of crazy thing that the Management would have in his vaults, for the historical value, though to Brother Death the real value would be if it was the same curse that Circe had used to turn Odysseus' men into pigs. I made a note not to get barbecue anywhere near where that bottle might have been.

Lucinda gave a triumphant laugh, and a mummified hand appeared on the board. It appeared ancient and must have belonged to a small woman or older girl. Brother Death looked toward that nave. "Is that . . . ?"

"Indeed." She sounded very impressed with herself. "Behold, the hand of Fatima."

I didn't have any clue what that was, and yet, I still held my breath. Brother Death seemed really pleased. I looked to Hansel who, despite being so stoic, had begun to tremble. His leg was bouncing nervously. Whatever it was, he'd not been expecting it.

"Did we just get outbid?"

"Maybe," he said. "I don't know."

Brother Death looked back and forth, long and hard, between the hand and the potion. "Decisions, decisions," he muttered.

Then Susan's nave lit up. Her offer was a statuette of some sort. It looked repulsive and it had African art lines, but I didn't recognize the sounds spoken to name it.

Brother Death gasped. "Does it still work?"

"Would I pawn off a counterfeit in a place such as this?" Mother asked, indignant.

"What is it?" I demanded of Hansel.

"I . . . I don't know."

Brother Death began to laugh, a deep, malicious sound. He looked at the board and made a gesture, swiping our offering right out of consideration. "I'm sorry, but there are some things that cannot be passed up. The baby is yours. You may claim your prize."

There are things you can't process. There are shocks or grief so great that all you can do is sit there, feeling like someone has upended a bucket of cold water over your head, and it has somehow turned you to ice.

Susan came strolling out. She really did look like me, only her skin was vampire pale, her body immortal perfect, and she didn't bother with a mask. Why? She was a rock star in this crowd. There was grumbling from just about every booth up and down the way.

Mother's smile turned feral. "I just want all of you to know that I won him fair and square and that, unlike my daughter, I'm not going to be so careless as to let anyone—anyone—steal him from me." The threat was clear to all the other monstrous guests.

"It's long been a dream of mine to bring my family together again, to make them all immortal, and this is the beginning of that. I'm going to take this powerful little guy and raise him up right, so he's a credit to the Shackleford name." Then she approached the table. "Hey, Ray, it's Grandma."

Ray looked up at her as though it was the first time he'd seen anyone inside the church. He seemed doubtful. For a moment, it hung in the balance how he was going to react.

Here I should note that my mother and I look very much alike, and since becoming a vampire had rejuvenated her, we could pass for the same age.

"Come to Grandma, honey," she held out her arms.

Ray chose to give a fat, little, rolling chuckle. I wanted to believe there was doubt in it, but really there wasn't. My son didn't know anything of vampires or evil, and this creature looked like Mommy, so she was probably the most comforting thing he'd seen in a long, long time. He extended his chubby arms toward her.

We'd lost. It was time for plan B. "Wait!" I shouted.

The vampire stopped. She turned toward my nave, incredulous. She couldn't see me, but she could recognize my voice as well as I could recognize hers. "Julie?"

"Get away from him."

Brother Death scowled in my direction. I couldn't tell if he could see me through the magic or not. "The bidding is done. The dragon's offering was insufficient. My decision is made." He began to grin needles. "Unless . . ."

"Hold on," Susan snarled. "I already won."

But Brother Death held up one hand to silence her.

It turned out the *Adze* was as greedy as the legends made them sound. "Perhaps I was hasty. Let us see if the other Shackleford has anything she'd like to bid."

"There's one more thing." I reached into my stole, pulled the real artifact from where it had been suctioned onto Mr. Trash Bags, and held it up. "Offer it," I snapped at Hansel.

I don't know how the magic worked, but the image behind Brother Death changed to show my shaking hand clenched around the Kumaresh Yar.

If there had been gasps at some of the offerings before, this positively floored them. Of course, most of the regular humans had no idea what it was, but the monsters knew.

"This is the Kumaresh Yar, the artifact used by Lord Machado to open a portal to the Old Ones, and by Owen Zastava Pitt to break time."

"You only have that because you stole it from me," Susan spat.

Then the spell around the Condition's nave shimmered as Lucinda stormed through it. "Wait a bloody minute! My people hired you to steal that from her. She can't bid what's rightfully mine."

"Back off, girl," Susan warned the high priestess, "or I'll finish what I started and rip off your other hand."

"Bring it, cunt. I'm ready this time." Lucinda raised her metal prosthetic, opened her fingers revealing that the symbol of Asag had been carved on her palm. Susan recoiled and hissed. Apparently an unholy symbol could work as well as a holy one, provided the bearer had sufficient faith, and Lucinda was a fanatic.

Susan and Lucinda appeared to be in a standoff. The transformation was subtle, but the vampire had gone into a predatory mode, crouched just a bit, like she was ready to pounce. Except she didn't because there appeared to be sparks snapping between Lucinda's fingers. An energy was building in the air, and the tiny hairs on my arms stood up.

"Now, now, ladies. Please, keep it civil or my security will have to get involved." Several of the clay men stepped into view as Brother Death said that. "I'm sure you would not want any harm to inadvertently come to the baby before you take possession."

"My men hired you to steal the Kumaresh Yar from her, Death," Lucinda spat. "You made a deal."

"And I kept it, Priestess." Brother Death seemed amused by all of this. "I fulfilled my part of the contracts. It is not my fault your men lost it again immediately afterward."

"Hang on . . . *Contracts?* What do you mean contracts plural?" Lucinda asked.

"Hey," I shouted. "You assholes want this evil thing or not? I'll just leave it here, take my kid, and you can sort it out."

Most eyes were on the necromancer and vampire who were about to throw down, but my words got Brother Death's attention and, I assumed, every other monster's here who knew just how incredibly valuable the artifact was. The other items put up for bidding were useful for all sorts of evil, but in the right hands, this thing was take-over-the-world super evil. Brother Death wasn't the only greedy thing here tonight. I'd been counting on that.

I lowered my voice and told Hansel, "Give me your jacket."

"Why?"

"Because your pockets are full of ammo and I'm not going to make you follow me for what comes next."

He hurried and shrugged out of his jacket, with an expression that said something like, *I didn't see anything, and I won't see anything even if I see anything, so don't do anything that I have to see or respond to, please.*

Brother Death turned back to address Lucinda. "Yes, Priestess. I fulfilled two contracts that day. One for your foolish minions to get the artifact, but the other...was so that I could repay a longstanding debt."

"To whom?" Lucinda demanded.

"You wear his symbol upon your palm."

"What? No. Explain yourself!" She looked like she wanted to aim her killing hand at Brother Death, but to do so meant that Susan would attack. The vampire was pissed off and ready to fight. And I'd seen her move before. It would be like a flash of lightning followed by blood painting the church.

While most of the participants were fixated on the two powerful supernatural forces who looked like they were about to slug it out, I lowered my hand. Once the artifact was no longer in view on Brother Death's magical display for the bidders, I slipped the real artifact back to Mr. Trash Bags to hide and palmed the fake rock.

Brother Death chuckled. "Asag does not reveal everything to his servants. You should realize by now he enjoys his games. It seems the father of this child vexes him, so he retained my services. I took the artifact for your minions. I took the child on behalf of your god."

I'd felt like this when I saw my brother die at the

Christmas Party. It was like the world had ended and there was nothing, absolutely nothing I could do about it. It had taken me years to come out of that stupor and even think of fighting monsters again. It had taken a vampire outbreak to shake me out of it. Now that feeling of helplessness hit me all over again. Ray was still sitting there, eating his raisins, blissfully unaware.

When my brother had died, I'd been unable to stop it. But that was then, this was now and I'd get my baby back by *any* means necessary.

I threw on Hansel's jacket. The pockets were heavy with mags. Then I untied the frilly mask, put my glasses back on—*much better*—and took the custom pistol out of the purse.

Hansel gave me a dubious look. I remembered what he'd said earlier, about if we lost the auction, Management couldn't be seen as lending me aid, because that would cause troubles for him in the world of supernatural villains, or something.

Right. Watch me.

"You'd better get out of here, Hansel," I said as I did a chamber check.

He nodded. "Good luck." And then he fled.

The vampire and the necromancer were glaring at each other. The security golems were moving to get between them. Surely the bidders were watching the potential conflict between two powerful supernatural forces to the point Ray was forgotten. Or so I hoped. It was now or never.

Only Brother Death looked back at me. Apparently he could see through the concealing spells just fine; he knew what was coming and, worst of all, seemed amused by it.

And poor little Ray was just sitting there, oblivious, between a bunch of monsters, stuck in the potential crossfire. He was in danger, but better to die human and innocent than to let Susan twist him into something horrible.

Stepping out of that nave was the hardest thing I've ever done.

"You want the Kumaresh Yar? Here it is!" Then I tossed the fake. It landed between Susan and Lucinda with a thump.

They both looked at it, and since they'd both possessed it before, it was obvious that neither of them was fooled. However, I was hoping that in the heat of the moment every other evil, conniving, power-hungry thing there would go for it.

The church went nuts.

You've got to want something pretty bad to get between a vampire and a necromancer, but monsters— humanoid and other—rushed, shambled, or slithered out of their naves.

I punched the gun out in both hands. The Grayguns Sig had a compact optical sight on it, just a window in a box, but on that glass was a glowing red dot, and the instant it was floating over Brother Death's chest, I pulled the trigger twice.

He took a step back, not from pain or shock, but just a small reaction. He put one big hand to his sternum where there were two holes, glowing green. The look he gave me wasn't one of pain, but more like he was surprised by my audacity. Then I shot him in the face.

The loud noises hurt Ray's ears and he began to wail. Lucinda glanced toward my gunfire and that tiny distraction cost her. Susan launched herself at the necromancer, so fast she was practically a blur. Only something else collided with the vampire to fling her violently away. Susan was sent rolling across the grass, but she popped right back up. Her dress had been shredded by claws.

The thing that had saved Lucinda's life had come from seemingly out of nowhere, and it appeared to be a jagged, seven-foot-tall clump of pure shadow. So dark that it was *almost* solid.

"Meet my plus one; he's one of my father's finest creations." Lucinda said. "Now pluck the arms off that vampire bitch so she can know how it feels!"

I'd let those two work it out.

As the other bidders and guests either fought over my rock or went for the exits, I headed straight for Ray. Brother Death had shrugged off a gunshot wound to the head and simply turned his back to walk away.

One of the clay men stepped in my way. He was reaching into his suit, acting just like a regular security guy, probably to draw some sort of weapon from a shoulder holster, but I shifted over and put a round in him.

It turned out they weren't bulletproof. In fact, the impacts were rather dramatic as the side of his head *shattered*. The sunglasses went flying. The space where the eyes should've been was open; there was nothing there, just a dark hole going into the body, except what seemed like a good ways inside, there was a tiny flame dancing. It gave both the impression of a pupil and a sense of animation.

But then I put another round in his forehead and the whole top of his skull burst into pottery fragments.

Fireflies came out as the body collapsed in a pile of dust.

The church was chaos. It turned out the two Russian dudes were some sort of were creature because they were getting hairy and ripping out of their suits as they claimed the rock, only to get swatted aside by a woman in an evening dress whose skin had just turned to fish scales.

As Susan clashed with the shadow monster, Lucinda began screaming, "Move in! Move in! Julie Shackleford's inside the church! Get me that bloody artifact *now!*" She'd brought a radio. That meant this whole place was probably surrounded by cultists.

Then I had to duck because it turned out the clay men *did* have firearms, and they opened up.

Bullets dug holes in the grass or splattered off of stone. The tentacle monster let out an obscene bellow as it was struck with a stray.

And poor Ray was still in the middle, crying his head off. Every second this went on, he was in danger of getting hit.

I'm not as good with a handgun as my husband is. I'm more a long-range kind of girl. But right then I was so angry and hyperfocused that time seemed to slow down to a crawl, and I was running and gunning like Owen on his best day, because these assholes were standing between me and my son.

I moved to cover and kept shooting as clay men staggered and broke, crumbling to pieces in their fine suits. Some of my bullets passed through and hit some of the fleeing human guests. *Serves them right.* As soon as my slide locked back empty, I pulled back just as several bullets smashed into the pillar I was hiding behind. I calmly reloaded while they pounded the historical site full of holes. If I lived, my ears were going to be ringing for days. I should've put some earplugs in my purse.

Suddenly, there was a sharp pain around my ankle, my foot was yanked out from under me, and I went down hard. I rolled over and found there was a tentacle wrapped around my leg.

A coiled mass of *something* came shimmering through the other nave. It was the thing Hansel had hit with the snack tray. I had no idea what it was, but I just did a rapid-fire mag dump into its center, fifteen rounds, fast as I could pull the trigger. Then I had to grab another mag out of the coat pocket, only I fumbled my reload because everything had gotten turned around and twisted up. Pocket reloads are stupid. That's why professionals always use mag pouches. Stupid dress code.

Another tentacle reached for me, but before it got there, there was a scream of, *"Protect Cuddle Bunny!"* and my little tentacle monster attacked the big tentacle monster. Mr. Trash Bags was tiny, but he was super aggressive. The other bidder had to let go of my leg to try and defend itself.

I sprang back to my feet, went around the pillar, and nearly crashed headfirst into a clay man.

They weren't quite human. They were just a bit too slow. If this had been a trained gunman, I'd have gotten shot. But instead, I shoved his gun to the side just as he fired, and I jammed my muzzle into his chest, blowing a hole clean through him. I shot him twice more as I pulled away, and then put a controlled pair into the one standing behind him.

I heard that awful, high-pitched voice again as

another bidder revealed itself. "Such chaos. I'll just take that fine, delicious young man off your hands." Sadly, some of the bidders were more interested in children than in world-conquering artifacts because this thing was heading right for Ray. Fat, greasy, ponderous, it was the same species as Marchand, a *bicho-papão*. It stretched greedy hands towards Ray, gross belly dragging, voice alternately shrilling and gasping. "Oh yes, mine, mine, mine."

I couldn't reach him in time. It had taken a grenade to put a dent in the last one of these I'd met and I didn't have anything like that. Ray's eyes had been closed tight because of the gunfire, but he opened them now, saw the horrible, slavering beast coming his way, and screamed harder. He may be an innocent, but there was no mistaking this thing for anything but pure evil.

"Ray!" I wasn't going to make it in time.

Then my mother came out of nowhere. "Back off, asshole!" She slammed one hand *into* the *bicho*, right through the skin. Its all-too-human face grimaced. Pale blue eyes went very wide. And then he convulsed as she ripped his heart out. It was coal black, pouring out green smoke, and still beating. The *bicho* fell, convulsing at her feet, and Susan took a bite out of its heart.

Blood ran down her chin as she roared, "Any of you other sons of bitches want to try and take what's mine?"

Then the shadow monster rose behind her, encircled her in its serrated arms, and lifted her into the air. It didn't give a damn about Ray, but Lucinda had given it an order which it would follow until it won or was destroyed. If I'd learned anything from fighting the man, Martin Hood's shadow magic was relentless and dangerous as hell.

The volume of gunfire suddenly went up dramatically with the addition of a few automatic weapons. Clay men twitched and split apart as they got shredded with bullets. For one brief moment, I thought that maybe by some miracle Hunters had arrived, but from the look of the scraggly bastards running into the church blazing away at anything that moved, it was just Lucinda's cultist backup. But at least Brother Death's security now had someone to shoot at besides me.

Gun up, I moved toward Ray. I dropped another clay man, stepped through the dust, and then put two into a running cultist. He crashed into the buffet table. One of the guests rushed me with a knife. Man or monster, I couldn't tell, it just looked like a guy in a tux, so I shot him twice in the chest. He fell and skidded across the grass on his face. Man then.

Almost there.

And then a bullet hit me in the leg.

My knee buckled and I fell. I screamed, more from the frustration than the pain. I rolled on my side, found the cultist who'd shot me, just some punk in jeans and a T-shirt at the far end of the church, and opened up on him. He stumbled back against the stone, and then slid down it, leaving a red smear. I fired the rest of my mag at his buddies, clipping one, and forcing all of them to take cover.

Unfortunately, one of them took cover next to where a Russian had landed, and that unlucky bastard got his face bitten off by what I was pretty sure was a werebear.

Ignoring the agony, I shoved myself back up. My leg wouldn't support my weight. So while I reloaded again, I hopped along, dragging one foot behind me.

Ray saw me and reached out, like *Momma, save me from the scary noise!*

"It's gonna be okay." I scooped him up with my left arm and held him to my chest, trying to put my body between him and the threats, then I limped for the back. He was warm, heavy, soft, and thrashing around, strong as an ox. This was the real Ray. It was him! It was really him! "I got you."

The cultists popped out, but I swung my right hand back and fired wildly, trying to force them to keep their heads down. At each loud *bang* Ray screamed. My poor kid was going to be deaf. So was I, but right then my health didn't matter.

I was heading for the lamias' lair, but that was better than going out through the wild gunfight that was consuming the front.

Except I didn't quite make it.

One of the clay men shot me in the back.

As I fell, I managed to turn my body to protect Ray from the impact. I hit the ground hard and lost my pistol. It was like a red-hot lance had just pierced through my shoulder blade, but all I cared about was making sure he was okay. The poor little guy was terrified, but unharmed. He wasn't going to stay that way for long though, so I desperately tried to drag myself further.

A pair of high heels stopped right in front of my face. I looked up to see Susan, her arms tinged with dark blood, face dripping supernatural gore. She must have gotten away from the shadow creature.

The face that used to be my mother smiled down at me. "See, sweetheart. That's why I can't allow you to keep the little one. You've really got no concept of how to keep children safe, do you? You're going to get him killed with this foolishness."

She reached for the baby. I reached for my gun. And then something hit me on the back of the head. The world went black.

CHAPTER 18

"Thou art the worst Guardian ever."

I was in a grey, foggy place, and the man speaking to me had been dead for years. Unlike the last time I'd seen him, he was in one piece and not having his skin peeled off by a Great Old One. He was a big, muscular man. Like me, he also bore the marks of the Guardian, only he had a lot more of them, covering most of his body, and his kept moving around in a very unnerving way. But they'd done that back when he was alive too.

"Am I dead? I've got to go back. Ray needs me."

"In time," the last Guardian said.

Then I wasn't dead? Good. Because if this swirling grey wasteland was heaven, it was a real rip-off. But time was the last thing I had. Last I could remember I'd gotten shot, and Ray was in danger. "Look, my husband's the one who talks to ghosts. That's not my thing. Send me back or wake me up or whatever. I've got to get him before Susan does. Please."

"'Tis not my decision." But the way he was giving me a disapproving scowl, that told me if it had been his decision, he still thought I was wrong.

"Well, screw you then." I started walking.

I made it through a few hundred feet of fog only to find myself back at the exact same spot, with the Guardian standing there, arms folded and grumpy.

"What is the life of one child, even thine own flesh and blood, when weighed against the fate of the world?"

I wasn't going to take any shit off a funny-talking, dead Viking conquistador whatever the hell he was. "I never asked to guard the stupid artifact. That was your job."

"'Twas my duty," he agreed.

"You volunteered. I didn't." Even though the fog was moving, I couldn't feel any wind. I couldn't smell anything. I couldn't *feel* anything at all. All I could see and hear was a sanctimonious dead guy, and I wasn't in the mood for a lecture. "I appreciate you saving my life, but I never asked for any of this Guardian stuff. I don't know how it works, I don't know who it comes from, and I don't know what the hell they want from me."

Some of the fog parted, revealing a still, black-and-white vision of our battle on the pyramid where Koriniha had telekinetically ripped all his skin off, and she'd also stabbed me in the throat. Old Ones were real assholes like that.

"'Twas fate that brought us to that moment, for the passing of the mantle. Dost thou wish to understand the powers granted to thee?"

"If I'm stuck here while my kid's in danger, can't you at least talk normal?" But he just kept frowning at me. "Fine. Yes. Tell me how it works then."

"Thou art nigh unkillable, should thy will be sufficient."

"Unkillable?" I snorted as I pointed at the three-dimensional fog vision. I don't know what to call it. This was more Owen's kind of thing. "Koriniha peeled you like a grape."

"*Nigh* unkillable. Old Ones are not to be trifled with. The Others hold no sway over them. The Great Old Ones are treacherous and cunning. Though sometimes they trick the Others to do their will, the factions remain bitter enemies."

"The Others... That's one of the groups in this great cosmic war that's supposedly going on all around us. They're the ones who created these marks. Who are they? What do they want?"

"The Others are not of this world. They do not wish to conquer it, yet it does not behoove them to let it fall to the likes of the Great Old Ones, or be consumed by the madness of Asag. Thus, they meddle."

The fog vision changed. Now it was an unfamiliar scene, but it was the same old Guardian, massacring what looked like a bunch of Nazis. From the skulls and SS pins, they deserved the ass-kicking the Guardian was dishing out. I recognized one of them as that psycho Jaeger, though he was still human at the time and not yet a vampire.

"In times of great peril, when this world may fall, each faction chooses a champion."

This time the grey vision was a jungle, and a bunch of conquistadors were having a very bad day. It looked like they'd interrupted a human sacrifice. I'd never seen Lord Machado in his mortal form, but I spotted him because of the morion helmet and that terrifying axe, and from the trail of limbs behind him, he'd not appreciated the interruption.

"A vow I made to the spirits of my ancestors, the Others heard. Things of vital importance must be guarded. Only the vigilant are chosen."

"Since I let Brother Death steal my son, I've bombed in the vigilance department."

I realized that the last man standing against Lord Machado was the Guardian, only it looked like he was still human at the time. But then it swirled into another vision, of an even older battle ground and another Guardian fighting some menace, and then another, and another... They began to flash by, faster and faster, a parade of black-marked strangers, fighting clear back to the beginning of time.

"Thus it is. Thus it has been. Thus it must be until the final battle, the end of time, when even death may die."

"That's a lot of poor suckers all drafted to protect one evil artifact," I muttered.

"Nay. 'Tis not always that cursed device. That which is guarded varies. The Others provide the mantle. The Guardian decides how best to use it."

"Hold on. I get to pick what I'm supposed to protect?"

If anything, that annoyed him even more because he knew exactly what I was thinking. "Choose wisely what thou wilt guard, flippant wretch, for each use brings great peril. The more thou vows to protect, the faster thy humanity will be consumed."

That's right. There ain't no such thing as a free lunch. "What's the cost?"

"A coarsening. The stripping of all that is good and kind. With each new line, thou wilt become less human, more weapon, until the forfeit of thy very soul."

The visions changed to other unfamiliar Guardians—or more like what was left of them. They'd fought too long until the marks had consumed all their humanity. They looked more like Lucinda's shadow monster than a flesh-and-blood human being.

"Thus is thy fate . . . unless thou perishes first."

"Was it worth it?" I asked, staring at the vision of a female Guardian, where the right half of her face was beautiful, and the left half was a twisted nightmare of pitch-black spines.

"If thou must ask, then what thou hast chosen to protect is unworthy."

Whatever she'd been protecting, she'd been willing to make the sacrifice to save it.

"I understand now. Send me back. I've got work to do."

I woke up to cold and silence in the dark.

There was a scent I remembered, but I couldn't make sense of it, except to say it brought images of warmth and something moving. But nothing moved here. It also smelled weird and musty like an old, abandoned tomb. The fact that I knew exactly what an old and abandoned tomb smelled like should tell you how messed-up my life was.

My head hurt. I remembered getting shot in the leg and the back . . . I felt weak, but I didn't feel *shot*. And I felt like I had actually slept for a few hours.

It took me about a second to remember where I'd been: the old ruined church and the auction. And then I remembered Ray. I'd had him in my arms, his little body against me. I'd had him, safe and secure. But I was alone now. I'd lost him. A wave of grief washed over me and I closed my eyes.

When I opened them again, I could see a bit better.

I think my eyes had just gotten used to the darkness. It wasn't a good thing.

I was in a sort of basement that must once have been part of the church. It was enormous and very dark. It must have taken up the entire space, not just below the church, but below the whole plaza. There were a couple of tiny light bulbs above, but they were weak and distant.

Several big columns supported the floor above. I was tied to one of them. I could feel the rough stone against my bare arms. Pulling and struggling against the rope showed me only that it was thick, made out of some orange synthetic material, and very tightly knotted. Whoever had tied me up wasn't an amateur. I was never going to get out of this by my wits alone, and it didn't seem like the stone was rough enough to cut through that thick a rope—not in the next year or so.

In this area, directly under the church, the walls were sturdy and intact, and the floor looked like the old Roman mosaic you see in every old building in Europe. After that, beneath the space that wasn't the church proper, there were ruins, where it looked like houses had fallen into the area, and then been built over. Across from me, there was a stairway leading up to something I couldn't see clearly—it was just too dark—but which looked like the door of a manorial house, with statues on either side. I couldn't see what the statues were. There was movement around the edges.

Was this the lamia den that Management had told me about? Probably. But if they were still here, they were holding back for some reason.

"Goddamn it, son-of-a-bitch cultists," a very familiar voice said.

I'd looked around in a general way, but not at the floor right next to me.

It was my mother.

I nearly jumped out of my skin.

All vampires are evil, but this one was something special. Not only was she a Master vampire and power broker in the dark networks of villains, but she was... Okay, she was straight-up crazy. Perhaps it was impossible, at any rate, for a vampire to occupy the body and mind of someone like my mother, someone genuinely good and kind and loved by all, and to still have all her memories and most of her feelings, and not go batshit insane.

She was lying on the floor, next to my feet, with nothing to hold her back.

Shit. I'd rather they had fed me to the lamias. Instead, they were about to feed me to the crazy-ass evil vampire. She couldn't turn me—the Guardian's marks prevented that—but she could easily kill me.

Then the vampire moved... but weirdly, in a crabbed way, as though her middle were pinned to the ground. It wasn't. I could see it wasn't. Or at least there wasn't a stake protruding from her back. Just her back, moving and spasming, as if her stomach were glued to the ground. She tossed her head around. Since she'd become a vampire, she'd rejuvenated some, and her hair looked just like mine, only perhaps even darker and shinier.

She twisted her head around in an unnatural way, and I wondered why she wasn't just shape-shifting into mist and drifting free from whatever had trapped her. I'd seen her do it before.

Instead, she turned her head up, kind of sideways, so she could see me. It looked wrong. The head turning, I mean. It was not quite as bad as seeing someone turn their head all the way around *Exorcist*-style, but it was the same sort of thing: wrong, like she should be breaking bones. And maybe she was. Vampires, particularly Master vampires, just regenerated superfast, and maybe she didn't care if she broke vertebrae, if they just came back together.

She was staring at me, with her eyes very wide. As I stared back, she blinked. "Oh, calm down. That shadow thing messed me up enough that Brother Death got some kind of curse on me. I'm trapped as much as you are."

It had to be some kind of magical binding instead of ropes, but I still didn't trust her.

"Are you okay? Did they hurt you?"

"What the hell do you care?" I flung back, because it was almost unbearable to see this creature wearing my mother's flesh, and it was unbearable to hear it talk to me as if I were still the little girl Mom had raised, way back. This is the way she'd talked to me, when I'd come back from school upset about something; or when some boy I liked had told me I was just too weird or something. From her voice, if I closed my eyes, I'd expect her to bring me cookies and lemonade.

Only this was the vampire that had set fire to my home, changed and killed my daddy, and made my life a living misery.

She made a soft sound. "Of course I care, honey. No mom ever stops caring about her baby. I thought you'd know that by now."

Ray. I thought of Ray in my arms, and my voice caught in my throat as I spit back, "What would you know about being a mother? You're no one's mother."

"Honey—"

"No. I know you have her memories, and you think you're my mother, but you're not. You're just a crazy-ass vampire."

I could almost hear her weighing different responses. I don't know how, because I sure as hell couldn't read her mind, and I couldn't be reading her breathing because she didn't have any. Perhaps I could hear rustles as her body tensed or something. She said, "Bless your heart, if that's what you think."

"My mother would never help take my baby away from me. She'd have given him back to me. My mother would have cared about how worried I am and how scared Ray must be."

She chuckled. The bitch actually chuckled, a kind of rich and satisfying chuckle. "Oh, honey, that's not true. Sure, I want you to raise your baby, but I want you to do it right and under my protection, so that neither of you will be in danger from all the evil things that want to hurt you."

"Evil things like you?"

"No. Not like me. I'd never hurt a precious hair of your heads. But there are things out there, Julie, things like Brother Death, who only care about your power, and little Ray's power too, and they'll take you and hurt you badly, just so they can get at it. I could keep both of you safe from all that."

I had to actually close my eyes and take deep breaths because there really was no point talking to the crazed thing who wanted to turn us into vampires, which, by definition, would kill us, but she was too insane to grasp that.

"You think my wanting to make you immortal is a bad thing," she said, and I jumped, because it was like she could read my mind. "Don't be so scared. That weird curse on you makes it so I can't really get in your mind, but I can still read your expressions. How could I not? I've been looking at them ever since the day you were born." She shook her head, and this time, I swear I heard a sound of grating bones. "I know you think that turning you would be harming you, but that's because you don't know. You don't know!"

"I know that you got a demon inside you, talking through your mouth and thinking through your brain, you old hag."

She didn't even blink. She continued looking at my face, but her eyes were all misty-soft and it was like she was looking into the distance, into something unutterably beautiful. "I was scared once too."

"What . . . of being turned? I should hope you were scared."

She shook her head, just a tiny movement, with crunching bone again. When she talked, it started in a whisper. "That too, of course, but I was so scared of so many things. When I found out there really were monsters out there, and then I had a family, and I was so scared for all of us, all the time. Even your daddy. He wasn't very strong, you know. Oh, sure. He was strong physically. One of the best Hunters ever. And he was strong mentally. Smart as could be. But I always knew that I was his emotional strength. He used to hold me all through the night, saying he didn't know what he'd do without me."

"And you killed him!"

"No. I saved him! That's what you don't understand. The night I woke up as a vampire was the first time I was really alive. I could see. I could hear. I could feel like never before. It was like all my life I'd lived in a sack at the bottom of a dark cave, and now, suddenly, I was awake. And I was strong. So strong. Strong enough to protect my family and those I loved. Strong enough to make sure nothing ever went wrong for them."

"Like my brother?" I spat. "Ray got killed by a bunch of demons because Dad was trying to bring your skanky ass back to life!"

"Oh, honey. I'm so sorry about that. Yes, I should have contacted your father earlier. I should have stopped his bumbling attempts to bring me back. Thing is, at the time I had obligations that—you'll never understand. I couldn't be there for you then, okay? But when I learned what happened, I knew I had to be more involved. I had to help my family."

"Help? You bit me! It's only because these marks burned your stupid mouth off you didn't kill me! You wrecked my house, turned my Dad into a vampire, kidnapped my ex-boyfriend... tried to murder my husband! You helped Lord Machado try to blow up time! You've got a weird idea of *help!*"

"I've helped you," she insisted.

"How?"

"Like that vampire outbreak at your college, Julie!"

For a moment, for just a moment, I was back there, with the blazing science building behind me. I thought of Cynthia Anne Aiken, with the baby blue eyes, and her stupid tattoo with a quote from Anne

Rice, and then my having to chop her head off and carry it around in my book bag.

"What do you mean?"

She laughed, the type of sound she used to make when us kids were just figuring humor out and told her a knock-knock joke that wasn't really funny. She'd laugh like that, partly to acknowledge the joke and partly because the fact that we were trying at all was funny in a way. Just not the way we thought.

"What're the odds there'd be a vampire nest formed at your school, just when you were there, pretending to be like the rest of them?"

"I wasn't pretending."

"You can't lie to me, Julie. You were miserable. It was like watching a full-grown woman trying to squeeze herself back into kindergarten clothes. You wanted to be a Hunter. You've always wanted that, more than anything else in the world. But you were so eaten up with guilt, blaming yourself for Ray's death and your father's fall, you were torturing yourself living a life that wasn't even yours."

"It was you . . ."

"Sure was. I turned this dweeby English professor. What was his name again? Jan, I think. Something like that. He made a lousy vampire. Always full of himself. But I turned him because I knew he was just the sort of cocky fool who'd start a mess big enough to bring you back to your senses."

I remembered something about a professor who had left on sabbatical around that time. A lot of the kids had been fond of him because he'd always shared his weed.

"You bitch."

She shrugged, or something that passed for a shrug while her stomach was pinned to the floor. "You had to be reminded of your place. What were you going to do otherwise? Finish your degrees and become isolated, teaching in some university? And what would that do? Nothing. I forced you into a moment of clarity. Spare the rod and spoil the child. Tough love. You needed to wake up and remember your legacy."

There was something there. I didn't want to believe it. I didn't want to admit it, but in a sick and twisted way she was right. I'd been miserable before that, though I'd kept telling myself I was in no way miserable and that I was doing exactly what I wanted to do and living the life I wanted to live. It's easy, particularly after a great loss, to tell yourself stories and to avoid acknowledging the truth.

"You caused a bunch of stupid kids to die! Cynthia Aiken was my friend, and she—"

"She was a sheep. They would've all gotten killed sooner or later—if not by Jan, then by something else. There's predators and then there's prey. Prey always die. That's their *job*. What's slaughtering a bunch of sheep if it means making sure my little girl was all right and not living a dead end life?"

What did I tell you? Crazy. Bonkers. Bat-guano insane. When the pure evil of the vampire met with the pure good of my mother's soul, it had splintered into this nightmare.

"Why are you crying?"

I hadn't realized I was. "Because you're a monster."

"Don't cry." She was actually trying to *comfort* me. "It'll all be okay."

With a shock I realized that in the depths of her

black heart she really did love me. It was a corrupted and twisted love, one that no sane creature would understand, much less bear, but it was love. She really thought she wanted what was best for me, to protect me and guide me.

That's how much my real mom had loved me, that even Susan the vampire couldn't help but feel a twisted shadow of what had been. My eyes were overflowing, and my throat was too tight to swallow.

She might love me and my family, but her regard for humans and the things of humans was negligible, and her moral compass was gone. This Susan was pure evil, yet there was still something of my mother in there, and that something made me want to believe it was really her.

Above us, a door opened, and people began entering the cavernous space. No. Not people. It took me a moment, and then I realized they were the clay golem things that Brother Death had used as bodyguards.

"About damned time," the vampire said. "Unbind me!"

Fully a dozen figures came down the stairs. Ten were the security golems. The remaining two: one of them was Brother Death, who looked human mostly, but for some odd reason was now dressed in a period-accurate cavalier costume, including plumed hat; the last was one of the weird green gnomelike creatures, about two and a half feet tall, with the big ears that twitched as he walked. He was dressed in a matching outfit to his master's and carried a metal folding chair in his hands.

As they walked toward us, I randomly thought that it was amazing Brother Death didn't also have a bunch of golem women fanning him or throwing rose petals in his path. The whole thing had that kind of feel—staged to show he was a very important personage, deigning to come and talk to us lowly prisoners. Who was he trying to impress and why?

Susan watched them carefully. I truly believed that she was stuck somehow, but she looked angry enough to peel herself off the floor right then, even if it meant leaving half her body behind. She was furious and barely holding back.

Brother Death stopped about four feet away. His golems stood at parade rest, while the little guy scurried around with the chair, set it directly behind his master, and then got out of the way. Brother Death took his seat . . . and smiled. It was a ghastly look with all those extra rows of teeth.

"So . . . are you two lovely ladies ready to listen?" The smile increased in size. "You could say that you're my captive audience."

I groaned. "Just kill me now."

"No kidding," Susan agreed.

Brother Death removed his big hat, set it on his knees, and gave us a very stern look. "I drove off the Condition and their shadow creature, and brought you both here, safe from harm. I've secured you both for your own protection. I can't have my guests killing each other, especially before I had the chance to offer my deal. Sadly, there is only one prize to give, so whoever comes to an agreement with me first, I will remove the ropes or the curse of Quintus Emilianus, and that one will be free to take the child and go."

"And if we don't come to an *agreement*?" Susan demanded.

"I am a businessman and a respecter of deals. I have a reputation to uphold. There is always an agreement to be struck... But if pride gets in the way of cooperation, then I will result to baser options."

I was sure all of those baser options would prove fatal, and probably hurt a lot too. "Where's my son?"

"Somewhere safe. I didn't want his presence to agitate you further. For a woman with a reputation for being cool during negotiations, you certainly become rather violent and irrational when your child is involved."

I'd show him violent and irrational... But despite being a bundle of nerves on the inside, I tried to appear calm and collected.

"Now to business." He tilted his head to address the vampire on the floor. "Susan—may I call you Susan?"

"Whatever floats your boat."

"Good. As I revealed upstairs, the Condition asked me to retrieve the Kumaresh Yar, but it was mighty Asag who commissioned me to steal the child."

I died inside as he said that, because while most of the world's Hunters were laying siege to Asag's house, he'd decided to get his revenge on poor little Ray.

"Susan, you have allied yourself with the one called Stricken, in the hopes of thwarting Asag's plans, yes?"

I couldn't believe my ears. "What?"

"When there's a war coming, better to pick a side than get drafted. I'm done being a slave to cosmic horrors. Asag, Stricken, they're both assholes, but Stricken puts Earth first. And I live here. So what? You going to execute me for your boss?"

"You wound me." Brother Death feigned hurt. "I'm no mere hireling. I'm an independent contractor. I sent word that I had you in my power to see if Asag wished to bid for your life, but he declared that killing you would be a waste. Instead, I was told to convey a message. You have become a powerful entity in your sphere. Asag would much rather be your ally than your enemy."

"Go on . . ."

"Hold on." I guessed where this was heading and couldn't keep it in any longer. "I made an offer too."

"Ah," Brother Death said, managing to make a moue of distaste that would do credit to a society matron. "Julie." He said my name in exactly the same tone as he'd refer to something sticking to his shoes and, unlike the vampire, he didn't ask my permission before getting all familiar. "Yes, the Kumaresh Yar in exchange for your child. For such a precious thing, you might have won the bidding, yet we never closed the deal. You failed to deliver. Your pathetic trickery even caused a few of my more gullible guests to kill each other. Perhaps if you told me where the real artifact is now, we could come to terms."

So Mr. Trash Bags had followed instructions and hid with it. Good. "I bet Lucinda grabbed it."

"Don't try to fool me. You know very well the Condition doesn't have the artifact. If Lucinda had gotten her metal hand on it, she would already have tried to kill us all. Last I saw of her, she was very angry." Then he turned back to the vampire. "As I was saying before I was rudely interrupted, Asag would prefer to have you as a friend rather than an enemy. So he wishes to present a peace offering. A gift, consisting of your life, your freedom, and your grandson."

I suppressed an inarticulate scream.

"Oh really?" Susan smiled, all fangs and crazy. "And what's in it for Asag, the world-ending chaos demon?"

"He simply asks that when the time comes, and Stricken and his otherworldly allies call for your aid, you remember the merciful kindness shown to you by Asag, and abandon them."

It must not have been a very strong alliance because it took Susan all of three seconds to think it over. "Buddy, you got a deal."

"No!" I shouted.

"My associate will now remove the Quintus curse, and you will be free to go. The child will be given to you at the top of the stairs." He gestured towards the manor door standing open far above. "My associates will escort you out."

One of the golems approached Susan, squatted down next to her, and slid his hand between her body and the ground. He pulled out what appeared to be an ancient coin. She immediately sprang up and landed on her feet.

Indignant, she looked like she was thinking about ripping everyone apart.

But Brother Death was too clever for that. "If you wish to take the child home in one piece, you will behave."

For a moment the vampire hesitated, and there was that odd look of the concerned mother in her eyes as she looked at me. "What're you going to do with Julie?"

"She's not part of the package."

Then she looked towards the lighted doorway across the vast underground space, and I could see her worry. Somewhere in that messed-up head she was doing the math, trying to figure how best to reach her unholy goal of protecting her family.

The marks made it so she couldn't turn me. Ray on the other hand...

"Fine." Susan looked back at me, a little sad. "Sorry things couldn't work out, honey."

"Don't hurt him!"

"We've got a different definition of hurt. I'm going to love him and raise him right. Once he's full grown I'll give him the gift of eternal life. I wish you could understand this is for the best."

She walked out flanked by two golems she could easily break with a gesture, casting only one look back at me.

Brother Death waited until she was all the way through the plaza—her footsteps echoing hollowly on first cobbles and then packed dirt—and up the steps. Then he waited a while longer, perhaps to make sure she wasn't listening in.

Once the door was closed, he turned back to me. There was malice in the smile which didn't quite obscure the abundance of teeth. He gave the impression of rearranging his body, of settling more deeply into the folding chair, like a person getting more comfortable. It wouldn't be half as creepy, either, if his body didn't seem to fold and stretch in the wrong places.

"Now you...you are a very special case. You taunted me with the artifact, and then took it away. I try to keep things professional, but that sort of thing offends me on a personal level. Where is it?"

"Go to hell."

"Last chance."

"I don't know where the artifact is. You're the one with mind control powers. You should be able to tell I don't know."

"There are two ways I can possess someone. A gradual, slow invasion of their dreams, a subtle twisting if you will, picking through their thoughts, steering their emotions, breaking down inhibitions. Then I use them as my unwitting servants until I am ready to fully take control... Yet that takes some time and only works on the weak-willed."

"I've been accused of many things, but that hasn't been on the list."

"No, it is not. Then there is the more violent, direct approach, where I simply kill your body and then seize control of it. Yet that leaves only an empty husk. And a husk has no memories to steal." The *Adze* leaned back on his chair. "You know, you're not the first Shackleford I've encountered in my long life. I met your grandfather many years ago, in the Congo if I recall correctly. He tried to kill me, nearly succeeded too."

I remembered what Albert Lee had said about that mission. "Sucks it didn't take."

"For him especially. Seeing him again after all these years, and finally being able to murder him? Now that was an unexpected bonus."

I'd never wanted to kill anyone more. I pulled against the ropes until my wrists bled, but it didn't do a damned thing.

"You Shacklefords are canny yet unreasonable. Unlike me, you are not honorable in your dealings. So now I'm going to leave you to be tormented by the lamia."

"Where are your stupid snake vampires?"

"Still devouring the bodies of everyone who died upstairs. We simply dump the corpses down here for disposal. It is very efficient. I've given them permission to bleed you, to hurt you in ways you can't even imagine, but to leave you alive."

He stood up. The gnome thing picked up the chair and folded it.

"We will speak again when you are ready to tell me where the artifact is."

CHAPTER 19

I watched as he and his entourage made their slow and stately progress across the sunken plaza, the plume on Brother Death's hat bobbing as he walked. *Why that costume?* I wondered, and then was sure I didn't want to know. Things of consummate evil tend to be weirdly sentimental. But what they remember . . . let's say it's not a first kiss or a first love.

While Brother Death and his entourage walked up the steps and out of sight, nothing happened. I don't know what I expected. An explosion of snakes with human faces, perhaps, rushing on me.

But nothing happened. I was left tied to the column. The pair of security golems he'd left behind stood still, watching. They were probably there to alert him when I was ready to talk.

In the vast underground space where every sign was magnified, there was almost no sound. Just a rustle and slither from across the area, and the sound of my breathing. The golems didn't even have the decency of pretending to breathe. They stood absolutely still, like statues in Armani suits wearing their dark glasses.

I wondered what they were wired to report, if Brother Death could see through their eye holes, or if they were only coded to activate at the scream declaring I wanted to talk. I wondered if I should say I wanted to talk. If I were untied, I could perhaps . . .

What? Without a gun or really anything but hands and teeth, how was I supposed to take out golems? But what was the alternative? I didn't know where the artifact even was. I could feel the loss, a sense of being bereft. It wasn't real or sane, like my feelings about losing Ray, but it was there all the same, worked upon by the ghost-Guardian's sermon in my . . . was it a dream?

So, what did I have to offer?

Maybe, I thought, *once the vampire who'd been my mother figured out that I couldn't get out, maybe once she had Ray secure, she would come back for me.*

And then I realized I was hoping for an evil vampire to save me, and I felt like screaming. I felt like screaming anyway. My son. I'd had my son in my arms! I hadn't been able to keep him.

And now Susan had him.

I let out a scream, a howl of frustration and rage. The golems didn't even react, which at least told me something. They didn't react to just anything.

Back in the shadows, I saw a snake tail scuttle back into the deeper dark at my scream. I tried to remember: did they not like loud noises? Well, that was one way to keep them at bay, at least for a little while.

I needed to focus on getting out of here. Maybe the column was rough enough to wear through the rope, but not fast, and the rope was thick and looped a number of times.

Hell, what did I have but time? Gritting my teeth because rubbing the rope on the column meant rubbing my wrists on the column, I started moving them up and down as much as I could. Frankly it wasn't much. Maybe a quarter of an inch. It was going to take forever.

Meanwhile . . . meanwhile, all I had to defend myself was my feet, and I didn't even have shoes on anymore.

I caught movement from the corner of my eye. At first I thought it was one of those little hairball yippy dogs bounding my way, but then it said, "Cuddle Bunny!"

"Shhhhh."

"Cuddle Bunny, I is mammal!" Under the furs I'd been wearing earlier, Mr. Trash Bags was in *disguise*.

He dashed up to me extruding little eyes on stalks that seemed to come from the middle of the now-filthy fur. At least now he was trying to whisper. "Cuddle Bunny must flee. Bad things come."

Okay. This was more like it. I looked back toward the golems, but they were still staring off into space.

"Snake things. Many teeth, eating!"

"I'm tied up. Can you eat through these ropes?"

One tentacle stuck to the rope as if tasting it. "Material not digest."

"Just biting through them is fine. How long?"

"Not meat, bone, or ground. Minutes to take."

Sure, he'd eat the ears off somebody's head, but ask him to eat through a nylon rope . . . I almost snapped at him that now wasn't the time to be a picky eater, but then something man-sized moved in the shadows where I'd seen the snake tail.

"Go find me something to cut through these ropes.

It looks like a bunch of houses fell down here during an earthquake; there's got to be something."

He looked at me very intently, then left, moving so fast he almost lost his disguise. I couldn't tell where he was going, but I could see that my torturers were beginning to venture from the corner.

Mr. Trash Bags came right back. He held up, with a look of great triumph—an egg.

Shoggoths weren't known for their high IQs, even those who hadn't been frozen and mostly killed. "No, no, no. Cut. We've got to saw, or break it, or something. *Cut.* Go!"

More shapes were rising from the darkness of the sunken plaza. Bodies low to the ground, they came toward me, slithering. The barely audible sound made all the hairs on my arms stand up. One of them crossed beneath the feeble light.

They truly were horrendous to look at.

According to legends, lamias would often lure men with their charms to places where they could be killed. All I can say is they must be the kind of men who would find a hole in the ground attractive. Either that or there was some illusion at work which could make them look better. If so, that magic didn't work on women, or they didn't have it turned on right now, because more were entering the light, and they were *ugly*.

Imagine a great big snake, dirt-brown to unpleasantly moist black-grey, to patchy moist green—you have the right picture. But when you get to where the snake's head should be, it starts to widen out and turn into a sort of human torso, still covered in snakeskin. Despite looking reptilian, they had what looked like human breasts. They didn't have legs, but they certainly had arms, which were too long and ended in claws. Their faces ran the gamut of features that even a Roman mother couldn't call beautiful, from hatchet noses to no noses at all, to overbroad foreheads to skulls that were downright pointy. And all of them—all of them—had beady little snake eyes and a mouth that more closely resembled a chicken ass than human lips.

And the reason their mouths looked like that—I knew from my training days and one of our teams' report on an incident in Little Italy in Cleveland—was that inside there wasn't anything even vaguely resembling a human mouth. Instead, it was like a tunnel, lined with sharp teeth all the way down their gullet.

They could expand their mouths like anacondas, to swallow something twice their size or more. By the time their prey made it through all those teeth, it had been cuisinarted to death.

And while their bites wouldn't make you into one of them like a vampire, it would inject a weird narcotic poison into your bloodstream.

So if they were supposed to torture me into compliance, this was going to be a long slog of being in pain and not being able to react, and being in pain some more, world without end.

Moments later he was back, carrying a . . . cat. Which he held up to me hopefully while the stray cat hissed and spit.

"Damn it! Something that'll cut through rope!"

"Mammal has claws," Mr. Trash Bags explained.

The instant Mr. Trash Bags let go of the cat, it hit the ground running.

"Nonononono," I screamed, as I saw the horrors

drawing nearer. There were too many, too densely packed to count, but the closest one had her mouth slightly open and was drooling poison down her chest. It wasn't even so much being tortured. Did I have to be tortured in an unspeakably gross way?

The cat ran straight to the stairs, past the lamias, past the golems, and out of sight. The tiny shoggoth curled one tentacle almost like he was shaking a fist. "Useless mammal!"

"Just go! Find something!"

As the lamias approached, they started making a snickering sound. Maybe it was just their breathing, but it made them seem even more unspeakably nasty. It was weird; as they kept their bodies close to the ground, the snake halves slithered, but they used their arms to crawl. It seemed a weird, disjointed, creepy method of getting around.

The nearest lamias used their arms to shove themselves upright. The snake parts curled, powerful muscles lifting them so that they could see me better. I got hit with a gagging stench, like the reptile house at the zoo crossed with rotting death. I realized that some of the lamias looked stretched out, tummies bulging, because they'd just got done feasting on the remains of everybody I'd shot upstairs. At least they were a little sluggish after the big dinner.

"Cuddle Bunny!" Mr. Trash Bags came bounding between the monsters, and this time, whatever treasure he'd found was dragging along the rocks behind him, making a metallic clanking noise.

Holy shit. Mr. Trash Bags had found a sword.

This wasn't some rusty relic that had been lost down here for centuries. It looked new and rather decorative. One of the auction guests had probably been wearing it for the ceremonial flash, or maybe one of the Condition morons had thought it looked cool to bring a sword to a gunfight. I just hoped it was more than decorative and sharp enough to cut thick rope. Who knows? I was just glad to see he'd not brought me another alley cat.

"Yes! Perfect. Cut the ropes!"

The sword was much bigger than Mr. Trash Bags, but shoggoths have a great power-to-weight ratio. He stuck the blade against the pillar and started sawing back and forth, like an angry, furry buzzsaw.

The security golems were still on the stairs. Surely they'd heard Mr. Trash Bags by now, but they'd not sounded an alarm. If Brother Death could see through them, then he knew what was going on. Either he didn't know, or he found my attempts at escape amusing and didn't care enough to get involved.

The ropes frayed, then snapped.

"Flee, Cuddle Bunny!"

I rolled away from the pillar, struggling to get my hands free. The lamias slithered my way. Some were moving to the side to encircle me and cut off all avenues of escape. My wrists hurt and my hands tingled from the lack of circulation, but I managed to snatch the sword from Mr. Trash Bags.

A lamia swayed toward me. I slashed the sword hard across the chest. The glistening skin split open, revealing red muscle underneath. The lamia hissed and reared back.

"Let's go," I shouted at Mr. Trash Bags as I headed for the stairs.

The lamias swarmed.

I don't know a damned thing about sword fighting. I had an adopted uncle who was a master at it, who'd tried to teach me stuff when I was little, but it hadn't stuck. When it came to monster hunting I'm a fan of shooting them from as far away as possible, and for me, that was really far. Up close and in your face isn't my style.

But right then I didn't have a whole lot of choice, so I just started swinging.

A lamia clawed at my face, but I lopped off two of her fingers on the way in. One swept around behind me and got a handful of my already torn dress. I spun the sword around and stabbed her right in the mouth. The blade sunk deep and I yanked it out of her cheek.

But then it was wall-to-wall snake flesh, and I had the terrible realization that the only reason they hadn't ripped me to shreds was Brother Death had commanded them not to kill me. I slowly turned in a circle and saw that I was completely surrounded by hissing, twisting, snake women reaching for me.

Suddenly there were a bunch of gunshots from above.

All the lamias and I looked up to see that someone was coming down the stairs, blazing away with an automatic rifle at the two security golems. Whoever it was wasn't much of a shot because he tore through what must have been a 30-round magazine and only hit the golems once or twice each. Still, rifle bullets do a number on hardened clay, so they burst into pieces and fireflies as they tumbled down the stairs.

I used the distraction to my advantage and started chopping at the lamias. I clipped one in the neck and she sprayed blood. I hit the next one in the bulging snake belly hard enough to split her wide open. So wide open in fact that the chewed-up cultist she'd eaten spilled out.

Mr. Trash Bags might not have been big on eating rope, but he had no problem eating lamias. Still cloaked in furs and squeaking his battle cry of "*Consume*" the little shoggoth bounced across the floor, latched onto a snake tail and attacked.

Claws ripped through my dress but missed my skin. I didn't have a good angle to stab that one, so instead I punched her in her ugly face with the sword's hand guard. That one lurched away, but I screamed as her friend's teeth latched onto my shoulder.

Lamia venom *burns*.

I stabbed right past my head and stuck that lamia in the face. Her teeth released and I fell. Rolling forward, I barely managed to dodge more claws, winding up on my back with a lot of hissing vampire bitches right over me.

"Julie, catch!"

Hansel?

Now that was a surprise. I'd not expected him to come back. I looked up just in time to see him toss a pistol my way.

Now judging by how inaccurate the lawyer's aim had been against the security golems, it was probably good that he'd thrown it to me, rather than tried to help by shooting, because I probably would've gotten plugged. Problem was, he wasn't that accurate at throwing either, so the gun bounced off another lamia's head and landed in the dirt a few feet away. Somehow Hansel had found the Sig I'd lost upstairs. Before I could reach for it, though, I discovered that lamias aren't just biters, they're also constrictors. All of a sudden a lamia wrapped her lower body around my legs. The crushing pressure was incredible. Another grabbed my sword arm. It compressed the bones together so hard it felt like they were going to be ground into powder. Then there was another terrible flash of awful chemical fire as a lamia bit into my hip.

Head swimming from the poison, I got buried in snake vampires . . . but not before I got my left hand on the pistol.

I jammed the muzzle against the temple of the one on my legs. *Pop!* Then against the forehead of the bitch sucking on my hip. *Pop!* Then the one on my right arm. *Pop pop!* She got two because I didn't have a very good angle on her brain.

The pressure released and the lamias flopped around, twitching. I stumbled up, gun in one hand, sword in the other, bleeding, poisoned, and with most of my clothes torn off, and shouted, "Come on!" Then I was shooting and chopping my way toward the stairs.

The poison was really messing with my head. The world was swimming. I don't even remember how I got to the stairs, but it must've been by spilling lots of lamia blood and leaving a trail of severed hands and pissed-off hissing snake ladies.

During all that, Hansel had been trying to figure out how to fire one of the submachine guns dropped by the security golems.

Even terrified, the lawyer was still well-spoken. "Forgive my late arrival. I was trying to reach you, but I couldn't keep up with your little helper."

The lamias were slithering up the stairs behind me. "Here, trade you." I pushed the sword to him and took the little B&T subgun away. "Run!" Unlike Hansel, I knew how to deactivate a thumb safety, so I extended it in one hand and opened fire, working the muzzle back and forth as bullets tore into the tightly packed monsters in the narrow stairwell. When it was empty, I dropped the gun and ran after him.

"Let's go, Mr. Trash Bags!"

The now blood-soaked fur jumped off a lamia's partially eaten head and bounded up the stairs.

I don't know how long we ran for. The underground area was a whole lot bigger than I first thought, and with the poison pumping through my veins, I was really dizzy. My vision was blurry, and it wasn't just because I'd lost my glasses. I had a sneaky feeling that if it wasn't for the Guardian's mark, I'd either be paralyzed or unconscious by now.

I rounded a corner, and Hansel was there, leaning against the wall and breathing really hard. He probably didn't get a lot of cardio in his line of work. There weren't any lamias directly behind us, so I stopped to catch my breath.

I gave Hansel an incredulous look. He'd told me from the beginning he wasn't doing this for me. He was doing this for Management, to whom he owed loyalty or at least some obedience as a client. "Why'd you come back?"

"Let's say I didn't feel right about leaving you to your fate. I've had many clients, and helped many people for other clients, but your quest is probably the only truly righteous one I've ever had. There is no higher calling than helping a mother protect her child." He paused to cough. "It is a far better thing than I've ever done."

"Well...huh...thank you!" That was really nice of him, but I'd get sentimental later. I ejected the magazine from the Grayguns Sig. It was too dim to see the witness holes in the dark, but from the weight remaining, I only had a few rounds left. "You got any more magazines for this thing?"

I'd lost his coat, but Hansel fished around in his trouser pocket and handed me over one more mag. "That's all I have left. There is a way out. I came through it, from a small building across the plaza. It's quite possible that on the way back we'll find something else blocking our way." He looked down at the sword in his hand. "I'm afraid I don't really know what to do with this."

"Join the club," I said as I loaded the fresh mag and did a chamber check. "Brother Death has got to know I've escaped. He'll be down here looking for us too."

"I'm not so sure. A few minutes ago Hunters from the Portuguese government raided the church above. He's more than likely fled."

So Albert had gotten ahold of Grant after all. "Great. Then let's get out of here before their Feds mistake us for cultists and shoot us. You first."

It wasn't just because I was injured and poisoned that I wanted Hansel on point. He felt genuine, but I'd already been tricked by Brother Death's mind-controlling people before, and I didn't intend to fall for it again. Mr. Trash Bags obediently bounced alongside my bare feet. It's strange to say, but covered in filthy blood-matted fur, he was actually more frightening than his usual look of tar-colored blob with extra eyeballs and teeth.

I didn't want to say anything in front of Hansel—just

in case he was possessed and this was all another scam—but I needed to see if Mr. Trash Bags had the artifact. So I picked him up. "Good job, Mr. Trash Bags."

"Cuddle Bunny love Mr. Trash Bags?"

I gave him a squeeze. It was like the furs were filled with a bag of jelly. He kind of *smooshed,* but in there was the hard rectangular lump of the artifact.

"Yes. Cuddle Bunny loves her Mr. Trash Bags."

If a shoggoth could purr, he probably would have right then.

Nothing else tried to kill us.

It took us what seemed like forever to stumble blindly through the ruins.

CHAPTER 20

The exit was just a plain wooden door which was, thankfully, unlocked. I emerged from the tunnel and blinked because after hours down there, the streetlights were really bright. It took me a minute to realize that the door was on the back side of a gurgling stone fountain, set almost against a wall but not touching it. That's the weird thing about Old Europe: you can have an unremarkable door on the street lead to a bake shop . . . or catacombs. Flip a coin.

Then I noticed there were a lot of men with guns and flashlights nearby.

We hadn't been spotted yet, so I crouched next to the fountain and tried to take stock. The plaza the ruined convent was in had been sealed. Orange traffic barricades had been put up to block the streets around it. Thankfully we'd come out on the other side of the cordoned-off area. On this side of the barriers was a cacophony of sirens and arguing voices, as the Portuguese motorists weren't having any of whatever they were being told had caused the closure of the plaza.

Manning the barriers were what looked like World

318

War I generals in polished brass helmets and elaborate uniforms, but inside the plaza, it was all men dressed in black fatigues and balaclavas, holding serious hardware and skulking around, looking at everything, particularly the old church.

I was certain the ones in black were Agencia de Segurança Sobrenatural and, despite their incredibly unfortunate English acronym, they looked like they knew what they were doing.

Hansel was still in the tunnel. I put my finger to my lips, warning him to be quiet.

"Mr. Trash Bags pretend to be mammal," my shoggoth said helpfully.

Without even looking, I used my foot to shove Mr. Trash Bags back into the tunnel.

Hansel took a turn poking his head out of the tunnel to see what was going on.

"Who are the World War I generals?" I asked, my voice low.

"The Republican Guard. They're basically police. They are the excuse to clear the plaza. If anyone heard the shots, I'm sure they'll blame it on terrorism. It's ASS we have to worry about."

I felt my face contort in a grimace. "I don't think I'll like a Portuguese prison any better than a German one." I sure didn't like feeling cornered.

Most of the bystanders were looking toward the commotion in the plaza, not our way, which meant we might not be seen sneaking out. Well, less likely, since my dress was hanging in tatters, and I was covered in dirt and drying blood. I couldn't just hide in the tunnels waiting for them to leave while Susan was getting further away with Ray. Even though getting caught here—especially with the artifact—wasn't going to end well, we had to go for it.

I made a gesture for Hansel to stay quiet, not that it was needed. The one who needed to be quiet was Mr. Trash Bags, but good luck with that. There weren't that many people around, but if they turned around, they were going to see me in my bedraggled evening dress, barefoot, clutching a gun in one hand, with a bloody nightmare poodle at my feet.

Luckily, nobody saw us sneak around the fountain. I let my breath out.

Then Hansel whispered, "That gate to the left. Open it and go in."

There was an arched wooden gate, set in a seven-foot-tall pink-painted stone wall. When I'd scanned, it hadn't even registered. It had a massive lock on it, and in the middle of a large city, I assumed it would be locked.

"I went through it earlier. Go."

So I went. I didn't know if the gate led to a house or what, but it seemed like it would be easier to go through a house, even if I had to take hostages, than it would be to not be spotted on the street looking like this.

I had, in fact, walked into a vegetable garden. A tiny one. There were things staked and things on stalks, and a bunch of hydrangeas colonizing a corner. This time of year most of the garden was dead. There was a path leading straight through to another wall and a gate.

"Wait a moment. I'll be right back." Hansel wasn't nearly as dirty or messed up as I was. There were a few mystery stains on his nice white shirt, but he still mostly looked respectable and not nearly as likely to be noticed by the law. He went out the opposite gate into the street.

I got really impatient. Every minute I hid in this garden was that much farther Susan was going to get away with Ray. But it wouldn't do me any good to get arrested.

I still hurt everywhere, but the effects of the poison seemed to be wearing off. I had no way to see, but I couldn't feel any bullet holes in my back, so I could only assume there were new black dots back there. The nonlethal fang punctures in my hip were still bleeding though. Thanks a lot, stupid curse.

Waiting there gave me time to think about what Susan had said. She was responsible for the vampire outbreak at my school. She'd manipulated me and meddled in my life, pulling my strings without me ever realizing it. Even though I had a happy life and loved my job, without getting back into monster hunting I never would've met my husband nor had my son. The knowledge that Susan had played some part in influencing my decisions made it all feel tainted.

About ten minutes later a car horn honked on the other side of the gate away from the plaza.

I stepped through, trying to gather my dignity...

And found myself in the middle of a tree-lined city street. Nearby was a little sidewalk café, with the early morning crowd having their morning espresso and croissant.

I put my gun behind my back, trying to hide it in the folds of what was left of my dress trying to look nonchalant. I expected a scream for the police at any minute, but luckily the gate was in shadows.

You'd think honking a car horn would draw more attention from all the nearby cops, but there were a lot of honks since Portuguese seemed to believe making noise was an essential part of driving. They made New York drivers seem polite and reserved.

The honking was coming from a white luxury sedan. I didn't recognize the driver, but Hansel, looking like the canary that ate the cat, got out of the backseat and held the door open for me.

I tried to look like this was my car, and it was perfectly normal for very wealthy people to run around Lisbon barefoot carrying a gun while wearing a bedraggled evening dress.

I got in and Hansel slid in after me.

"I called for a car and told it to wait before I went back in for you. I just came around another way, after giving one of the ASS agents a suitable bribe." Hansel shoved something at me.

It was a business card. It read LUISA LOPES. INVESTIGADOR PROFISSIONAL. AGENCIA DE SEGURANÇA SOBRENATURAL and a number.

"I suspect she knew who I was working for, and I do not mean Management. She said she wishes to talk and to help."

"You mean help arrest me?"

"I do not think so." We were already moving down the street. Hansel glanced through the back window. "If that were the case, they would be following us now. It appears to be clear."

"But I though all the EU supernatural agencies were linked and allied."

He shrugged. "Portugal is a case of oppositional defiant disorder with borders. They certainly know you are wanted in Germany, and that might be exactly why this Agent Lopes wishes to help you. All of the institutions in Portugal are a sort of Swiss cheese of genuinely honest agents, time-servers, and very corrupt people."

"You mean just like my government?"

He gave me a weird look. "Not even close. You have no idea."

"So, this lady you just gave a bribe to wants to meet? Why?"

"If she's corrupt, then further bribes may get her to pass on intelligence. If not and she is one of the honorable ones, she might do the same for entirely different reasons. It is not my place to weigh the risk, merely to convey the offer."

"I'll think on it." I slipped Lopes' business card into my décolletage. That's cleavage for those of you who went to the University of Alabama. There's a reason that women from time immemorial have used it as an additional pocket. There is this space in the front of the bra, between your boobs, that will hold anything securely for at least a little while.

And then Hansel's phone rang.

He pulled it out of his pocket, "Yes?" And then, "No, sir. But you see, I couldn't let her— No, sir . . . Yes, sir . . . No, sir. Here she is."

He handed the phone to me, and then Management said in my ear, "From the chatter, I assume the auction did not work out as you hoped?"

"Not even close. Susan Shackleford has Ray. I need to figure out where she's going."

"Of course. Hansel is taking you to another one of my properties in Lisbon. You are welcome to stay there and enjoy my hospitality while I set my minions on this search."

"Thank . . . thank you. I thought you'd said if we didn't win the auction, I'd be on my own because you didn't need the trouble."

"That was before Brother Death insulted me and attempted to murder my employee," the dragon said in a cold and cutting voice. "Oh yes, I take it Hansel did not tell you how Brother Death's guards set upon him when he attempted to flee. Your hideous blob monster intervened and saved him from certain execution."

"He left that part out." I gave Hansel a sidelong glance. The lawyer shrugged. So maybe his motives might not have been quite as heroic and pure as he made them out to be, but help was help.

"I know that you are unfamiliar with the supernatural communities which live well outside man's law, but believe me, such an insult cannot go ignored. To do so would indicate that I no longer have the power to keep safe my employees. I'd lose all my holdings." There was a pause. "Also, I must confess that, given how much she's grown in status since the death of Martin Hood, it doesn't please me to have Susan Shackleford's might increase further by her harnessing the powers of your child."

"The things at the auction seemed to think he was magic, but I've never seen any indication Ray's special." Beyond rolling over, having a chubby little laugh and, of course, being capable of filling his diaper with absolutely room-clearing stink.

"It would be nearly impossible not to be, given whose son he is. And whatever gifts he has inherited, I do not want a Master vampire controlling them."

If Monster Hunters were paranoid, we had nothing on the monsters we hunted. They were constantly measuring themselves against each other and playing games to not let the other one get any advantage. We'd already made one business arrangement with Management because he hated Asag. Hating Susan was a happy bonus.

"While you recuperate, I will see what I can do. I've instructed Hansel to return to his regular business. I do understand his desire to assist you beyond what he was contractually obligated to do, but I do not pay him to have a heart or impulses. He's supposed to do exactly as he's told, not play at being heroic. Leave the heroics to the heroes. I'll excuse this instance of his going off script, but my employees are of no value to me dead." A pause. "I do not employ foolish employees."

I hung up the phone and looked at Hansel. "Your boss is pissed."

"I gathered that."

"I'm sorry if I got you in trouble."

"Don't be," he said. "A man has to do what— Never mind. For once in my life I wanted to fight, not just with words. I'm glad I helped get you out. Even if your little companion might have done it all on his own." He looked down at where Mr. Trash Bags was getting the floor covers dirty. "What is he, by the way?"

Normally I'd try to hide the fact that I was hanging out with a monster, but Mr. Trash Bags was practically a saint compared to some of Hansel's clients. "Pocket shoggoth. It's a long story."

"Cuddle Bunny. Made of stars," Mr. Trash Bags explained.

Hansel proved that he was worthy of being Management's employee by making no comment at all, not even the raising of an eyebrow.

We drove to the edge of the city and stopped at an isolated property belonging to Management. The car pulled around to the back.

"Management thought perhaps you should go in through the private entrance. He believes it would be better if you are not seen."

I got out. Hansel stayed in the car.

"This is as far as I go with you."

"Thanks. If you're ever going to get involved in monster hunting again, take some shooting lessons. Seriously." I looked down at my hand, which still held the gun. "Tell your client I'm keeping this. Bill me for a replacement."

"I shall do so. Best of luck to you."

There was a doorman waiting, the sort of thing one expects in high-class condos. Management must have warned the staff because he didn't even change his expression when he saw how beat-up I was.

The doorman led me to a private elevator that went directly to the penthouse. This wasn't as grand as the place in which I'd gotten ready for the auction, but it was still pretty fancy.

There were servants waiting in the penthouse. I was asked upon arrival if I needed help bathing and changing which, to be fair, I hadn't needed since I was three, but I got them to point me toward the bathroom, and then they asked whether I wanted a meal and when.

I hadn't even thought of food, which was when I

realized I was famished. I asked for a meal heavy on the protein, I didn't particularly care what. Then I asked for a needle, thread, iodine, and bandages. I was so weary I was having trouble thinking, but I had to keep going.

I found that my room already contained clothes in my size, ranging from sundresses to jeans and varying types of T-shirts and blouses to evening attire. There were even three new pairs of glasses in different styles. Of course Management even had my correct prescription. I wasn't sure what Management thought I'd be doing in Lisbon or how long I'd need to stay, but I had the sudden disquieting feeling that should it come to me needing to stay here for years while tracking down my son, Management and his employees would act like this was no more than expected, and I'd be perfectly welcome here.

I took off my clothes, left Mr. Trash Bags, in his much-the-worse-for-wear fur, on top of the artifact, and got in the shower. It was warm and prickled on my skin, making me realize that I had been severely hurt in several spots. There were scrapes and bruises all over, most of which I didn't even remember getting. I'd been knocked out and my head throbbed. That couldn't be good.

I'd done all that, gone to that evil place, been attacked by monsters and tied up in a dungeon by Brother Death, and all for what?

My baby was gone. My evil mother had him. She was going to—

I couldn't even think of what she was going to do. She probably wouldn't hurt him physically—yet. She'd want him to grow up first before she turned him—Susan was too pragmatic to want an immortal baby—though it was difficult to guess what a vampire would do, because their sense of what is good for people is all off. But even if she was going to keep him alive and in one piece, he'd still see horrible things, feel horrible things, be taught all sorts of crazy, and then, when he'd finished growing up, she'd turn him.

I leaned against the tile and bawled my eyes out while the water ran over me, making every little bruise and scrape hurt like hell.

I'd had Ray in my arms—warm against me—I'd had him! I should have kept him safe. I sucked as a mother. Despondence washed over me, and then I punched the tile. No, to hell with that. I was still alive, which certainly hadn't been in Brother Death's plans. I still had the artifact. I was going to find that vampire bitch, I was going to take my baby from her, and then I was going to make her pay.

I soaped and shampooed as if I were washing away the fear and the pain and the angst of missing my baby. I knew it wouldn't work. I was still crying after I rinsed, but I was going to call Dorcas, find out where my backup was, and get them to help me. Now, if not yesterday.

I dried myself, bandaged the puncture wounds, and put on jeans and a T-shirt. Breakfast was already waiting for me. I ate while I grabbed the Management's secure phone and dialed Dorcas. For some reason I expected it to ring a long time, but instead I got her voice almost immediately, sounding all snuffy like she had a cold, and even more hostile than usual.

"MHI. What do you want?"

"Dorcas? It's Julie. You said you were going to send—"

I stopped because a wail interrupted me. "Oh, honey, I'm so sorry."

For a moment I wondered how she knew I'd lost Ray again, but in the next second I knew. I knew. "What? You...you heard from the siege?"

"The Russians just nuked Severny Island."

"What?"

"It's all over the news."

There was a TV in the room, and I turned it on and flipped through, until it landed on CNN. Yeah, they're trash, but they're in English and pretty much everywhere. I read the scroll. *Surprise nuclear test violates treaties.* They were showing what had to be a stock photo of the island. The talking heads were going on about UN outrage, saber-rattling, nonproliferation, all that smoke-screen nonsense.

I turned the TV off and sat on the bed. It was all gone. Owen, my brother Nate, and all my friends were gone. I'd lost Ray, and everyone else was *gone.*

I don't know how long I sat there, my face all wet and tears dripping from my chin. Dorcas was yelling, "Honey?" from the phone, and Mr. Trash Bags cuddled up to my arm.

I picked up the phone. "Oh, Dorcas. They're all gone."

She said softly, "Maybe." But she'd had more time to process this than I had. "But maybe not. There's been a communications blackout. Everything's being jammed up there. We know what was really on that island, but we don't know the circumstances of them dropping that bomb. There were a mess of Russians at the siege too, so maybe they let our guys get out first."

"Then why haven't they called?"

"I don't know. I've been trying to get hold of that scumbag Krasnov's people. If Earl and the rest are dead, *if*, and that's a mighty big if, then we'll make it work. But trust me, kid, Earl's hard to kill, and your husband ain't no slouch either! It ain't over 'til the fat lady sings."

But I was so tired and so wrung out that I simply had no hope left. Owen was dead. It was just me, and I sucked. I sucked as a mother, I sucked as a Hunter.

I must have started blubbering that out loud because she snorted rudely in my ear, "Yeah, right. Sure, you suck at monster hunting. You've only been doing it all your life, and all that PUFF in the bank just came because people really like your pretty eyes, right? Stop being a fool, girl. I take it you don't have your boy yet?"

I told her what had happened.

"Okay," she said, her voice like molasses over grits or perhaps like acid over something really gritty. "I tell you what you're going to do: you're going to call that ASS agent, and then you're going to find that crazy vampire, get your son back, and kill that bitch. Got it?"

"I don't know if—"

"I didn't ask you what you could or couldn't do, girl. I told you what you're gonna do. The group I sent to help should be there in"—I heard paper flip at the other end of the line—"a couple hours. Tell me where you're going to be, and they'll meet you. And then you get Little Bubba back. We need you, Julie, and you need him. You're going to get your ass back here and run the company like your grandpa intended. And you're gonna train Little Bubba to be the best damned Hunter that ever was, better than all the other Rays who ever ran this company combined. You hear me?"

I heard her. "Yes, ma'am."

I hung up and walked around the room to the window. I'd been living in such a way that my meals and sleep had absolutely no relation to the time of day. All I knew was that it was early morning. We were at a high point in the hills surrounding the city, and though I knew there were skyscrapers nearby, the view out this window was tile roofs, the occasional tall, golden stone building and church spire, going down to the blue sparkle that I assumed was the sea.

In any other circumstances it would be beautiful. Right now this was the saddest sight I'd ever seen.

My husband was probably dead... I could either dwell on that, or I could keep fighting to save the rest of my family.

"Salt water drips from your face eyes." A tentacle wrapped around my arm, and two little eyes on tentacle stalks stared up at me. "No more," Mr. Trash Bags commanded, trying to be helpful.

He looked so goofy it actually kind of distracted me from the pain. "Hey, let's get you out of that fur coat."

"Mr. Trash Bags not pretty?"

"Yes, you are." He looked like a terrifying reject from *The Muppet Show*. But what the heck did I know about shoggoth fashion anyway? He was actually kind of adorable—except for the pelt being all dirty, torn, and covered in dried blood. I don't even know how he'd managed to keep it on through all the excitement; he must have suction-cupped himself to it or something. "But I like you better without the coat."

That was enough. He parted from the pelt. "Mammal no more. Retrieve Cuddle Bunny Cuddle Bunny. WILL EAT ALL TOES."

"That's the spirit," I said as I dialed the number on Lopes' card.

It was answered immediately. "Agente de Segurança Sobrenatural Lopes."

I hoped she spoke English. "This is Julie Shackleford. You wanted to talk?"

"Yes." There was a pause as she mentally switched gears. She had an accent, but luckily her English was pretty good. "Some important men were killed last night at that church. There are many searching for you right now."

"I've already heard about how I'm upsetting the delicate balance of the EU monster hunting agencies."

"To hell with them. This isn't Germany. I'm glad those rich bastards got shot and murdered last night. I want to help you."

I was desperate and sad, but not a sucker. "How much is that going to cost me?"

"No. I'm not on the take. Well, not exactly. Okay. A little, but not much. Mostly I want these assholes out of my country. You shaking things up is good. I'd prefer not to say anything more over the phone. We need to meet."

"And you'll tell me something for my benefit?"

She hesitated. "I think so. I believe there is a way I can help you and you can help me."

Right then I needed something—anything—some tiny spark of hope so I could keep going.

"Let's meet."

CHAPTER 21

I drove myself to the *Museu dos Coches*. Apparently taking the city bus simply wasn't done for any guest of Management, and there had been a garage full of new cars with the keys in them.

I had to sit in the parking lot for a minute to compose myself before going in. I wanted to believe that my husband was still alive, that by some miracle most of my remaining friends and family had gotten off the island before the Russians had bombed the City of Monsters, but right then I really couldn't.

Nothing looked suspicious. None of the other cars looked familiar. I didn't think I'd been followed.

The entrance to the museum was dispiritingly modern, with glass doors and then smoked glass doors to the interior. I paid the ticket price to the bored-looking man at the entrance. He tried to make small talk. "Kind of early in the season for tourists," he said, in heavily accented English because apparently I couldn't even buy a ticket without revealing where I was from. "Most of our visitors now are elderly people and school groups."

I smiled and told him I was in Portugal visiting family, and he gave me a dubious look since I didn't look in the least Portuguese, then I went in through the smoked glass doors.

Inside, if I hadn't been there on a mission of far more importance than gawking at historical artifacts, I would have been impressed. Putting on my art historian hat, I could have spent several happy hours inside the carriage museum. Most of the carriages were from the late nineteenth century, but there were some from the eighteenth that looked like the worst excesses of Baroque churches on wheels.

There were a few people wandering around inside, but I didn't see anything that looked like an SJK hit squad there to arrest me.

I was walking around a carriage which had been painted with panels representing mannered pastoral scenes, and then ornamented with rococo carvings covered in much too much gold, when a small, neat woman approached. She was dark-haired, dark-eyed, early forties, wore the cheap business attire that is the international symbol for a government agent, and walked with the kind of gait that let you know that, yes, despite being kind of frumpy, she actually was in great physical shape.

She approached me with her hand out, "Mrs. Pitt? I am Luisa Lopes." She flashed an ID with the letters ASS emblazoned across it in bright red. Then she looked at the nearest carriage, "You are admiring some of Portugal's history, no?"

I reminded myself not to piss off the nice foreign government agent who supposedly wanted to help me. In our marriage, Owen and I had a strict division of labor. Pissing off government agents of any and all nationalities was his job. Mine was to make sure that it didn't end with us dead. So I remained polite.

"I'd love to come back and look at all this properly, at a better time, when I'm not worried about my son being kidnapped by a Master vampire."

She sucked in air through her teeth. "Very sad. If we can't protect our children, who will be safe?"

"You have children, Agent Lopes?"

"No."

"Then you have no idea what I'm willing to do to protect him."

We walked along between the carriages.

"So, Mrs. Pitt, before I share too much, tell me, what cause do you have to think he's even still alive? Vampires are not known to keep babies alive. They are too young to be turned, and normally—"

"The Master vampire used to be my mother."

"I see."

"You have to understand, the human version was a very good mother. She still wants to be a good mother and, worse, a good grandmother."

She gave me a look of pity. "You tell me the truth. I already knew who she was. The MCB shared their file with us, but it counts in your favor that you tell me the truth."

I'd been so fixated on not trusting her that I'd not even thought about her not trusting me. Either way, I didn't want pity.

"Truth is I want Susan dead."

"We believe we know where she is hiding in this country. ASS is not pleased at this incursion into our territory by foreign vampires. We have trouble enough as a country, we do not need foreign vampires too. It's in our best interest to eliminate her before the tourist season starts. Too many disappearances are bad for the economy. And then the politicians yell at me."

I was glad Agent Lopes had her priorities in order. "So why haven't you raided this hideout yet?"

"It's complicated. It is a very isolated estate which belongs to a monster who has been protected. Up until now it has been off-limits."

Dealing with corrupt officials was nothing new for me, so even though I was tired and frustrated, I did my best to sound sweet. "So how much will this information cost me?"

Lopes grinned. "No, no, you misunderstand. You see, the creature you killed in France had made many arrangements. It turns out much money was being paid to government officers in Portugal. Big people. Even ASS couldn't go against them. If ASS had tried, we wouldn't have a leg to stand on. But now Marchand is gone, there is no one to pay protection for his clients."

Maybe I had read her wrong. "So I've already done you a favor."

"For me, yes. For our politicians who will be poorer now, not so much. The French searched Marchand's home. One of his clients is a wealthy Portuguese businessman: a man we have been keeping an eye on, who has never once been seen outside during the daytime. Starting an investigation on this businessman got my predecessor fired. Now I know why. Can you believe that? Politicians sparing a vampire for money?"

My government would make deals with certain monsters and give them PUFF exemptions, but a vampire? They needed to kill humans to live. Sparing one of those was pretty much inconceivable to an American Hunter. "How sure are you this guy's a vampire?"

"Fairly sure. I continued my former boss's investigation, but in secret. I've paid informants and sent men to spy on the property. My hands have been tied to challenge him directly but if I were to get real proof, my superiors would have no choice. A day ago we got word this vampire was hosting a guest . . . from the deference shown, a yet more powerful vampire. The description by my informant matches your mother who arrived right when there was a very valuable baby kidnapped and auctioned, bringing all sorts of supernatural scum to Portugal. And we can't have that. ASS is not a plaything."

Even as messed up as my day was, that still made me smile.

Lopes was getting worked up. "The rest of the European agencies, they say arrest Julie Shackleford because we don't want private Monster Hunters here, disrespecting us. But you know who disrespects ASS? All those stuck-up EU sons of bitches. We have a very difficult beat here. Ancient country, Portugal. Very ancient. Old ghosts. Old Roman gods. Monsters brought back from Africa and India." She waved a hand around like the monsters had personally arrived in these old carriages. "ASS doesn't fall down on the job but they treat us like we're the awkward little brother. To shit with them, I say. ASS will help you. You did nothing to cause this. It's not your fault. Why the hell should I arrest a mother who wants to save her son? It would make the Virgin Mary cry." And she crossed herself.

I still hadn't decided where on Earl's scale of Asshole

to All Right the Portuguese government Hunters fell, but this one at least seemed earnest.

"Then how about you give me the address of this businessman, and I'll go take care of another problem for you?"

"Again, you misunderstand. This is my country. ASS will kill the vampires." Lopes held up a hand to stop me before I could protest. "But I can take you with us to where this *vampira* resides, so you can help in rescuing your little son."

As territorial as government Hunters were, she had to have some angle where bringing me along helped her, but I wasn't about to argue my way out of getting another shot at Ray.

"Then we should strike fast. Last night Susan got injured by a shadow creature enough to be temporarily imprisoned by some kind of curse. From what little we know about vampires, she'll probably need time to feed and regain her strength. If she's there, it won't be for long. The second she thinks anyone is onto her, she'll move."

"I agree. My raid team will be ready by this afternoon. We will strike while we still have daylight."

"Even wounded, Master vampires are no joke. How good is this group of yours?"

"We are few, but very good. People say Portugal, small country, their ASS is a joke. They say you can do whatever you want in Portugal, and ASS won't get in the way. We have no budget. No training. All you have to do is give them some gloves... some—how do the Spanish say?—*mordida*, and they'll bend over backwards for you. And ASS doesn't get invited to any gatherings of governmental monster hunting agencies.

They don't even call us if they can help it. Right now, one of your MCB is here, Grant Jefferson, acting like we're beneath him. He acts like we're the mat under his feet, the rug on the floor."

"To be fair, he acts like that to everyone."

"Yes, well, what I say is it's time ASS proves itself. I got promoted to run Lisbon and I've kicked out all the bad elements. I copied the rules of the MCB. I want to run a tight ASS."

I bit the inside of my cheek. Dear Lord, couldn't they have called their organization something else? I answered as seriously as I could, "I'd be happy to have A—the agency's help." Then I thought I'd better come clean. This was a small and prickly bunch, the last thing I wanted to do was insult this little old country's pride, so I'd better mention my backup. Though I wasn't going to give any details yet, the last thing I needed was for them to get locked up like my guys in Germany.

"MHI is sending a team over to help me. They should be here soon."

Lopes looked at me, suspicious, "You too think ASS is not good enough to do the job on its own?"

"Of course not. No insult was intended. When I called for help, I didn't even know who you were. If you're going to conduct a raid anyway, I can provide some extra muscle. The last time MHI took out a Master vampire, we used artillery."

"But if we win, everyone will say it was the Americans and not the Portuguese. We'll still be disrespected."

"You can say my people were never here. I promise to give all the credit to ASS."

There was a moment where it hung in the balance. At first I'd thought that Lopes was just a regular rank-and-file type, who could get me some intel, not an agent in charge who could get me an army. But you didn't get to a rank like that unless you were a political animal.

Then she put her hand out, and we shook on it. "And you'll speak well of ASS to MCB?"

I promised. I didn't tell her that my opinion meant jack to the Monster Control Bureau. I mean, normally when we crossed paths, either the excrement was about to hit the rotating object, or we had other, worse problems. But I didn't have any objections to praising the Portuguese agency to the MCB in the unlikely event the opportunity should arise.

"Good, good. Then we will work together because, honestly, when I said my group is good...eh...yes, but we've never even seen a Master vampire before, so help will be nice."

That's when the schoolchildren came in. They must have been from some sort of private academy or else Portuguese public schools dressed like the stereotypes of Japanese schools. The kids ranged from six to eight or so in appearance. They were small and dark. A lot of the girls had pigtails. All the girls wore white blouses, plaid skirts and black patent leather Mary Janes. All the boys wore white shirts, blue pants and blue blazers.

There were about twenty of them with two teachers, and they chattered like tropical birds. The kids, not the teachers. If it hadn't been for the teachers silencing them now and then, we'd not have been able to hear ourselves think.

The teachers were saying things like "This is the carriage of King Luis the Boring—" although probably not literally that, since royal nicknames are never that honest, and the kids were instead wandering around and looking at everything in awe, just because it was pretty and gilded. They were doubtless too young for this type of museum visit, but I could see myself walking around like that with Ray in a few years.

My eyes were suddenly wet, and I had to turn away so Lopes wouldn't see that I was a barely functioning wreck.

Which was when I heard the rumbling. It took me a second to recognize the sound because, you see, we were in a museum, with carriages that were quite obviously not only stopped, but had no driver or horses. So, who the hell expected to hear carriage wheels?

The growing noise was coming from the dim recesses of the museum, composed of squeaks, the sound of wheels turning, and horses' hooves striking the floor.

"What in the world?" Lopes said as she reached beneath her jacket to rest her hand on her gun. "Did something from the church last night track you?"

"I don't think so. Were you followed?"

"Eh . . ." Lopes shrugged. "Maybe? I was obviously in charge."

Great.

Something was coming. The children had heard it, but they were standing there paralyzed, their teachers too. I started shooing them out of there. "Move! Run!"

Then the ghost carriage burst through the wall.

I've got to hand it to her, Lopes was quick on the draw. She was firing before I even saw the carriage clearly. It was being pulled by black steeds with fiery eyes, with a shadowy driver in outmoded attire, bowling towards us at full speed. Animals, rider, and carriage were all translucent, and I could see the far wall of the museum through them.

Lopes' bullets went right into the horses, but the impacts simply rippled like water. They weren't actually here, but the floor behind them was left glittering with ice crystals. As the horses collided with one of the adult museumgoers, he fell *through* the carriage but hit the floor twitching like he was having a seizure. His skin turned grey. It was as if just the touch had sucked the life right out of him.

Everyone screamed. The teachers reacted and began herding the kids away.

Except there was one little boy standing there, frozen with fear, right in the path of the ghost horses.

I just reacted.

The ground was shaking. The cold was like walking into a freezer. I wasn't going to make it, but I ran directly at the danger anyway. Scooping the child up, I hurled myself to the side. I landed on my back to protect the kid, but a ghostly wagon wheel rolled right over my foot. Except rather than a nasty crunch and squirting blood, it passed through like fog, only where it touched was *so cold*. It was like all the strength went right out of my body.

All I could do was lie there shivering. I tried to ask, "Are you okay?" but the kid was obviously fine. I'd taken the hit for him. He started wailing and flailing about, broke free from my cold, numbed hands, and ran for his life, thankfully in the direction opposite the ghostly carriage.

Lopes was still shooting, but it wasn't doing anything.

The carriage narrowly missed her, but then the ghost driver whipped the demon horses and the carriage turned, passing right through the real carriages. It was coming back around to run us down.

In my perception, time seemed to slow down, so the screaming of the kids, the rolling of ghostly wheels, all the noise, the cries of the teachers, everything got weird like when you play a recording at one tenth the speed.

I noticed that even though every other bystander was running or hiding, one burly older man was off to the side watching, amused, almost gleeful. Son of a bitch looked like he would be eating popcorn. He saw me looking at him and smiled back, and in that expression I recognized Brother Death.

Hands trembling, fingers like blocks of ice, I pulled the Sig. As the red dot crossed his torso, I jerked the trigger.

Brother Death laughed as I killed yet another of his possessed victims.

The ghost carriage just vanished. One second it was there, terrorizing the school children and giving everyone frostbite; blink, and it was gone.

Shaking and weak, I managed to get to my feet, and stumbled over to the man I'd shot. He was lying on the floor with a hole in his abdomen. My guess was that I'd hit him in the liver. The sudden cold snap had really messed with my aim. His eyelids were squeezed shut against the pain, so I couldn't tell if they were that unnatural green, so right then all I could do was hope that I'd made the right call and that I hadn't just shot some innocent man who just happened to really like carriages.

Brother Death would've hurt me far more by leaving me with those doubts, but he was so cocky that the idea probably never even crossed his mind. It was like he was compelled to taunt me, and the voice that came out of the dying man was clearly that of the *Adze*.

"There was so much latent psychic energy here to take advantage of, how could I resist summoning a shade?"

"What do you want from me now?" I shouted.

"Before, it was business, but last night's debacle was a personal insult."

How many poor fools did he have wandering around who he had already gotten his hooks into, where he could possess their bodies and use them like this? Had he followed me? Or had he been tailing Lopes? Had he overheard our plan?

"I don't give a shit about you, Death. I only care about my son."

"But I care you about you, Julie. I'm enjoying myself. Toying with you has been the most fun I've had in years. Everything needs a challenge. You will be mine."

And then the monster was gone, and it was just some poor man bleeding out from a fatal gunshot wound.

Lopes joined me, wide-eyed, frightened, and trying not to show it. She'd heard the exchange. "Are you hurt? You're very pale."

The warmth was already starting to return. "I'll be fine."

"I recognize this man," Lopes muttered. "He was one of the bystanders ASS questioned last night. A spy! Go. Get out of here. ASS will take care of it."

"Just don't shoot the kids," I mumbled through chattering teeth. "Okay?"

"What?"

"The witnesses."

"Ah, no. I'm trying to make us more professional like the MCB, not brutal like the Germans. Who cares if there's a bunch of press out of Portugal talking about ghost things? It's good for tourism. I mean, we're not as lazy about it as Brazil. Those guys, anything goes! Never mind. Get out of here. My superiors can't know I met with you."

I started stumbling for the door. "Don't forget our deal."

"Call me in an hour and I will tell you where to meet. Go! I promise no shooting school children."

CHAPTER 22

An hour and a half later I met Lopes at a private hangar at the Lisbon airport. The guards at the gate had let me through with no problem.

There were an assortment of government cars, Toyota Land Cruisers, and a couple bigger military trucks parked out front. A whole bunch of men in black fatigues were loading equipment into a large cargo plane. Mortars, flamethrowers, explosives—you know, the usual stuff.

This would be a great time for Lopes to arrest me to turn me over to the SJK to curry favor, but I parked Management's car behind the trucks anyway. This was my best bet to get Ray back, so it was worth the risk. *Here goes nothing.*

As soon as I got out, Lopes spotted me and jogged over. She was dressed in black fatigues and had put her hair up in a bun. The first thing she did was hand me an iPad.

"Here's a summary to read on the flight." She had to raise her voice to be heard over the engines, and we weren't even that close. "Your mother is a couple

of hours away. To the south there is a province called
Algarve. Many beaches. Most people there are retired
British. It used to be all fishermen villages but now
there's a lot of buildings, but not so many tourists to
the part we're going. It's still too cold."

I made some kind of noncommittal sound, saying
that, yes, it was cold. I tried not to think how cold it
must have been on Severny Island when the nuke—
Focus. When I had Ray back, I could mourn my
husband and all my friends. I didn't know how, but
I would. The plaques on the wall of memory would
outnumber the ones from the Christmas Party, but
we'd get by.

She'd kept talking, and I realized that I'd gotten
distracted and missed something. It made sense: I was
emotionally wrung out, injured, tired, and running on
caffeine. "I'm sorry, what was that?"

"I said that when I was little, everyone vacationed
in Algarve, but because of all the foreigners, no one
can afford it now. It doesn't matter. Not relevant."

"Are we going to get there in time to hit the place
before dark?" Only an idiot hunts vampires in the dark,
and only a suicidal idiot would try that with a Master.

"I don't like it being this close, but yes. We have
to move today before the network realizes Marchand
is gone. Look, I'm not going to make excuses. Portugal is a Latin country. In every Latin country there's
the official government, and then there's the network.
It's all godfather, *padrinho*—a network of godfathers,
compadres."

"The mob?" I said, now thoroughly confused.

"No, no, no. Those stupid movies. No, I mean
real *compadres.* Like when people are your child's

godfather and become family. Family, influence, you know." Ah yes. Good old boys. We understand good old boys in Alabama. "There are important men who got rich making us turn a blind eye. If this is a vampire's house, that will be very embarrassing to them. Word of Marchand's death has not spread far yet, so we must strike before the network tries to stop us. We must kill this vampire now or never."

We were both in a hurry, but for entirely different reasons. "Works for me."

Lopes looked in the backseat of my car, but it was empty. "So about you bringing that help..."

"I wanted to make sure this wasn't an elaborate plot to arrest me first."

Lopes shrugged.

"Radio your guards at the gate and tell them to let my friends through," I suggested. As Lopes got on her radio and spoke some rapid-fire Portuguese, I got out Management's untraceable cell and called a number. They picked up immediately. "We're good. Come on up."

"How many Hunters?" Lopes asked.

"Eighteen of mine. Plus I don't know how many more who've come in from other countries." Dorcas had been scrounging up everyone she could. Apparently some of Grimm Berlin were ticked that their guy Fabian had gotten thrown in jail, and Darne's people were thankful I'd just scored them a free bounty on a *bicho*. "But we're going to need to borrow equipment for most of them."

Lopes nodded appreciatively. "As long as you understand I'm in charge, and that they will follow ASS commands without question."

"Of course." My baby's life was at stake. I could swallow my pride. But if it looked like ASS was going to screw this up, I wouldn't hesitate to frag Lopes myself. She seemed like a pro, but I'm goal-oriented. "Tell me about the target."

"Those with no passport, no money come to Algarve to sleep on the beach. So who cares if five or ten disappear a year? No one even notices. As long as this vampire never takes locals, the network takes Marchand's money and says look the other way. It will be the end of my career, the end of funding for ASS if we don't."

I was getting the picture, and it took my breath away. For as annoying as the MCB could be, at least they didn't turn a blind eye to vampires.

"This team here is supposed to be on cleanup duty at the convent. By the time my superiors find out what we are doing, it will be too late. I'll be honest. That's why I invited you."

I had pieced that together on the drive back from the museum. "So if this all goes horribly wrong, you'll tell your bosses that you went there because you got a tip I was going to be there so you could arrest me. Where I'm from we call that plausible deniability."

She actually laughed. "That, and eighteen more shooters will be nice too. I've got twenty, counting me."

And here I had been getting my hopes up. Occasionally working alongside the MCB and their seemingly bottomless toy box had given me an unrealistic view of what other government Hunters' resources were like. "Don't you guys have private hunting companies here you could contract?"

"A few. Dark Fate. The Legion of Mary. The Aguas

Santas Slayers. Not very big you know. Nothing like your company. But I told you we're a very old country, lots of outbreaks. Little ones, big ones. We could have hired one, probably in Algarve: the *Pescadores de Polvo*. But their hands are tied even more than us. Going against pressure from above would destroy our funding. We believe in protecting people, but you can't do that if you can't eat. But private Hunters? They would go to jail."

That would have pissed me off, giving something that evil a pass, just because it didn't rock the boat too hard. "We'll make this work."

"The target's name is Sergio Saturnino, millionaire shut-in. He throws parties like your—what is it?—Playboy Mansion. But only at night." She showed me a picture on the iPad. The house was huge. It looked like something I'd expect out of Morocco or certain parts of Greece, a sprawling construction, painted white, with a couple of round towers that looked like they belonged on Cinderella's palace. There were a few chimneys sticking up from the center that looked like they were made of ceramic and then cut and recut, with curlicue openings, so they were elaborate enough to match the towers.

Lopes flipped through more pictures, probably taken by her spies. "The beach immediately near it is not as sprawling and its sand not as white as the other beaches nearby, so it hasn't been colonized by tourists and expensive restaurants. The house does have stairs for access to the beach, and more stairs within the garden walls." The backing up allowed me to see that the house did have a substantial garden, with mature trees and eight-foot-tall white walls.

"Nice swimming pool."

"Which the owner only ever uses after the sun goes down."

I hated vampires. I won't say that of all the undead they're the worst, because honestly, it wasn't like I'd met them all, but I'm not sure there are any good undead. There are all sorts of different kinds of curses out there, things that twisted people into something different, though some people learned to turn them around and use them almost like a superpower, like Earl...or hopefully me—if I could prove the previous Guardian wrong—but undead were different.

Earl did still have his anger issues, though that made him more human, not less.

But vampires...

They were stuck between worlds. Not really alive, but jealously clinging onto this world that didn't want them. Taking life from the innocent, just so they could stick around, being miserable just a little bit longer. Vampires were like immortal vermin.

I had no idea what pool parties meant for vampires, but something I was sure of was that beautiful mansion would have feeding pits, filled with terrified, mistreated humans used as fodder by vampires till they died, and then chopped up and served to their fellow sufferers until they were all gone and a new batch of fodder brought in.

"There's going to be hostages besides Ray. You say they feed on transients."

"Yes. Runaways, prostitutes. People with no papers. Many from Eastern Europe, but we even get them from France and England," Lopes said.

And Lopes had to go to work every day, suspecting

that people like that were getting eaten in her juris-
diction, and that there wasn't a damned thing she
could do about it. For any real Hunter, that would
be torture. I bet she had ulcers.

"Saturnino also has servants, but we don't know
what they are."

"Even if she's by herself, Susan is the bitch whore
from hell."

"Now for good news and bad news," she said, as
if a Master vampire wasn't bad enough. "Because it
was once a place for smugglers, this mansion is built
over caverns. They are under sea at high tide. The
bad news is that we don't know what Saturnino keeps
down there now."

"And the good news?"

"We know about them and can use the caverns as
another entry point. Or at least make sure they don't
escape out the back." Before I could ask her how they
planned on covering underwater tunnels, there was a
noise on Lopes' radio. "Have them drive right into the
hangar." Apparently my backup had arrived. "Come on."

Lopes led me inside the unremarkable building.
One area had been set apart for operations planning.
There were pictures and maps of Saturnino's estate and
the surrounding area on a cork board, and somebody
had been drawing up an entry plan with dry erase
markers. It took me all of three seconds studying it to
tell that I was going to need to try and gently offer
as much advice as I could to get Lopes to alter her
plan, before she got Ray and the rest of us killed.

I was getting the impression ASS had a lot of
enthusiasm, but not a lot of actual experience against
this level of threat.

Inside, there was a lot of equipment on shelves plus racks of guns. She probably thought that I would be impressed, but the first thing I noticed was that everything was old, dated, military surplus. Their radios and night vision were a decade out of date.

"Nice, huh?"

"Very nice," I lied, realizing that MHI's operating budget probably dwarfed poor ASS. Another thing I just kind of took for granted.

"Technically for operations like this, ASS is supposed to call the army, but if I call the army, the network finds out and—"

"Your ASS is grass."

Lopes looked at me for a moment. "I don't get it."

Luckily, before I had to try and explain the American idiom, the rental cars arrived, and Hunters began getting out. The Americans had arrived on a couple of different flights. Dorcas had managed to hook them up with some of the foreign Hunters who'd been arriving at the same time.

They were all dressed low-key, jeans or cargo pants, T-shirts or casual shirts, that sort of thing, but even when Hunters try to look normal, most of them can't help but stick out a little. It wasn't just that even the sloppiest of us tended to stay in good physical shape, or that there was a much higher than average number of scars and militant looking tats on them, or that their luggage tended to be brown or olive drab with a whole lot of extra straps on it . . . Naw, it was that people who are constantly prepared to inflict violence tend to carry themselves in a certain way. Not cocky. That's for posers. More like alert and confident.

I spotted the MHI guys right away because I knew

every single one of them, at least from interviews and performance evaluations, so I knew about their skills and backgrounds. And I also knew why each of them hadn't been picked for the siege. Inexperience mostly. The majority of these had been in our last or second-to-last Newbie class. The others were because they'd been injured or out sick when the siege had been put together, but in a couple of cases, they'd been the healthy, experienced ones who'd been unlucky enough to get picked to hold down the fort because somebody had to.

But since the rest of us might have just been swept away in a nuclear fire, they were probably feeling lucky right now.

Then the next van arrived. There were also... My jaw dropped open.

Look, I couldn't tell who all of them were. I recognized some, others were familiar, but it had been a long time.

She was so desperate to find me help that Dorcas had called up some of our retirees.

Hunters do retire. Well, sometimes. Lots of us tend to die on the job, but most don't. Like any other career, eventually you get too tired and beat up to do it anymore or, in our case, you've made enough PUFF bounties that you don't need to work ever again.

Keep that in mind next time you see an elderly white-haired lady knitting or playing bingo in a retirement home. She could be a retired Hunter. In which case, I guarantee she still has a lot of weapons somewhere around her person and is ready to put you down if you look like a threat.

None of these were as old as my grandpa had been,

but there sure were a bunch who could collect social security. Dorcas must have told them to disguise themselves as typical tourists. There were lots of Hawaiian shirts—one of them with naked girls on it—and some of them were wearing big floppy straw hats.

I did recognize Steven Daniel Roberts. Twenty years ago he'd run Kansas for us, and I remember him visiting sometimes and bringing bottles of whiskey for my dad. Hell...if I was remembering right, he and Dorcas had *dated* like thirty years ago. She had probably called everybody she knew who was still in decent enough shape to handle a gun, who she figured wouldn't want to die of old age.

It wasn't just Hunters who'd retired due to age though. It was hard to miss the buff Indian guy with a cane. That was Doctor Nikhil Rao. After a bad back injury in a fight with vampires, Dr. Nik had left MHI, and was now working to help monster attack survivors with their PTSD.

They were on the far side of the hangar, and even from here I could see the near instant animosity between my people and the European volunteers they'd just barely met. It wasn't anything personal, but just like that casual violence thing, we tended to be cautious about working with people we didn't know. And you should have seen the Euro Hunters' reaction when they saw half my people belonged in an old folks' home.

I must have been really tired because I hadn't even started thinking through the logistical and tactical challenges we were going to face. We were throwing together a bunch of Hunters, most of them inexperienced or over the hill, who had not only never trained together, who probably all didn't even speak the same languages, to perform a complicated hostage rescue under the nose of a Master vampire, in a few short hours...

"Oh shit," I muttered to myself as the reality of the situation sank in.

But Lopes overheard me and had apparently been thinking along the same lines. "It's going to be difficult...but we've done difficult before."

Problem was I didn't know if she actually had.

"Do you mind if I talk to my people for a minute?"

"Sure, sure," Lopes said.

I walked over to where they were taking their bags out of the trunk.

It looked like Jonathan Dinger was in charge of the currently employed bunch. He was in his late twenties, wore glasses, and had a buzz cut. He was a solid enough Hunter that he'd been picked to go on the siege. Only a climbing accident while training at Camp Frostbite had gotten him injured and Earl had sent him home.

"Julie." He nodded. "I'm so sorry about the Boss. We'll do everything we can for little Ray."

My other employees and ex-employees gathered around me. They might have been the ones who'd been benched, but right then they looked as pissed off and determined as any Hunters I'd ever seen.

"Thanks for coming. It's been a hard couple days. I'm thankful you're here. This is going to be dangerous, and normally vampires this high up we'd get paid a PUFF bounty, regardless of the borders, but because of the legal problems—"

"Dorcas already warned us. This one isn't about the money," said Kenneth Bell, who was a Newbie I'd sent to Team Haven just a few months ago. "This is about getting your kid back."

"The Boss would've expected nothing less," declared Steven.

There was a chorus of agreement.

I was suddenly very emotional, but I did my best to hide it.

"You all know about the bombing at Severny Island... I don't know if everyone else is okay or not. All of you have friends there. My husband's there, my brother's there. I just don't know what's happened. All I do know is that this company has been killing monsters for well over a hundred years, and no matter what happens today, because of heroes like you stepping up to hit evil in its bitch face, we'll be doing it for a hundred more."

"Amen!" shouted another Newbie.

"You being here means more to me than you'll ever know. Thank you. Now, let's go rescue Ray!"

We had all gathered at the front of the hangar for Lopes to give a briefing. The Portuguese were trying hard to puff themselves up. I could tell they were a little intimidated by the arrival of my people. MHI had a reputation for being the premier eradication company in the world, and the locals didn't know this was scraping the bottom of our talent barrel. That's right. Let them think that half of us appear to be grandparents, and we'll still kick your ass.

Lopes had found a bunch of old real estate photos from when the house had gone up for sale ten years ago. The pictures had been taken to accentuate the red tile floors, warm cream walls, ocean views, and Arabesque tiles in the bathrooms. We were using them to plan our attack.

"How big is this place?" asked Dinger. He was one

of my smart ones, so of course he'd ask the pertinent questions.

"Eighteen thousand square feet including the base-ment. Twenty bedrooms, ten and a half baths, eight-car garage, and lots of other rooms. Plus we don't know what renovations have been made since Saturnino bought it," Lopes replied.

"Bet you ten bucks he's installed a torture dungeon," said Bell. He was another one of my employees, but I hardly knew him. He hadn't even been with us for a year yet . . . What had his introduction been? Zombies, if I recalled correctly.

The Newbie meant it as a joke, trying to lighten the mood. I should have let it go, but I was just too weary. "There will be feeding pits for sure. Guaran-teed. When a vampire sets up shop like this, there always are. It's like an instinct for them. They can feed off a single victim a whole lot longer that way. It'll either be a secured room in the basement or a hole the victims can't climb out of in the cavern. Even if we can get them out alive, they'll probably be in bad physical and mental shape."

That little ray of sunshine certainly killed their spirits. *Way to go, Julie.*

Lopes continued her briefing. Over half of us spoke English, so that's the language she used. While she talked, a couple of Hunters translated for their friends into Portuguese, French, and German. "Within the property, there is also a boathouse, pool house, and the tunnel which leads to the beach cavern which is of unknown size."

I scowled at the dry erase board. That was a whole lot of ground to cover.

"Defenses?" I asked.

"Sergio Saturnino has an entourage, as does your mother. We are unsure on the numbers, eight to ten maybe, or how many of them are enthralled humans, and how many may actually be other lesser vampire slaves."

"How can human beings live there and not freak out and run away?" someone asked.

"Vampire bite and enthrallment would be my guess. They are probably scared and fascinated in equal measures," Lopes answered.

"Don't forget that powerful vampires often create other types of undead to serve as their daylight watchdogs, usually wights," I said. "But there's another serious complication. Agent Lopes and I were spied on earlier today by an *Adze* known as Brother Death. It's possible that he might warn Susan and Saturnino that we're coming."

My experienced Hunters shared an uneasy glance at that. A few of them had been at the battle for DeSoya Caverns. They were the only other ones here who actually understood the sheer murderous power of a Master vampire. Especially one who was expecting company.

"He might have told them, he might not. He's not loyal to Susan, but his primary motivation seems to be that he enjoys screwing with people. It'll just depend on who he wants to screw over more—me or her."

"Do not worry, everyone," Lopes said. "I have men watching the property. If the vampires attempt to flee, we will know. That would be even better because then we could take down their transport in the daylight!"

Dr. Nik, who had dumped a belt of fifty cal into

a Master at DeSoya Caverns and still got his back broken by it afterwards, whispered to me, "I was more worried about her looking forward to our visit than her running away."

"She'll work as hard to protect Ray as I should have," I whispered back.

There was genuine concern in his eyes. "When's the last time you slept?"

"I'll sleep when I'm dead."

Lopes had kept talking, and she pointed to one of the mansion's top-floor windows overlooking the sea.

"I believe this is where they will be holding Raymond Pitt."

That certainly got my attention, but it didn't make much sense. Vampires were harmed by sunlight. Even though Lopes' intel indicated that all the windows had been tinted and heavy blackout curtains installed by local workers, from what I'd seen, vampires had an almost instinctive desire to stick to the shadows and stay low to the ground.

"Yesterday afternoon, the Saturnino estate called a few local stores and purchased high-end nursery furniture, a truckload of stuffed animals, and a lot of diapers and formula. The delivery was made, signed for by someone we believe to be a human servant, who had the workmen carry everything up the stairs. They assembled the crib in this room."

Lopes flipped through the pictures on her iPad until she landed on one that had been painted a colorful blue, with a mural of little yellow ducks playing in a stream. "On the real estate listing, it was labeled the nursery."

Son of a bitch. I'd been thinking about Susan like

she was a typical vampire. Sure, she was a monster, but she was still terrifyingly *motherly*. Of course she'd put Ray in the room best suited for him. Then I realized something even worse. She'd ordered the crib and baby stuff *before* the auction. That was how confident she had been. She saw Ray as rightfully hers.

I hadn't admitted it, even to myself, but I'd been afraid that my mother wouldn't care if he stayed forever a child. She had once, when human, while looking over an album of pictures of me and my brothers when we were little, said that every mother secretly wishes she could keep her babies forever.

Thinking back to that—at the time innocuous— conversation filled me with dread. She might very well decide it would be fun to have a baby-doll vampire forever. The clock was ticking.

"Our equipment is nearly loaded and the aircraft are prepped. We will rendezvous with more of my men at a small naval base not far from the target. Please continue to go over the action plan during the flight. Each of you will be given an ASS handler to"—Lopes scowled as all the foreign Hunters laughed at her—"to tell you where to go." She put her hands on her hips. "Need I remind you, you are guests of the Portuguese government and we will not be disrespected!"

Even though we were very much *not* guests of the government, but rather one rogue agent with a chip on her shoulder, I glanced over at my guys and gave them a subtle head shake in the negative. *Be cool.*

Lopes might have been prideful, but she was also savvy enough to recognize who got the most respect in this room. "Is there anything that you would like to add, Julie?"

"Sure." I walked to the front. The Americans knew me. I assumed most of the Europeans at least knew of my résumé. "Thank you for doing this. My baby's life is in your hands... But here's the deal: most of you have never seen a Master vampire before. They can soak up an incredible amount of damage and keep fighting. They heal unbelievably fast. They move like a hurricane-force wind. Blink and you'll miss them. For them, ripping your limbs off is like you plucking the leaf off a tree. Susan in particular also has some psychic powers. She'll cloud your thoughts and screw with your head. She may be able to read your mind. She can change shape. We have documented her being able to turn into mist to pass through walls. And when we get close, she *will* sense us coming."

Some of the Portuguese Hunters had been smiling when I'd started. They weren't now. *Good.*

"Susan Shackleford has all those nasty vampire powers, but she's worse because she used to be one of us. She knows how Hunters work. She knows our tricks. She used to teach this stuff for a living. The other Master vamps we've killed? It's because they got proud. They got stupid. They underestimated us. Susan won't. She's way too young to be as strong as she is, but she is. Whether it's from black magic, her sucking the life out of monsters that vampires normally wouldn't prey on, or who knows what, she's damned strong. Pair that with a flexible mind and a killer instinct, and she's quite possibly the most dangerous thing you've ever fucked around with."

The room was real quiet now. I'd been worried about Lopes arguing with me, but I could tell that even she was starting to feel worried.

"That said, we have a chance today because she was injured yesterday and probably hasn't fully recovered yet, and this plan?" I went to the board where Lopes had drawn a bunch of lines and arrows. "It's pretty good," I lied. It was terrible. Even if they'd had time to build a mock-up and do trial runs, it would've sucked.

"Thank you," said Lopes, completely oblivious.

"But since I'm one of the few people in the world who has fought Master vamps more than once..." I trailed off, because if the siege had gotten nuked, I was the *only* one left, but I just shook my head and continued, "Would it be okay if I make a few tweaks? It isn't like any of us have wasted time practicing this."

"I value your input. We can revise on the plane," Lopes agreed.

That was a small victory, though honestly I was so damned tired I'd been hoping to use that opportunity to sneak in a nap.

"If this Master's that tough, then how we gonna kill her?" asked one of the Portuguese Hunters.

I thought about what the Guardian had told me. It was all about what I wanted to protect, and what I was willing to sacrifice. For my baby, I was willing to sacrifice *everything*.

"I'll face her. If I fail, the rest of you back up and blow the entire place to hell."

CHAPTER 23

Screw sleep. I'd sleep when I had my son back in Alabama. Right now, right this moment, I was getting ready to hunt monsters. I'd spent most of the plane ride trying to gently nudge Lopes into an entry plan that wouldn't get all of us killed. From what she'd drawn on the map, it was obvious these guys didn't do very many big raids, and she had teams blundering into each other's fields of fire with big sections left uncovered. She even had teams breaching the doors and entering before they smashed in the windows to let in daylight, which was a no-brainer when dealing with vampires. It seemed to have worked. She accepted a bunch of my suggestions, and we'd just passed out new assignments.

The cargo plane's seats were basically nylon baskets down each side. In the middle, the out-of-town Hunters were picking through crates and getting kitted up. A couple of our retirees had gotten too fat to buckle the borrowed load-bearing vests over their Hawaiian shirts.

"You know, your Hunters are not what I expected," Lopes mused.

Whatever. I wasn't about to tell her that these were the dregs of the dregs because everyone else was at Severny or in a German prison. "They're good. Worry about your men."

"Mine are excellent. Very many experienced Hunters. Then there's three men from Paris, the very best, and four men from Germany. I am commanding a very large operation. This is a great honor."

I closed my eyes and made a vague prayer in the direction of whoever might be listening that ASS wasn't going to make this all, well, ASS backwards. There is something you learn in this business. You don't put rookies in charge of big operations. I suspected, when it came to operations of this size, Lopes was very much a rookie.

From what I'd gathered about this culture, to have a woman in charge of something like this was really odd. American women like to complain about equal opportunity, but we've got nothing on Latin countries. She had to be really competent and hard-working to overcome that. Or, this was a dead end position and she'd annoyed someone enough that they'd stuck her here. Either way, Lopes appeared to be trying to make the most of it. She clearly didn't agree with her bribe-taking, vampire-ignoring superiors. Maybe by being this crazily in your face, she thought that no one would suspect her of anything underhanded, like taking a notorious American fugitive on this operation with them.

My internal clock was still too screwed up to tell what time it was, but according to Lopes' watch, we reached our destination just after noon. As our plane descended into a small airfield just off the ocean, out my window I saw the other vehicles we'd be using to hit the mansion. The trucks were lined up and waiting to carry most of us, but the air transport for the team that was going to hit the roof was a Huey helicopter that was probably older than I was...and unlike MHI's ancient Russian Hind, ASS probably didn't have a magic orc to keep theirs running.

"I'll watch the operation from above in the helicopter," Lopes said. "I like helicopters."

"How good's your pilot?"

"The best."

"You're going to fly it too, aren't you?"

"Copilot." Lopes grinned. "I always wanted to fly. When I was young, no women in Portugal's Air Force. Very backward. Besides, they use such old airplanes you take your life in your hands every time you go up. You see, once you do that, and assume you're going to die every time you fly, there is nothing else to fear. I said I like helicopters. The government gave this one to ASS; I'd be a fool not to take lessons!"

I'll admit that made me a little glad that I was one of the Hunters going in by sea.

The beach was deserted. There were signs everywhere saying something or other in big red letters. Even without knowing Portuguese, I could understand PERIGO and INTERDITO. Lopes had explained that the cover story was that there was a gas leak from an underground mine that trickled out here, and if you inhaled it you could die suddenly. But in reality it was to keep people from seeing her "secret weapon."

The submarine pen was basically a big concrete shed built into the hillside. The room was lit with a weird blue light.

"This is the secret weapon of ASS," Lopes said proudly.

Frankly, their little submarine looked like a rusty piece of shit. MCB agents wouldn't be caught dead in this thing.

"You understand the traditional danger in Algarve is of Deep Ones. They love to settle just off our shores, especially in this part of the coast for some reason. Twenty years ago they carried off too many tourists, so the government secretly bought this so we could hunt them and not be seen."

Either that was extremely practical, or it was the only way these people could get some perks from their job and somebody thought it would be cool to have their own submarine.

It was probably half and half.

"We're Portuguese." She said that in a way that it seemed to be a major brag. "We have one of the longest coastlines relative to the landmass in the world. We've got almost as much coastline per area as any island. We—"

"So you bought a submarine?" I asked, incredulous.

"Three. They bought three submarines. Little ones."

I was starting to suspect that the reason that Portugal was the P in the PIIGS—the countries most in debt in Europe—might have something to do with the enthusiastic spending of their supernatural agency.

Then Lopes got sad. "But the other two sank... But anyways, this one is still good. And even with super vampire senses, she will not be expecting us to strike from under the sea."

Could Susan's thought-sensing abilities get through solid steel and all that water? This might be the only way we could actually gain some element of surprise. If so, a submarine would be ideal. I wasn't fond of the idea of consigning myself to a can that someone else would be driving into an underwater cave, where a small screwup meant drowning. I'm always a little uneasy with flying too, not so much because I'm up in the air, but because I'm not in control. Unless, of course, Skippy is flying, because then I'm not nervous at all.

Lopes nodded toward the crew, who were waiting on the catwalk over the sub. "That's Captain Pereira. He will deliver your strike team."

Pereira was an ugly little man, and he just kind of frowned at Lopes. It was pretty obvious that somebody didn't like the fact a woman had clawed her way up to being his boss.

Lopes talked to the crew hurriedly in Portuguese as Pereira occasionally grunted something back. At length, Lopes turned to me and said, "I believe this will work. Unless you hit the rocks of course."

But apparently Pereira did speak English too. "I'd be honored to have you in my craft. I'll get you there all right."

This might be an empty promise, but what else did I have to go on?

My "strike team" consisted of me, three of my Hunters—Kenneth Bell, Nik Rao, and Joshua Radick—and three of Lopes' men. Because she'd warned me it would be a really tight fit, I was the tallest one there.

Lopes called three names, "Coelho, Justino, Anuncio," and the three locals started climbing down through the hatch.

"The submarine will arrive first. Hopefully it will be a surprise. Your mother will sense your presence in the cavern and surely go to fight you. She won't want to endanger the baby, so she'll leave him upstairs. Once you radio that she is fighting you, that is when we will land on the roof and secure the baby," Lopes explained, which was kind of silly since I'm the one who'd talked her into that plan, but she probably said it like that to try and impress Pereira with her tactical brilliance.

"Susan's powerful, but she can only be in one place at a time."

"I want you to appreciate the diversionary tactic, like Hannibal with the herds of cattle with lanterns on their horns."

I had no idea whatsoever what Lopes was talking about. Hannibal had two files in my sleep-deprived brain: one having something to do with Rome and elephants, and another a movie about a serial killer. I couldn't even imagine how either applied in this case, so I just nodded.

"Time to go," Pereira said, "while it is still sunshine."

Which was kind of funny, since there was no daylight where we were going.

The submarine was indeed small and . . . let's just say that I really hoped it wasn't nuclear because, if it was, then I was compromising the health of all my future progeny.

Honestly, the interior looked like it was entirely covered in random metal plates. The appearance was that of a much-mended garment, and it seemed to me—though I knew next to nothing of submarines—that it was a bad idea to have things that were designed to be submerged be all patched up with visible rivets.

And I wondered how all of this was going to work, and if ASS had any idea what they were doing.

There were three things I'd already learned while dealing with Portuguese: first, they didn't take orders very well. Even though these were their country's equivalent of MCB and, therefore, presumably more disciplined than the private Monster Hunter orgs, they were more unruly than MHI.

The second thing is that Portuguese really weren't that good at understanding the chain of command thing. They argued everything and barracks-lawyered everything possible. On the plane, and right there in the sub, they were arguing and rearguing the plan, trying to turn it all upside down.

In fact, Lopes had even warned me during our planning session, "It's like we say here. Our plan always ends up being all in a pile and may God help us."

I can't say that filled me with confidence.

And, finally, the third point was much in evidence as they elbowed and jostled each other inside the sub. Even such spontaneous forms of organization like standing in line seemed foreign to them. They weren't really good at self-organizing, but they were very eager, and joking and laughing as we sailed toward our potential suicide.

It wasn't so much they were fearless, it was that fear, and possibly sanity, were nowhere near their mind. And I thought leading my people was like herding cats. Frankly, I didn't know how an entire country of people like that could ever work out, but I liked the stubbornness and the refusal to bend.

The little I knew of the Portuguese system of government was that it's the same kind of controlling, super-regulating state as most of Europe. But the feeling I was starting to get from the people told me that while they vote for jerks who regulated everything, they were convinced this was needed so *other people* behaved properly, while each individual by himself had the absolute certainty that rules didn't apply to him or her. Each individual was an anarchist in a country that wanted to control everything.

I'd been in submarines before. I knew what they were supposed to smell like. The stink of motor oil and old socks had only bothered me for a moment. But there was an undertone of fish in this one that really disturbed me. The fish were supposed to stay on the *outside*.

"It's a short ride. Not too bad," the one named Justino warned us as he sealed the hatch.

I was standing, squished between Radick and Bell, both of whom were relative Newbies, but Justino looked like a freaking little kid compared to them.

"I've never fought vampires. Lopes says it will be easy because it's day."

I demurred. "Not necessarily. Newly created vampires tend to be really sluggish during the day, but older vampires might be awake and frisky." And I worried, of course I did, because the kid had never fought vampires, despite me asking Lopes for her best men. Normally we tried to give the Newbies an easier job, and saying that he wasn't *my* Newbie really didn't help. He was going on this mission because of me.

The metal hull made a terrible groaning noise as we went beneath the surface. The interior lights flickered. There were no windows close to me, which I was kind of glad of. Pereira was sitting up front with another sailor named Silva. They seemed relatively competent, even though I had no idea what any of the controls they were working did. This thing wasn't much bigger than a van, so it couldn't be *that* hard to drive. They had the only window, though it was really more of an armored-glass bubble. That view wasn't too bad...at first. It was nice and blue, and fish swam by, but as the minutes passed, it got darker and darker until all I could see was darkness, and little bits of silt and seaweed floating through our headlights. That view somehow made everything worse, so I had to look away.

We moved sluggishly through the water, in the stink of motor oil, with the engines making an infernal electric hum, listening to the occasional metallic *pop* as something shifted under the increasing pressure. The kidding around stopped. The jokes ended. No matter how hard you thought you were, riding in this thing was unnerving.

I'm not normally claustrophobic, though right then, I think I understood how people who suffered from that felt. Between us and our equipment—and we'd brought a ton of stuff—there was no wiggle room at all. There wasn't much airflow back here, so within minutes it got really warm, and we were all sweating through our black fatigues. The inside of the submarine heated up until I was wondering if it was an easy-bake submarine.

There wasn't a good way to distract myself from the stifling heat and lack of air, because everything I looked at inside seemed rusty or wrapped together with duct tape, which just added to the general unease. Glancing forward, it was just shadows and floating bits of dead fish. That didn't help either.

My regular team was talkative before a mission. It kept things loose. You needed a sense of humor or you'd go crazy. Earl had taught me that a long time ago. Don't let your Hunters stir inside their own heads, because that's when the fear and tension starts to eat at you. Keep them talking. Only it was hard to make witty banter when my kid was in danger, and my husband and all my friends and family probably just died. I needed to put that aside and try though. Burdens of leadership and all that.

"You know, once this is all over I should introduce these guys to Milo."

"Good idea," said Nik.

"Who's Milo?" asked one of the Portuguese Hunters— Coelho. I'd started thinking of the three Portuguese Hunters as Huey, Dewey, and Louie.

"Who is Milo? Only the best mechanical genius in all of monster hunting."

"I bet he could fix this thing right up. Install some air conditioning, some good speakers so we could listen to some tunes." Nik wasn't very tall, but he had the build of somebody who lifted a lot of weights, so he was squished in behind me and obviously hating life. I'd requested him for the sub because he was one of my experienced guys—even if he was out of practice now—and he had actual medical training. There were bound to be vampire feeding pits down there, and if there were any survivors, they would be in really bad shape. Also, he was pretty handy with a flamethrower.

"Oh, that Milo guy is nuts. He's also in charge of the Gut Crawl. Grossest thing ever," Joshua Radick said, and every one of us MHI people shuddered at the same time. Radick had one of those weird résumés that tend to make good Hunters. He'd bounced around the world, being a school teacher in places like Guatemala and Kurdistan, before he'd had his run-in with the supernatural. Then he sadly added, "Except Milo was on the island too."

Well that certainly killed the mood. We chugged along in silence for the next minute.

In DeSoya Caverns, Susan had used the dark, the vast size of the place, and her incredible speed to her advantage. "Speaking of Milo, his faith was sufficient to knock the hell out of Susan once. Any of you guys devoutly religious?"

"I'm Catholic," Justino said, proudly grabbing the chain around his neck and pulling out the crucifix from beneath his shirt. "Maybe I can scare her off."

"No offense," Nik said, "but are you like super Catholic, faith like a rock, never any doubts, obey all your commandments, stroll right through the pearly gates because you're so righteous Catholic?"

"Uh . . ." Justino looked a little embarrassed as his two buddies snickered at him, and one of them mumbled something about him and a *puta*. "What are you implying?"

"That if you waver in your commitment, even the tiniest bit, then it's just a trinket," I explained. "She'll take that necklace and choke you to death with it."

Justino gave me and Nik a sheepish glance. "Okay, maybe not that good."

"Don't blame me, kid," said Nik. "I didn't make up your rules. I'm Hindu."

I suppose I could've asked Lopes if she had a priest on the payroll, but in my experience, even professional clergy usually choked and failed miserably when they actually came face to face with a legit vampire. It's that whole theory versus practice thing.

"Then we'll just be doing this the old-fashioned way. Watch your angles. No incendiaries or explosives until I give the go-ahead." Meaning that I wasn't going to let these guys unleash hell in an enclosed space until I was sure Ray wasn't present and I was pretty sure the roof wouldn't cave in on us. I had a terrible thought as I eyeballed the three Portuguese guys. "Y'all speak English, right?"

Justino nodded. "They're okay. I'm real good."

"Then make sure Dewey and Louie get the message. No blowing shit up until I say so." We were the distraction and they knew it, but they'd all volunteered anyway. They had guts, but smart was more important than brave. "Any vampire is deadly, but Susan will be a beast. Do exactly as I say and we'll have a chance."

The problem was we didn't know anything about the caverns. Lopes' predecessor had sent divers to sneak up to the entrance to measure it to see if their sub would fit, but we didn't know how big it got past the entrance. If Susan had room to maneuver, she could hit us from all sorts of angles before we'd ever see her coming. If the space was tight, then we could make her approach through a wall of silver and fire.

We spent the rest of the journey going over everyone's responsibilities. Pereira and Silva would stay with the sub. If everything went horribly wrong, they were our way out. Either that, or we'd be swimming for it. Nik had a messed-up back, so he'd be the last up the ladder. He also had our most dangerous close-range weapon, but that was okay because I needed to make sure Ray wasn't down here before we used it.

Pereira's idea of a short trip was anything but short, but I could tell when we got close because the groaning and popping noises changed as we went up, and the murk out the front turned blue again.

Now the hard part: steering between the rocks to get to the cavern entrance.

Our captain snapped something in Portuguese. Justino helpfully translated it for us. "He said that if we crash, don't panic. We're close enough to the surface we can pop the hatch and swim... But not to pop the hatch until he says to, or we all die."

"Fantastic."

Lopes had made it sound like they'd trained for this sort of thing, like submarine entries into underwater caverns were no big deal for ASS. But the way Pereira's hands were shaking and by the sweat rolling down his bald head, that wasn't the case.

CRACK!

That noise was a lot worse than all the previous sounds. It had come right through the hull next to me. We'd hit the side. Silva started shouting. I didn't need to be fluent to tell that Captain Pereira told him to shut up.

"He says everything is fine," Justino assured me.

"That didn't sound fine."

"Uh, Julie." Bell got my attention. He gestured for me to look down.

The floor was wet. Then it went from damp, to an inch of water. Then two.

"We've got a leak!"

"Is fine, is fine." Pereira waved one hand dismissively. The view out the front was our headlights bouncing off slime-covered rocks seemingly right in front of us. "Almost there."

I had to hand it to them—nobody panicked. Their eyes were wide. They were breathing fast. But nobody freaked out inside our metal coffin as the water slowly rose up our boots.

Silva stood up, flipped down a lever, and peered through a viewfinder. I realized that he was looking through a periscope. *"Chegamos!"* He began giving Pereira more detailed instructions.

"Going up." Pereira began to giggle like a madman as he flipped a switch and turned a knob. The passengers went from clenched-up terror to all smiles. *"Preparem para abrir a portinhola, tres, dois, um."*

At his signal, Justino popped the hatch.

Actual air came in. It was like Christmas.

CHAPTER 24

The Portuguese Hunters went through first. Pride demanded that. Even burdened with ammo and carrying machineguns, they scrambled up the ladder like it was nothing. They might not be that experienced at hunting in general, but they had at least gotten a lot of practice playing with their stupid death-trap submarine. I went next.

Outside, I took a gulp of cool, clean air.

Actually, the air smelled like salt water, rot, and death, but it was better than being inside that metal tube.

Everybody had a powerful flashlight mounted on their weapon, and there was a spotlight on the top of the sub. We'd come up inside a cavern. The top was ornamented with magnificent stalactites which were way closer than I'd been expecting. I'd have to be careful not to crack my head.

The sub was rocking and slowly drifting toward one side. I got to my feet and immediately regretted it, because the top of the sub was really slick. Bell shoved my borrowed weapon up through the hatch.

I grabbed hold and hoisted it the rest of the way. It weighed a ton.

Okay, not a ton. Even with the giant plastic ammo box on it and other crap bolted onto it, the gun was only like thirty-something pounds, but still, at that angle, an MG 3 is one serious chunk of steel, and it made me regret that I'd been neglecting the gym since I'd had the baby.

Anuncio was wading toward a shelf of visible rock while his buddies covered him. I turned the flashlight on, worked the charging handle on the German beast, and got ready to help. It was awkward as could be, but half of us were carrying big old belt-feds like this, because I hadn't been joking when I said that I wanted Susan to approach through a wall of silver.

My guys were hurrying up behind me. Anuncio shouted as he found the tunnel that theoretically would take us to the mansion. As the sub bumped against the shelf of rock, I leapt across, fast, because if you're going to do something stupid, it's best to do it fast.

Susan might not have sensed us underwater, but I was certain she knew we were here now.

I'd really wanted to be on the helicopter. I should have been the one roping down onto the roof and smashing out those nursery windows to let in vampire-roasting daylight, and then going through to grab my baby... but the sub team was the distraction to draw Susan off. She might have ignored anyone else, and left Saturnino or his minions to deal with them, but she wouldn't be able to ignore my presence. She'd also leave Ray behind because she'd try to keep him from danger.

Or so I hoped. To beat Susan, I couldn't just think like a vampire, I had to think like a motherly one.

As my guys crossed over to the tunnel, I grabbed my bulky radio to report to Lopes. The Portuguese radios weren't nearly as good as MHI's. They would've been state of the art when I was in grade school. No integrated hearing protection earpieces either, so we were all going to be deaf shortly. But with all the rock overhead, all I got was static.

The sub had a bigger radio, so I shouted back that way. "Hey, Captain. Can you reach Lopes? I've got nothing."

He stuck his head up through the hatch. "A little. I told her. She never listens to anyone, but I told her."

She needed to wait until Susan was down here before swooping in. "Then I'll relay the go signal to you, and you tell Lopes, got it?"

"Got it."

Anuncio had more guts than sense because he'd already started up the tunnel by himself. *Fucking amateurs.* "Back him up, damn it!"

Justino hoisted his big HK21 and ran after his stupid friend. Then it was Coelho, and then it was my turn. At least the space was narrow. The vampires wouldn't be able to flank us after all. The short guys were okay. I had to crouch and shuffle along behind.

This was a country of short people. Even their smuggling tunnels were too short. Sure enough, I hit my head. On missions like this, MHI usually used a lightweight hockey-style helmet just to keep from braining yourself. But ASS had either big ballistic helmets, which was kind of cumbersome and pointless if nobody was shooting at you, or berets—nothing in between. It's hard to crouch and gracefully carry a gigantic gun that was totally never intended to be used in enclosed spaces, so by the third time I hit my head, I was really wishing I'd grabbed one of those Kevlar helmets anyway.

I made sure my guys were moving up behind me, and then I started climbing. The tunnel went up and it was steeper than I'd expected. This might have been Saturnino's emergency escape route. It was so slick with wet moss that I bet even the vampires rarely went all the way down to the sea. It was only wide enough that maybe two people could squeeze in side by side.

I tested that theory when Coelho's boots slipped and he went tumbling down the rocks. He slid about four feet until he crashed into me. Thankfully he was enough of a professional to keep his finger away from the trigger so he didn't accidentally kill us all, though from the way his weapon-mounted light blinded me, he'd failed to control his muzzle. I used my free hand to grab the wall. He outweighed me by quite a bit, but I managed not to lose my footing when we collided. "Watch it."

"Sorry." He then kind of in slow motion kept sliding past me, while his now slime-covered gloves tried to grab hold of something. While he got his shit sorted out, I stepped over him and kept climbing. I had a baby to rescue.

Anuncio's shouted warning echoed down the hole. He'd heard something. We had company.

Our point man was armed with a paratrooper Galil, a much more compact and more maneuverable weapon than mine, which had made sense since we didn't know how tight this place was going to be. "Anuncio, move back. Justino, let him by."

Thankfully, Huey and Dewey didn't argue with me. Anuncio made his way back and squeezed past the two of us with heavier weapons, while Justino and I got side by side, braced our machineguns as well as possible, and got ready to meet the welcome wagon.

Our lights revealed that the tunnel was a straight shot for about thirty yards, sloping upward at about a thirty-degree angle. It was like the dictionary definition of fatal funnel.

I flipped open the bipod and went prone. We were using frangible silver bullets. Lopes had said they're the same brand the MCB buys.

There was a noise coming our way, a sort of wet shuffling. It must have been what Anuncio had heard. Kid had good ears. Then I almost gagged as I smelled them. Unfortunately for me I had a good nose.

That was the stink of undeath. And I wasn't talking pretty and well-groomed vampire undeath. I'm pretty sure I knew what happened to all those people who'd disappeared in this region over the years, and it explained why ASS had never found any bodies. Why drain somebody and dump the body when you could drain them and just use necromancy to turn them into an undead guard force? Luckily for Hunters everywhere, only the strongest of vampires seemed capable of doing that. Sadly for us, right now we were dealing with a *strong* vampire.

I don't know how I knew. It wasn't like I could feel the tremors of their footsteps. It wasn't like I could tell volume of bodies by the smell. But somehow I knew that there were a whole *lot* of monsters heading our way.

"Everybody listen. We'll lay down fire. When we run dry, we'll slide down, next shooter takes our place . . . Repeat. Reload. Take a turn. Don't shoot until I say so!"

And that's when the wights started moving into the tunnel.

They'd been human once, but what was left was rail thin, with bones sticking out in places. They were dressed in filthy rags or buck naked. Their fingers ended in blackened claws. Their mouths were jagged rotten holes filled with black teeth. Their eyes reflected our flashlight beams. The tunnel slowly, painfully, began to *fill* with them.

They were so hideous and torn up that your institutive reaction was to just start blasting as soon as you saw them. "Hold your fire, Justino," I ordered.

"But . . . but—"

"Hold." I wanted as many of them as possible in this tunnel before we started shredding them. I raised my voice so the whole team could hear. "Wights. Don't let them touch you or you'll be paralyzed. They're tough. You've got to completely tear them to pieces before they'll stop."

They were shaped like people, but they no longer moved like people. The creatures began to scramble up the walls and along the ceiling, suspended somehow, like their hands and feet were sticky. They were taking their time, investigating, a sort of glacial crawl of spider-crawling rot. They were all jagged edges and twisted limbs.

Justino was breathing so hard I was worried he was going to hyperventilate. Oddly enough, I was cool. No matter how bad it got, Ray was just on the other side. "Hold."

The wights heard my voice. Every undead head

simultaneously turned right toward me. Their eyes glowed as they reflected the beam of my flashlight. I couldn't even tell how many there were, they were bunched in so tight.

Their creeping was done. There was an explosion of movement as the undead charged.

"Now!" I squeezed the trigger.

The roar was deafening as both 7.62 belt-feds opened up. My vision was filled with orange fire as I worked the muzzle back and forth across the narrow tunnel. Justino was screaming incoherently as he fired. Hot shell casings and the disintegrating metal links that had held them together were raining down on me.

The Rheinmetall MG 3 was a crazy-fast bullet hose. The Germans had used this thing's predecessor during World War II. It was the one the GIs at D-Day had described as making a sound like ripping cloth because of how fast it ran. It had so much cumulative recoil against my shoulder that it started sliding my body across the moss.

The tunnel was packed so full of rotting meat above us that we literally couldn't miss. MCB ammo was made out of compressed powdered silver. At close range, delivered in a heavy bullet going this fast, they pretty much exploded on impact. Against the emaciated wights, that meant tearing off limbs and chunks. Heads exploded. Jaws flew off. Just what we needed.

Wights fell from the roof. They bounced off the walls. Destroyed bodies rolled and slid toward us. Gun smoke and vaporized blood filled the air.

And then I was empty. One hundred and twenty rounds in one continuous burst.

Yet the wall of meat was still coming.

"Backing up!"

I hadn't realized, but there was so much foul black blood leaking down the tunnel that it had basically turned into the world's grossest water slide. All I had to do was pick up the machinegun, roll over onto my back, and gravity did the rest. As Justino and I slid down the tunnel past Anuncio and Coelho, those two started shooting. Only their guns held a whole lot fewer, smaller bullets than ours had, so it wasn't nearly as impressive.

"Nik, move up," I shouted as loud as I could, hoping to be heard over the pounding gunfire.

Either he'd heard me or he knew what to do anyway because he climbed up past me, grimacing because of the heavy weight on his injured back and the canvas straps digging into his shoulders.

Levering around the heavy-ass machinegun, I started to reload. I hinged the top open, then I ripped open the Velcro top of the bag at my side to get out another ammo belt.

Multiple eyeballs blinked inside the bag. "Now, Cuddle Bunny?"

"Not yet, thank you," I told Mr. Trash Bags as I squished him to the side to grab more ammo.

Radick and Bell were shooting now as Coelho and Anuncio retreated. Somebody screamed as a wight managed to touch him. I looked back. It hadn't even been the whole wight. Just an arm that had gotten blown off. But it had rolled, thrashing down the tunnel, and had sunk its claws into Coelho's leg. That was enough to paralyze him, and when he fell down the hole, it was as an out-of-control mess. Most of my guys managed to get out of the way, but he crashed straight into Nik. With the heavy tanks on his back, our doc never had a chance to keep his feet. Both of them fell, rolling, until they landed clear back next to me.

And the monsters were still coming. *How many bodies had Saturnino collected down here?*

They might have overwhelmed us then, except an angry, ear-piercing shriek filled the cave. It was a terrible, inhuman noise, but there was a tiny bit of it there that reminded me of my childhood, when me or my brothers had done something horrible which had really pissed our mom off.

"You'll never have him, Julie!"

The sound made the remaining wights freeze in place: missing limbs, black blood pouring from the dozens of fresh holes just punched in their bodies, but still dangling from the walls and ceiling.

"He's mine now! I know what's best for him. I won't let you hold him back!"

She was getting closer. I grabbed my radio and mashed the transmit button. "Come in, Pereira. Tell Lopes she's here. She is here!"

"You've left me no choice. If it means killing you, then that's what I'll have to do."

"Copy," came the distorted reply over the radio.

I went back to reloading the machinegun as Susan kept screaming threats. Once I got the belt in place and thumped the lid back down, I reached over and smacked Nik on the arm. "Wait to make sure she doesn't have Ray." I really doubted she would bring a baby down amongst a pack of nasty wights—that wouldn't be *motherly*—but I had to be certain.

Nik nodded. He'd heard me. *Good.* I started climbing past my guys again, and he followed me with the flamethrower.

"Fall back," I warned each man as I passed him. The wights were paused. Now was our chance. "Fall back! All the way to the sub."

Susan came strolling down the tunnel, looking elegant in a red dress and heels, a colorful ensemble that really stood out among the mottled greys and blacks of the wights. Somehow she didn't even get so much of a speck of dirt or blood on her.

"Give me my baby, Susan!"

"No, honey. Ray is somewhere safe—"

That'll do. "Burn her! Burn them all!"

Dr. Nik didn't hesitate. He raised the big nozzle, pointed it up the tunnel, and pulled the lever.

The Vietnam-era M9 flamethrower was an antique, but Lopes had assured me that it worked great. ASS had refurbished it . . . which meant that it would either work great, or it would explode and kill us all the second we tried to use it.

Thankfully it worked.

Brilliant scalding fire filled the tunnel, boiling up through the wights and engulfing Susan. The vampire screeched as burning napalm clung to her skin.

Heat smacked me right in the face. It was unbelievably hot. I almost fainted as it sucked all the oxygen away, but instead I just flopped back down, held my breath, and let the MG 3 rip, aiming it right at Susan. I must have hit her fifty times before there was so much fire I couldn't even see what I was shooting at. Then I just worked it back and forth.

The tank on an old flamethrower like that can go through several bursts, but keeping it sustained like Nik was emptied the whole thing in just a few seconds.

The heat and lack of air in the enclosed space must

have stunned me, because the next thing I knew, I'd let go of my machinegun, was dizzy and coughing, and somebody got ahold of my ankles and was dragging me down the tunnel. Good thing, too, because I realized that all those dead wights we'd just set on fire were now sliding and rolling down the tunnel on top of us, still ablaze.

My team spilled out of the tunnel. Bell was pulling Nik. Radick had me. Everybody was drenched in sweat, hacking or gasping. If you thought wights smelled bad before, try setting them on fire. Then I had to struggle to my feet and get out of the way as the tunnel vomited out burning body parts and flaming ooze. The fiery, rotting mess spilled into the seawater and immediately gave it an oily sheen.

I glanced over and did a head count. It was darker because we'd lost a couple of flashlights, but everyone was still alive. Justino was looking at me, face black with soot and grime, wide-eyed. Coelho was starting to move again, paralysis shaken. But they looked happy, like we'd just had some success or something.

They didn't realize the magnitude of what they were facing. "Get ready. Susan's not dead."

"But you burned her to ash!" shouted Justino. To be fair, we were all shouting because our hearing had taken a pounding from running machineguns inside a tunnel.

"Yeah. We've burned her before. It's only a temporary setback. She'll either come after me or return to Ray. Either way, she ain't done."

Justino made the sign of the cross.

Now that the tanks were dry, Nik shrugged out of the flamethrower straps and managed to gasp, "That was fun. Just like old times. Reminds me why I retired."

It would take Susan a minute to regenerate, but hopefully Lopes had gotten the message. Right about now the helicopter should be hovering over the mansion roof. I'd made sure Dinger was aboard for that because I trusted him. Despite his accident in Alaska, he was one of our best climbers, so he'd be the one hitting the nursery windows. I could only pray that Ray was actually there. The rest of our crew should be rushing up the road in trucks. They'd bail out, start smashing out ground-floor windows, and cause lots of mayhem. Vampires couldn't go out in the sun, but wights could, so hopefully we'd just roasted most of Saturnino's guards. Once the perimeter was secure, Lopes would bring up a track hoe she'd had her local guys rent, and they'd use that to start knocking more holes in the walls. Sunlight was a Hunter's best friend.

"As soon as the fire dies down, we can head up to help," Bell suggested.

I wasn't going to wait that long. "Grab a rope from the sub. If they're still burning in our way, we'll hook 'em, drag 'em down, and dump them in the water." I opened the ammo pouch and grabbed a hand full of squish. "Nobody freak out. He's a friend." Then I pulled out Mr. Trash Bags.

"Greetings, horde of Cuddle Bunny," he squeaked.

"What the hell!" Radick yelled. Well, they all said something to that effect, but you get the idea. But they didn't start shooting, which was what mattered.

"Don't worry. He's cool. Listen, Mr. Trash Bags. I know you're vulnerable to fire, but you're small enough to find a path. I need you to go up this tunnel and go look for Ray. Cuddle Bunny's Cuddle Bunny. Do whatever you can to protect him. Ray needs to go with the nice humans. The humans are all on our side. Avoid the humans. Don't hurt the humans. Find and protect the baby. That's the most important thing. The vampires and undead are the bad guys. Hurt them all you want."

"Eat noses? Eat toes? Consume?"

"Exactly. But only the bad guys. Got it?"

"Consume!" Mr. Trash Bags agreed with great enthusiasm as he leapt out of my hands and bounded up the tunnel. If it were possible for a shoggoth to be gleeful, this was it. I'd basically just given him a license to kill.

Bell came back from the sub, and he'd done me one better than a rope. He had a telescoping pole with a hook on the end. Probably for docking purposes. "I'll start clearing a path."

"If it's still moving, yank it down, and then somebody else hack its head and hands off. It's the teeth and claws that get you. And remember, they don't need to be attached. Just ask Coelho. At least one of you stay on lookout with a gun pointing down that tunnel in case Susan comes back."

While my guys went to work, I tried my radio again. Lopes' channel was still just static. So I went back to the sub, hopped across, and climbed down the hatch. I landed with a splash. There was about a foot of water in the bottom now.

"Are you gonna sink?"

"It's fine. We've got a pump." Even though he looked like he wanted to complain because I was getting undead blood all over his submarine, making it smell like death and smoke instead of oil and fish, the captain immediately handed me the radio.

I only had to listen for a few seconds to tell things weren't going according to plan. The nursery had exploded.

At first I had a panic attack, like somehow we'd screwed up and accidentally launched a rocket at Ray's room or something. But from the furious shouting back and forth, it sounded more like it had been a booby trap. Then I realized Lopes' people had interviewed the workers who'd dropped off the crib. Only Susan had been one of us. Even if she'd not suspected that ASS was on to Saturnino, she'd still be paranoid. Humans had gotten a glimpse into her terrain and lived to talk about it. So of course she'd switch it up and move Ray somewhere else, then set a trap just in case.

That sneaky bitch.

I'd been too tired and too rushed to see that coming. From the air, Lopes couldn't tell what shape the guys who'd tried to enter the nursery were in—maybe dead, but at least badly injured. That was my fault.

And that meant Ray was hidden somewhere else inside the mansion. And in short order Susan would be healed up and heading his way. I dropped the radio microphone, leaving it dangling by its cord, and headed back up without another word.

CHAPTER 25

Luckily most of these wights were so old and dried out that they didn't burn for long. Set a recent undead with a lot of fat on them on fire, and those could burn for hours. The skinny ones not so much. So it was only a matter of minutes before we were able to go up the tunnel again.

And it was horrible.

In Newbie training, we have an event called the Gut Crawl. The nastiest bit of psychological torture we do, it's basically making our people crawl through a long, dark, muggy pipe, which has been filled with aged cow guts and entrails. It's gross. It's messed up. And it's designed to weed out those too squeamish for monster hunting. At times Milo has actually handed out coins and certificates to people who made it through that declared: "I survived the Gut Crawl."

This was that times a thousand. Because at least in the Gut Crawl, the stuff you were crawling through wasn't half burned and still *twitching*.

I took point. No matter how awful this was, it didn't matter, because on the other side was my baby. Plus, if Susan attacked, better to hurt me than anyone else. They were here because I'd asked them. While the other guys had to stop to gag and puke, I just had to think about Ray, and then I could keep going.

My machinegun had been buried in flaming undead. When I'd found it, the action was covered with baked-on gore to the point it was sure to malfunction, and I didn't have time to clean it. Plus it was a cumbersome pain in the ass and Susan wouldn't be dumb enough to come straight at us again, so I'd left it. I'd grabbed a spare paratrooper carbine from the sub and had that slung over my back. I made my way up the tunnel with pistol and mounted flashlight in one hand and a borrowed tomahawk in the other. Whenever anything stuck to the wall reached for me, I'd hack it until it stopped.

I was wearing some of the replacement glasses Management had gotten me—the sporty, safety-goggle kind—but nasty crap kept dripping from the ceiling and getting all over them, and I didn't have time to stop and clean it off. I was covered in slime, wight chunks, and burnt hair.

The tunnel flattened out and got wider. The walls went from rough stone to ancient crumbling bricks. From the looks of things, this is where they stored their wights. There was a big doorway. Our lights revealed that the other side opened up into an old, unused wine cellar. We'd reached the mansion's basement.

My team immediately took up defensive positions while I tried my radio. Without all that ground in the way, I actually got some reception.

"Come in Lopes. This is Shackleford. We're out of the tunnels and in the basement."

Lopes replied, but I missed half the words from

the static. She was trying to update me but it was something about unexpected resistance.

"Say again, Lopes. That wasn't clear."

"We had to evacuate some injured. Your mother left a bomb in the crib."

That sounded like something she would do.

"We can't break most of the windows. I didn't know Saturnino installed metal security shutters. We only got a couple, then they dropped when the alarm sounded."

"I installed those on my house. They're great. What're you doing now?"

"We're bringing up the tractor thing you said to rent."

Good. Because nothing could rip the wall off a house like a big steel bucket on the end of a powerful hydraulic arm. Explosives were faster, but that meant more danger for Ray. The best way to hunt vampires was to tear the place apart, brick by brick, letting in light until you found where they were hiding.

"Whoa," said Nik as I started walking into the wine cellar. "Hang on. Where do you think you're going?"

I pointed toward the ashen trail visible on the floor. Mr. Trash Bags had gotten really filthy climbing over the burned wights so it was easy to see which way he'd gone. "I told him to find the baby, so that's what he'll do. He's not super sharp, but he's committed."

"The plan was for us to guard the tunnel until they clear the upstairs," Justino protested. "It's the only way the vampires can escape during the daytime."

"It's the only way ASS knows of," I snapped. "You didn't know this place had armored shutters and a small army of wights either. It's obvious Saturnino has been making improvements. If there's another secret way out of here, we've got to find Ray before Susan sneaks him out. We can't just stand here picking our nose while she does."

"We have our orders," Justino insisted. "You can go ahead, but ASS must hold this position!"

I got on my radio. "Come in, Captain Pereira."

"This is Pereira."

"Is your sub still seaworthy? No bullshit assessment."

"Yes. We can make it back out. Eh, and it is better to sink off the beach than down here anyway. Easier for salvage."

"Good. Unload all your explosives. Get out of there, and then collapse the cavern. Blow it to hell."

"Understood."

I put my radio back in the pouch and glared at Justino. "Position *held*. Now let's go."

The kid didn't argue. Susan might be able to shape-shift into mist and float through the cracks, but Ray couldn't, and he's what mattered. We started following Mr. Trash Bags' trail.

"Keep moving. I've got point. Nik in the middle." In a situation where you were dealing with creatures who could pluck your limbs off, you really wanted to try to keep your doc in one piece. "Justino and Coelho, bring up the rear."

"But—"

He probably took it as an insult. It must have been a Latin thing. "I guarantee there's going to be sleeping vampires down here, and we can't stop to clear every possible hiding place. They're going to be waking up and coming after us, so shut up and watch our six. Debate with me again and I'll shoot you in the kneecap and leave you for the vampires."

Justino nodded. *Good.*

"I don't know what the deal is with your little blob thing, but this beats wandering around in the dark," Bell said. "Is he like a bloodhound?"

"I don't even know if he's got a nose."

We moved quickly across the basement. The place was a dusty, cobwebbed mess. Of course, if there were any lights down here, they were all off. There were piles of old furniture and boxes. Not having the time to search through the junk meant that we could be passing by vampires who'd rise up to hit us from behind, but there just wasn't time. This was a hostage rescue first and eradication mission second.

In the next room we found where the vampires fed. Everybody winced when we shined the light into the hole in the foundation and saw what was there. I'd been hoping for survivors. There weren't any. From the condition of the bodies, I figured that after Susan had returned from the auction, she'd had a celebratory feast. We'd have to come back here later to chop all their heads off so they wouldn't come back.

There was a loud crash from above. It shook dust from the ceiling. Lopes had started ripping off the walls. "The more daylight up there, the more it's going to force the vampires our way. Get ready."

Mr. Trash Bags' trail went right past the feeding pit and toward the stairs. I kept the stubby Galil shouldered as I moved in that direction.

Someone leapt down the stairs, and when I say leapt, I mean they covered the last ten steps in one jump, and landed in a crouch like it was no big deal. He was wearing black attire, like a butler. "Vampire!" I shouted, which was confirmed when he raised his face, opened his mouth crazy wide, showed us his fangs, and hissed.

Then we blasted him.

Only four or five of us had an angle, but we lit that vamp up. He twitched and jerked as dozens of bullets ripped through his body. He crashed back against the wall. Dust and chunks flew.

The thing about vampires, they're tough and they heal crazy fast, but if you damage them enough, you can overwhelm them. Then while they are recovering you can take them out permanently.

"Cease fire, cease fire. Radick, stake. Bell, chop." I pulled the tomahawk I'd been using in the tunnel from my belt and tossed it to Bell. "Everyone else, cover your zone."

The vampire was still struggling to rise, but we'd pulverized too many bones. Black blood was squirting out his chest and neck. I reloaded, but moved past the temporarily helpless vampire to cover the stairs. Bell grabbed it by the legs and dragged it away from the wall. It flopped over on the concrete. Radick kicked it in the shoulder to flip it onto its back, and then immediately rammed a sharpened stake right into its heart.

The thing let out a terrible wail, but once staked, it stopped them from regenerating and left them pretty much helpless. Which was good, because then Bell started hacking through the neck with impunity. It only took him two enthusiastic tries before the head went rolling away.

From the way the Portuguese guys were staring, they'd never seen anybody take down a vampire that fast and smooth before. That's right, ASS, these are our Newbies. That's why MHI is number one. "Quit gawking and cover your zones."

And I swear, the instant I said that, a vampire rose up behind Justino. He screamed as its claws sunk into his shoulder.

I simply reacted and shot it right between the eyes. It was so close my bullet actually cut a bloody crease out of Justino's ear. Not bad, considering the first time I'd used one of these was today.

The vampire lurched back as half the contents of its skull sloshed out. Got to give the kid credit, Justino leaned forward, and then side-kicked the vampire in the chest. As it stumbled away, Coelho started shooting it. And when Justino fell down, everybody else had a shot too.

It was a near perfect repeat of the first vamp we'd dropped, only this time Nik was busy trying to stop Justino's bleeding, and Coelho and Anuncio were clumsy as hell on the stake and chop. Coelho had to jab it in the chest like four times before he got it through the heart, and then Anuncio awkwardly sawed its head off while it flopped around.

Still, thirty seconds after it had appeared, everybody from ASS was sitting on the ground gasping for air, and one of them was moaning in pain. Justino had four perfect finger holes in his shoulder.

"It's bad," Nik warned. "He needs evac."

There was more crashing and shooting upstairs. The whole mansion shook. Walls were coming down and Hunters were coming in. "Okay, get him up. We've got to get him outside. Warn Lopes we're coming out."

We rushed up the stone steps.

On the first floor, it was pandemonium. There was a massive great room with a spiral staircase leading to the upper floors. The front entryway was gone, and in its place was a massive jagged hole. Hunters were using the stone pillars on the porch for cover. The Portuguese ones were dressed all in black. Mine were the ones with load-bearing vests tossed over Hawaiian shirts.

Suddenly a giant orange chunk of steel tore through the wall. Wooden beams burst. Steel shutters fell and glass shattered. Pipes split and sprayed water. More sunlight came inside. There was a beeping noise as the track hoe was put in reverse, to move to another wall.

Inside, crouched behind the furniture, were the defenders. You could quickly tell the vampire servants apart from the enthralled humans, because the vamps were the ones steaming and screeching as sun from the new hole hit them. The humans were the ones busy shooting at my people.

I'd seen Grant when he'd been enthralled by vampires, and he'd tried to kill us when we rescued him. From what I understood, being bitten and enthralled was kind of like a drug. That made sense considering their accuracy. It was obvious that they weren't so much shooting at Hunters as at the ceiling, the wall, and that interesting shadow that kind of reminded them of a Hunter.

I don't like to kill innocents. I mean the whole point of monster hunting is to protect innocents, right? But every Hunter knows sometimes you can't save them. Sometimes it's them or you. It's just survival. Even idiots can hit you by accident. And with all of these stray bullets, my *baby* was in here somewhere.

I was all out of fucks to give as I moved up behind them. I shot one of the enthralled in the back before he even knew I was there. A woman in one of those French maid costumes turned toward me, pistol in hand, and I fired a controlled pair. Unlike vampires, humans are squishy, and a couple of 5.56 rounds to the chest tends to put us right down.

My team moved across the great room, shooting vampires and their slaves. They hadn't been prepared to get hit from this side. I reached the corner of the wall and sliced the pie, working my way around, shooting everybody who wasn't on our team. Nik and Bell were carrying Justino between them, who had passed out from blood loss. They were heading for the front, but then I saw movement on the balcony above and signaled for them to stop. They managed to, right before someone hung a shotgun over the edge and put a bunch of buckshot holes in the hardwood where Nik would've been standing.

"Reminds me why I retired," Nik shouted at me.

"Hang on," I warned as I leaned out and looked for a target.

The enthralled pumped the shotgun and an empty hull flew over the edge. When he leaned out again, I was ready...and shot him right in the face. He flopped over the railing and plummeted to smash wetly into the floor right in front of us.

"On Monday, I'm retiring again."

"Clear. Move!"

Nik hoisted up Justino and ran for the porch. We'd killed enough of the defenders that the Hunters there were able to rush up to cover them. The burned, blinded vampires were being taken down and beheaded. No matter how tough vampires are, sunshine is the great equalizer. There were others, smoldering and sparking, but they were retreating deeper into the mansion.

Upstairs, a baby cried.

CHAPTER 26

My squad rushed up the circular staircase. Coelho was shouting into his radio, warning the others so they wouldn't accidentally shoot us through the walls.

I'd heard him. I knew that was Ray. But then a door had slammed and his cry had been cut off.

Mr. Trash Bags' trail was faintly visible on the wooden steps, but really obvious on the white carpet of the next floor. White carpet... Saturnino must have had a rule for his minions: no feeding upstairs unless you put down a tarp first. We were still filthy from the tunnel climb. These stains were never going to come out.

Unlike the basement, this area was kept immaculate. There was art on the walls and healthy potted plants. This was where Saturnino held parties and invited guests over, to wine and bribe politicians while pretending to be human. I didn't know how that worked. Apparently, some vampires liked to live in the darkest, mustiest hole they could find, and others still tried to play-act like they were still people.

The stairs kept on going up to the top floor and so had Mr. Trash Bags. So we kept climbing too.

Off the top balcony was a long hallway. There were several doors on one side. All of them were closed. There were windows on the other, but all of them had been sealed with the armored shutters. It was still dark up here so we turned on our lights again. Below us I could hear more Hunters rushing into the house. I was down to five with me, but more would be coming to help.

From the sound, Lopes' helicopter must have been hovering right outside.

There was a door at the very end of the hall. Over the ringing in my ears and the noise of the helicopter, I could barely hear Ray's muffled cries coming from the other side.

"The hostage is in the northwest corner room, top floor," Radick said into his radio. "Watch your fire."

I shouted, but my voice came out harsh and hoarse. "Give him up, Susan. There's no way out." Almost as if to accentuate my point, there was a loud bang as the metal bucket smashed another of the downstairs walls. "Neither of us wants Ray to get hurt."

Susan responded immediately. "Y'all know the story of Solomon's judgment?"

I tried to pinpoint where her voice was coming from. I couldn't. All of my guys had heard it and were looking around confused too. But then I realized it was *in* my head. It was like she was talking and psychically broadcasting at the same time.

"That's when two women went before the king. They were concubines of the same man and each had a son. Only, one of their babies had died and now they were both claiming the living baby as her own."

"I know the story," I managed through clenched

teeth. She was messing with our minds. It was some kind of trick. My head felt like it was going to burst, and it looked like the other Hunters were getting hit even worse.

"But Solomon was a clever one. He said he couldn't tell who the real mother was, but since the mother of the surviving heir would have great power and status in the household, he had to make a call. So he declared that he'd cut the baby in two."

The room was spinning. My vision was getting fuzzy. Anuncio stumbled and fell. Bell clumsily dropped the big SPAS 15 shotgun he'd taken from the submarine. Radick had to brace himself against the wall to keep from falling over.

"When Solomon said that, the woman who'd already lost her son said she was fine with cutting the baby in half. The real mother said that she'd rather the baby be given away because she only cared about his life. And so, she got the baby."

Through watering eyes, I saw Susan was walking toward us. She was perfection. This was the sainted mother. She was an angel. I tried to lift my gun, but my arms wouldn't respond. One of my Hunters fell over on the carpet. I was so dizzy I couldn't tell which one.

The Guardian's marks began to heat up.

"Let him go, you crazy bitch!" I screamed as I fell to my knees.

She extended one gentle hand toward me. "This is exactly like Solomon's test. You're here risking Ray's life, Julie. You're the one forcing it, willing to let him get ripped in half. If you were a good mom, you'd let him go."

The marks got so hot they felt like they on fire. The pain was intense, but it was a cleansing fire, and I could see and think again.

Which meant that I could clearly see the horror standing right in front of me.

All illusions of humanity were shed. Susan had turned herself into something that looked like a hairless bat. Her kind mouth was really filled with fangs, and her gentle hand ended in claws like knives. This twisted nightmare was the true form of a Master vampire.

"So beautiful," Anuncio whispered.

Susan must not have realized that the spell had been broken on me, because she began to softly stroke my hair, like I was her baby again. "You have to be willing to let your children go to save them, and to save yourself."

The marks must have given me supernatural strength because it was the fastest I'd ever moved in my life as I yanked one of the wooden stakes from my vest and drove it into Susan's heart.

Her glowing red eyes widened in shock. "How—"

"You should've taken your own advice!" Twisting the stake hard, I shoved her away.

Susan let out an unholy wail. The sound seemed to break the hold she had on most of my men. Bell scooped up the shotgun and let her have it right in the mouth.

But unfortunately not all of them. "No!" Anuncio shouted as he lifted his gun to shoot Bell. In his charmed and befuddled mind, the other Hunter had just attempted to murder a beautiful angel.

I quick drew my pistol and shot Anuncio in the leg. He stumbled as he jerked the trigger. Bell still got hit, but he only got winged in the arm instead of getting his head blown off. Anuncio stitched full-auto holes up the wall and into the ceiling as he fell.

Shooting your teammate is harsh but it worked, because as he lay there clutching his leg, he screamed something at me. I didn't know the language well, but it was something to the effect of *what the hell?*

I turned back just as Susan hit me hard enough to send me flying. I crashed into Bell and we both went rolling across the carpet.

A stake through the heart paralyzed a lesser vampire, but on Masters, it only slowed them down. She spit out a mouthful of silver buckshot pellets and started toward us.

Coelho and Radick started shooting. Susan walked right through the bullets and grabbed Coelho round the throat. The Hunter thrashed as she squeezed. Blood exploded from between her tightened fingers. She nearly popped his head off.

"Shit!" Radick tripped over his own feet as he tried to back away. "Shit!" He kept firing as he fell.

Susan reached down for his kicking legs, but then she winced and flinched back hissing.

I noticed a tiny beam of sunlight coming through one of the bullet holes Coelho had punched in the wall. Just that had been enough to scorch her skin.

Susan wasn't going to let a little burn stop her for long though, because she still grabbed Radick by the boot. Bones crunched and Radick screamed. Then she swung him by the foot against the interior wall. He hit so hard that he smashed right through the sheetrock and out the other side, disappearing into the next room.

I picked up Bell's shotgun, pointed it at the wall next to Susan, and fired.

At that range, a buckshot pattern isn't much bigger than a fist, and it blasted a hole through the wall, letting more light in.

Fire danced down Susan's unnaturally long arm as the sun hit her. She reflexively pulled back. But there was a lot of boards and dangling insulation in the way, so it wasn't enough light. "Shoot the wall!"

Anuncio and Bell were both hurt, but they listened and went nuts. Anuncio picked up the Grayguns Sig I'd used on his leg. Bell pulled his pistol. I emptied the shotgun. Dust and splinters flew through the new beams of light as the hall brightened.

Susan was full-on smoking. Wherever the sun hit her, skin crisped and blacked to ash, and sparks drifted upwards. "You think this will stop me?" She grabbed the stake in her chest and started grinding it back and forth, trying to yank it free from her ribs. "I've been kind. I've been patient. I've been merciful to you for the last fucking time. I'm sick of your shit, Julie. Now you die."

This still wasn't enough light. I grabbed my radio.

"All outside Hunters, open fire on the top-floor hallway, north wall. Four feet high. Only the hall, not the room on the end! We need daylight."

Susan ripped the stake out. Black blood sprayed across the white carpet.

Lightning quick, Susan lifted the stake and hurled it at me.

I caught it with one hand.

Both Susan and I stared in disbelief at my fist holding the stake. Thrown at full, uninhibited, Master vampire strength, every bone in my hand should've exploded. That stake should've gone *through* my whole body.

My palm didn't even sting.

I'd pay the cost.

"Say again, over."

"Shoot the third-floor hallway, north exterior wall. We're hugging the floor. Now, damn it! *Now!*"

Lopes listened because, all of a sudden, the top of the wall above us was torn wide open. There was a minigun mounted on the helicopter and they let it rip. On the receiving end, it makes an unholy roar. It was like a super-intense hailstorm, only the hail was made of metal. All we could do was hug the carpet tight as we were pelted with fragments and cut by pieces of broken bullet jackets. I just hoped the door gunner didn't aim low or at the room at the end of the hall as the wall got turned into Swiss cheese.

Susan had been the only one upright. Bullets shredded her, but they were nothing compared to the damage from the sudden abundance of sunlight that followed them.

Nobody knew why sunlight hurt vampires, but it hit her hard. Susan burst into flames. And it wasn't like when we'd got her with the flamethrower. This was far worse. It was like every exposed molecule turned into a molten dot and started eating its way inward.

But she was still standing.

"You want to tear the baby in half. So be it."

She moved so fast it was as if she'd disappeared, but the doorway at the end of the hall was torn off its hinges as she crashed through it.

"Ray!" I jumped to my feet and ran after her.

"Cease fire! Cease fire!" Bell shouted into his radio.

I didn't care about the bullets zipping past me. Ray was the only thing that mattered.

By a miracle I didn't get hit before the gunner let off. Through the door, it was just another bedroom, but placed in the center of the bed was a pile of blankets. As Susan reached for Ray, bits of her burning flesh fell off and set the sheets on fire.

"If I can't have him, nobody will." Her skull was visible through the fire. Her eyes were burning pits. "This is your doing, Julie."

"No!"

Susan drove her burning fist into the mattress.

I screamed.

My whole world ended.

I can't even begin to describe the feelings that struck me just then. It was despair and hopelessness and the worst pain I'd ever experienced, like someone had grabbed my heart and squeezed.

But Susan was confused. Burning feathers drifted through the air. The lump in the middle of the bed hadn't been Ray at all. The thing beneath the blankets was just a pillow. "Where is—"

"Cuddle Bunny Cuddle Bunny!" Mr. Trash Bags bellowed from up above. *"Protect!"*

The little shoggoth was stuck to the vaulted ceiling. Dangling beneath him was Ray. Mr. Trash Bags had wrapped his tentacles around Ray's body like a harness. My baby was actually giggling, but that turned to fear when he saw the burning vampire below him.

If the feeling that I'd just had was the most powerful sadness in the world, then what hit me now was the greatest rage imaginable. This time I didn't feel it in my heart, but rather in the evil black marks etched on my neck and body. They flashed with an energy beyond understanding as I hurled myself at her.

I'd never hit anything that hard in my life. No regular human being had ever hit anything that hard in history.

Susan flew back like she'd been nailed by a truck. She hit the metal security shutter on the giant window so hard that it curled around her.

The two of us stood there, facing each other, her on fire and me beneath my baby, furious and consumed with dark magic.

Susan's body was falling apart, but she was still deadly. "What has my little girl turned into?"

"I'm his Guardian."

Susan looked up at Ray and prepared to leap. But even as fast as a Master was, as she left the ground, I tackled her around the waist. We hit the broken shutter which barely slowed us as we fell out the window.

I had my arms wrapped around the burning vampire as we crashed onto a narrow lip of roof. We rolled across the shingles. Far below us, waves crashed against rocks.

If the indirect light before had burned her, direct sunlight hit her like the wrath of God. I had to let go of her as the wave of heat burned my arms. Susan was screaming as she was consumed. I was screaming as I realized I was sliding to my death.

As I grabbed for something—anything—to hold onto, Susan went over the edge. My legs went over, then my torso. I about tore my fingerprints off trying to get purchase, but by some miracle I managed to stop my momentum, and I hung there, desperate.

As I pulled myself back up, I saw the fireball that

had once been my mother sink into the ocean. She disappeared in a cloud of steam as what was left of her sunk beneath the waves.

The Huey roared by with a rush of wind. The door gunner clearly saw me and, luckily, even as filthy, torn-up, and blood-soaked as I was, he didn't mistake me for an undead. I pointed toward the ocean and made finger guns to indicate that he should shoot a bunch of silver at where Susan had gone down.

As Lopes' Huey machine gunned the surf, I climbed back through the window. Mr. Trash Bags was gently lowering Ray from the ceiling. Shoggoths can stretch like a Slinky.

Hanging from the end of that bouncy strand was my baby. Ray saw me . . . and *smiled*.

CHAPTER 27

I took him in my arms. It was him. It was really him. He was still crying a little, but almost soundlessly, like he'd damaged his voice. I kissed his forehead. He looked unharmed, but he was going to need medical treatment. I needed to check him over and make sure there was no other damage.

I couldn't help it. I started sobbing. It was stupid. There was still shooting downstairs, which meant the situation was still dangerous, but I was wrung out, and I had my baby back.

There were more Hunters in the bullet-riddled hallway now. They were performing first aid on Radick, Bell, and Anuncio, but everyone stopped what they were doing as they saw me walking along with Ray in my arms. I think at first because of the tears cutting a track through the grime on my face, they thought they'd failed and that I was carrying his body, and crying because of the loss. There was that moment of fear and uncertainty, but then they saw he was moving, and the Hunters grinned.

411

Coelho was clearly dead. The barely conscious Anuncio looked at me as I went by, and said, "Make sure he grows up worth it."

"He will. I promise."

Without another word, I was surrounded by a protective cordon of Hunters. It's a testament to the flexible minds that none of them even said anything about Mr. Trash Bags riding triumphantly on my shoulder.

I wasn't going to let anyone else touch Ray. I wasn't going to put him down. I wasn't going to let him out of my arms. This young man would be lucky if I allowed him out of my sight when he was college-age.

With the hostage secured, there was no reason to stay inside. We rushed down the stairs, me carrying a baby, and the others carrying the wounded. There were a lot of bodies in the great room. Human slaves, wights, and the ones whose flesh was melting off their bones were the vampires. My newly appointed bodyguards got us out on the porch. One of them was shouting into his radio that the hostage was coming out. I'd lost my radio nearly falling off the roof.

Outside, the Hunters had pretty much locked everything down tight. The track hoe was tearing down the next wall while a bunch of men with guns protected it in case any more wights rushed them, though it appeared we'd killed all those already. With a rumble, another fifteen feet of beautiful mansion came tumbling down. The resale value on this place was toast.

Mr. Trash Bags must have been learning, because when we got around all the people, he slid down into the empty ammo pouch and hid.

There were several ambulances waiting. It was obvious the poor Portuguese paramedics had no idea what was going on, but all the government men with guns were shouting orders at them. Radick, Bell, Anuncio and others I didn't know were loaded in, and the ambulances took off with sirens blaring. The driveway had been blocked off by regular police.

There was a vast lawn, which was now the Huey's landing pad. The rotors were still turning. Rather than scare him, Ray seemed fascinated by the noisy helicopter. The air hitting him just made him make a gleeful expression.

As she ran toward me, I didn't recognize Lopes at first because of the flight helmet, but then she spoke: "Is that your young man? I'm so glad you managed to rescue him."

"So am I." Reaction was setting in. I just wanted to sit down, or lie down and sleep. I was so tired and thirsty I could barely function, but I couldn't think about myself yet. As much as he'd been crying, surely Ray needed water, probably food too—who knew what Susan had been feeding him? "I just want to get him home."

Lopes nodded. "Come with me. This is in hand. For you the battle is over. The last thing you want to do is risk your son now. Come." She grabbed my arm and steered me toward the helicopter.

"We're taking that?"

"It's out of ammo and needs to go back to refuel anyway. I'll drop you at our base. My superiors called. They found out about the raid."

"So am I going to get arrested when we land?"

"No, no. They're very upset, but I guess some friend of yours called Management paid them enough to not turn you over. He's sending a private jet there to take you back to America."

With the entire team on Severny gone—no, I tamped that thought down. That only made it more imperative I get Ray out of here and back to Alabama. I wanted to be home. Of course, what I really wanted was to be with Owen, to know my little family was reunited and nothing was wrong. But that was impossible, and right then I would give major pieces of my anatomy to just be back in Alabama, in my house, with my familiar things. I wanted to put little Ray in his little bed, and look after him. He was all I had left.

"What this little man needs," she said. "Is to be home, and peaceful."

I had to cover Ray's ears as we got closer to the Huey. The door gunner was a young man who helped me in, and then handed me some big earmuffs to put over Ray's head. Then I put on a set for myself. The gunner petted Ray's hair and Ray started to cry again, which just tells you how tired he was.

Lopes sat at the controls and checked the instruments with the sort of glee that made me think she was as crazy about flying as Skippy. "Sorry. No car seat," she said over the intercom in my headset. The pilot glanced back at me to see that I was strapping in, then we lifted off.

We got above the trees, turned north, and we set out for the naval base, flying right down the beach. We were only a couple hundred feet up; out the right side was land, and on the left was water. Even though this was the first time Ray had flown, he seemed excited that the doors were open. And it was *really* windy with the doors open. The kid was a natural Hunter.

There were some water bottles under the seat. They were the kind with a twist top you could suck the water out of but not spill. I opened it partway and let Ray suck on it, which he did, desperately. I got another one for myself and drained it.

Ray had a few bruises and scratches, but nothing too bad. This is when I found one of the other convenient aspects of having a mini-shoggoth as a babysitter, in that Mr. Trash Bags stuck a tentacle out of his bag and held the water bottle in position. This allowed me both hands to look for the first aid kit.

That's when I noticed something off about the door gunner. I was so exhausted, the sight so odd, that at first I wasn't absolutely sure what I was seeing.

Even though the minigun was empty, he was still sitting at the open door, his back toward me. In the middle of his back, right about where his heart would be, there was a bullet hole.

It wasn't a scratch. It wasn't a boo-boo. It was an actual gunshot wound. He was wearing the same black fatigues as everyone else from ASS, and there was blood soaked into the fabric all around the injury.

I felt as if my entire body had just gotten covered in ice.

The vampire's servants had been shooting at the helicopter. Lopes and the pilot must not have noticed when their gunner had gotten killed. Especially since from the location it had been instantly fatal, yet he'd kept on doing his job.

There were a lot of things that took over dead bodies. In fact, you could say a lot of supernatural creatures were like hermit crabs, looking for some discarded thing to occupy. But there was one thing in particular I'd been dealing with, who'd stolen little Ray from his crib, who'd tried to sell him for profit, who'd run me over with a ghost carriage, and who had vowed to make the rest of my life as miserable as possible, who had a predilection for taking over dead bodies.

Brother Death.

I slowly reached for my handgun, only to grab a fistful of air. The holster was empty. That was because Bell had picked up the Sig off the floor and been using it when I'd gone running after Susan.

The door gunner looked back over his shoulder. With the helmet and tinted goggles, I could only see his mouth, but he gave me a wry grin. He'd shown me the fatal wound. He wanted me to see it. Brother Death wanted me to feel that dread, to know how screwed we were.

I keyed my microphone. "Lopes! The gunner is Brother Death!"

"What?"

But then Brother Death turned, raising a pistol, and fired several times. The pilot jerked as bullets struck, then his head was flung forward violently and blood splattered across the cockpit. The Huey lurched hard forward as the pilot slumped over the cyclic control. Lopes had to fight her controls to keep us out of a sudden dive. Brother Death reached forward and yanked the dead pilot back by the shoulder straps.

Lopes looked back to find a pistol pointed at her head. Brother Death reached up with his other hand to key the mic clipped to his chest. "Keep flying." I didn't know what the gunner had sounded like when he was alive, but it probably hadn't been with an African accent and a really deep voice.

I put my hand on the combat knife at my belt,

but I didn't draw it. Inland seemed to be an arid landscape, with groves of olive trees and expanses of straggling grass. If he executed Lopes, we'd definitely crash before I could grab the controls.

"Remain calm, Julie. If you do something rash, your child may be hurt. I know you are too good a mother to want both of you to die."

I was getting sick and tired of people telling me how to be a good mother. "I'm calm," I lied as I shifted the mic button to my off hand, so I could pull my knife with my strong hand. "What do you want?"

"We creatures who aren't protected by man's law have only one thing keeping our peers from turning on us, and that is our reputation. How would it look if I allowed you to meddle in my business without repercussions? My honor has been damaged."

"Spare me your bullshit. It's obvious you didn't warn Susan we were coming. You could've protected your client. You must've overheard us talking at the museum because you even tagged along to watch."

Brother Death laughed. "True. I didn't tell her. Honestly, it amused me. I wanted to see what would happen."

We were crossing over fields with some kind of low-growing crop, which was being watered by a mechanical contraption that was like a long metal pole with watering hoses attached to it. The whole thing moved around slowly from end to end of the field, and for inexplicable reasons made me think of storks. If he wanted us dead, he could've just shot both pilots or set off a hand grenade. Brother Death must have had a plan.

"Your buyer's dead," I said. Though perhaps "croaked" would be more accurate, because the voice that came out of me was strangled by fear. I was trying to sound confident and normal, but my body wasn't cooperating. Keep in mind we were having this conversation via intercom and headset, because there's way too much rotor wash to speak normally.

"I wouldn't bet on it. Susan Shackleford didn't become the second biggest noise in the vampire community in only a few short years by being easy to kill. She'll be back. If I take either of you alive, maybe she'll even have another opportunity to bid for your lives. You thought you could cheat me, escape my dungeon, embarrass me in front of my clients and there would be no punishment? That was foolish."

"What have you done with Andre?" Lopes demanded. That must have been the gunner's name.

"Catch up, fool. He died ten minutes ago. Since you are the ones in charge of patrolling one of the countries I like to make my home, I've sunk my hooks into various people within your Agencia de Segurança Sobrenatural. That's how I knew you would be at the museum. When I overheard your scheming, I knew I simply had to watch. When this one was killed, I saw my opportunity and took it."

From the way she kept nervously glancing back, I could tell that Lopes was thinking about trying something, but sadly I didn't know what that would be.

He laughed, that horrible, smug sound. "You'll never escape me, Julie. These bodies are just vehicles. You cheated from the beginning, following the artifact to Cologne. You've never dealt fairly with me, yet because of your tenacity, I've discovered a renewed love for my work. Even now, I can see the defiance in your eyes. You're trying to plot some way to turn the tables. Only it doesn't matter. Even if you destroyed this body now, I'll come at you with another. How long could you escape? Wherever you go, I'll find you. I'll be your mailman. I'll be your son's kindergarten teacher. Even a mind as paranoid as yours won't be able to predict my actions. I will take your child simply because to do so amuses me. And once he's gone, then I'll come for you."

Brother Death was trying to watch me and Lopes both as he spoke. I waited for his eyes to move back toward the front before I drew the knife and hid it behind my leg.

"I have a new hobby, Julie. You can delay the inevitable, but you'll never win. I'll never let you feel safe again. You're used to being the Hunter, of having creatures fear you? Well, I'm the hunter now. I will never let you feel safe again."

And that was when Lopes made her move. Everything tilted violently as she turned the helicopter hard on its side, trying to dump Brother Death out the door. I held onto Ray for dear life as I was flung against my seat belt. Only Brother Death had been ready for that. The gunner had a safety harness bungee-corded to the helicopter, but he didn't even need it. He held on with superhuman strength with one hand, and he used the other to shoot Lopes.

"Hold the baby, Mr. Trash Bags!" I shouted as I struggled to unbuckle the straps holding me in place. "Don't let Ray get hurt!"

I don't know if he could hear me or not, but my shoggoth immediately popped out of the bag and wrapped himself protectively around Ray. Tentacles shot out his side and stuck to the wall.

The sudden change in gravity's direction had at

least thrown off his aim because Brother Death hadn't blown Lopes' brains out, but she still cried out as she got hit. I couldn't get the buckle undone with all my weight pushing against it, so I slid the combat knife inside and sliced right through the canvas.

I fell across the compartment, collided with Brother Death, and held on for dear life as the beach flashed by below. I slashed the knife across his arm as he tried to shoot Lopes again. The bullet put a hole in the instruments instead of her.

He hit me. Hard. I jammed the knife between his ribs. Again and again and again. He shoved me back against the wall. I hit the metal, but Mr. Trash Bags had already clambered up the side with Ray, so he was safely out of the way.

Down was down again as Brother Death started toward me. I kicked him in the stomach and shoved, trying to knock him out the door, but he was too strong. He swung the pistol toward me, but I intercepted it with the knife. He seemed almost amused as three of his fingers got sliced off and the gun fell to the floor.

I dove for the gun, but it was just out of reach. Lopes must have been struggling to remain conscious because the Huey was banking hard left and right. Centrifugal force kept pushing us in different directions. Down was rapidly changing directions. The pistol slid out the door.

Brother Death's remaining hand grabbed me around the throat. He hoisted me up and slammed me against the wall. He was saying something, surely gloating or mocking me, like he'd be continuing our conversation if it hadn't been for this minor interruption, except I'd lost my headset and couldn't hear his crazy nonsense over the rotor, so I just slashed the knife across his throat instead.

Glowing fireflies poured out.

The insects filled the cabin. I saw that Mr. Trash Bags crawled up to protect Ray's screaming face to keep the bugs from flying into his open mouth.

Lopes' helmet was rolling around on her neck like she'd passed out. The Huey tilted hard again as we corkscrewed toward the ground. The glove slipped from my throat as Brother Death fell away. He reflexively grabbed for a handhold, but had forgotten he was missing most of his fingers. Brother Death fell out the door, but then the gunner's belt snapped tight, and he was flailing around just outside.

I slid across the metal floor, caught myself at the edge, reached out and slashed the cord.

The possessed body flew into the rotor and exploded in a red cloud.

Sad part was, Brother Death would be back.

But worse, our rotor was seriously damaged. We were now basically a rock.

All I could do was look over and check that Mr. Trash Bags still had Ray. Not only did he, he was climbing down the wall, back into the safety of the seat, and had grown two more tentacles to pick up the seat belt, and was trying to figure out how to buckle them both in.

Lopes was either unconscious or dead.

I tried to make it to the controls, but we were going down.

I yelled at Mr. Trash Bags to make sure Ray wasn't hurt.

We hit the ocean.

When I came to, all I could hear was waves.

I opened my eyes.

The helicopter was at a weird angle, partly on its side, half filled with salt water. The windshield was broken. Almost everything was broken.

I was lying in the water. I didn't know how long I'd been out. It didn't feel like we were sinking. We must have hit the shallows. The dead pilot was submerged. Lopes was hanging from her chair, unconscious and dripping blood. A wave came through the front and hit us.

I thrashed around, searching for Ray. I didn't see him. Fuel must have been leaking because there was an oily sheen on the water. "Ray! Mr. Trash Bags!"

"Cuddle Bunny!"

They were outside. I clambered out of the wreck and fell into the surf. When I thrashed upright, the water came up to my chest.

Mr. Trash Bags had wrapped himself entirely around my baby, trying to protect him like an air bag. They were floating on top of the waves. The shoggoth was wiggling, trying to swim. Ray wasn't moving.

The mouths asked, "Cuddle Bunny okay?"

I was sure, just as absolutely as sure as I could be, that I'd sustained injuries that would have killed a normal person. But I wasn't a normal person anymore. I was the Guardian. But me living didn't matter as I splashed toward Ray.

"Cuddle Bunny Cuddle Bunny not okay."

"It's okay." I dragged Ray close and kept wading toward the shore. "I've got him."

Mr. Trash Bags retreated. It was like watching plastic melt away.

I got onto the sand, but Ray wasn't moving. He was still and very, very pale.

I'd seen dead people before. I knew what that looked like. And Ray looked dead.

. It hit me like a train. I heard a voice cry and realized it was me.

"Come on, wake up. Please, wake up for Mommy." But I knew he wasn't going to.

When I touched his chest, I couldn't feel his heartbeat. I couldn't give up. I just couldn't give up. Ray was the only thing I had left. He was the most important thing in the world.

I'd learned about what to do with an unresponsive baby while I was pregnant, and now I did what I'd been taught by rote.

Ray wasn't breathing. I opened his mouth to make sure he wasn't choking on his tongue, and he wasn't. There was foam in his mouth, and it was pink.

He couldn't have bit his tongue. He had no teeth. He didn't have any external injuries. I took his little shoes off and flicked the bottom of his feet while shouting, "Ray, Ray, please wake up." They'd told me if the baby is just passed out, sometimes that works, but he wasn't breathing.

Damn it, he wasn't breathing.

Baby CPR was dangerous. They were so frail. You could break their little ribs. But I couldn't see anything else I could do.

I laid him on the wet sand and put my hand on his still chest. It didn't feel right. I put the pads of two fingers in the center, just below the nipple line. I compressed, pushing straight down about an inch and a half, and then let the chest return to its normal position. I was so scared I was going to hurt him, but I had to do this. So I did it again. And again.

Hard and fast, hard and fast. I remembered the instructor saying that the compressions should be smooth, not jerky. And that we could use the rhythm of the chorus to "Staying Alive" to do it. I counted out loud while the song played in my head. Two compressions per second.

"One and two and three and—" I pushed down as I said the number and came up as I said "and."

I'm a-stayin' alive, stayin' alive
Ah, ah, ah, ah, stayin' alive, stayin' alive
Ah, ah, ah, ah, stayin' ali-i-i-i-ive

I tilted his head back, to straighten his airway, took a deep breath, then put my mouth over his nose and mouth and breathed into him. *Come on, baby, staying alive. Stay alive.* His mouth tasted like blood.

I started doing compressions again.

I could not give up. He could not die.

I don't know how long I kept it up, only that I ended up sitting on my heels, crying. My son was dead and I couldn't wake him. I couldn't wake him.

A wave washed over us. The water hissed into steam when it touched the mark on my neck.

Deep down, instinct told me I wasn't done. Ray wasn't done. The Others had given me this power, but it was up to me how I'd use it.

A coarsening. The stripping of all that is good and kind. With each new line, thou wilt become less human, more weapon, until the forfeit of thy very soul.

Was it worth that cost? That was a stupid question.

I was giving my humanity away, bit by bit. But it didn't even matter. This I would save, this I would keep. This I would do. I picked Ray up and held him tight. He was so cold.

The Guardian's marks burned as they consumed more of my soul. As I held Ray close, I watched a black dot form on the back of my wrist. The darkness grew. It crawled up my skin, wrapping itself around my forearm.

Only then all that heat seemed to flow out of me and down into my baby's body.

He gasped and gave a choked cry. At first I thought I was dreaming, but then he opened his eyes and looked right at me.

"Ray?"

His eyes widened in recognition, and he gave me his happiest little laugh.

EPILOGUE

Two Weeks Later

Brother Death was laying low.

He'd found a lovely resort in the Swiss Alps, a place where no one but the very wealthy or the very famous knew about. Movie stars came here to *rest* and cure their various addictions, be they drugs or sex. In fact, they were merely going to an inaccessible place, where no one could track what they were actually up to, to take a nice little vacation without anyone checking on them, and then return to play whatever repentant part they needed to get back in the good graces of the public.

At this time of year, well past the ski season but before summer, the resort wasn't full, although everyone who was staying here was beautiful and rich and famous.

Brother Death liked that. He enjoyed basking in the company of the most successful mortals, pretending to be one of them. It amused him to manipulate and tempt them.

This was a much-needed rest. His last venture hadn't gone according to plan, but he hadn't exactly lost, either. His most valuable business associate, Marchand, had been killed, as had many of his servants. Those were setbacks. Some power had gotten reshuffled, but in the end, he'd made new alliances and found an interesting new long term project—tormenting Julie Shackleford.

He hadn't given up on his prey. He'd not lied when he'd told her that she could never be sure when he would strike again. Even while doing nothing, he was making her worry. It was delicious.

Just a little rest, and then he'd find a way to take the child again, and with such a bargaining chip, this time he'd be able to demand an even higher price.

Brother Death walked out of the resort and towards the pool, his towel draped over his shoulder. It was a beautiful clear day, high upon a rugged mountainside, surrounded by evergreen trees. He could see miles in every direction, and so could the resort's security, which kept out the undesirables, fans and paparazzi or, in his case, Hunters.

As was his fashion, he'd changed his body to suit his surroundings. His skin was just dark enough to incite curiosity from the pampered Europeans, muscled but not freakishly so, tall but not a giant. Today he appeared to be a confident young man, extremely good-looking. His persona was that of an international model.

It was amazing how he could lie to these people who attended all the fashion shows, and yet they never realized that they had never seen him before. Vacuous, all of them. They paid no attention to the face of the people showing off the clothes, no matter how pretty they were.

"Hello, Gitonga." A leggy blonde who was the new up-and-coming thing in Hollywood called to him from one of the lounge chairs by the pool.

That was the name he was going by here. Gitonga meant *wealthy one* in Kenya. Brother Death had prepared many human identities he could hide behind, though he'd been forced to sacrifice all of the ones Marchand had set up for him. They had likely been compromised when his business associate had been killed, but Brother Death had many more to choose from.

The actress was sipping something from a glass ornamented with a paper umbrella. "You got up late this morning."

"I'm here to rest, am I not?" he answered in the accent most of them found so charming. He walked to the chair next to her, folding his towel carefully and setting it on the ground.

He was well fed, too. For a creature who grew fat on human misery, these neurotic stars were the closest thing to a banquet. They all wanted to take him to bed, and as soon as he was alone with them, all he had to do was say something that fed their body insecurity. Oh, then how the misery would flow. And despite his cruelty and abuse, they never cut him off after. No, the more miserable he made them, the more they tried to please him.

Brother Death was formulating a plan on how best to seduce and destroy this one when a phone rang.

He was certain he hadn't brought his cell phone—any of them—outside with him.

"Sounds like your phone is ringing," the Hollywood star said. "It's not mine."

He noticed that a cell phone had been left beneath the lounge chair.

Curious, he picked it up. The screen read *Guardian*. A moment of alarm. How had she found him?

"Did you see who left this here?"

The actress shrugged. "I wasn't paying attention."

Of course not. She was a useless, vapid cow. He glanced around, but saw no sign of danger. The phone continued ringing.

Then Brother Death smiled at the audacity. If it was a trap, then it was not a well-thought-out one. His ability to shape-shift would enable him to easily escape if necessary. Julie Shackleford had brought an interesting new challenge into his life. Before taking on the Raymond Pitt contract, he had grown complacent. When you've lived for centuries, it was rare to find an actual challenge. Her tenacity was remarkable. In a way, this was better than he expected. Much, much better. The prey was delivering itself. To be honest, he had gotten bored sucking the life out of the rich and famous.

Feeling some excitement, he answered the phone.

"Good afternoon, Julie."

"Brother Death."

"I trust you are well?"

"Right now, I'm feeling great."

Interesting. She sounded far too relaxed. He'd expected her to be angry and emotional. It was a bit of a letdown.

"And your child? He's a jovial sort. I miss his company."

"He's fine, no thanks to you."

He scanned the windows and the woods, looking for Hunters, but saw no danger. "How did you find me?"

"I'm good at my job."

"As am I. We are both professionals. I think that's why I've enjoyed our time together so much," he answered truthfully. "But really, how?"

"You pissed off people with a lot of connections, and a friend of mine in the MCB took this personally for some reason. You'd be amazed at their resources. You're not nearly as clever as you think you are. We actually found you a couple of days ago."

"I'm disappointed. Why has it taken so long for you to reach out?"

"Remember when we first met, and you shot a friend of mine in the chest?"

"I do," he chuckled. "You should have seen the look on your face. You didn't see that coming."

"That was a big mistake. Albert's our researcher, and he can fixate and hold a grudge like you wouldn't believe. He's been busy."

"Doing what?"

"Combing through every old record of every Hunter who'd ever chased an *Adze*, trying to figure out what my grandpa had started scratching into the floor with his hook while he was lying there bleeding to death . . . Aluoch."

The name "Born on an overcast morning" in Luo was impeccably pronounced, said exactly the same way it had been centuries before at his naming ceremony.

His name. She had his *name!*

It was in the contract—the one which had given him his immortality—that his true name could temporarily bind him and strip away his powers. It had been a tool of control, created by beings who had long since abandoned this world, yet their contract remained in force.

He couldn't change shape. He was powerless. He was *mortal*.

Aluoch looked around, panicked, for anyone who might attack him at this vulnerable time. It was in that awful instant that he realized the many flags and banners along the resort's fence were lying perfectly still.

There was no wind.

The bullet came out of nowhere and obliterated his skull, splattering the Hollywood star in bright-green-glowing blood.

On the opposite side of the canyon, eleven hundred and fifteen yards away, I watched Brother Death die through my scope. *That was for the Boss.*

"Hit," my spotter confirmed. "Target is down."

"O ye of little faith. I told you I'd get him first try."

"No kidding. You blew his head clean off." Owen squinted as he peered through the spotting scope. "It looks like that name worked just like Albert thought it would."

The hard part had been finding experts to make sure I was pronouncing it right.

I glanced over at Owen and smiled. My husband looked a little different now, thinner and bearded, still bruised and battered from his escape from the Nightmare Realm, but it wasn't just the physical aspect. He'd also seemed a little haunted since he'd gotten back from Severny Island, but right then he gave me a giant grin. "And he landed right in the pool. I bet that's gonna suck to clean."

I'd thought my husband had died. I'd thought they'd all died. But they'd been ordered to evacuate by the Russians and watched the bomb go off from their ship. As soon as they'd gotten away from the communications blackout, I'd gotten the happiest phone call of my life.

It's amazing how much more you appreciate your family after believing that you'd lost them forever.

"We better get moving," I said as I stood up and dusted myself off. MHI wasn't supposed to be here. Hell, I wasn't even supposed to be on this continent. From her hospital bed, Lopes had assured the EU that I'd surely fled the continent. Grant and the MCB would be claiming credit for this one.

I watched as Owen gathered Ray up from the little towel, where we'd left him sitting between us. He looked silly, with the giant squishy earmuffs covering half his head, but even a suppressed .50 BMG is still pretty loud.

Ray had been a little strange around Owen for the first couple of days he'd been back, but now he laughed at Daddy almost as much as at Mom. Which was good. You can't take yourself too seriously when a baby is laughing at you.

I glanced down at the new black mark curling around my forearm. *Totally worth it.*

"How come I'm carrying this howitzer back to the car while you get to carry the baby? That's not very chivalrous."

"I'm making up for lost time," Owen explained as Ray kicked one bare leg at his midriff. "Ow. Super Baby has a kick like an elephant."

"Yeah, that's nothing. You weren't around for the part where he thought my bladder was a football."

Owen put his arm around my shoulders and drew me in, warm and protective. Ray cooed and grabbed a handful of my shirt. There we were, just a happy little family, together again, taking a walk through the woods after a successful assassination.

"We should find someplace to get lunch," Owen suggested, "but not that resort. I think they're too busy."

"Let's just go home."

I didn't know if home would be safe anymore. My family was fine for now, and the artifact entrusted to me was secure, but there'd be more threats. We'd made too many enemies. I suppose that was inevitable for those of us who choose to hunt monsters.

All I could do was make sure my family continued to survive.

I'd stand guard.

Monster Hunter Memoirs: Sinners
9781481482875 • $7.99 US/$10.99 Can.

Monster Hunter Memoirs: Saints
9781481484114 • $7.99 US/$10.99 Can.

THE FORGOTTEN WARRIOR SAGA

Son of the Black Sword
9781476781570 • $9.99 US/$12.99 Can.

House of Assassins
9781982124458 • $8.99 US/$11.99 Can.

THE GRIMNOIR CHRONICLES

Hard Magic
9781439134344 • $15.00 US/$17.00 Can.

Warbound
9781476736525 • $7.99 US/$9.99 Can.

MILITARY ADVENTURE
with Mike Kupari

Dead Six
9781451637588 • $7.99 US/$9.99 Can.

Alliance of Shadows
9781481482912 • $7.99 US/$10.99 Can.

Invisible Wars
9781481484336 • $18.00 US/$25.00 Can.